The Mistress of Lilliput

Also by Alison Fell

FICTION

THE GREY DANCER (1981)
EVERY MOVE YOU MAKE (1984)
THE BAD BOX (1987)
MER DE GLACE (1992)
THE PILLOW BOY OF THE LADY ONOGORO (1994)

POETRY

KISSES FOR MAYAKOVSKY (1987)
THE CRYSTAL OWL (1988)
DREAMS, LIKE HERETICS (1997)

ANTHOLOGIES

THE SEVEN DEADLY SINS (1988)
THE SEVEN CARDINAL VIRTUES (1990)
SERIOUS HYSTERICS (1992)

THE

MISTRESS OF LILLIPUT

or

THE PURSUIT

ALISON FELL

Doubleday

LONDON · NEW YORK · TORONTO · SYDNEY · AUCKLAND

TRANSWORLD PUBLISHERS LTD
61–63 Uxbridge Road, London W5 5SA

TRANSWORLD PUBLISHERS (AUSTRALIA) PTY LTD
15–25 Helles Avenue, Moorebank, NSW 2170

TRANSWORLD PUBLISHERS (NZ) LTD
3 William Pickering Drive, Albany, Auckland

Published 1999 by Doubleday
a division of Transworld Publishers Ltd

A catalogue record for this book is available from the British Library.
ISBN 0385 410514

Typeset in 11/13pt Adobe Caslon by Kestrel Data, Exeter, Devon.

Printed in Great Britain by
Mackays of Chatham plc, Chatham, Kent.

Thanks are due to:

Ruthie Petrie, for editing me once again

Dennis Reinhartz of the University of Texas, author of *The Cartographer and the Literati – Herman Moll and his Intellectual Circle*, for enthusiastic conversations about Mr Moll

Joachim Schwend of Leipzig University for his delicious mistranslation of *beeren* as 'bears'

My son Ivan Coleman for the 'rough and ancient sketch' in Chapter 20

The staff of the North Library, Map Room, and late lamented Round Reading Room in the British Museum

Credit is due to Clarissa Pinkola Estes, author of *Women Who Run with the Wolves*, for the notion of the Scapecoat

Apologies are due to the eighteenth-century naturalist Antoine Duchesne, for biographical liberties taken to suit my own fictional ends

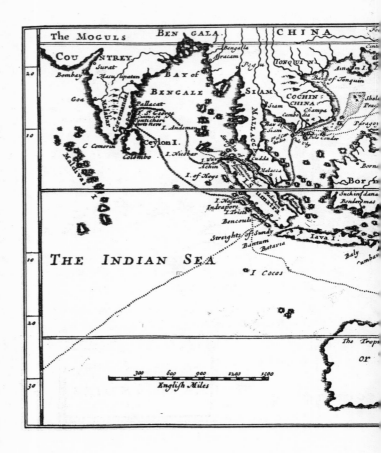

A Map of the

EAST INDIES

I have long awaited an opportunity to give some public testimony of the esteem and respect I have for the lady, modest in the extreme, in whom I have found all that is valuable in our sex, and who is, without flattery, the most prudent, most humble, and most accomplished woman I ever met. Her virtues are her own, her small vices occasioned only by her misfortunes; indeed, had she been a man, she would be considered without fault. But the charter of our sex being more confined than that of the other, what is not a crime in men is considered scandalous and unpardonable in woman, as the eminent Mrs. Manley herself has observed on divers occasions.

Madam, allow me to say that I am charmed with your conversation, and extremely proud of your acquaintance. The world may often condemn those who are too partial in their friendships, but I am of Horace's mind, and take no pleasure in variety of association, two or three persons of worth being quite enough to make life pleasant. I do not write for bread, nor am I vain or fond of applause, but I am very ambitious to gain the esteem of those who seek truth with assiduity, and it is on this account, madam, that I entreat you to accept the little present I here make of the life and adventures of a lady who shall ever find me

her devoted servant,

L.M.

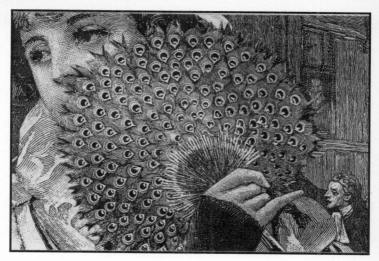

CHAPTER I

*Being an Account of Mistress Mary Burton and her Family . . . Her
Early Years . . . An Introduction to her Dolls . . . A Presbyterian
Mother . . . Divers Thoughts on Time . . . A Society Occasion . . . A
Decisive Encounter with Mr. Lemuel Gulliver . . .*

Let us begin, then, in the proper manner, with a genealogy
of our heroine, which contains neither squires nor
scholars, but which will none the less reward perusal. Her
father, Mr. Edward Burton, was a merchant and proprietor
of a hosiery concern in Newgate Street, a prosperous business he had come upon after some years as a master hosier
with the New Mills Company near Edinburgh, having been
drawn north by the very favourable contracts then being
offered to English weavers and frameknitters. It was at

Edinburgh that Mr. Burton met one Eliza Kerr, the daughter of a farmer in the Scottish Borders who, fleeing the rigours of sheep-moor and cattle trough, had apprenticed herself to a milliner in Tollcross. After four years in Scotland the industrious young man was in a position to lend money rather than borrow it, and he removed himself and his new wife to London, where he established his own workshop. So rapidly did he turn his business to account that by the year his eldest daughter Harriet was born he employed as many as fifty hand-frame knitters to manufacture the finest quality silk, worsted- and fancy-hose as could be found in the capital. Mary's birth followed within the twelvemonth, and although her father had wished for a son, his generous heart made such easy compromise that we should not consider it overly vain of Mary to hazard that she had always been his favourite.

Into a world of hose, then, she came, for the newborn was instantly hoisted to her father's shoulder and toured like a victor's trophy through the workshop. The first sound her tiny ears encountered was the whispering clack of the combs, and the first sight her eyes beheld was the multicoloured lengths that issued like magic snakes from the conjunction of man and machine. Indeed, I myself can vouch for the fact that the very first word she spoke was 'stocking', and that before she was three years old she could parrot the names of all the patternings, from zigzag to intarsia, and from horse-shoe and honeycomb to bird's eye and lover's-knot.

(You may be curious, reader, as to my identity, but let me be bashful for the moment, with the promise that all will be revealed by and by. In the meantime only ask yourselves who in a young girl's life is made accessory to her earliest experiences; who observes her at her games and listens to her childish prattle; who on the one hand is entreated to talk, yet on the other is sworn to silence? Who is hurled from the cradle on a whim, or smothered by the sweats of infant fever; who above all others is lived and dreamed exhaustively, even as far as the folds of delirium? No matter, I assure you, if you cannot immediately answer; ponder the question no longer; indeed, waste no more time upon it, for it is not my intention to push myself to the forefront, thus diverting you from the proper heroine. Rather my place is to stand like a humble servant in the shadows of the narrative, there to hold the lamp that shines its light on Mary.)

Sooner or later children will come out with questions about their provenance, and Mary was no exception to the rule, piping up one day in the workshop, 'Papa, when I was a baby, where did I come from?' Now a mother may avail herself of several stock responses, from gooseberry bush to obliging stork, but she does not have fifty workmen hanging on her answer. Since it was Mr. Burton's nature, when abashed, to play to the gallery, he pointed to the knitting-frames and laughingly declared, 'Why, Papa knitted you, my precious!'

So fertile is the infant mind, however, that even a light-hearted joke may bear serious fruit. Some days later, on a visit to the nursery, Mrs. Burton was shocked to discover the little girl rocking her naked rump industriously upon her close-stool, her face quite red from her happy exertions, while with her tongue she mimicked the rhythmic racket of the frames. To the Presbyterian mother no pleasure so intense could be entirely blameless, and so she interrupted her daughter in the throes of it, scolded her roundly, and forbade her to play such naughty games again. 'But Mama,' cried the delinquent, quite baffled by this behaviour, 'I am knitting me some babies!' Eager as she was to explain herself, her precocity only earned her a hearty slap, and the further indignity of being put to bed without supper, as if hunger pangs would help her fathom her disgrace.

Mr. Burton, meanwhile, was quite confounded by the reproachful wife who hinted darkly at improprieties but could neither name the criminal nor, for the life of her, prosecute the case in plain English. Since there was as little prurience in the man as there was piety, all innuendo was lost on him, and though he be upbraided, he made no more sense of it than did his tiny daughter.

Now while a husband may solve a paradox simply enough by forgetting it, a tender girl will not so readily untie the knots of perplexity, but will be hobbled and hindered ever after, youth being a time when the spirit may be easily bent, if not so easily broken.

What should Mary do, then, in her dejection, but turn for solace to her dolls, those little Buddhas of the bedchamber who had dried her mother's tears and her grandmother's before her, and who knew far more than was given them to reveal? (Do not think for a moment, reader, that a doll is a mere mannikin without eyes to see or ears to hear, nor that her humble status dooms her to dimwittedness. On the contrary, her very lowliness, as you will see, assures her of a privileged understanding. Do not imagine, either, that a slap will stop dead at the first recipient, however woebegone she may appear. Rather it will go on to knock many a wig sideways, and leave its devil's brand upon a china cheek, for it hath a long life, I warrant you, and more incarnations than any Buddha of the East.) But I shall not dwell for the moment on such distasteful matters, since I am hardly embarked upon my tale. Let me record, rather, that while Mary wept at her own wickedness, and raged at the spoil-sport who was her darling, sweet Belinda cooed, and Charlotte comforted, and the Lady Mary kissed and did not tell.

Presently the pain, if not erased, was pushed aside, for Mary had a nature as incorrigibly affectionate as her father's, and she forgave her mother everything, as children will, but did not forgive herself.

No scolding in the world could have stinted Mr. Burton's delight in his young apprentice, however, or the pleasure he took in amusing her. If the workshop was his palace, then she would be its princess, and test its finest wares. Blindfold, she must pull the silk stockings through her childish fingers, and judge whether the gauge be 26 or 30, and the yarn single- or two-fold, and even what number of needles composed the frame. Try she did, but dared not please him, on pain of displeasing her mother, so that if her touch was nice, her grasp of mathematics would be sadly wanting. Thus an intelligent child may choose stupidity if it seem the lesser evil, and cultivate deficiencies so stubborn they will persist in the face of every patient effort to correct them.

But for this convenient disability I do not doubt that Mary's sex would not have deterred Mr. Burton from training her up in the hosier's trade; as it was, for the first time in his life he was disappointed in his daughter, and abandoned her regretfully to the schoolroom, where a more conventional education in French, Music and Classics awaited her.

Thus with some relief the little girl exchanged the hectic

felicities of the workshop for the sober tutelage of Mrs. Bainbridge, and settled to her lessons with her elder sister Harriet. Very often the sisters would also have the bonus of their mother's company, for thanks to Mr. Burton's industry their estate had grown quite elevated and Mrs. Burton, seeing that she must come up in the world, had prevailed upon their teacher to coach her at elocution. With great determination the matron set about eradicating the accent of the Scottish Borders, and substituting for its age-old music the stricken vowels and abrupt consonants of the south. Painstakingly Mary and Harriet helped her to her new sounds, having first obtained the promise that she would reward them with a rhyme or a song in broad Scotch dialect.

As soon as all three had escaped the schoolroom a wild twinkle would light up their mother's eye, while from her mouth came utterances foreign as a bagpipe's drone or the wail of a banshee, which were guaranteed not only to give the girls delicious goosepimples, but to send the maids scurrying in fright from the eccentric oracle. A firm favourite with her daughters, and one they requested again and again, was a vulgar monologue on 'mucking oot the byre', which ended invariably with the majestic admonition, 'Dinnae get mairrit tae a fairmer, lassies, they're a' too near tae the coo's backside.'

As Mary and her sister advanced towards womanhood, however, these engaging shenanigans were firmly set aside, and it was in vain that they pleaded for their reinstatement. For middle age had come like a wintry blight upon their mother, driving her ever deeper into devoutness, so that she turned her back on levity, denounced its romps and frolics, and even, in her rigour, renounced the display of natural affection. If the effect of this change upon Mary and Harriet was cruel beyond a doubt, suffice it to say that it was but a symptom of the larger cruelty Nature holds in store for mothers, who must watch their own charms wither in the exact moment of the daughters' flowering. Suspecting insurrection even in her own devoted daughters, Mrs. Burton countered the threat with constant vigilance; thus she who had been the queen of their hearts became their fiercest critic as, turning her mind to their moral education, she strove to imbue them with the faith of Mr. John Knox.

They submitted, as girls must, to their mother's governance, but in vain did they seek the companion of their youth in this stern and sober matron who watched over them with a jealous eye, and set about preparing them for marriage. Moreover, since the worship of the stocking absorbed Mr. Burton to the exclusion of all other religions, no mitigating influence saved the young women from the full force of the Thundering Scot, so that they learned to fear God rather than love him, to abjure anything that smacked of Romish idolatry and, above all, willingly to bear the yoke of womanly duty.

Now, if Mrs. Burton chided her husband for his heathenish interest in fashion, he could truthfully return that the health of his business depended upon his sharp eye for a trend. No such excuse, however, could legitimize his daughters' aspirations to be decked out *à la mode*. No matter how fashionable the occasion, Mrs. Burton dressed invariably in a dark silk mantua over an unribboned petticoat, a plain tucker and modesty-piece, and a mob-cap without lappets, and obliged her daughters to adhere to the same modest code.

Though by now well versed in meekness, Mary chafed inwardly under such a restraint, for naturally enough her vanity yearned for expression. At her monthly times, when she was much afflicted by melancholy, the leather-covered Testament crawled through her dreams like a great black beetle, and the Book of Common Order was its companion centipede. At such times she would steal up to the musty attic where the wind rattled the windowpanes and the slope of the slanting roof was a sail for the ship of her heart.

Here she took command of a naughty crew: Charlotte, Belinda, Arethusa, and, if I dare say so, her favourite Lady Mary, all of whom were in a very ordinary condition, our gowns threadbare, our petticoats cobwebbed, and our limbs still clad in the stockings that Abel, the most adroit among the master-hosiers, had knit for us some years ago.

'Mutineers you are,' she scolded us, 'to the very last man!' And she lashed her midgets to the mainmast, scrubbed our smutty cheeks with brine, and prodded us along the plank like pirates. Yet if I, who was the closest to her heart, must suffer the most rigorous correction, by the same token I was fortunate, for I was to be singled out for improvement.

In Mrs. Burton's marriage-trunk Mary found the fineries she needed for the renovation, for she had decided I must be decked out to suit my given rank, and done up in the highest degree. And just as Mr. Burton, of an evening, opened his ledgers and totalled his receipts, so his daughter, spellbound at her sewing, made good her heavy deficits, and balanced her secret books. All in diminutive she worked a green silk petticoat bordered in red and white calico, a cherry-coloured stomacher, and a red satin gown trimmed with white persian. This elegant ensemble was completed by a velvet tippet lined with ermine, and swansdown muffettees to show off my fragile wrists. My complexion was then enlivened by rouge applied with Spanish wool; my lips and fingernails were reddened; my eyebrows, which had once been arched, were shaven clean away, to be replaced by narrow strips of mouseskin (a fashion Mary had observed at a chamber concert, her mother having joined with other charitable ladies to raise monies for the relief of sick prisoners in Newgate). Black velvet patches adorned my chin, and cork plumpers filled out my rosy cheeks. From locks of her own hair glued on with mastic, Mary contrived a memorable wig, with frizzed front curls on the forehead, and those stray curls at the temples the modish ladies call 'favourites', and the whole powdered edifice topped with a high *fontange* of Brussels lace.

Having painted and prinked and coiffed me to her heart's content, my mistress stood back to consider her handiwork. 'How charming you look, you little minx!' she cried. 'I daresay no gentleman on earth could fail to admire you!' Indeed, I was every bit as thrilled as she to imagine the glances which might greet my entrance into society. I would surely take the capital by storm; why, I might even conquer hearts at Hampton Court, and vanquish royal rivals!

As long as it took the day to fade Mary stood rapt in contemplation of my successes, while the clouds which had been but brief moths against the brightness of the sky gathered and glowered at the window. She saw the chandeliers and the sparkling suppers, she heard the music of the *bal masqué* and the soft whisper of my satin feet as I curtseyed in the cotillion . . . she touched the silver locket at my throat . . . she smiled with downcast eyes, seeing, in the shadows, vase upon vase of huge gardenias . . .

Reader, I would elaborate further, if Mary had not now checked herself, deciding, in a rapid turnabout, that the room was dull and dark and the dream was foolish. Nothing would please me more than to tease your fancy with girlish fairytales, to give you silks and suitors and Spanish lace, to shower you with *billets-doux* and sail you to Richmond on a moonlit river-barge. But sadly the door is shut fast, and it will do no good to plead that it be reopened, for Mary is her mother's daughter, and can indulge you no farther than she dare indulge herself. As for the poor doll whose charms she had flaunted, I regret to say that she pricked me hard with a hat-pin, lest I become swell-headed, and get above myself!

When a vogue swept the city for garters woven with mottoes, Mr. Burton wasted no time in having Abel work up a line, which he advertised with some success under the appellation: 'Trophies Sought by Bold Adventurers.' This occasioned a bitter quarrel between Mary's parents, for her father would indulge religious scruple only insofar as it did not discountenance profit, on which matter he was utterly intransigent. The sins committed by her father, then, in the pursuit of capital, Mary mimicked in the secrecy of the attic without warrant or excuse, lavishing on me a pair of little garters with the bridal motto:

> *My heart is fix'd, I cannot range,*
> *I like my choice too well to change.*

Had Mrs. Burton ever set eyes on the above I venture that Mary would not have escaped without a whipping, yet fear alone was not sufficient to deter her. For though the female instincts be dammed and diverted they will never be entirely quelled, and no doubt Mary was not the first daughter of the Presbyterian Church, nor will be the last, to lay out the plain hymn books by day, and by night to salve her vanity by dressing up her dolls like veritable harlots.

In the spring of her seventeenth year Harriet married Mr. Joseph Brierley, a worthy if struggling advocate, thus clearing the way for her younger sister. As soon as Mary had passed her sixteenth birthday, then, her mother prepared to launch her ship upon the sea of marital prospects. Seeing, with the realism of her race, that to make sure of a suitable catch she must set scruple aside, she contrived to cast her net more widely than the Sunday services at the Scots Church in Lothbury and the Concerts of anthems in the Stationers' Hall. Lady Chesingham, who was a patron of St. Bartholomew's Hospital and sat with Mrs. Burton on several committees, was also a hostess of some distinction; therefore it was an excited, if apprehensive Mary who accompanied her mother to a garden-party at her Ladyship's summer house in Greenwich. The opulent colours and stuffs of the gowns, the gaiety of the young people who frisked on the sloping lawns, the silver liveries of the little *mustee* boys Lord Chesingham had brought back from Guayaquil – those details alone would have sufficed to fix the occasion in her memory, had it not also been the very day she first set eyes on her beloved Lemuel. The eminent surgeon, Mr. James Bates, introduced this gentleman to the Burton ladies in the most glowing terms, telling them that Mr. Gulliver had been his prized assistant at St. Bartholomew's before studying physick at

Leyden, and proceeding thence to a career as ship's surgeon on the high seas.

Mr. Gulliver, who stood stolid and unprotesting under the welter of praise, was a man of strong build, with a complexion much freckled by wind and weather, and a gaze uncommonly stern and direct. He wore the sober black coat and full wig of his profession, and carried the surgeon's gold-topped cane; in short, despite his youth – he was around twenty-five years old – he was an imposing figure, and one on whom a young girl of sixteen would have hoped to make a good impression. Yet since her mother had trained her in no womanly arts but modesty, Mary was at a loss as to how this was to be achieved, for she was keenly aware that her plain gown and tucker cut no dash at all in the elegant crowd on the lawn; and being far too young to know that blooming youth is its own finery, and needs no enhancement, she could not help but feel both rivalrous and dejected.

A short distance away from their party, a group of young bloods had commandeered a swingboat that hung from the branches of a tall cedar tree, and were disporting themselves noisily.

'Young Henry Chesingham and his friends from Oxford,' observed Mr. Bates, with an indulgence born, perhaps, of wistful memory, but Mrs. Burton gazed on the unruly group with open disapproval – for in her strict opinion students were without exception drunkards, Mohocks, and frequenters of the gambling dens and bawdy-houses of Covent Garden.

Just then a fellow not much older than Mary, of meagre stature and with a complexion already sadly pock-marked, hoisted himself up on the ropes, and with playful kicks banished the other occupants from the contraption. As he propelled himself to and fro, his companions egged him on with jests and laughter, crying: 'The wig, Joseph, give us the wig!'

Yielding at last to popular demand, the youth raised his reedy voice and addressed the crowd sarcastically:

'If, gentlemen, through some magnificent invention of modern science the men of the next century could fix us in some magic eye and look back on us, what judgement would they make upon the mincing gait, the frown of concentration, the rigid and unnatural pose of the head and neck? With what perplexity will they observe that we move as slowly as tortoises merely out of respect for *The Wig*, that we abjure ball games and other healthful sports that risk dislodging it?'

With a bow which required him, at the risk of capsizing, to release one hand from the rope in order to steady his own wig, thus raising cheers of delight, he continued, 'As to a catalogue of the positive effects, they keep heads warm and barbers in business, and, unlike natural hair, they shelter no vermin and conceal the passing years. Along with the sash window and the wainscoted wall, are they not in fact a prime comfort of the modern age? – Honour the animal, too, for its longevity, for it is well nigh indestructible. First it is left by will to son and heir, next, it goes to the coachman, eventually it passes to the gardener, thence to the second-hand shop, and onward to the sixpenny lottery in Rosemary Lane, until finally it ends its long and useful career in the shoeblack's box, where it buffs up the toes of theatre-goers.'

The speaker had been swinging higher and higher, his capers growing ever more outlandish as he tried to keep his head fair and square and his wig in its proper place. But now, throwing caution to the winds, he let his head loll back and thrust his feet heavenwards, so that the item spiralled into space like a leaf in autumn and fell among the rushes at the river's edge, leaving a shaved and shining pate for all to see. This prank brought Lady Chesingham hurrying to remonstrate with her son, who seemed no more sobered by it than did the orator, for the two young fellows quickly drummed up a rescue party and set off in pursuit of the quarry as assiduously as if they had been boar-hunters in the swamps of the Orinoco.

'Hardly seventeen and a pamphleteer already,' said the jovial Mr. Bates. 'I do believe we are over the hill, Lemuel!'

'Mr. Addison has an exceedingly high opinion of himself, I hear, and a correspondingly low opinion of all others,' said Mr. Gulliver so testily that Mary quailed before him. Setting her mouth in a line as strait-laced as her mother's, and her mind as levelly on gaining his esteem, she swore that she had not gleaned a moment's amusement from the undignified exhibition. All would have been well, no doubt, if Mr. Gulliver's hand had not strayed nervously to his own handsome wig at this juncture, thus rousing in her mind such a string of unworthy thoughts that she had cause to bless the fan which spared her blushes.

Fortunately the Reverend Fleming chose this moment to pay his respects to their little group – a visitation Mr. Gulliver appeared to find less than congenial – and under cover of the diversion Mary slipped away to cool her flaming cheeks at the river's edge.

A flight of stone steps took her out of sight of the lawn,

and led her down to a wooden pier which jutted some distance into the river. Since there was but little breeze on the bank she followed the jetty to its end, where coolness rose from the waters, and the noise of the throng was but a distant murmur. As she stood in contemplation of the scene, a swan glided regally from the shallows, its neck brilliantly silhouetted against the sunlight. The creature delved its head beneath the calm surface of the water, and when it emerged again, drops of molten gold showered from its beak and cascaded down its graceful neck. It was as if water had dared to meet with fire, and far from destroying each other, the two opposing elements had fused in a sublime marriage!

So susceptible was Mary's state of mind that she stared transfixed at the bird, and had some sage chosen this moment to interrogate her I daresay she could not have told him whether it was the swan's soul or her own held cupped in that momentary hand of light. Youth and lovers, of course, are greatly given to epiphanies, and it should not surprise us if there flashed upon her at this very juncture a sudden understanding that Time, far from being horizontal, was this deep dazzle she saw before her, this vertical deceleration into brightness.

So intent was she on the swan that she did not notice Mr. Gulliver until he was far advanced along the jetty, leaving her no avenue of escape.

'A fine sight, Mrs. Burton,' he ventured boldly, startling her with his sudden appearance and, in addition, so exalting her with his address that she trembled like a leaf, and responded with the barest of nods. 'And a lofty aim, moreover,' he continued, 'to improve our knowledge of the position of the celestial bodies. I take it you have visited the Royal Observatory, where Mr. Flamsteed labours day and night to chart the motions of the heavens?'

Mary blushed extremely, realizing that he referred not to her swan, but to the distant dome which was reflected in the glassy surface of the river. 'I regret, sir, that I have not,' she murmured, feeling his piercing gaze upon her.

'A penny for your thoughts, Mary,' he begged. 'I had the impression that they were most uplifting.'

'I was thinking . . .' she faltered, almost struck dumb by fear that he would laugh at her. 'Forgive me, sir, but . . . are we not mistaken when we say that Time forms a continuous sequence, like a line? For surely, Time is vertical. You see, I have been observing that swan . . .'

Mr. Gulliver entreated her to continue, but to her chagrin she found that she could continue no further with her explication, and must stand there stuttering like a ninny under his quizzical gaze.

Mr. Gulliver turned his attention now upon the swan. After considering the lovely creature at some length, he said with a smile, 'I think you are a Platonist, perhaps, and wish as he did to preserve the realms of perfection from the laws of Time, reserving their depredations exclusively for the material realms of decay . . .'

With a blush Mary confessed that she had read little Plato, and had not attempted the Timaeus, at which Mr. Gulliver, rather than heaping scorn on the limitations of Mrs. Bainbridge's instruction – which, while comprehensive in French and fair in Latin, left a deal to be desired in Science, Greek, and Philosophy – seemed to relish the opportunity to make good the deficit, and proceeded to regale her with a lecture on Mr. Newton's laws.

'Universal Time,' he explained with enthusiasm, 'is obtained in *theory* from the motions of bodies subject only to the force of gravitation, and in *practice* from the orbital motions of the planets, for which non-gravitational forces are negligible.' Mary listened obediently as the lecture ran on, until despite all her efforts her head was fuddled with dry terms. She could not tell Epoch from Interval, failed miserably to grasp the concept of Ephemeral Time, and could but dimly comprehend the need for an Ideal Rate-Measure based upon the Mean Solar Time of the Meridian. Meanwhile her swan swam placidly on its own meridian and answered, perhaps, to absolutes she could not have begun to explain to her instructor, had she read every word of Mr. Newton and Mr. Locke and Mr. Leibniz besides.

Even as she berated herself for possessing a mind more given to ecstasy than enquiry, she could not help but notice that her stupid silence did not in the least deter her companion, whose features grew increasingly animated and whose gold-topped cane waved ever more vivaciously in the course of his exposition. Had she been older or more worldly, reader, she might have drawn the plain conclusion that the last thing a man of reason requires is too much cleverness in a woman; as it was, her heart, unsullied by cynicism, could only marvel at his generosity and complaisance.

At the conclusion of the day's festivities Mr. Gulliver asked if he might call upon her family at Newgate Street, and, to the astonishment of all of us at that establishment, made a formal request for her hand within the week. Mr. Burton, of course, had never been one to tarry, for business, like the high seas, fosters a spirit of decisiveness. Having established that Mr. Gulliver's father had a modest estate in

Nottinghamshire, and that if the young gentleman, being the third son, had no expectation of fortune, his profession nevertheless assured him a reasonable prospect, Mary's father gave the match his blessing, and a date was speedily set for the nuptials.

Although it would be fair to say that in Mr. Gulliver's opinion Popistry was a disease of the mind and Presbyterianism even more deluded, he kept his dislike of Mrs. Burton's religion well concealed, and suffered himself to be married by the Reverend Fleming at the Scots Church in Lothbury. The stark ceremony completed, the wedding guests proceeded with relief to an extravagant reception at Newgate Street, which was attended also by the stocking-knitters, the girls in streamers of pink and blue, and the men with ribbon cockades. In vain had Mrs. Burton tried to inject moderation into the proceedings, begging her husband not to add fuel to the old adage that a London tradesman may not speak like a gentleman, but he can assuredly buy one! Mr. Burton, however, was quite set on prodigality, and indeed had excelled himself, for that day he presided over a feast fit for Queen Anne herself.

For meats there were hare and coney, and a roast kid stuffed with forcemeat of figs and raisins, and pigs' maw with almonds. There were blackbirds and boiled capons and crab-appled goose, and for the second time in their brief acquaintance, Mary and Mr. Gulliver gazed upon a swan – only this bird was well browned and crisped and swam not upon the waters of the Thames but upon a glistening river of oysters and prunes!

Finally came the great bride-cake, iced with almond sugar

and *crocant* paste, tiered like a pyramid of Egypt, and surmounted by a masterpiece of confectionery which won loud
acclaim from the tipsy hosiers. For there in pride of place
beside the bridal-shoe was a stocking with its garter, both
rendered in perfect miniature, and fashioned down to the last
knitted filament in sugar-plate paste.

My mistress was very touched, and the tears she wept into
her swansdown muff were both grateful and sorrowful, as it
struck her for the first time that she must leave the parental
nest for ever, and live henceforth entirely under the aegis of
her husband.

But Time stays its march for no man, and all too soon the
hour of departure arrived. The carriage was brought round;
the bridegroom, as is customary, distributed the broken
meats to the street-beggars, and the butchers struck up with
their marrow-bones and cleavers. In the clamour Mary saw
her father wipe a tear away with his glove, and her heart bled
to think that the poor man must wanly wave away his
favourite, as if the steps of the family home were a Bristol
quay, and her carriage a bark bound for the far-off Colonies.

CHAPTER II

Marriage . . . A Cabinet of Curiosities . . . Mary receives advice from Divers Quarters on the Correct Behaviour of a Matron . . . Some Wonders of the Wide World . . . A Catastrophe . . . The Eyes of the Argos . . .

Let me preface this brief account of Mary's first years of matrimony with her own strict proviso that Mr. Gulliver was at all times the best of husbands – thus rebuffing the reader who seeks in these pages the anti-masculine polemics made fashionable by Mrs. Astell and her quarrelsome sisters. In intimate matters her Lemuel was from the outset very respectful, and showed all the consideration due to a young and inexperienced wife, never foisting himself upon her, and withdrawing immediately afterwards to his own quarters, so that she might never have the slightest occasion for disgust.

Now that they were joined by the most sacred and in-dissoluble of bonds, Mary did her best to curb her girlish fears and comply with Mr. Gulliver's wishes, as her mother had enjoined her. Yet if at first her husband's embraces did not entirely ravish her senses, she soon found that they were very far from being a burden to her. When, after several months, and with many a blush, she confessed this partiality to her spouse, asking if he would not postpone his exile and stay a little longer in her chamber, his stern frown alone would have convinced her of the immodesty of her proposal, had it not also been accompanied by a lecture on the qualities which were reprehensible in a woman, as well as those which were most becoming.

That evening after he had retired to his chamber Mary copied a list of these stipulations, committing them first to her diary, and later, by rote-learning, to her memory, so that many years later she was able to set down, without the slightest effort, a faithful reproduction:

prized: *artlessness, docility, clear complexion, restraint, slenderness of limb, gentleness, propriety*

loathed: *pride, artfulness, a masculine thrust of mind, gossip, powdering and patching, lust, scheming and calumning, tooth-picking, strong opinions*

Vanity, he had said, was also to be avoided, as the enemy of virtue and reputation. Now if the truth be told, Mary had fancied that, freed from her mother's authority, she could not only dress as she pleased, but by dint of fine robes and laces could also – for she was not one of those unfortunate women to whom Nature has been niggard of her bounties – legitimately please her Lemuel. However, she was now forced to recognize that, although her husband reviled all that was Presbyterian, he retained more than a little relish for what was Puritan, for he swiftly let it be known that simplicity was the one *bon ton* his wife might aspire to. She had escaped parental strictures only to be presented with a parallel censure, but since, as you have seen, she could bear nothing less than to incur displeasure, she vowed to knuckle down and let obedience be the watchword not only of her wifehood, but also of her coming matronhood. And indeed her efforts did not go unrewarded, for presently the birth of her daughter Caroline ushered in an interval of domestic happiness and tranquillity.

Reason and duty, however, cannot over an extended period be other than fitful guardians of the natural passions. Accordingly, the more the young wife discovered her ardency, the more strenuously did she attempt to conceal it, and to practise, long after its natural timespan had elapsed, the blushing innocence of a virgin. Perplexed as she was, Mary knew better than to turn to her mother for advice, and since her sister Harriet had removed with her family to Norfolk, I was the one in whom she confided, being the only soul she could count on to receive her without the slightest reserve, and tolerate her lapses.

She addressed me gloomily, envisaging the freedoms and felicities enjoyed by other married ladies, and regretting that her own lot had been cast so vastly different: 'Well, my Lady Mary, am I fated by invincible necessity to be punished for the excesses of my nature?'

This question was not entirely rhetorical, given that those

who are greatly afflicted by loneliness will always make tenebrous pacts with dolls, or kittens, or house-plants – for which I own I am very grateful, since it is a hard thing to possess wisdom yet lack a tongue with which to impart it. I beg you, then, do not concern yourselves with *common sense*, or the facts of so-called science, but rather ponder the universal need for relation, and the mystery of those messages which longing will always contrive to wring from shadowed silence.

Of course it is the devil's own business to advise a young matron on her conjugal affairs, for too much candour will surely bring about divorces, and if one's counsel is to err at all, better that it be on the side of caution. So, while I heartily commiserated my mistress's hard fate, I advised that Mr. Gulliver, though a man of honour and distinction, was not one to look kindly on a wife's complaint. Accordingly I warned her to keep mum for the moment, however disagreeable she found her situation. How many ladies, I declared, had learned from the imperatives of matrimony sterling lessons in self-command, while at the same time allowing their native liveliness of mind and body to co-exist in the shadows, like a treasure chest secreted in the attic of the soul, or a dark pool in which one constantly and invisibly refreshes oneself?

This last speech was delivered with a certain irony, which I believe served to remind my mistress that her loyal confidante had spent a drab year in the darkness of the marriage trunk, since Mr. Gulliver would not permit the display of childish relics until his wife had furnished the unassailable excuse of an infant. Although I could see that she was not best pleased with my advice on this occasion, she thanked me nevertheless, gave me a shamefaced kiss, and set me, not in the interior of the trunk, but on the sunny window-seat for the duration, where I could not only gaze upon the delights of rose-bush and snap-dragon, but also display myself like a bright blossom to the eyes of the passersby.

If Mr. Gulliver's bedchamber was as small as the meanest ship's cabin, his study, by contrast, was prodigal, occupying as it did the largest south-facing room, which otherwise would have served very handsomely as a withdrawing-room. On the shelves he had marshalled his library of philosophers and geographers antique and modern, while on his desk were assembled his almanacs and instruments of navigation. Between the two tall windows stood a glass-fronted Cabinet of Curiosities, in which were displayed the prizes taken on the high seas, or bartered for in the ports of all the oceans.

In the promiscuity of the Cabinet, cups carved from African rhinoceros-horn rubbed shoulders with obsidian wine-coolers from ancient Phoenicia, and coco-nut shell boxes from Taheete with Spanish *reales* struck at Lima in the reign of King Philip the Second. If, under the guise of reading the classics of literature permitted to her, Mary had often watched her husband poring over his favourites, fondling a black ebony fetish from the Orinoco river, or running a callused finger over a mother-of-pearl powder-box engraved with Nereids, it had been impressed upon her that these were no playthings for idle amusement, but the objects of a study aimed at enlarging the general understanding of the human species. As such, little Caroline – who was quite at liberty to tear my Brussels lace or hang me by the heels from the apple tree – was not permitted to tinker with them, nor the housemaid Maria to dust them, and although my mistress was charged with the upkeep of the study, she was not entrusted with the key to the Cabinet.

Upon the provenance of its contents, however, Mr. Gulliver lectured her regularly, with the boyish fervour of the true scholar, his eyes sparkling and his spirits exhilarated. In this way she became acquainted with many wonders of the world, from the roebuck-serpent of the Cape Verde Islands, which is thirty feet long and broad as a barrel, to the strange customs of the cannibals of Brazil, whose women follow their husbands to war carrying their entire household luggage, a child hung about them on a piece of calico, a parrot or ape on their shoulder, and a dog on a string, while the idle lubber carries nothing but his club or bow-and-arrow.

Attentive as she was, like many of her sex my mistress was more interested in the mysterious continents of her own nature than in regions farther flung; in this matter, thinking to find a fellow-mariner with whom to pore over her charts and align her sextant to the angles of the stars, she had, for better or worse, appointed Mr. Gulliver the Captain of her Heart.

One spring evening shortly after her second pregnancy had been confirmed, she sought to steer her husband on to her own path of enquiry. He had been discoursing – with less vivacity than usual – on the Cordillera of Chili, where he had observed meteors at times so high on the mountain top that they resembled stars, and at other times so low that they frightened the mules and buzzed feverishly about the ears of the explorers. Setting aside her embroidery, she ventured timidly, 'Tell me, Lemuel, are you happy?'

Mr. Gulliver stood at the open doors of the Cabinet, his fingers snapping open and shut a sapphire ring which contained a silver skull. 'I assure you I am content,' he answered absentmindedly. 'Why, I have a dear wife and daughter, and shortly, perhaps, a son . . .' At this he stopped short and, stricken, fixed a ghastly gaze upon the window, through which could be glimpsed the tall rigging of the ships on the river. His face, which normally bore the ruddy glow of health, turned white as a bedsheet, and with wild hands he wrestled with his neckcloth as vehemently as if it had been a common cutpurse out to strangle him in the back alleys of the Strand.

'Are you unwell, Lemuel?' cried Mary, for he had the appearance of a man in the first stages of asphyxia. Shaking his head vigorously, Mr. Gulliver threw open the casement and inhaled the evening air with rasping breaths. 'Will you not tell me what concerns you?' she begged, for she was aware that his practice had suffered some diminishment of late, and hoped to assure him that she was no fair-weather wife, but one who would gladly stand shoulder to shoulder with him in any adversity. If he should ask for aid, she would be his helpmeet; if he required economies, he would find her as frugal as her Scottish mother; indeed, if he would only tell her the occasion, she would wholeheartedly rise to it.

Mr. Gulliver, however, was not a man to confide his worries, preferring to ponder them in solitude and present the world with a *fait accompli*. Thus, bestowing on his wife a dour and resolute look, he delivered a broadside to the sloop that was her marriage, informing her that since he could not see that his business in London would soon mend, he had accepted an advantageous offer from Captain William

Pritchard, Master of the *Antelope*, and would sail on May 4th from Bristol, bound for the South Seas.

At this my mistress let out a shriek and, careless of her condition, flung herself at his feet, imploring him not to absent himself from a wife who loved him so dearly. While plunging Mary into despair, however, the confession seemed to afford Mr. Gulliver immediate relief, and the sunny colour returned to his cheeks just as her own countenance took on the pallor of the moon. In fact, dear reader, had she been less distressed, she might have concluded that this sudden turn of tempo – and the outburst of planning which followed thereupon – was a sure indication that her husband feared the entrapment of marriage as much as he relished its comforts, and, having secured his release, had set his joyful heart once more upon the far horizon. 'Come, come, Mary,' he chided, raising her up gently. 'We are not sweethearts to mewl and be mawkish, but husband and wife, and must conduct ourselves accordingly!'

Reader, I will bear witness to the nights of grief that followed, and the days spent striving to regain some small composure. In this adversity, of course, I bore my mistress up as best I could – although I cannot say I got a great deal of thanks for it – and on the first day of May it was a dignified young matron that bade a fond farewell to Mr. Gulliver at the garden gate, and suppressed her tears until the chaise had passed out of sight. Then she flung herself down on the arbour seat under the honeysuckle and, clutching little Caroline to her breast, gave way to a grief so violent that the nursemaid overheard the infant's cries of fright and hurried out to rescue her.

*   *   *

Now, as the reader will no doubt be aware, the self-esteem of a woman deserted will hold up only insofar as she can persuade herself that her beloved has included her in his plans. And so my mistress applied herself to that study so dear to the female imagination, which consists in deciphering the intentions of the male, and calculating on the basis of her insights the part she is intended to play in his grand design. If Mr. Gulliver had wished to set her a test of character, he could not have contrived a better than this extended absence: or so she told herself in these first weeks of loneliness, her one consolation being to discern in his departure not careless selfishness, but deliberate wisdom.

In the idleness enforced by her approaching confinement Mary spent many hours poring over the list of qualities her husband had commended, and resolved to progress each day in virtue and self-command. In this mood of obedience she hurried eagerly to discharge the small duties he had charged her with at parting. The first of those was to trace on his charts, by a series of markers, his progress across the globe. This indulgence he had begged of her, saying that it would please him, while on the unpredictable seas, to think his course so solidly plotted in the confines of his study – as well as providing easy intelligence of his voyage to enquiring friends and relations. The second task, which was even more precious to her, consisted in caretaking the objects in his Cabinet.

It will not surprise the reader to hear how timorously my mistress turned the key in the lock, and how she wielded her duster as gingerly as if her fingers had been the girth of mahogany logs. Now she found much that previously she had not been privileged to view, and many things to marvel at: numerous Nereids and Leviathans, and Aphrodite rising from her conch, and Nymphs who rode the waves on dolphins and seahorses. So much was of the sea, in fact, that to open the Cabinet was to sniff the salt air and hear the creak of rigging. Many was the night, I assure you, that she stood with her Lemuel upon the tilting deck and watched the gently rocking stars, and many the night that she and I fell asleep to the soft lap of waves against the pillow, and dreamed again and again of the sea. And while I do not believe that Mary had in her nature any ingrained tendency to jealousy, within a few short weeks of separation she had come to know her greatest rival as intimately as she knew herself, and could name her as none other than that cool-eyed daughter of Cytherea, Aphrodite herself, High-Priestess of the waves and winds.

Having made it plain that he frowned on the type of temperament given to sullen fits and excitable humours, Mr. Gulliver had voiced a fear that in his absence Mary would vex herself with solitariness, languor, and an excess of ungovernable grievances. Before leaving he had recommended the avoidance of melancholy by the useful occupation of mind and body, and now she took this counsel to her heart. In the words of a more famous Burton, whom the hosier, regrettably, could claim as no relation: *as bracken grows in neglected fields, and all manner of coarse weeds, so do gross humours in an idle body. A horse in a stable that never travels, a hawk in a nest that never flies, are both subject to diseases; as indeed is wit that wants employment.* Or again, in the words of Galen: *evil and corrupt thoughts multiply in an idle mind like worms and noxious creepers in a standing pool.*

In pursuing the aim of balance, busyness, and good sense my mistress did not restrict her labours to supervising the kitchen, stockroom and nursery, but also, inspired by Mr. Dryden's translations of Ovid, applied herself to a study of Latin, and to refreshing her imperfect Greek. Whenever her resolution weakened, and she lay on her couch in a dream of antics and chimeras, Mr. Gulliver rose up ahead of her to urge her on. What was she, indeed, but a *lifeless lump, unfashion'd and untrain'd, Of jarring seeds, and justly Chaos named*, and how else was she to give form and shape to her universe but by invoking her absent watchman and keeper?

Like the head of the Argos with his hundred eyes was Mr. Gulliver's regard, and poor Mary would gladly have had the whole constellation wide awake at their station that she should never for a moment be out of his sight. And indeed she thought that the entire hundred would hardly be sufficient to oversee those aspects of her life that sadly wanted correction and encouragement. It would take half a dozen eyes alone, she fretted, to keep her boisterous Caroline on the straight and narrow, and twice as many to command her to her own stumbling studies. Another dozen to overlook her as she hemmed linen under the lamplight, or scolded the parlourmaid for pertness. Yet others, surely, would observe the pleasures of the bath and the snowy froth of suds from which she rose as virginal as Venus; still more would commend the artlessness with which she rode up her petticoat to pull on her new silk stockings, or bent of an evening over some scholarly text, her hair glinting gold in the firelight, her bosom white and dimpled as any Andromache. How dearly she wished that her husband's gaze, which had seen such marvellous cities and momentous shores, which had rested on distant Chili and Cathay, should turn on her not sternly, but constantly; not coldly, but with the warmth of approbation; regarding her with eager chivalry, like a man smitten and bitten; or even jealously, like a man spellbound and bewitched.

There are readers, of course, whose knowledge of the Classics will tempt them to be clever and quarrelsome at Mary's expense. Recalling that Juno's Argos, lulled by Hermes' song, was heavy-lidded and delinquent at his post, they will quiz her with wishing his grisly fate on her own keeper – to be slain by the sword and his all-seeing eyes mocked for eternity on the tail of a peacock! To these cavillers I retort that it may be no bad thing if a young wife sweeten a bitter absence by convincing herself of her husband's tireless vigilance, for it may well serve to keep her out of mischief! Certainly the lady herself had no doubt that her Lemuel was superior in resolution to any beast of antiquity. Thus safeguarded, she was no longer prey to fits of inconsolable weeping or childish rebelliousness, and the comfort gained thereby was to stand her in good stead in the severe trials which lay ahead of her.

When the marker-flag on the sea-chart stood at the Cape of Good Hope, Mary was able to dispatch to her husband, by way of an agent of the Dutch East India Company, the happy news of the birth of their son William, but it was not until many months later that she received from Batavia a reply which contained many messages of congratulation and esteem. From that date hence, however, she heard nary a word for two long years, until the arrival of the dread intelligence that the *Antelope* was feared wrecked in Equatorial waters, and all officers and men given up for lost.

For some weeks my mistress lay sick and adrift, for without her Captain she could find no direction, and though I offered what consolation I could, I was listlessly repulsed; indeed, not even the sight of little William's countenance could rouse her from her torpor. Mrs. Burton would have had Mary in widow's weeds directly, and begged that she should give up the house at Redriff and remove the children to Newgate Street. Her father, meanwhile, sought to lift her spirits with the tale of Mr. Alexander Selkirk's rescue from the lonely isle of Juan Hernandez, where he had dwelt four years as a castaway. It was the comfort of the latter that sealed my mistress's resolve to resist the efforts of the former, for at Redriff she was privy to the comings and goings of sloops and merchantmen, a view which the narrow streets of the city would not have afforded her.

Year followed upon year, and although Mary occupied herself in overseeing the care and education of William and Caroline, still she watched and waited daily for news of their father, and at nights scanned the map of the globe as if her eager instincts might discern Mr. Gulliver upon some coral strand, mother-naked with a rude spear, or garbed ingeniously in goatskin like the resourceful Mr. Selkirk. Not a day went by, I assure you, on which she was not convinced that she remained within the compass of his gaze, and accordingly she resolved that all must be well, and her husband hale and hearty. So, despite all attempts to persuade her to the contrary, to divert her with charity balls and hints of remarriage, she would not allow that Mr. Gulliver was dead, and vowed that when he returned he would find everything as he left it: his small bedchamber like a temple, his study without alteration or speck, and his Curiosities in their self-same place in the gleaming Cabinet. She would watch over them with the same jealous eye with which he had watched over her, and should her traitorous dreams depict her beloved in the arms of a fish-tailed Aphrodite, all the more assiduously would her heart, fanned by rivalry, keep alive its attachment, and refuse to abandon him to the voluptuous deeps. Which leads me to hazard the proposition that even an imaginary rival may be a godsend, insofar as she keeps a woman on her mettle, for when on a December day in the year 1715 a ragged stranger stood before the garden gate, he found not a twice-married matron with her brood, but a wife in whose faithful heart he reigned supreme, and whose ardency, moreover, was perfectly undiluted!

The shock of this encounter was so extreme, I assure you, that I should not have been surprised if Mary had fallen into a faint at the sight of him, yet this was not in fact the upshot. As soon as Mr. Gulliver entered the porch my mistress took him in her arms and kissed him heartily, at which he started back with a furiously affronted expression, giving her immediate cause to reproach herself about the gay *coquelicot* ribbons on her bonnet, which were a sure offence against simplicity. To her astonishment, however, after uttering a few words in a language she could not at first recognize as the King's English because of the whinnying sound which accompanied each syllable, her husband fell at her feet in a swoon, and lay there unconscious for a full hour. Having revived him with vinegar and salts, moreover, she found her ministrations forcibly repulsed. With a high toss of the head and in a tone of voice much deformed by a harsh neighing, Mr. Gulliver declared that he could tolerate neither the sight nor the odious smell of a *Yahoo*, and begged her to withdraw directly.

Thinking her husband delirious, and hoping to awaken in him a natural fatherly affection, my mistress drew forward her handsome William, and her gold-haired Caroline, who at seventeen was already considered a *nonpareil*. Fortunately her dear ones were well-bred enough to conceal the alarm such a wild-eyed stranger might have inspired in them, and welcomed him prettily with a bow and curtsey, and fondly called him father. Far from soothing him, however, the sight of the young folk appeared to drive him to despair, and he declared with a dreadful neigh, 'Will you force me to consider that by copulating with one member of the *Yahoo* species, I have become the parent of more?' And with the appearance of being struck by the utmost confusion, shame and horror, he hid his face from his family and hurried out to sleep in the straw of the stables.

CHAPTER III

Mary is Passed Over in Favour of a Horse . . . Geographers Antique
and Modern . . . An Account of the Catastrophic Weathers in the
Reign of the late Queen Anne . . . Mary Studies a Map and sees a
Magical Vision . . .

Readers who have studied the recent account of Mr.
Gulliver's sojourn among the horse-beings dubbed the
Houyhnhnms, will be familiar with the unnatural privations
suffered by my mistress on his return. During the first year
the gentleman could hardly endure his wife and children in
his presence, saying that the very smell was intolerable to his
greatly enlarged and sensitive nostrils. Much less could he
suffer them to eat in the same room, but, having made a
permanent lodging with the carriage-horses in the stable,

would have his collation – which must consist entirely of vegetable matter – served to him in the manger. This state of utter seclusion appeared to be the only one tolerable to the long-lost patriarch, who banished bridle and saddle as an affront against equality, and lived with his equine companions in amity, conversing with them for at least four hours each day on philosophical matters.

In vain did Mary and Caroline attempt to approach him, for even though their toilet grew increasingly fastidious, and their skins were raw and red with scrubbing, and the laundrywoman came and went each day with veritable mountains of linen, he would not permit them to take him by the hand, and suffered their proximity only by stopping his nose with rue, and lavender, and tobacco leaves. William's filial attentions, on the other hand, gained rather more reward, so I cannot but draw the sorry conclusion that the intimate odours of the female *Yahoo*, as opposed to those of the male, caused Mr. Gulliver the more profound distress!

Any suggestion that he might renew his acquaintance with his former circle was greeted by a stubborn sang-froid, for the hermit would suffer himself to be visited neither by his colleagues Mr. Arbuthnot and Mr. Gay, nor even by his dearest friend Mr. Herman Moll, the cartographer. All inquiries were rebuffed and all calls expressly forbidden; indeed, Mary was roundly scolded for letting it be known that he had returned to Redriff. As for myself, I have no doubt that had it not been for William's persistence Mr. Gulliver would have regained neither the bare lineaments of civilized behaviour, nor one half of his previous command of the English language – a task which was finally achieved by holding before his face a glass wherein he could make a constant study of the motion of his lips, thus correcting any eccentric or equine tendencies in the vocal expression. Under his son's tutelage he also learned the arts of supping, sitting, and handshaking, and in the same mirror would rehearse the gestures of an English gentleman, mimicking his lessons until they became second nature, and thus building up some degree of tolerance towards the species he professed to abhor.

It was a measure of William's success that the debutant was persuaded to pass an hour in the study with his family on Christmas Day, on condition that the maids screen off the scullery door with blankets, for all greasy roasting smells were anathema to him, and that he seat himself at some remove, by a window thrown wide to admit the caustic gales of December.

Consider, then, the excitement with which the household, on this most holy of festivals, gathered round its head. After the exile that had been imposed upon her, my mistress could not have aspired to a higher felicity – although it is true that she found the surfeit of fresh air something of a blessing, as Mr. Gulliver settled himself to discourse upon his travels, straw-haired, beetles in his beard, moths in his jerkin, and smelling profusely of dung!

Thanks to William's diligence, however, the eloquence of his expression was but little impaired, and his political pronouncements, in my opinion, were more rebarbative than ever. He would address us, he said, on the provenance of His Majesty's Dominions, and the method of their enlargement by new discoveries. 'For example,' he declared, a deep frown contracting his brow, 'a crew of pirates are driven by a storm they know not whither, at length a boy sights land from the topmast, they go ashore to rob and plunder, they see an harmless people, are entertained with kindnesses, they give the country a new name, they take formal possession of it for the King, they set up a rotten plank or stone for a memorial, they murder two or three dozen of the natives, bring away a couple more by force for a sample, return home, and get their pardon.'

Mr. Gulliver drew back his lips from his teeth, and let out a neigh of disdain. 'Here commences a new dominion acquired with a title by divine right! Ships are sent at the first opportunity, the natives driven out or destroyed, their princes tortured to discover their gold . . .'

A fleck of froth rose to the orator's lips, and his eyes rolled up in their sockets to reveal the whites. Fearing that he had become overheated as much by his polemic as by the unaccustomed heat of the hearth, Mary signalled to William to offer the water-jug. Breathing harshly, Mr. Gulliver took a gulp from the jug, and, having slaked his thirst, poured the remainder over his head. Dripping, but with no evident cooling of spleen, he continued, 'A free licence is given to all acts of inhumanity and lust, the earth reeks with the blood of its inhabitants, and this execrable crew of butchers employed in so pious an expedition is a *modern colony* sent to convert an idolatrous and barbarous people!'

At this the patriarch, able to contain his ire no longer, reared up and, narrowly avoiding a catastrophic collision with his Cabinet of Curiosities, galloped from the room. Out on to the wintry lawn his unhappy family followed him, all of us concerned for his safety and his sanity, and afraid that the head of the household might by accident or design dash his brains out against the garden wall.

Providence, however, intervened to aid us at this moment, for a halloo at the gate announced the arrival of Mr. James Bates, the famous surgeon. On the pretext of paying a seasonal call, he had come to satisfy himself as to the veracity of certain disquieting rumours regarding his colleague's frame of mind, and now he advanced upon the shocking scene with a purposeful if gouty step, astonishment writ large upon his countenance. 'Easy, old fellow!' cried Mr. Bates, joining in the pursuit. 'Compose yourself!'

The sight of his old friend and mentor, however, served to further inflame Mr. Gulliver, who backed away behind a sweet-smelling rosemary bush and, greeting him with horribly bared teeth, let out a stream of abuse as squalid as any that ever assailed my ears, calling his patron *cider-sot* and *stinkpot*, and his entire race *horse-bridlers*, *marrow-guzzlers*, *poxy turdipoles*, *catchpenny pimps*, *bumsuckers*, *blighters*, *colicky curs*, *gaping lollies*, *nettlepedlars*, *hare-fuckers*, and *camel-eaters* . . .

Caroline and William had fallen back in dismay and my mistress, convinced that Mr. Bates' presence could only madden her husband further, drew the surgeon aside. 'Let us leave him,' she urged in a whisper, 'and allow a speedy return to the stable, where he may find repose among the inmates.'

Once inside the house the physician strove to regain his composure, while Mary hastened to acquaint him with the occurrences of the past year. 'My dear Mary,' he exclaimed, mopping his brow, 'yours is a life the very saints would shrink from!' After drinking the glass of Madeira she pressed

49

on him, he professed himself calmer. 'Hippomania,' he declared, with a scientist's gleam in his eye. 'I have seen but one case of it, and at least that poor wretch confined his delusions to a supposed expertise in the pedigrees of the turf! Dear madam, you must put up with this distressing business no longer. Indeed, I absolutely forbid it!'

'Oh, it is not so terrible,' parried Mary, stung by his high-handedness to a defence of her situation. 'I am not the first woman, I wager, who was ever passed over in favour of a horse!'

'All the better if you have the spirit to make light of it, my dear,' said Mr. Bates with a sorrowful shake of the head, 'but to my mind here is a poor lost soul who will be best succoured at the Bethlehem. With God's grace and our human skills, perhaps we may yet restore him to his senses.'

Fired by his determination to incarcerate Mr. Gulliver in Bedlam, and brooking no opposition from Mary, the surgeon sprang to the door with a step uncommonly virile. With a cry of 'To Finsbury, dear madam – I shall return with keepers directly!' he took his leave like a gallant, giving the distinct impression that, had he had a cloak and a sword, he would have flourished the one and brandished the other, as heralds every rescue in the best romances.

Immediately he had gone my mistress could think only of the impending disaster and how it might be averted. She could not bring herself to surrender her Lemuel to chain and pinion, ice-bath and blanket-gown, nor to the wanton and indolent curiosity of common horde and Charitable Commission alike. Yet she knew that the fervent Mr. Bates would never allow that a man may better recover his wits in the solitude of his own stable than in the zealous clutches of modern medicine.

Conceiving a desperate plan, she sent William post-haste to the Smyrna coffee house in Pall Mall with a note for Mr. Moll – who of all men could be depended upon to furnish his old friend with a sanctuary – intending, on the surgeon's return, to inform him that his putative patient had absconded in the interim. Then, helped by her dear Caroline, she hurried to pack linen, books and necessaries to ease her husband's exile in Devereux Street. On entering the stable to apprise him of her stratagem, however, she found to her horror that although the door was fastened and the horses safely therein, of her husband there was neither shadow nor trace.

When William returned from the Mall many were the reproaches he heaped upon himself, for in passing the stable he had hastily told his father of the plan, hoping in this way to set his mind at ease. Poor tender-hearted William! How was he to have known what we must now regretfully assume to be true – that Mr. Gulliver, terrified by the prospect of confinement, and failing to make a distinction of quality between the bars of Bedlam and the hospitality of Mr. Moll, had panicked and stampeded like any high-bred Arabian, and had gone we knew not where!

The tears wept by Mary and her daughter were bitter ones, while William, with touching manliness, attempted to console and succour his womenfolk, so that when Mr. Bates returned with two burly guardians he was met with no masquerade, but a family united in genuine sorrow at their loss.

The surgeon was quite out of countenance with the whole affair, for he had been engaged with Sir Hans Sloane and the Reverend Stukeley to dissect a young elephant which had died in the town that morning, and had missed his appointment due to his exertions on Mr. Gulliver's behalf. After proffering his condolences, he took his leave curtly, observing that the fugitive would no doubt tire soon enough of the perilous alleyways of the Riverside, and come running back to his stable – in which instance my mistress was to summon him without delay.

The afternoon, however, brought no chastened Gulliver creeping back to claim his comforts, but instead the agitated person of Mr. Herman Moll. On hearing a rapid summary of the events, the geographer took Mary's hands in his and gazed at her with eyes which brimmed with tearful sincerity, giving the lie to the belief that the Germans are of all races the most phlegmatic. 'Thank God!' he exclaimed, 'that my dear old friend has escaped those ruffians.'

Mr. Herman Moll was a tall, handsome man, long-armed and broad-handed, with fingers cracked and blackened by the inks and acids of his profession; his cheeks were patched with scarlet, as if they had been rouged, and his yellow hair, unpowdered, was clubbed carelessly back in a tail. More important to Mary than his agreeable appearance, however, was the fact that her husband had described him as the best fellow in the world, a man utterly lacking in malice, and above all one to whom she might confidently turn in adversity. Here, then, was a broad and trusty shoulder to lean upon, and the little composure that remained to her threatened to desert her at the very thought of it; indeed, her redoubled efforts at self-command made her tremble violently as she ushered her rescuer into the study.

On entering the room, however, she saw not only that the Cabinet doors stood open, but that the Cabinet itself had been emptied of all the smaller and portable objects, leaving the shelves laid as bare as was Mr. Gulliver's intention in that horrid instant. She could hold back her emotions no longer, and, breaking down, cried bitterly, 'Oh yes, Mr. Moll, he has certainly escaped. He has escaped all of us!'

The cartographer could only agree that Mr. Gulliver's action in furnishing himself with valuables dashed all hope of an early return; as for the whereabouts of his friend, he professed himself at a loss. To set off on the trail of the Curiosities would be to embark on a veritable hare-and-hounds, and most probably to no avail. To dispose of such artefacts Mr. Gulliver must needs be dressed like a gentleman, and to present himself in such a distressed condition at the abode of any respectable antiquary would invite a speedy removal to Newgate Prison. Only in the thieves' dens and receiving-shops of Limehouse could he pass unnoticed, except by the press-gang and the crimp.

At last a downcast Mr. Moll ventured, 'Forgive me, dear lady, but is it not most likely that your husband will seek passage to the South Seas, to the island where by your own account he was received with such graciousness and magnanimity?'

My mistress regarded her ally angrily, for the heart will defend itself to the last against discomfiting truth, but finally, recognizing the likelihood of his supposition, she fell into a despairing fit of tears. Such sorrow was not to be borne by the kind-hearted German, who leapt to his feet and swore that he would go immediately to scour the alleys of Lime-house and every one of Wapping's wharves, in the hope that he might gain intelligence of the fugitive, or even intercept him in the act of embarcation.

That night my mistress slept but an hour or so, for anxiety woke her in fits and starts with dreadful visions of the Riverside, and try as I might to soothe her, her restless mind would not be turned from its torment, but was compelled to imagine again and again the perils faced by Mr. Gulliver and his pursuer among the repugnant swarm of footpads, deserters, and fences.

At first light, however, the loyal geographer arrived at the door, pale-faced, with his lace torn, but otherwise unscathed, and with the following news.

While pursuing his enquiries in a low tavern on the wharf the landlady had referred him to a night-watchman who was taking his dinner of broiled red herring in the company of an old lighterman. When Mr. Moll had described Mr. Gulliver, the watchman said that he had found a wretch of that description sleeping among the tobacco bales in his ware-house. Upon rousing the ruffian, however, he had been surprised to find him well-spoken, quite the gentleman, in fact, and one who did not object to parting with a few coins in exchange for his illegal lodging. The gentleman had then begged to be introduced to any lightermen of his acquaint-ance . . .

'But here,' said Mr. Moll, 'the watchman's dining-companion took up the story, he being the very one who had conveyed Mr. Gulliver to the Pool, and set him aboard an East Indiaman sailing for Cochin on the dawn tide.' The German sunk his head in his hands and appeared as wretched as if he had been not merely the bearer of bad tidings, but the very author of them. 'I daresay I would not have believed the rogue,' he muttered, 'had he not boasted that his passenger paid him not in coin, but with a carved ivory of a sea-goddess, which brought him £20 last night in Cheapside.' He regarded Mary with a glance doleful in the extreme. 'What on earth are we to do, dear madam?'

In this matter my mistress was ahead of him, having pondered through the long and gloomy watches of the night, wherein the years of her marriage passed before her for review and were judged, if not exactly wanting, then hardly as conjugal as might have been expected. For fifteen of these seventeen years she had been left entirely to her own devices – and let me say here, dear reader, if Mr. Gulliver's is the tale of derring-do, then we stay-at-homes had also been exposed, if not to mortal danger, at least to the risks which are faced by any ordinary Londoner. I speak here, of course, of the queer inclement weathers encountered in the reign of the late Queen Anne, as if Nature herself suffered from a royal contrariety of humours, and must spew forth excess of gaiety or spleen upon the heads of her hapless subjects.

In 1703, you may recall, the first of the great storms wrought destruction throughout the kingdom, and the damage sustained by the city of London alone was estimated at £2 million sterling. Twenty-one persons were killed and two hundred wounded by falling masonry, and of the ravages let me detail the thousands of chimney-stacks blown down, the lead of church roofs rolled up like parchment, and every river barge between Hammersmith and Wapping sunk or staved. In the year 1708 Nature showed herself in another aspect, that of tumultuous heat with its attendant drought, during which such a prodigious quantity of flies fell on the city that they covered the streets like a quilt, and kept the impression of people's feet as plainly as upon thick snow. That summer's fearsome fires, and winter floods are but a sample of the hazards that fell to the wife's lot in the husband's absence. In addition, she had laboured at childbirth and lessons alike, sacrificing the bloom of her youth and a great part of her vivacity, and might therefore be forgiven for expecting that some small measure of happiness might reward her trials. Yet on the threshold of her maturity my mistress had had returned to her not a husband whom separation had fired with passion, not an Argos-eyed lover to whom her every move was a marvel, but – forgive me, reader – a half-man in a rabbit-skin bonnet, with a brain quite broken down, and a nose too nice to approach her!

Now a woman will put up with untold privations for the sake of love, will brave ill-use, penury, and any amount of inconvenience, but the one circumstance which will vanquish devotion is to be disappointed in the object of her passion, for then her noblest sacrifices will shrivel in her own regard and take on a far less flattering aspect. Suffice it to say that this is the brink on which my mistress teetered: whether to keep faith with her exalted sentiments, or cast them off like laddered hose, and with them all hope of Mr. Gulliver.

Mr. Moll was quite ignorant of the lady's tergiversations, which were not evident on her countenance, and could only admire what was discernible to him, that being, in order of importance, her handsome brow, her heightened colour, and her air of prideful intent.

'What I shall do,' she declared, with an accent on the 'I'

which did not escape the German, 'is to follow Mr. Gulliver, to the South Seas if necessary.'

Mr. Moll was greatly alarmed, and hurried to advise her against any such endeavour, but at that moment the door burst open to admit William, who thrust out a sheaf of stained and tattered papers. 'Mama,' he cried, 'I found these notes of father's in the stable. Do you not think they might be calculations of latitude and longitude?'

The cartographer asked if he might examine the figures, and pronounced William's hypothesis entirely correct. 'Dear lady, this is a stroke of luck!' he exclaimed. 'I do believe my old friend may have left us a clue to his destination.' Inviting my mistress to accompany him to his workshop, he declared that he would attempt to plot the readings on a map of the South Seas he had completed a day or so previously. William begged to go with them to Devereux Street, whence they were rapidly conveyed by a chaise, and entered a low room lit on one side by a long window and lined with benches over which artists bent at their colouring, surrounded by brushes of sable and rabbit's foot, by pots of red lead, copper green, and indigo, and by leaves of gold so ethereal that to sneeze was to send the will-o'-the-wisp a dozen yards across the room, and to breathe in sharply was to run the risk of gilding both throat and nostrils.

While Mr. Moll brings out his slide-rule and dividers, and laboriously transfers Mr. Gulliver's figures to the grid of lines on his brand-new map – a process not as straightforward as he anticipated, for it soon became evident that his friend had had at his disposal neither quadrant, sector, nor astrolabe, and had availed himself, with some ingenuity, of home-made instruments – let us take a moment, reader, to consider the enormous advance of geography since the time of the ancients to its present flowering. Is it not marvellous how the clean blade of science has hacked away the thickets of superstition, by stringent method pushing ever outwards the frontiers of the known world, while the Terra Incognita, home of all chimeras, shrinks back into the shadows? No longer can a Solinus induce a gullible public to believe in the Hercynian birds of Germany, whose feathers glow in the dark, nor persuade us that the River Niger is so hot that it boils constantly, nor, to be sure, that in Libya lives a terrible creature called the cockatrice, who creeps along like a crocodile on his front legs while his hindquarters are held aloft by wings!

No longer need a cartographer be an Isidore or an Ososius, and strive to reconcile geographical fact and theological dogma; no longer must he sniff at the wind or whistle in a pig's ear to establish his position, for now the stars and planets are all but accounted for, and the dimensions of the earth measured, and whether the Prime Meridian be at Antwerp or Padua, or, as on Mr. Moll's new map, bisecting the city of London, he will know just where he is, and just where he is going.

As the German laboured in the dusty sunlight, my mistress could not help but marvel at his craftsmanship, at the coastlines shaded with fine *hachures*, and the stippling which indicated shoal water; at the cities bricked in red lead, and the lakes shaded in pale blue bice; at the tiny ostriches and elephants which grazed peacefully on the plains of Africa, and the Leviathans which sent up white spouts from the Atlantic Seas. At the four corners of the map the wind-blowers sat astride Aeolus' bags, their trumpets in their hands: Eurus, cheerful Zephyrus, and bleak-browed Boreas, and Auster the south wind spewing forth rains and frogs across the oceans.

In the Southern Hemisphere was an artfully illuminated compass-rose of thirty-two points, with its north point adorned by the fleur-de-lys. It was here, in the centre of an indigo ocean, that Mr. Moll was applying his expertise. But even as Mary peered at the blue expanses, it was as if an islet appeared on the bosom of the sea, with shores of scalloped silver, and a bright cloud of mist which trailed like a fine white nightgown from its mountainous shoulders. At that moment, however, Mr. Moll's dividers pounced on a spot some degrees to the west and, quickly checking his measurements, he sketched with his stylus a small island shaped like a lozenge. Clapping William on the back as if he had been a long-lost brother, the cartographer cried out gladly, 'I believe we have it!'

Mary was overjoyed, and though she thanked him very gratefully for his efforts her heart, demurring, whispered that science was at fault, and that this was not the destination of her runaway. Turning her gaze instead to the place where her hopes now lay, she scanned the page with a magnifying-glass, only to find to her dismay that the islet of her discovery had vanished without trace. It was almost as if the island ordered into being by the masterful strokes of the cartographer had caused its shyer sister to sink down with a sigh and let the waters close again above her head, the better to preserve her modesty. Yet despite the precise dimensions and fixed position of the former, Mary could not escape the belief that her own island, however evanescent, was in all ways more substantial than Mr. Moll's, and stood in the same relation to it as does the solid globe to the discredited notion of the flatness of the earth. Moreover, its dazzling lineaments so reminded her of the swan which had foretokened her Lemuel that she took it as an omen, and plotted her course towards it without compass or sextant, knowing that only the rightness of Time would summon the islet once more from the seas. She expressed none of those far-darting thoughts, however, for caution persuaded her to betray its existence neither to the faithful Mr. Moll, nor even to her own beloved William.

Reader, that a matron of modest means should contemplate such a voyage may seem as preposterous as if a chambermaid should visit the Pyramids, or a common ostler presume to gaze upon Gibraltar's Rock. But no such considerations were sufficient to hold my mistress back when the bit was between her teeth, and she set herself to prepare for her departure with all the energy and tenacity of her Scots forebears. Seeing that she was adamant, Mr. Moll had kindly undertaken to enquire of Captain Fitzallan, who had circumnavigated the globe with the famous Mr. Dampier, whether a passage might be obtained for her aboard the *Aphrodite*, which was bound for the South Seas by way of the Horn. He had even gone so far as to volunteer his own services as aide and escort, but this was a sacrifice Mary would not allow him to make.

Accordingly, having equipped herself, at a cost of £150, with the foodstuffs and necessaries for the long voyage, she embarked at Bristol on the 4th of January, and stood alone and all atremble on the creaking deck, with her heart aching for the four strong walls of her house and the loving arms of her children. 'This, then,' she said wonderingly, 'is what a man does constantly without conscience or cavil!' And she shivered in the chill sleet of the Channel as her homeland slipped away behind her, for she could no more comprehend the life of action, with its thrust and swagger, its dangers and hardships, than she could decipher the run of the rigging or the calculation of current and tide. 'What courage must a man have at his disposal,' she marvelled, 'that he can turn his back upon the past, upon the familiar comforts of memory, and propel his mind ever onward and outward, towards the thin inhospitable line of the horizon?' Needless to say such a train of thought succeeded only in making her berate herself for her timidity, and she was so preoccupied by the shame of her own shortcomings that she failed to consider that even brave Achilles had his heel, and a man who is a paragon of courage on the ocean crest will certainly, in other circumstances, be every bit as lily-livered!

So, dear reader, as the Atlantic prospect stretches ahead of her, and the gulls squander their pitiful cries on the empty heart of the sky, let us refuse to be accomplice to her self-abasement, and rather give her credit for her achievements. But here let me surrender the narration to the lady herself, who, with the aim of occupying her idle hours and taming her timorousness by self-discipline, resolved to set down as best she could a log of her voyage. It is to this manuscript I now refer you, having excerpted from it such passages as may be judged fitting to the tale and of some interest to the layman.

CHAPTER IV

*A Cruising Voyage . . . On the dimensions of the Chilean Strawberry
. . . Virtue expects no Reward . . . A Valentine's Toast . . .*

Jan 6th, 1718

The weather having turned fine, I was invited to take a turn
on the quarterdeck by Captain Fitzallan, who was kind
enough to answer some of my queries about the ship and its
crew. The *Aphrodite* is a frigate of 260 tons, having 26 guns
and 108 men, although we are to take on additional crew in
Cork. While carrying no letters of marque, and licensed only
for trade and discovery, Captain F. confided that, since the
situation in the Mediterranean is volatile in the extreme, his
friends at the Admiralty have given him to understand that,
in the event of Spain reneguing on the Treaty, privateering

would not be looked on with undue harshness. Seeing how I blanched at this, the Captain hastened to say that I would be in no danger, and impressed upon me that it was his duty to protect His Majesty's subjects, as well as to advance the interests of his owners. From our conversation I concluded – not without some difficulty – that privateering is as far removed from piracy as a High Court trial from a common brawl, being conducted within the law, and that the booty taken from ships captured or detained is considered as *legitimate spoils of war*.

The ship carries above the usual complement of officers, for one quarter of the crew are foreigners, and of His Majesty's subjects several are tinkers, pedlars, fiddlers and the like, as well as two negroes, and about five boys. But the Captain assures me that I will be well protected, and so, reminding myself that my Lemuel has never shrunk from peril, I am heartily ashamed of my vapours, and resolve for his sake to show more fortitude in future.

Jan 7th

As to my quarters, they cannot be said to be spacious, but are no more confined than the cabins of the senior officers, and similarly equipped, although the Captain has kindly added a small escritoire, at which I also take my breakfast, brought to me by one Lionel Sims. The bunk is narrow, but mercifully high-sided, so that I may not tumble out in a storm, and the small window affords me a view of the main deck and forecastle; all in all, there is room for myself, Lady Mary, and my dressing-chest, and even a little to spare. The sanitary arrangements – which I confess were of some concern to me – deserve remark, for, being the only female aboard, I am privileged to possess a close-stool, rather than a mere necessary-bucket. The disposal of this, I am glad to say, is the responsibility of one of the boys, who also attends to the lamps etc., and seems a harmless enough little fellow. All the same, I have taken notice of Mr. Sims, who warns me that it would be prudent to keep my valuables under lock and key.

Jan 8th
While at anchor in Cork H.M. *Brighton* entered the harbour and ordered us, it seems, to strike our pennant, which we immediately did. A great roar of guns broke out which greatly affrighted me, until Mr. Sims assured me that it was but a salute, for all privately commissioned ships are obliged to pay respects to His Majesty's ships and fortifications! This morning we took on extra seamen, and let go some of those who had embarked at Bristol, as well as losing some who simply ran away. Captain Fitzallan seems little concerned by this, dismissing them as ordinary fellows, and not fit for our employment. Extra provisions were also loaded, to supply the immediate needs of the officers, those being several firkins of butter, 2 gallons of sweet oil, casks of bread and rusk, 100lb. weight of flour, 5 cheeses, as well as Arrack, hogsheads and cider barrels.

Jan 10th
To my great surprise, all the time we were at Cork the crew were continually marrying, despite the fact that they expected to sail immediately! Given such an abbreviated courtship, many of the weddings were conducted without banns or bouquets, in full view on the windswept quay, in the very

hour of quitting the harbour. Among these was a Dane coupled by a Romish priest to an Irishwoman, without understanding a word of each other's language, so that they were forced to use an interpreter. Yet I perceived that this pair were more afflicted at separation than any of the rest, the young bride having to be restrained by her family when the ropes were cast off, lest she hurl herself bodily from the quay, and the bridegroom, I am told, continuing melancholy for several days after we were at sea!

Jan 15th

After making good speed in a following wind, we put in this morning at Madeira, to pick up liquor, for, as the Boatswain said when I chanced to comment that the crewmen seem but meanly clad for such weather, 'good liquor to sailors is always preferable to warm clothing'. I was able to dispatch letters to my father and my dear William and Caroline with the landing-party, for there is a ship of the South Sea Company returning to Portsmouth on the dawn tide. I would write also to the good Mr. Moll, but I fear he will find me deficient in the buccaneering spirit, no matter how I try to foster it in myself. I may pick up my pen with the best of intentions, but my thoughts are sticky as mastic, and I cannot conjure up a single word. As time goes on, God grant I will be able to repay his kindness in the priceless coin of information concerning undiscovered territories, without which his geographies must fall short of perfection.

(Reader, if Mr. Moll received no scientific data from my mistress, he was generally the recipient of a large correspondence, much of it from overseas, and in this period he received from his dear friend Monsieur Antoine Duchesne a letter which greatly excited his interest.)

Mon frère,

Fortune and fool-headedness bring me to the shores of Brasil, en route for Chili, on a wild goose chase if ever there was one. It will not surprise you to hear that I am in search of the most splendid of strawberries, owing to a chain of uncommon circumstances which I shall sum up as follows. In brief, my quest began when Monsieur Nouettes-Grou drew my attention to several passages contained in a manuscript by one Monsieur Frézier. This gentleman returned last year from the Spanish Americas, where he had been sent by King Lewis to take plans of the most considerable ports and fortresses along the coasts, details of which might be of use to France should war break out once again between the two countries. Monsieur Frézier was set aboard a merchant-ship, and passed as a trader, the better to insinuate himself with the Spanish Governors, and to have all opportunities for learning the disposition of their defences. In a word, dear friend, the man was a spy, and a good one, too, judging by the very elegant plans he executed – his chart of the fortress of Angria being particularly fine. These items will come to you by and by, and I am certain you will find them useful; needless to say my own interest in the fellow is less cartographical, and pertains, as always, to my dear fragaria.

Imagine my excitement, dear Herman, on hearing that this M. Frézier – the name is such a pretty coincidence that I confess I took it as a good omen – had found on the coast of Chili a brand-new strain! Doubt me not, Herman, for I have seen the scale drawing! 'Fragaria chiloensis' *dwarfs all our* hautbois, *makes pygmies of the* vesca, *and far outstrips the English* virginiana, *not to mention our own* moschata. *I am assured by Monsieur Jussieu, who received two plants for the King's Garden, that the* frutillar, *as it is called in Chili, grows big as a walnut, or sometimes even a hen's egg!* (*The two plants received by M. Jussieu were all that remained of the batch which undertook the arduous homeward journey, and survived only because our M. 'Fraisier' — is he not a heroic fellow, who deserves our utmost admiration? — stinted his own meagre water ration on their account.*)

So, have I set eyes on these giants? Have I weighed them in my hand, and inhaled their heady scent? Have I worshipped at their floral axis, and prostrated myself before their fleshy altar? Alas, dear friend, herein lies a tragic twist! For I had every intention of doing so, and rode like a brigand to Versailles, I assure you, only to discover that some weeks before, while M. Jussieu was attending on his sick mother, some village children had dislodged the nets and gobbled up every one of the berries. M. Jussieu was distraught (*though hardly, I think, as distraught as I*) *and thereafter tended his precious immigrants as lovingly as his dear mama, watering them every day with his tears, and mulching the plants with a special compost of three parts burnt-turf to one part each of lime-rubbish and rotten dung. When four weeks had passed and no new berries had appeared, he suspected the worst, and on examining the roots uncovered the depredations of the* hanneton — *the dreaded cockchafer!*

The tragedy of it is that this glorious 'frutillar', or 'frutillier', as he has called it, is not hermaphrodite, but possesses both male and female flowers. The separation of the

*sexes, Herman! You will remember, of course, that my
hypothesis is that our little French* capiton, *unlike all other
European species, is not universally hermaphroditic, as is
commonly held . . . And so, a godsend! Had our pale native
at last found a potent partner, a sturdier stock with which to
interbreed? Might I yet be proved right?*

*Imagine my excitement, and my despair! Hopes raised and
hopes dashed, Herman, thanks to a few hungry urchins and
the hateful* hanneton. *So there you have it. If my conceit
knew no bounds, I was soundly punished for it. I sulked like
a jilted lover; I took no food for days. But finally, impelled
by Cupid's dart, you might say, I saw that the mountain
must go to Mahomet, and directly took ship from St. Malo,
quite resolved to follow in M. Frézier's footsteps and procure
some breeding-plants of my own from those foreign fields. As
added insurance, I have carried with me some of my most
vigorous* capitons, *so that I may make my experiments in
situ, if necessary. As you see, I have become so foolish that I
cannot bear to be thwarted! Only think, though, of the
possibilities for improvement, and of the countless new
varieties which might spring from this* conjunctio! *In the
meantime, dear friend, be kind, be wise, be brave — and
marry, for God's sake. Above all, bless my endeavour,
and bear with your addle-headed*

Antoine

Jan 17th
This morning a hoar frost stiffened the sails, and the men
could be heard crying out for caution, for the ratlines (these
being the transverse ropes of the shrouds, up which the
sailors clamber to gain the yards) were perilously slippery

with black ice. That a seaman's life is one of extreme hardship I no longer have reason to doubt. Mr. George Appleby, the Surgeon, attending me for a painful boil under the armpit, told me that one of the Dutchmen fell yesterday from the mizzen-top to the quarterdeck, breaking his skull, and although he examined him and did whatever could be done, the poor man expired this morning. Indeed, I had heard a commotion, but since diffidence and the deteriorating weather kept me to my cabin, I failed to witness a tragedy which might have improved my understanding of the emergencies Mr. Gulliver has undoubtedly faced in the course of his career.

Jan 18th
The wind strengthens daily, and the swell is got so bad that sickness constantly threatens. I wish often that I had the constitution of the Lady Mary, since a stomach stuffed with straw would sustain me more reliably than one which gurgles uneasily with a mixture of salmagundi and ship's biscuit. Yet the long dark nights give me ample opportunity for study, and in this I endeavour to rejoice. Despite my bodily discomfort – exacerbated by the nauseous odours which rise from the bilges – I strove to keep a clear head to puzzle over the problem of the two Aphrodites, as posed by Pausanius. In Plato's opinion it is the elder who, being born of no woman, and stemming from Uranus alone, is named the Heavenly. Whereas the younger Aphrodite, who is the daughter of both Zeus and Dione, is called common, and the Love who is her fellow-worker is also called common, moving as it does the meaner sort of men, who are apt to love the body rather than the soul . . .

Jan 19th

This morning I was awakened to a noise and disturbance, which on spying out of the window I found to be caused by some of the fowls we took on board at Madeira having got loose. A negro they call Bluebottle, since they cannot pronounce his given name, was in pursuit, but no sooner did he pounce than the birds eluded him with a hop, skip and jump, squawking mightily and shedding many feathers as they flew. Seeing that the hunt met with no success, a fellow from Dorsetshire who goes by the memorable name of Leopold Scurrup, and is very full of country lore, brought out the Cockerel. Swearing that this patriarch would call the hens to order, he set the bird on the rigging, where he roosted proudly and crowed fit to burst his lungs. Yet the mischievous chickens, far from gathering around to meekly play the mating game, kept a good distance and continued to elude their pursuers, who were now several in number, and making quite a sport of it. At last, as it must, came the *dénouement*, and I regret to say it was a sad one, for a spruce wind whipped up, catching two of the hens in their unsteady flight from rail to ratline, and tossed them overboard, where, not being swimming birds like ducks or swans, I imagine that they met a damp and gloomy fate. Whether it was a worse one than the soup-pot I am hardly qualified to say; but assuredly it came sooner. On questioning Mr. Sims about the stately negro, who is above six feet tall, I learned that the man was taken some years ago from a Spanish slaveship in the Gulf of Guinea, and has since been proud to sail the seas as a free Englishman.

Jan 20th

I am not pleased with the stiffening winds, nor is my stomach. Nevertheless studied some hours at Hesiod and Plotinus, who are of a different opinion from Plato. Hesiod says that Aphrodite sprang from the severed genitals of Ouranos, after he was castrated by Kronos; Plotinus, on the other hand, ascribes her parentage to Kronos. As to the *Aphrodite* who conveys this poor diarist across the wayward seas, I care little who her father is, or whether she have mother or no, if she be but broad-bottomed, and well ballasted, and rock her human cargo with a gentle hand.

Jan 21st

The main topsail is reefed for the first time in the voyage – Mr. Sims says that this is a measure of the foulness of the weather. He prevailed upon me to take soup but I keep nothing down.

Jan 22nd

'*Love born of Poverty and Plenty*' . . . Plenty, her father, is reason, intellect. Her mother Poverty is need, aspiration, the material . . . My head swims. Mr. Appleby has prescribed belladonna.

Jan 28th

The storm does not abate. The boy came to light the lamps, but I am too weak to read.

Feb 5th

My yearnings for calm weather are become so strong that I dream again and again of walking on the surface of a placid sea. Of this type of dream Artemidorus says: *'To a young man this dream means love of a delightful woman; to a woman, however, it represents the dissolute life of the body, for the sea is like to a harlot, which hath a fair appearance but in the end brings many to evil.'*

Feb 6th
Anchored at the Cape Verde Islands, in the hope of respite from the gales. Since I was still too weak to accompany the officers in the longboat, I saw nothing of this land, wreathed as it was in mists and storm-clouds. Yet by all accounts it is charming, and very rich in produce such as maize, dates, hogs, water-melons, and bananas. Mr. Appleby very kindly brought me a tot of the fine strong brandy distilled there, the Captain having traded some calicoes and plate for several casks.

Feb 8th
In the open sea once more, where the squalls do not lessen, so that, after beginning to recover, I am instantly brought low again. In between turns I seek diversion in the cosmogony of the ancients; I would even study the stars and the planets, if I could but see them! Failing a clear view of the heavens, then, I light my lamp and turn to Anaxagoras, who, in his study of the great stone of Agiospotamoi, first speculated on the stars that fall to the earth, which he called aeroliths. Anaxagoras proposed that the whole sky consists of glowing stone clods which have united as a consequence of their vehement rotation, and that these *nydroi* will eventually become larger and heavier, and finally too heavy. The sun, like every other star, is a *nydros*, though

of enormous magnitude, and accordingly it must share their fate, and in some far-off future crash down to the earth.

That my mistress's days are neatly diarized should not lead the reader to assume that her internal life was ordered by a corresponding self-discipline. In fact, the more she strove to keep her head high and her spirits stoical, the more violent were the squalls which convulsed the oceans of the interior – as if the storms of the Atlantic were not in themselves enough to rattle her bones, tip her topsyturvy, and swill the very soul out of her stomach! Reader, forgive her, for I cannot plead youth – which may always be pardoned its self-absorption – in excuse for her excesses, and extend a similar tolerance to the self-pity which attends on maturity like the bad fairy come to blight the Princess's wedding. Alone, as far from hearth and home as she is from her husband, she is tossed hither and thither by tempestuous thoughts. Surrounded by sailors, spied on by seagulls, she thrashes in her narrow cot as if she were a Carmelite in her solitary cell.

You will be eager to know if her condition became more congenial as she accustomed herself to the journey; you will be eager to hear of improvement. Alas, this happiness I must for the moment deny, as it was denied my mistress, for she had been instructed not to fraternize with the crew, and plain shyness kept her from the officers' table, so that in those first long weeks she saw no one but Lionel Sims, who brought her meals to the cabin, and the ship's Surgeon, Mr. George Appleby, who attended her in the most severe period of her sickness. Indeed, I was her sole and constant companion, in whom she lodged complaints and sought advice on intimate matters.

One night when black rain lashed without mercy at the rigging and the portholes were blind eyes washed by sorrowful tears, she asked me in despair, 'Tell me, are my hopes in vain? Will my search come to naught, will I perish in the course of it and, entangled in the sea-wrack, float for ever on the ocean like a broken oar?'

Hope itself is never in vain, I answered gravely, but only a liar will give a guarantee as to the outcome.

Reader, there is a time for flattery, and equally a time for frankness, and believing – albeit mistakenly – that I had been asked a serious question, I responded in kind. But my mistress was incensed by such an unadorned reply and, striking the table a blow which made me jump into the air, cried rebelliously, 'So what price virtue? Have I not tried and tried to be worthy of him? Have I not suffered enough? Must I endure still more privation?' And she broke down in sobs, thinking that Job's fate was surely her own, and imagining what plagues the Almighty in his merciless wisdom might yet throw down upon her.

Thinking that I might as well be hanged for a sheep as for a lamb, I told her bluntly that virtue has no reward, and constantly to expect one is to embroil oneself in an everdeepening habit of depravity. This unwelcome truth – that all the improvements she had wrought in her character through years of application and study guaranteed nothing at all – vexed my mistress so extremely that I thought she might pick me up and hurl me bodily across the cabin.

That the matter could have been put more tactfully I freely grant, but a doll which is passed down as many generations as a gentleman's wig is privy to many secrets, and cannot help but accumulate, on the subject of womankind, a somewhat rebarbative wisdom. I should not have been surprised, then, if Mary was displeased, for it is never agreeable to be exposed as the sort who would strike a dubious bargain with fate in the hope of securing advantage!

Accordingly it was with vengeance on her mind that Mary turned, sneering, upon her alter ego. 'You are become quite the philosopher in your old age, my dear!' she jibed, as if mere spite would smash me to smithereens. It pains me to record, moreover, the satisfaction with which she remarked that I was as ravaged by the voyage as she, my eyebrows moulting, my velvet patches askew, and my powder streaked horribly by sea-spume.

With this parting shot, I regret to say, she turned my face to the wall and hardened her heart against me. At this point the doll was in danger of rivalling the mistress in self-pity, for if Mary always had her confidante for company, no such comfort was on hand for the latter, for I had been singled out for privilege only at the cost of losing companions of my own size and condition. And although at the outset I had been proud to be plucked from the pinching ranks, now I sorely missed my old confederates, for here on the high seas there was no willing ear to hear my complaint, nor fond arm to console me, nor advocate to fiercely bolster up my cause. In this larger world I stood alone, distinguished only by my disgrace, and for the first time yearned to be returned to that companionable litter, that lost conventicle of dreams and yarns and slanderous gossip.

Next morning Mary awoke to a great calm. The storm had at last passed over, and hardly a breeze broke the surface of the sea. 'Captain Fitzallan asks your ladyship if she'll do him the honour of dining with the officers tonight,' said Lionel Sims, setting her breakfast on the escritoire and informing her that it was St. Valentine's, and therefore a day for the ladies. Having at first thought to refuse, Mary decided that she was heartily sick of seclusion, and, after accepting the invitation with as much graciousness as she could muster, rummaged through her dressing-chest as anxiously as if she had been summoned to a royal reception at Hampton Court. By six o'clock she had sampled and discarded every garment twice over, leaving the cabin awash with fine silks and velvets and chintzes. Patches were affixed to her cheek, and hurriedly steamed off; rouge was applied and wiped away, gold-buckled shoes thrown angrily aside. My mistress had followed the path of modesty too long to readily abandon it, and each time she adorned herself to the full extent her mirror returned to her not a gaze of approbation or esteem, but a hundred Argos eyes which pierced her with poisoned darts of condemnation, that she should presume to be the peacock and take pride of place at the Captain's table.

Accordingly, when she knocked on the door of the state-room, she was scrubbed up like a Quaker's doorstep and costumed soberly, nay, with exceeding drabness, without a bow on her petticoat or a clock on her stocking, and with a modesty-piece hitched so high as to deny the inescapable facts of womanhood. Yet the senior officers attended on her as if she had been a *nonpareil*: Mr. Fry, the Chief Lieutenant, plumping up her cushions; Mr. Parsons, the owner's agent, filling her glass with best Madeira; and Captain Fitzallan smiling the breadth of his side-whiskers throughout it all. Mary could not help but be gratified, not only by these kind attentions, but also by the silver candlesticks, the fine china plate, and the excellent dinner which her stomach, having calmed like the seas, could now appreciate.

At length, when the cheeses were eaten and the plates cleared away, the cook fetched in a tureen of dark rum punch, the very aroma of which would have thrown a strong man sideways, and their glasses were filled once more. Well is it said that liquor oils the tongue, for now Mr. William Ballet, the South Seas pilot, would regale the company with every detail of his Louisa, and Lieutenant Oliphant would praise his peerless Abigail, until the Captain, calling a halt for fairness' sake, drew up a list of the wives and sweethearts of all the officers, and proposed a toast to put them in mind of home.

'To the fair ladies of Bristol!' cried he with his glass aloft, at which the company stood to a man, and responded in the most heartfelt manner.

Nor was Mary to be excluded from this solemn ritual, for Mr. Lancelot Parsons, a dapper gentleman who had toasted no lady by name, sprang once more to his feet, declaring, 'Gentlemen, let us not forget our charming passenger, Mistress Gulliver . . . your very good health, madam!'

So far removed had my mistress become from the small gallantries of everyday intercourse that a blush fired her cheeks and, thanking the Captain for his hospitality, she bade the gentlemen a hasty goodnight and fled in the direction of her cabin – not before having excused the eager Mr. Parsons from the necessity of escorting her there for her own safety!

Indeed, I must admit that on the teeming ship there were many who ogled my mistress, and who would doubtless have offered more than the small kindnesses they did perform for her, had they not been strictly forbidden on pain of penalty. That punishment fell swift and harsh on the heads of transgressors was unquestionable, for the cat o' nine tails was applied without stint to those who stole provisions of the meanest sort. We had already had the misfortune to witness a fight between Bartholomew Fish, the sail-maker, and Henry Viggars, the smith, which – according to Lionel Sims, who believed that a good officer rules with a rod of iron, and recounted the upshot with relish – resulted in Fish being lashed to the main-gear and drubbed, and then confined in irons for a week.

To her credit, Mary had nothing but contempt for the type of female who will drive a man to the duelling pistol to gratify her vanity, and though eyes regarded her from the topmast of the ship to the very bilges, they served only to remind her that, as long as her husband's gaze was lacking, she was a being without shape or substance, as invisible as the far horizon on a moonless night. 'What price Valentine's Day', she cried, as she slammed the cabin door behind her, 'if I cannot draw him back across the oceans, but instead must take the man's part and go in search of him? What price toasts when I cannot persuade myself that he will raise his glass this night and toast me as his sweetheart?'

There are some, dear reader, who in a similar predicament might seek consolation, at least temporarily, in the arms of another. But the very thought of such a stratagem was anathema to my mistress, who vowed to redouble her vigilance and thus rest secure in the knowledge of her constancy. The more he would flee from her, the more assiduously would she pursue him, even if he spurned her affections as sternly as had her own blessed mother!

As she reflected on this gloomy prospect her eye chanced to fall on me, and she imagined that in her absence her doll had not only dislodged the modesty-piece from her tucker, but had also – and here, dear reader, you will suspect my mistress of being in her cups – contrived to remove herself from the dressing-chest to the window ledge, the better to exhibit her décolletage to anyone who passed! Flying into a sudden fury, Mary ejaculated, 'So you would presume to be My Lady Fair, for everyone to gawk at! Well, doll you are and doll you will remain. Mark my words, as your custodian I will see to it!' And with that she whipped me more soundly than I deserved, and put me to bed without any supper, thus gaining the one release available to her.

But waste no pity, tender reader, on the recipient of the beating, for I can assure you it was nothing to what I had received from Mary's mother and grandmother before her, since, like any other servant, a doll soon learns that a drubbing is all in a day's work. As for the other treatments to which I had been subjected in the course of my long service to that family, let us examine those by and by, but only insofar as such revelations are occasioned by the needs of the narrative.

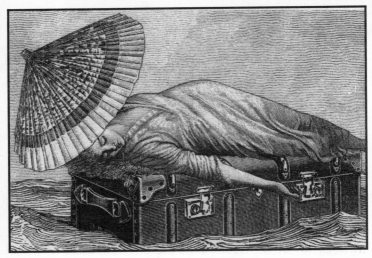

CHAPTER V

*A Doll's Dilemma . . . The Rounding of the Horn . . . St. Elmo's Fire
. . . On the Curious Nature of Heroism . . .*

If, as the latitudes grew shorter, and the days longer and balmier, Mary was diligent and kept dully to her diary, the same could not be said of my mettlesome self, whose spirits could not long be subdued by mere chastisement. Presently I grew exceeding restless, and if I could I would have bounced and jounced on the dressing-chest, thrust my bosom to the window, and even rubbed myself against the good Mr. Sims, for I was avid as a kitten for caresses. Starved as I was of masculine company – for I had been sequestered always with my own sex – I now found myself in proximity of 160 stalwarts, all stripped down for their work in the Tropic sun, their jackets thrown aside, their torsos spare and statuesque, their grey wool stockings rolled down to reveal calves worthy of a Phidias. There was much washing and shaving too, and oiling of pigtails and playing of harmonicas: all, in fact, that had hitherto been accomplished below-decks was now performed in full view of my inexperienced eye.

The sailor being his own sempstress, there were those who took advantage of the warm weather to mend their sailcloth breeches, and more than one who, forgetting there were ladies aboard, sat mother-naked in the fo'c'sle but for a belcher handkerchief festooned across the privates. Presented with such generous fare, I was quite overcome with excitement, my lips bone dry, my cheeks flushed up like autumn apples, and while my eye ransacked the feast spread before me, my heart was far too hungry to discriminate, and suffered the same painful indecision as the ass in Buridan's famous paradox which, finding itself between two equidistant and equally desirable bundles of hay, starved to death before it could choose. For there was not one of the men that was too portly, since the regime aboard would not allow it, nor had the gout, or the red-veined nose and rheumy eye that come of cold climates, dissipation, and the unhealthy vapours of the city. Here was a tender forelock, a shadowed throat, the arch of a naked foot; here a pair of surging shoulders freckled by the sun, and a broad arse straining mightily against the press of pantaloons. Here was night and day, light and darkness, mongrel and thoroughbred, solid age and blooming youth: here the salt-blond fleece on the chest of a Dane, here the bare belly of a Chinaman, smooth and brass-coloured and sleek as a doorknob, there the negro high on the cross-trees, his forearm a dark shield for his watchful eyes, his body curved taut as the bow of far-darting Apollo.

As my mistress sweated over the *Odyssey* of Homer, I took advantage of the opportunity afforded me to study a matter closer to my own concerns. Being without either the disadvantages or the benefits of body-hair, I was especially fascinated by the luxuriant growths revealed by such promiscuous nakedness. Not for seamen the privilege of wigs, and so I had already feasted my eyes on locks straight and fine, or crisp and greying, hair waved like the eddies of a tide-rip, or fronded in hyacinth-curls at the nape of a neck. Now, however, I was able to savour the whole gamut, from the small nosegays which sprouted on the joints of toes and fingers, to the sweet-springing sweat-damped hair of the armpits. Nor, as the sun glinted on downcast eyelash or sleeping beard, did I ignore the secret hairs, the bearish pelt hugging the small of a back, or the bush that nested like a great black cat between a pair of handsome thighs. For so well-endowed were the seamen that had they been citizens of a society in which *hair* was the common coinage they would have plucked gold guineas from their heads and fortunes from their nether parts, and purchased all the luxuries a rich man currently lays claim to! Even a doll, as you see, may daydream, and in my reverie why should not sailors be as prosperous as lords, for hair is a glory just like riches, which comes by heredity, and has no fairness to it, in that it cannot be willed or worked for.

Thus it was, from my peeping-post at the window, with my thoughts swinging back and forth between the lascivious and the merely acquisitive, that I witnessed the preparations for the Crossing of the Line, it being the custom to duck those who have never passed the Tropic before.

This ceremony occasioned the arrival on deck of the Lord Chancellor himself in the form of one James Cash, ship's barber, who fetched out shears and razor and set about lathering, pate-shaving, and delousing, so that I had cause to envy his intimate prerogative, and the nimble fingers which trimmed down beards and prinked up side-whiskers, and the feet which trod so carelessly upon a burgeoning Exchequer of curlicues and shorn-off locks. Watching, I sorely wished that for once in my life I might be crushed to a breast neither girlish nor soft, but rather one that was strong and stringy, and, like the bark of the cedar, both yielded and repulsed; and that my lips, which had had their fill of feminine kisses, might thrill at last to the bracing rasp of mustachios.

It was the former that I suffered now, however, for my mistress, who had come to the window to investigate the commotion, pecked her darling fondly and clasped me to her bosom by way of apology, half-smothering me in the process, and temporarily obscuring my view of the bacchanal.

By now the cross-bar had been lashed to the line, and Mr. Leopold Scurrup, that expert on husbandry, hoisted up to the yard-arm, thence to be dropped into the placid waters, and hauled out dripping from his baptism, as abashed as if he had lost his virginity; whereupon the men let loose a battery of vulgar sallies on the Dorset debutant, clapped him one by one on the back, and stopped his startled mouth with arrack.

The Captain, meanwhile, stood at the ready to shake the hand of each one who braved the ducking-stool, or else to levy a fine of half a crown on those who begged to be spared – a sum which most paid up cheerfully enough, on hearing that it would be spent on liquor for the ship's company on their return to England.

Where I had seen everything, my mistress saw nothing, but, Homer in hand, gazed on the seamen as vaguely as Penelope on her capering suitors, her heart brimming with her own lost hero, and *'that instant vanishment into blind silence, as though the Harpies, winged scavengers of the wind, had whirled him into their void'*. Thus, reader, were both doll and mistress preserved from temptation, and each in her own way lashed to the mast as firmly as Odysseus – the one by morality, and the other by immobility.

But let us abandon for the moment the all too familiar frustrations of the feminine and, taking the helm from the Bos'n, steer a course to the black-soiled Isles of Grande, in the mouth of the Amazon river. Here let us supervise the wooding and watering, and the carpenter busy at his trestles, and the sail-maker plying his skilful needle; let us even venture ashore to risk the lions, jackals and tigers, and share a hogshead with the Indians, who in the old days terrified the first *conquistadores* with tales of the gargantuan women who ruled the interior, so that the brave explorers fled back to their ships, and named the river after the one-breasted warriors of Queen Penthesilea. Then, when the work is done and the anchor is weighed, let us be pure *animus* and perch aloft in the cross-trees, where we may survey the South Atlantic and the Patagonian spires, and the penguins which flap their wings from floating icebergs like stranded Sirens begging to be rescued.

At the close of the month of April so southerly was our latitude that the frost of it penetrated the dreams of all aboard, from the boy huddled under the gunwale, who fancied that he slept on a market stall in Cheapside among frozen cobnuts and cabbage-stalks, to Mary in her narrow cot, who dreamed of a white ship like a wedding-cake on the dark ocean, lit at each mast by candles, with winged sails spun from sugar-plate, and a tiny mariner perched atop the cross-trees with his spyglass trained on the horizon and his heart ablaze for Ithaca.

So, as they drowse, let us steer them safely round the treacherous Horn, past the barren brute volcanoes of Tierra del Fuego, until dawn wakes them to a queer quiet and a sombre lowering sky. Now they rub from their eyes the encrypted sleep of polar regions, and creep about whispering, for though nothing can be seen to be awry, nothing is quite as it should be. It is as if an unseen element had entered by an invisible gate, something not quite silent, a hiss or a tremor, a small impulse felt clearly by the cooper in the iron hasps of his water barrels, and the smith as he beats a chainplate on the forge, and glimpsed also by my mistress who, engaged upon her toilet, sees that the hair will not wait for the stroke of the brush, but crackles up impatiently to greet it.

All unsuspecting in the meantime, Mr. Parsons and Captain Fitzallan chart a new course for the port of Valdivia on the coast of Chili, this being a destination agreed behind closed doors in Bristol and kept a strict secret ever since, on account of the gold to be got there, and the perils to be faced in the getting of it.

This town, as the story goes, bears the name of the first grandee who governed it, a man so covetous of the precious ore that he used the Indians in his employ most barbarously, taxing them beyond their means, and beating them so grievously if they came to him empty-handed that they often died from their injuries. Finally, we are told, the natives joined together and, taking 2lb. of gold, melted it down, and brought it to the Governor, saying, 'O Valdivia. Thou hast a very great and greedy desire after our gold. We have used all possible means to satisfy thee, but could not. Now by good hap we have thought upon a way. Here is gold; drink thy fill, for here is enough to satisfy the most covetous.' And they bound him with ropes, and poured it down his throat, whereupon the modern Midas died in agony. (A rousing tale, indeed, and yet I do prefer Ovalles' version, wherein the Governor was slain by rebels led by his former slave Lautaro, since it bears out the old adage that no man is a hero to his own valet.)

A metallic light on the brass vane of the astrolabe, a buzz like bees in a lilac bush, a current whispered between the two points of the dividers like treason between conspirators . . . now the phenomenon building in the stateroom reveals itself as the precursor of lightning-fork and thunder-clap. For a Nature which seeks release is yet reined in by contrary tendencies of the ether, rather in the way that opposing currents at the Equator result in those windless realms we call the Doldrums. Only here her power is neutralized but partially, and she discharges little by little what cannot fully be unleashed, touching the mastheads with a luminosity now moon-coloured, now ghostly pink, gathering her glittering energies on the yardarm until at last, with the hiss of a hundred angry swans, she flows like a molten river down the rigging to lick at the maindeck with cold tongues of fire. To a man the sailors scatter before her, for the Roman Catholics among them believe that the eerie light emanates from the body of Christ, and call it *Corposanto*, and cross themselves, and Protestant and heathen alike batten themselves below, for there is not a mariner on earth who does not hold that, if the light of St. Elmo's Fire strike a man's face, he will be dead within the day.

The ship, then, sailed on waywardly, with none to reef a sail or man a windlass, her helm aglow with a halo so mischievous that neither Captain nor Bos'n dared touch it. Nor was the slopping water in the bilges immune from the contagion, so that the rats rushed up to the mizzen deck with a great noise of squealing, but found no sanctuary, for not a single surface was left unscathed by the lightning, and if they would not throw themselves into the sea then they must dance the hornpipe, and die a death both luminous and lively. The breeze freshened, and the sails bellied, and for days and nights the ship scurried westwards on the wind, as if attempting to outdistance its affliction, but only in her own time would Nature blow out her light like candles on a cake, and set us free from her enchantment.

When that day of deliverance arrived, the boys were sent up first to empty the necessary-buckets, the long incarceration having done little to improve the odours below. Seeing that no harm came to the guinea-pigs, the officers surged forth to take a welcome breath of air and give the crew their orders, for the mainsail was tattered, and the bowsprit wreathed in sea-wrack, and the decks were thick with the crisped corpses of unlucky rats.

Although he had estimated that they were by now some eighty degrees to the west of Chili, Captain Fitzallan had not abandoned all hope of Valdivia, and accordingly made plans to provision the ship on the nearest island, and thereafter turn east to tackle the teeth of the wind.

My mistress, meanwhile, paced the deck in a state of great excitement, her hair and petticoats flying in the breeze and her eyes scanning the west horizon, for at last the great South Seas surrounded her, and each low white cloud in the sky might be the harbinger of *Houyhnhnmland*. Mirages rose before her, shimmering like hopes, and cliffs so close that she need only reach out her hand to touch the destiny which beckoned from their parapets.

So dazzled was she by this vision that a shadow of forgetfulness was cast over the emblem which had appeared to her in the German's workshop, whose lines were too subtle to be inscribed on any map, and whose existence was entirely without proof. That enigmatic island, whose substance had compelled her once, which had cried out to be husbanded, to be walked upon day by day and watered with tears like a garden, now sank back into immanence, and hid itself in the abysses of her mind. – Ah, reader, how easily she was diverted from her course, and not only by the machinations of the Captain! But to our tale . . .

In the stark light of noon the lookout sighted land to the north-east, and the Captain held the helm towards it. A great mist of surf veiled the promontories, and the southern fiords were so sheer-sided and inhospitable that he must run before the wind and seek a calmer anchorage on the leeward shores. Here, in an embrace of arctic and tropic, snowy peaks disgorged their glaciers, whose startling snouts, fringed by tree-ferns and oleanders, abutted the beach, and nuzzled at the turquoise sea.

My mistress was all agog to explore the place, and would

have gone ashore with the pinnace if she had not been forbidden by Captain Fitzallan, since by his reckoning the island was none other than New Zeeland, whose Indians, by all accounts, were warriors, and very jealous of their territory.

(Here, reader, I must concur with the Captain, for if Mary should be abducted at this stage in the narrative, I would be left as the sole heroine, and I venture that you would not be satisfied with the cruising voyage of a doll, no matter how edifying her adventures! Better by far that she stay aboard with her embroidery, and await the return of the longboat, with its stock of yams and tamarinds, casks of sweet water and fresh-caught crayfish, and giant turtles scooped live by Mr. Scurrup from the shallows.)

The loading was speedily completed, and as the Captain itched for the east and spun the wheel around, so Mary gazed impatiently westwards, and neither one saw what the sky said above them, nor how the white storm-birds signalled a warning with the scarlet stripes of their tails. Odysseus is not the only mariner to be dealt ill winds from Aeolus' bag, and scarcely were we out of the lee of the land than the first squalls hit us amidships and hauled us around. And no matter how a proud man hates to bow before necessity, the Captain must grind his teeth at the helm and give up all hopes of Valdivia.

Reader, you have travelled far, and suffered too many sordid realities, so I shall not weary you with the many leagues the bark was borne into the far west, nor with the days of ennui and disgraceful odours under the battened hatches. Suffice it to say that in the ensuing weeks eight of the crew were swept overboard, two bled to death in a murderous quarrel, and one expired when a great tunny fish, which had been thrown over the ship by the force of the waves, struck the poor soul square on the head and broke his neck.

Empty holds make bad ballast, and so unprofitable had the voyage proved that we were weighed down neither by silver nor gold, nor pepper nor pearls nor indigo. Thus the ship was at the mercy of every watery hill and furrow, and with each new buffetting grew weaker, until at last the typhoon triumphed and dealt the brave *Aphrodite* the death blow. Waves rose up tall as cathedrals, and the ship set her head at them like a horse ridden cruelly at impossible hurdles, and was immediately stricken. The masts that were her limbs splintered like kindling sticks, and the ribs of her hull caved in before the immeasurable might of Nature.

Chaos and seething darkness, reader! – Imagine the hue and cry as the crew ran hither and thither, ignoring the commands of the officers, and thrusting them aside to gain a swifter access to the boats; imagine my mistress's terror as she clung to the tilting walls of her cabin, believing she had been forgotten. Let us not lose our faith in human nature, however, but instead record that at this very moment Lieutenant Oliphant dashed down from the quarterdeck and hurried her towards the poop, which by now was at an angle that would have daunted an Alpine goat. Nevertheless they clambered undeterred up rail and rigging, until the boats lay below them, and willing hands reached out to help them to their goal. Yet now, within sight of safety, Mary remembered with horror that her dear companion, who had been overlooked in the emergency, was stranded in the sinking hold. 'I must go back at once!' she cried, and despite the furious objections of the gallant Mr. Oliphant, scrambled down to rescue me.

No one, I assure you, would be more embarrassed to be called a hero than Mary, who would simply say that one who was abandoned as she had been could not so easily abandon, and if all was lost – as she was convinced it was – she had rather go down with her doll.

You will decry such modesty, perhaps, protesting that she acted without a thought of her own peril: but to this I shall reply, nay, she acted without a thought at all. For if we are to examine the nature of heroism, we shall see that it is exactly the absence of reason that allows flashing instinct its freedom. And if exemplary deeds may be accomplished in this manner, then so will base ones, and one can no more ascribe virtue to a mere accident of temper than to the inborn colouring of hair or skin or eye. By the same token let us not take a moral stand and condemn those who lack such impulsiveness, for where no choice exists there can be no dishonour. Reader, I appeal to your intelligence! Is it not absurd that the stay-at-home who steels his courage for the daily dramas receives no plaudits, while at the same time men assign a false status to the heroic, and wrongheadedly strive after it, when by simple reason they could save themselves much sabre-rattling, and send a hundred Alexanders into retirement, and lengthen the lives of a million subalterns? That being said, I will refer you to Mary's ancestry, for I will allow that some nations, notably the Scotch, lack any talent for the humdrum, but rise to calamity with the style and relish of a gourmet before a fabulous table!

Having snatched me up safely, my mistress ran aft, where, seeing not only that the boats were full but that some had already capsized and tipped their occupants into the waves, she clasped me to her bosom and leapt into the tossing seas. At once the cold waters closed over our heads, and at once spat us out again, while all around the dismal cries of drowning men echoed above the roaring wind. Amongst the debris of broken spars pale arms waved ever more feebly as the currents dragged the sailors to their doom, and if Henry Viggars and Bartholomew Fish struggled, as they had in life, to the very last gasp, there were others who silently gave up the ghost; such a one was the negro Bluebottle, who, being unable to swim, shut his eyes and shrugged his shoulders and went down straight and stately as a totem-pole.

Saddened by this dreadful sight, Mary was certain that her fate was sealed, and muttered despairingly, 'Well, my dear, it is surely absurd to die, but between you and me I had rather drown than be torn to ragged lace and swallowed by a shark.'

Thus doll and mistress prepared to meet our end together, without a notion of what ceremony might see us properly on our way. Knowing no technique which might have expedited our demise, we lay supine on the waters like two Ophelias, and closed our eyes, and said our slight goodbyes, and since I could summon no wise words with which to dignify our final hour, I consoled myself with the thought that it was no more absurd to expire in decent silence than on a fulsome tide of rhetoric.

What Mary had hoped for was not to be, however, for as we two surrendered ourselves to the uncertain arms of the Almighty, her hooped petticoat filled with air and buoyed us up, so that despite the dreadful fathoms below us we floated on the rocking seas as comfortably as if they were a cradle.

The sea continuing to refuse us, and the sharks mercifully keeping their distance, we soon became bored with waiting, and took to inventing verses, singing lullabies, and reciting the nursery rhymes that Mary had learned in happier days at her mother's knee. And here the tale might ignominiously have ended, were we to depend solely for deliverance on Parfait Knight, or prancing charger, or even on Sindbad's blessed Auk. Rescue, however, has its own laws, and arrives always in the most appropriate, if not the most glorious form. In this instance succour took the shape of a large dressing-chest which, as it bobbed towards us on the waves, was revealed as the same brass-bound mahogany Mr. Burton had ordered for his daughter's wedding from Winterbourne's of Frith Street, and which contained all that a well-bred lady might require on a voyage to the Southern Hemisphere: her gowns of grosgrain and paduasoy, her muffs and mantles, her tippets and pinners and petticoats, her stays and stomachers, and her store of stockings knit in all conceivable stuffs and gauges. Needless to say such a gift-horse was not to be looked in the mouth, and stoic was swiftly turned to survivor as the chest hove to, was nimbly mounted, and bore its riders off on the westward current.

In the long nights that followed we were nudged amidships by amorous seals, and in the brief blue days penguins on the drifting ice-floes saw a strapping matron astride her luggage, and, in the small shade of a lace parasol, a pale-faced infant with her wig askew. Ten times frozen and ten times thawed, we traversed the southern ocean, and were borne, had we but known it, past the tip of Van Diemen's

Land, where Fortune filled the parasol with a fair wind and drove our odd bark northwards into balmier seas. At last we half-starved mariners, salted like kippers and swollen-lipped with thirst, were cast up on a milk-white shore at the end of nowhere, where we fell at once into blessed oblivion.

CHAPTER VI

Lady Mary's Luck . . . The Legacy left by Mr. Gulliver . . . A Narrow Escape from the Firing-squad . . . Great Power brings Great Responsibility . . . Fashion Notes for the Ladies . . .

If hitherto my mistress and I have been inseparable, it is no fault of mine that here, for a brief interlude at least, our narratives diverge. Reader, when I awoke, I was sure I had gone to Heaven, there to have my prayers answered, for not only had the Almighty rewarded me with companions of my own size, he had also equipped me with a trim throne of meet proportion, a silver goblet that suited my lips, and sweet-smelling flowers that exactly fitted my nose; in short, he had abolished the monstrous from every realm and tailored the world to suit me!

The well-read will be quick to deduce from these clues that we had arrived, by a strange stroke of Fate, on the island of midgets since made famous by Mr. Gulliver himself. Yet in this they will have the advantage of my mistress, since it was only after her departure from Redriff that the manuscript containing the details of his voyages was discovered by William, hidden in a manger of straw, dung-smeared, and much nibbled by cockroaches. It is true, of course, that a wife is often the last one to hear of her husband's doings, yet ignorance may serve her well if it saves her from worry, and certainly if it keeps her from the intelligence that her husband has pissed on Imperial palaces!

Innocent as a child, then, and delirious to boot, Mary woke on the strand with a loud drumming in her ears and in her heart a wild hope of horses, believing she had come at last to *Houyhnhnmland*, and would presently be reunited with her runaway. Small hooves do not thunder, however, but rather patter lightly, like rain on a pond or the absent-minded tapping of distant pencils, and the gross exaggeration of the sound was due entirely to her enfeebled state. When her eyes opened she found herself encircled by a miniature cavalry, all helmeted and halberded and with their lances at the ready. This sight so confounded her that for a moment she believed herself at Redriff, playing a game of lead soldiers; upon turning her head to look for William, however, she found that not only was she pinioned, but the slight movement her bonds allowed was enough to make the little horses steam and stamp and snort.

Presently the squeak of a trumpet sounded, announcing the arrival of a person whose plumed hat and proud medals marked him out as substantial. Mounting a rostrum no bigger than her jewel-case, this gentleman proceeded to read from a parchment the size of a postage-stamp, and though Mary could comprehend not a word of his address she concluded from his rancorous tone that it was more likely to be philippic than panegyric.

The handicap of language could only exacerbate a situation already irksome in the extreme, since her hooped skirt stood up before her like a bell-tent, and she could not see her feet. Thus beached and bondaged, she could do nothing to preserve her modesty, and must suffer herself to be a bowl upturned to the eager eyes of the citizens who moaned like mosquitoes behind the restraining barricade of lances. Being a woman of spirit, however, she gathered the rags of her dignity around her as she could not gather her petticoats, and declared, 'Your Excellency, I am Mrs. Lemuel Gulliver, an English gentlewoman, who has been shipwrecked on this shore by no fault of her own, and who wishes your citizens no harm. Please be good enough to unloose me, and accord me the courtesy due to any traveller in distress!'

The harangue from the rostrum ceased abruptly, and a deathly hush descended upon the crowd. Such a profound effect would have gratified a Greek Orator, let alone a London housewife whose words had never wielded a great amount of weight, and could not help but raise my mistress in her own estimation. Somewhat steadied in her spirits, she took stock of the scene around her, and was surprised to see that, despite his puffed-up chest and his fierce mustachios, the tiny *generalissimo* was quite decrepit in appearance, his lace yellowed, his plumes moth-eaten, and his hose so laddered that she wished in her homely way that Abel might be called upon to mend them. The scarlet uniforms of the lancers were similarly threadbare; as for the assembled citizens, they were so ill-shod and thin-shanked that her charitable heart went out to them.

Her reverie was interrupted by a squeal both irate and decipherable, as the general pounced on the name of Gulliver like a blackbird on a grasshopper, cracked it in his beak, and broke its back, and, shaking it asunder, tossed its remnants to the stirring crowd. An eerie ululation issued at once from the audience, for all unwittingly Mary had added insult to injury, thus playing into the hands of the demagogue, who shadow-boxed about the rostrum, stabbed a righteous finger at the air, and in short employed every technique which may exploit the discontent of the masses and whip them to a frenzy.

Such tantrums cut no ice, however, with one who still believed that size was on her side; indeed, she would have scolded the wee thing roundly had she not at that moment chanced to see the firing-squad which was drawn up six inches from her ear, with muskets primed and ready to dispatch her: an artillery, moreover, which was augmented at a distance by a solid cannon and a brace of bombardiers!

(Here the reader who is familiar with the *Travels* will note that the Lilliputians had abandoned their bows and arrows for superior powder and shot, and will deduce there-from that such an advance in military science could have been occasioned only by an alien example, that is, by a study of Mr. Gulliver's pocket-pistols. And whether we hold the gentleman liable or no, we shall surely find the upshot unfair and unfortunate, if it expose the blameless Mary to dangers far graver than those that were ever faced here by her husband.)

Reader, they say that travel broadens the mind, and I do not doubt it. And if the travel be bipartite, then so much the better, for then you will have two broad minds for the price of one. My point is this: I should do you a disservice were I to expurgate my separate adventures, so, having first made the promise that no harm will befall my mistress in the meantime, let me turn back the clock and rejoin my tale at its exalted outset.

Strange it is but true, that if the Lilliputians had had more than their fill of giants, their animosity did not extend to a *fetish* carried upon a giant's person, particularly if the fetish in question were a figurine, and that figurine a female, and that female borne like Aphrodite on the crested foam! Here it must be said that the natives had no concept of the doll as folk in England know her, and would have considered it blasphemous to use her as vulgar toy or plaything. In this they followed the peoples of antiquity, an examination of whose sacred sites reveals among the awls and axe-heads small female effigies scraped roughly from a round pebble, modelled in clay and powdered bone, or carved from mammoth ivory or alabaster. Since no earlier idol exists, even at the very dawn of Time itself, I believe I may be forgiven for contending that all other doctrines are no more than the jealous and heretical descendants of this primeval faith. Here then is a measure of how far the doll has come down in the world, and how strenuously her secret powers have been subverted, so that she who was once venerated is either thrust into obscurity or execrated, like the waxwork the witch impales with her malevolent pins.

Needless to say there is no doll on earth who would speak

openly of her heritage, lest she be accused, at the very least, of delusions of grandeur. Yet now by a strange stroke of Fate I found myself exalted beyond my wildest ambition, with a thousand supplicants prostrate before me, and a Priestess extolling my perfection, and two strapping attendants fanning me with the glorious tail-plumes of the moa-bird. My throne, reader, was of carved turtle-shell inlaid with lapis lazuli, and my grey silk cloak was glazed like silver fish-skins. Of my previous garments not a stitch remained, with the exception of the garter with its runic inscription, for the rags of my shipwrecked clothes and the broken buckles of my shoes had been salvaged from the flotsam, to be ensconced as sacred Relics in the temples of the land. And though my wig had been swept away by the waves, leaving me as bald as any babe, and one of my china arms had been snapped clean off at the elbow, I could be in no doubt that in the pious eyes of the pilgrims my beauty was supernal.

The memory moves me, I confess it. For does not the meanest among women carry in her heart the same aspiration, that though she be worn-down and broken, yet she may be remade, her body bathed in the revivifying oils of the tea-tree, her limbs massaged, and her weary feet anointed with aromatic balm? If in her dreams her eyes are luxuriously shaded with antimony, her ears adorned by rubies, and the universal light of Heaven drapes her shoulders with its golden shawl, why should it not be so, that on some real morning she wake worshipped in an arcane temple, with anklets of pearl and speaking Akkadian?

Reader, if here I strain your credulity, well so be it, for I do not make it my business to dice with the discourses of Divinity, there being enough sceptic scientists anxious to dismiss them, and depose the *anima* from her throne. Can we not allow for once the eternal sea of song, and ecstasy's seizure? Can we not allow that a doll may be ravished by the sunrays which enter through the open roof, and the soft air that laps at her skin, and the sight of the hummingbirds which dart among the blossoms on the trellises? Can we not allow one so long abased to be lauded as *Most Brilliant One, Who holds the Reins over Kings but dost Release the Bridles of Maidservants.* To be adored one hundredfold under the title of *Tireless One, Torch of Earth and Heaven, Whose Knees are Swift and Whose Vulva Sweeter than Date-Wine*? So let her enjoy it while she can, let her grow dizzy in the blue scent of incense, let her be icon and incarnation. To be a symbol of the Godhead, after all, is not to be sneezed at, for it is a pleasure not easily come by in England!

My gigantic mistress, meanwhile, lies as I have left her, accused incomprehensibly by the cocked muskets of the militia, condemned by the crowd, and sentenced to death by the wrathful demagogue. Yet even at the eleventh hour the voice of one just man may counter the collective prejudice, for now a shout rang out, and the crowd parted to allow the passage of a person running at full-tilt, who mounted the podium in a lather and proceeded to scold the general into silence.

The muskets, to Mary's great relief, were promptly lowered, and the complaints of the crowd quelled by a word from the civilian who, bowing tersely, pronounced in English: 'Principal Secretary Reldresal at your service, Madam Gulliver. I have the honour of being acquainted with your husband, who was kind enough to teach me something of your language. But please listen carefully, for I have won you but a brief reprieve, and must yet convince the Emperor it is shameful to sentence the wife for the husband's treason, and doubly so when the lady in question cannot comprehend a word of the articles brought against her.'

Mary gazed astounded at the Secretary who, having secured her attention, outlined the history her husband had withheld, with its catalogue of disasters and diplomatic incidents, and the intrigues which had culminated in his impeachment.

'Madam,' he concluded, 'I will be frank with you. Your situation is grave. I am afraid that our poor citizens, egged on by certain factions in high places, hold Mr. Gulliver responsible for their reduced condition, and are eager to punish him by proxy. I am to plead your case tomorrow with the Emperor and his advisors, but I am one against many, and in all honesty I can hold out little hope. I must ask you, therefore, to prepare yourself for the worst. In the meantime I have received a guarantee that you will not be harmed, but instead confined in the quarters your husband occupied, where you will at least be assured of a little privacy.'

This shocking speech plunged my mistress into the depths of despair. What a terrible trail Mr. Gulliver had left behind him, and what a pretty pass it had brought her to, if she who had done no wrong to a living soul should now lie with her life in the balance. 'Sir,' she said wretchedly, 'I am blameless, but I offer heartfelt apologies on behalf of my husband, as well as any recompense that may be required by Their Excellencies.'

Assuring her that he would convey this message to the

Palace, the Secretary fixed her with an eye bright and black as a sparrow's and said urgently, 'Forgive me, madam, if I beg that you do *nothing at all* in the meantime which might further incense the populace, for whom your very largeness is irritation enough!'

This admonition so alarmed my mistress that in the ensuing preparations for her transportation she lay motionless as a fallen log and scarcely breathed at all. How easily might the swell of her breast unbalance the midgets who swarmed about to cut her strings, and how easily a sneeze dislodge them, or a cough tumble them to the ground to break their heads! Such thoughts increased her physical discomfort beyond measure, until she longed for a sleeping draught to still her mind to silence, so that she might lie stupid as a queen bee in her bulk and care as little for the welfare of her workers.

Still her suffering continued without respite, and though the tiny feet of the servants tickled her abominably she must bear it without flinching, and in addition accommodate the engineers, who fussed around her with their pulleys. For a strange engine had now approached her, drawn by four score sturdy horses. This machine, which took the form of a platform about seven feet in length and four feet wide, raised three inches above the ground, and mounted on twenty-two wooden wheels, was brought parallel to where she lay, and the problem faced by the engineers was how to raise her up and place her safely upon it. Eighty poles, each of one foot high, were erected for this purpose, and cords the thickness of packthread hooked to slings, and girt around her head and body. Five hundred of the strongest men were employed to haul upon these cords and at last, aided by the pulleys, they succeeded in hoisting her on to the engine and there securing her. Two hundred horses were harnessed to the carriage, and thus she began her journey to the capital, although she might well have gone on her own two feet and saved her captors time and trouble!

But as she proceeded ponderously past dainty hedge-rows, and fields the size of table-napkins, and fence-posts no taller than hat-pins, she realized she could have walked more easily on eggs and done less damage. She felt then not only culpable by connection, but guilty of gross size itself, which would not admit of alteration or improvement.

Now it goes without saying that a woman like my mistress, who was accustomed to lament her weakness, should see her new powers in a purely negative aspect. Even as she lay there trussed like a goose on Christmas Eve and with, perhaps, as short a future, she could not help but picture herself as the agent of unspeakable catastrophes. If Mr. Gulliver, with the best will in the world, had flooded the Empress's Palace with his discharge of urine, what landslips of sewage might not his wife let loose upon the capital, and with what deluges of blood inundate it at her monthly time? What households might her great feet flatten like hedgehogs on the road, and what fragile matrons fall victim to her boundless temper, to be crushed in her fist like violets or obliterated like mayflies by a single slap? Why, even a single tear could soak a tiny gown and doom its wearer to a premature death by pneumonia!

Do not mistake me, reader, for it is not my intention that you should suspect her of a secret relish. On the contrary, such a capacity for destruction appalled my tender-hearted mistress, whose dread was eased only by the realization that while mighty power may harm if left to run amuck, it may equally be harnessed to serve the public good.

Thus encouraged, she applied her mind to the reparations she might propose to the wronged citizens of Lilliput. If the husband had eaten the country out of house and home, then the wife would employ her strength and ingenuity to restore the economy. With one stroke her pocket-comb might plough a cornfield; a flick of her wrist would sow it, and a snip of her nail-scissors gather in the harvest, while a flap of her fan would keep a dozen windmills grinding the flour and put the bakers back in business. Having solved the problem of the loaves, she turned her mind to the fishes, which were surely so minute that one scoop of her muslin petticoat might net an entire million. Moreover, should she be required to construct great dams, or divert the rivers to irrigate the plains, she would perform her labours gladly, for with her medicine-spoon she could move mountains, and uproot trees as easily as weed the willowherb from her own garden. Thus Poverty would be replaced by Plenty, and starvation by satisfaction, and the debt her husband had incurred would be discharged with interest.

Having set the record straight – if miraculously, and only in her mind's eye – guilt fell from Mary's shoulders like a fustian cloak which has concealed a dazzling gown. Virtue shone forth from her, and a fierce reforming spirit quickened her heart. If a woman be great, she must do great things, and how will subsistence satisfy her ambition, when her solitary labour can produce the surplus value of five hundred men? It was true that her appetite, being in proportion to her scale, must be included in the accounting, but if she did not eat, or was very frugal, it would entail but a small deficit in an otherwise prodigious profit.

Joyfully she contemplated the wealth that might be generated should she put mind and might to the question of milling, manufacturing, and mining, not to mention ship-building, by which trade with foreign lands might be effected, for presently the storehouses would be full to bursting with the fruits of agriculture and the products of industry, and this excess must be sent abroad to earn its keep. Thus Lilliput, like a favoured child, would go from strength to strength in self-improvement, and grow at last into a glorious prosperity.

The carriage was by now within a hundred yards of the capital, and so entranced was Mary by her own *largesse* that she could not help but smile at the throngs of citizens who lined the way, for it seemed to her that a grateful populace had gathered there to thank their saviour. Indeed, she would have raised her hand to greet them with a gracious wave, had she not been firmly pinioned. This annoyance, which she had temporarily banished from her mind, was as incontestable as the fury written small on a thousand faces, and the rain of missiles which pricked her pride – for though a broomhandle be as trifling as a toothpick, a bad egg will smell as rotten whatever its size. Such fervour as hers was not easily quenched, however, and she enjoined herself to be patient, for will not a good mother tolerate the tantrums of her child and do her best by it, even if she get no thanks? Though disappointed by her reception, she was no more deterred by it than any fledgling prophet whose teaching attracts the opprobrium of unbelievers, yet who forgives each trespass against him, convinced that History will bear him out.

What our philanthropist must bear in the present, however, was to be conveyed without ceremony through the great door of the domed temple that had previously housed her husband. This door was some four feet high and almost two feet wide, and the roof rose as high as the kingly head of the long-lost Bluebottle, so that she might have stood up as straight as he, had she been permitted. But such liberties were denied my unfortunate mistress, who, even as she was let loose from her slings, was attached again by a hundred chains as long as those you might hang a watch from in England, and padlocked to the walls as firmly as any lunatic in Bedlam. Straw, too, was her bed, and for victuals she must make do with a porridge of breadfruit served in an ox-cart, and slake her burning thirst with tepid water from a dozen thimblish rain-barrels.

Night fell, reader, and the new moon rose as high and handsome as it does in any other land, although its crescent was reversed, this being an eccentricity peculiar to the Southern Hemisphere, where one must suffer under unfamiliar stars, and turn to the North to see the sun, and feel for ever topsy-turvy. Nothing could have been stranger than this stripling moon which loomed so large in the Lilliputian sky, dwarfing the paltry turrets of the city, and nothing could have reminded my mistress more painfully of her displacement, neither the small howl of dogs in the distance, nor the lice-like foraying of rats. For it is above all the glimpsed familiar – whether the face of an acquaintance, or a phrase of his native tongue – that evokes in the traveller the keenest longing for home, and it seemed to Mary that this self-same moon which shone its full-scale light upon her children was her sole and soulful ally in an abbreviated land. Gone at a stroke were her wild improving plans, and here instead her plain predicament, and the deep dark homesick heart of her. She was not greatly destined, after all, but greatly alone, and could deny it no more than the infant powerless in his cot who cries and cries for elsewhere . . . Reader, she has borne the day bravely, and reached its bedrock, and if she weeps I shall not grudge her hard-earned tears, but hope instead that the moonlight comfort her as I cannot, until sleep steals through her weary limbs and restores her for tomorrow.

You may well dread to ask what the next day brought, and indeed I dread to disclose it. On entering the prison the Principal Secretary approached her dolefully, his eyes reddened by lack of sleep and his throat thick from a long night's disputation. A podium had been drawn up level with the head of the fallen Colossus, and from this Reldresal listened gravely to the detailed plan of works proposed by my mistress who, having put a heartfelt case, concluded passionately, 'Sir, I urge you to endorse these reparations, for not only will they put an end to pressing want, but also generate a healthy surplus, which may be distributed as His Majesty thinks fit.'

'My regrets, Madam,' said Reldresal with a sigh. 'The Emperor has spared your life, but under no circumstances will he grant your freedom! Be in no doubt that I have argued most vehemently, and have myself put forward a number of suggestions as to how the State might profit from your presence, but in this I have been frustrated by sworn enemies of your husband who have the ear of the Emperor. For instance, I have proposed the founding of a great museum wherein your person would provide a valuable locus of study for zoologists and anthropologists, and to which the general public might be admitted on payment of a modest fee . . .'

'A museum!' cried Mary in horror, but she had not heard the worst of it.

'Unfortunately,' Reldresal continued, with some evidence of distress, 'the Treasurer and High Admiral, being denied the death penalty, prejudiced His Majesty in favour of a harsher solution. Egged on by these gentlemen, the Emperor has endorsed the establishment of a Popular Pleasure-Palace, with opportunities for sport and leisure, and arcades for market stalls and penny amusements, for he is persuaded that such an enterprise will not only swell the coffers of the country but also distract the populace, whose minds dwell with resentment upon their penury.' The Secretary, who could no longer keep from his voice the bitterness of opposition, averted his face and spat rudely on the rostrum. 'Forgive me, but such men are a disgrace to a civilized country, and I am shamed even by association with them!'

While this display of temperament may have afforded some release to the Secretary, it was of scant comfort to my mistress, who was by now too stunned to speak. All hopes of agency were dashed, and she must face the fact that she would do no great deeds, but rather do nothing at all, and be instead an object to be gawked at by the curious. This prospect in itself was humiliating enough to make her grind her teeth and strain against her shackles; that the thing might be taken farther did not enter her head for a moment, and I own I am thankful on her account if she was thus protected, at least for a day or two, from the full apprehension of her fate.

*　　*　　*

How, then, was her person to be exploited for the amusement of the masses and the enrichment of the Emperor? Plans had been hastily prepared by the Chief Architect for reinforcements to the dome, arcades to abut the exterior walls, and interior galleries high enough to afford spectators a clear view on the captive, yet not so broad that they would be encouraged to tarry – on this point the architect had been forced to yield to the Treasurer, whose aim was to take the money from as many pockets as possible, and who was adamant that the optimum would be achieved by the creation of a continuous shuffling line. Although as a National Resource the giantess must be serviced, it was argued that the cost of her upkeep could be defrayed by an increased charge during the times of feeding, bathing, nail-trimming, or any other function that required an intensity of labour and the presence of a great number of attendants. The main walls of the temple, meanwhile, must be lined with marble sofas and basins for fountains, in imitation of a Turkish *bagnio*, so that the well-to-do could promenade or play their cards in comfort, and enjoy, at a price, the privilege of proximity.

As the renovations advanced, a hundred sempstresses were engaged on my mistress's costume, since her garments, like my own, were sadly stained and torn, and those in her dressing-chest were considered too drab and cumbersome for a prize exhibit – all but the stockings, that is, which were the marvel of the master-hosiers. Skilled as the sewers were, their budget imposed severe restrictions on the yardage, and though they rose to their task like artists, they could contrive from their materials only a gown bizarrely brief, like a circus-costume, and a Turkish waistcoat without sleeves.

So challenging was the question of headgear that a competition was held among the millinery students, the winner to execute her design with no other recompense than honour, and the knowledge that her reputation would thenceforth be assured. What took the prize in this instance was a headdress modelled on the pillbox cap of the *seraglio*, made of a light silvery stuff stiffened with buckram, and adorned with a hanging gold tassel, which was to be fixed to the side of the head with a pin and bound by the brow with a gold-embroidered ribbon.

When the time came for the fitting, the dressmakers brought the costume to the temple in twenty open ox-carts which were lashed together to avoid accident. The hat rode high behind them, and farther back followed the hairdressers and chambermaids, laughing and gossiping, and tossing their heads as nervously as horses. Timidly they entered the great door, their small shoes pattering across the paving stones, and scurried to their tasks like mice, all atwitch and atremble, and grateful for the sentries who stood guard with their pikestaffs and ogled and joshed, for the giant's garments must be cut off one by one with tiny scissors, and her entire person sluiced down with a hundred mops and buckets.

Yet as fear faded from the breasts of the attendants there grew in its place a sisterly feeling, and if at the outset some had tweaked the monster spitefully, as prejudice demanded, now they found that they touched her with tenderness, for what was she but a female like themselves, if on a somewhat startling scale? Thus their alliance slowly shifted, and the guards who had played their protectors, sensing this sorority, became their antagonists, and jeered as loud as will a cockerel when his brood of hens desert him. Since reproaches did not quell their lewd suggestions, the women downed tools, and stood in a firm rank with arms folded, until at last the Captain was brought to them.

'With respect, Sir,' said the spokeswoman, who had concocted the winning hat, 'we cannot work while these rascals torment us, and in any case it is unseemly to perform such intimate ministrations in public. We ask therefore that you remove your men for the duration, for we are in no need of their protection.'

Being a pragmatist as well as a gentleman, the Captain had the sense to see that no advantage would be gained by suppressing the rebellion. Accordingly he bowed to their demands and sent the sentries packing, although he reserved the privilege of remaining in the doorway, from which vantage point he could not only order prompt action, but also peek in at the curious *harem*.

If everyone has her Guardian Angel, my mistress now found herself with a veritable host, all of whom were in a high humour on account of their easy victory. Rolling up their sleeves, these handmaidens flew about her body on faery feet, crowing with triumph, and heartily congratulating one another. The Lilliputians being more scrupulous in personal hygiene than folk in England, every crevice must be lathered and scrubbed, and rinsed with warm water and cold, until Mary's skin was cheerfully aglow. Then followed the scented oils as the masseuses practised their earthy arts with all the strength at their disposal, pummelling her body with their fists and dancing upon her like dervishes. Notwithstanding that the goose receives the tenderest attentions before he is thrust into the oven, to be tended solicitously will always bring comfort, and Mary was no exception to the rule, for her mind was stilled and her senses soothed by the plucking and prinking and basting.

Greater pleasures are yet to come, however, for I wager there is not a woman on earth who does not relish the fluttering of fingers through her hair. I have already described the elegant hat, but before it can be fixed to the side of her head the *coiffure* must be completed, and here the hairdressers are at liberty to exercise their fancies. On the other side of the head the hair is smoothed flat and adorned with a nosegay of jewels fashioned like natural flowers: the buds of pearl, the roses, of rubies, the jonquils, of topaz, and all very well set and enamelled, no matter that they are but paste. On the crown of the head the braids begin, each discrete tress being the charge of three strong maidens, who plait as energetically as dancers weaving ribbons round a maypole, until they reach the nape, where the hair is left loose, and hangs at its full length behind. With what patting and pinning, frowning and squinting, adjusting and re-adjusting do they do their best for her, and bemoan the lack of a looking glass large enough to reproduce her image, and thoroughly engage themselves in the noble business of making beauty. Add to this the laborious shaping of the brows with a pair of hearth-tongs, the outlining of the eyes with a black tincture, and the trimming and tinting of the finger- and toe-nails, all of which were achieved with great skill and a minimum of discomfort. Mercifully Mary was spared the pain of body-plucking, since the women of Lilliput did not follow the Moorish fashion, and also of ear-piercing, for although rings in the ears were *de rigueur* for all classes, the outlay on such a quantity of silver could not be sanctioned, nor could the labour of the many smiths required to forge it.

Once the hat had been hoisted up and perched in position, all that remained was to fit the curious costume. But now the couturiers faced a dilemma, for fashion's laws apply exclusively to free-standing bodies, whatever their dimension, and here was one not only recumbent, but shackled at strategic points. The keys, moreover, were held by the Captain, and herein lay another quandary. Were he to recall his sentries as a condition of unlocking the giant, the modesty so strictly safeguarded by the sisterhood would once more be affronted, and the original sweetness of the rout would turn to the bitter gall of retreat. On one thing the women were agreed: the keys must be got by fair means or foul, and should the fellow prove recalcitrant, steps must be taken to distract him. Thus it was that two of the handsomest girls were chosen to accost the Captain, the first to spirit away the keys while the second sacrificed her material modesty for the sake of the larger ideal.

The deed was quickly done by the one lass while the other dallied, and limb by limb my mistress was unshackled. Then she must put her feet inside the flimsy garment, and suffer it to be hauled upwards by two companies of twenty women. With her lower limbs once more enchained, she must lift her hips skywards to allow its continued passage, until the brief sleeves settled on her shoulders, and the women laced her at the breast and buttoned her at the gusset, and sank down exhausted around her. Giant though she was, they had decked her out like any girl her doll, and they were happy, and sweaty, and spent.

*   *   *

Reader, is it not ironic that one who had longed in her youth to show off her charms should in her maturity be rudely obliged to exhibit them? What might once have been pleasurable indulgence was now a wholesale imposition, for though the attendants tried their utmost to encourage Mary, drying her tears with their tiny kerchiefs and praising her appearance in eloquent mime, she had no reason to believe that their countrymen would regard her with anything other than scornful hostility.

It is strange, is it not, to observe how patterns laid down in youth repeat themselves in the life of the adult? Disaster, heretofore, had invariably accompanied the expression of her feminine desires. She had grown from a girl to a woman under Mrs. Burton's disapproving eye, and though she had tried like a Trojan to avoid discomposing her mother, indeed had endured all manner of unnatural restrictions in a vain attempt to please her, still she had been repulsed. In recent years, as a matron, she had yearned to melt Cold Genius with her Cupid, and bask in the gaze of her beloved, but such desires had only earned reproaches, and a husband who sequestered himself in study or stable, and fled from her across the ocean. It is not surprising, therefore, that her present ignominy was all the more unbearable for being thus prefigured! As she had blamed herself then, so did she now and, persuaded by a peculiar logic that the punishment was a faithful measure of the crime, concluded that her transgressions had indeed been very monstrous!

You will protest that Mary's tale is become too sombre; you will be impatient, perhaps, with one whose disposition is so intemperate that she will rub the salt of severity into her open wounds. Ah, reader, would that we were all immune from such wrongheadedness! But who amongst you will swear that she has treated her own person with the unvarying courtesy and consideration she shows to the meanest parlourmaid, and has never gone wildly slashing at her hair with her scissors, aggravating invisible pustules with her fingernails, or otherwise wreaking havoc on her self-esteem? It is as if you will not be content with simple unhappiness which, left to itself, would eventually pass by like a fast-flowing river; rather you must divert it into lilyponds, shade it with laburnums, tease it through fountains, and dam it into ornamental lakes in which to intricately examine the multifarious reflections of your misery. Ladies! Answer me this! What price your great expertise in appearances when it is used to your detriment? What price your subtlest artistry if it turn a plain condition into an exquisite torture? Would it not be altogether better to break down the little dams, and let your natural feelings flow out like the waters, even if they should flood the lawns with froth, strike down solid oaks, and strew haystacks in the teeth of the hedges? For if you keep them imprisoned and perfect them like prettiness, they will afford the same safety as a cage, while inflicting prolonged and petty injuries.

Do not mistake me for a revolutionist, however, for I am very far from being the kind of Amazon who rains the arrows of polemic on her unlucky readers. I agree that the restrictions placed upon you are many, yet at the same time you are blessed with freedoms far beyond my wildest dreams! Moreover, and no doubt more importantly, let me remind you that unlike my mistress, you are not entirely pinioned, nor at the mercy of your own odours and ordures, nor washed by tears, investigated by rats, or dripped on by raindrops from a leaky roof. Look upon her, reader, and have pity! Pinned to a far corner of the world like a butterfly to black velvet, she spins helplessly with the turning earth, her womb tugged at by foreign tides. Even as her ropes ensnare her, she is adrift with not a thing to cling to.

Were she to have penned a list of her sorrows it might have gone as follows:

> *She could not pursue Mr. Gulliver or ape his exploits.*
> *She would do no great works.*
> *Her blood must flow out of her and puddle upon the marble.*
> *She must eat and drink and scratch and sleep and wake crammed like a poor pig in its sty.*
> *Her mind must be entirely at the mercy of her fleshly body.*

These were the unhappy imperatives that confronted my mistress, yet they may reward a closer inspection, for we may detect therein a saving grace. Life has many lessons to teach a woman if she will learn, the first being that the mind must not get above itself, for it is marooned in the body like a castaway on an island, circumscribed not by the ocean but by the mighty materiality of flesh. At first she may rail like a madman against the alien environment, against wild surf, strange fruit, and inhospitable thorn, but after years of rebellion she will begin to see the sense in coexistence, and will gradually desist from gazing at the horizon, building rafts, and screaming for rescue, and learn instead to savour the produce of the place, learn its livestock and its lineaments, and not only be reconciled with it, but even favour its rhythms above all others.

Reader, although my mistress had journeyed countless leagues across the sea, I promise you that, bound by the margins of her flesh and blood – indeed, immobilized by them – she was to travel a great deal farther!

Chapter VII

A Sojourn in the Pleasure Drome . . . Mary encounters the Eye of the Argos . . . A Surprising Apotheosis . . . Some Observations on the Land of Chili . . .

Meanwhile, on a couch strewn with frangipani petals, I dreamed surprisingly of the long-lost Bluebottle. He who had rolled his eyes to Heaven and surrendered himself to the deep now popped out of oblivion like a veritable cork and gazed around him with no evidence of surprise, decorous in death as he had been in life, his head held high above the waves, his wet body black and gleaming as a mussel shell. Presently, finding solid sand beneath his feet, he set out at a level stride for the Paradisal shore, fully expecting to encounter his ancestors.

If my mistress's copy of Artemidorus had been to hand, I might have taken a moment to explore the symbolism of the dream, with its motifs of death and rebirth. As it was, having half a hundred souls to bless before breakfast, I gave it no further thought, thus forgetting first principles, which rule that while dreams may be dismissed by the ordinary man, those of an Oracle are visions in which crucial information lies encoded. Yet the inexperience which made me remiss proved a great boon to Bluebottle, for it allowed him to land unadvertised on a secluded shore beyond the northern mountains.

(As to the adventures that befell him there, you must wait, as doll and mistress did, to hear them from the gentleman himself, for only then, in witnessing the telling of the tale, will you appreciate its radical effect upon the listeners, and thus upon the larger narrative . . .)

In the meantime, consider the contrariness of the fate which had been reserved for myself and my mistress: to be split asunder like the two Aphrodites, the one endowed by her faithful followers with the numinous wisdom of a Sophia, the other licensed by State decree as a Palace in which less devout citizens might indulge profaner appetites.

If Mary had ever longed to display her charms, here in the Pleasure Drome her wishes were most monstrously fulfilled, for although the dogged Reldresal had secured an undertaking that no harm should be done to her person, he could no more shield her from prying eyes than he could deliver her from the daily humiliations of the dung-cart. Such was the public demand to gawk at the giantess that the upper galleries were thronged with visitors from morn till night; in addition, those Societies which could provide accreditation in writing were allowed access to the body of the chamber, so that the exhibit must not only suffer the massed eyes of Lilliput, but submit to the closer scrutiny of Rotary Clubs and Sunday Painting Circles, and shrink under the slide-rules of Topographers and Trigonometrists, Anatomists and Apothecaries. She must even be swarmed over by the Society of Alpinists, who practised their ropework regularly on her nursery slopes, thus perfecting the basic techniques of a sport wrongly believed to have originated amidst our European crags.

While Sport laid siege to her virgin faces, Science set out to gauge her secrets. Within a few short weeks Hypsometry had established her altitude and azimuth, and Planimetry her ordinate and her abscissa; her curvature and cubic capacity were comprehensively calibrated, and her monthly flow, moreover, computed in Lilliputian quarts. Of her womanly mysteries hardly a one was left unrifled, and my poor mistress soon decided that she would far rather bear the mockery of the common mass than be a study-specimen for naturalists!

Catcalls, indeed, there were aplenty, for the citizens were encouraged to discharge their frustrations at her expense, and although large notices expressly forbade the throwing of missiles, the guards turned a blind eye as often as not on those who contravened the order. She might have been a scold in the Newgate stocks, to be pelted at will with mouldy turnips and rotten eggs, albeit they were harmlessly in miniature!

It was to the devotees in climbing-breeches, as it happens, that she owed her deliverance from such petty defilements. These young folk were scrupulous caretakers of their sporting environment, and so ethical that they would risk life and limb to retrieve a rope or a piton rather than leave a trace of tackle to profane a pristine slope. How galling, then, that they must wade among orange-peels, slither on the ordure hurled by others, and waste precious scaling-time on sweeping and scouring . . . Thus they argued eloquently in the highest echelons, and being in the main from the very foremost families, the rumpus they raised could hardly be ignored.

Reader, be thankful on Mary's behalf for small mercies, for I daresay you cannot imagine the lonely despair of her position! Around her the citizens gossiped and picnicked and took their pleasure, and though she was undoubtedly the centre of attraction, in her own palace the Princess had no place. No intimacy and no engagement, no affection and no relation, nor even a brief hour of solitude in which to shed her private tears! Here indeed was the head of the Argos with its omnipresent eyes, but how inhospitable its scrutiny compared with the loving gaze she had yearned for!

Yet as any doll could tell you, those who are starving will take nourishment wherever it can be found, and by and by, like the humble toadflax which draws moisture from the merest chink in a garden wall, my mistress adapted herself to a situation which was inimical in the extreme. Such was her hunger for love that her heart sought satisfaction in the unlikeliest places, and succeeded in turning to account the only attention available. Ambiguous as it was, the gaze soothed her and the gaze slaked her, just as if it had been the doting glance of a tender mother, and she turned her face towards it like a flower towards the sun, and if as time went by she noticed neither scorn nor blame in the eyes of the onlookers, though undoubtedly both existed, I can only conclude that the human spirit is most marvellously ingenious, for under the very worst of circumstances it may none the less disarm an inner enemy, and transform a critical eye into a friendly one! And so the sun rose and the sun set, and each day brought an increment in her curious content, as she savoured for the first time the febrile joys of the Thespian, whose soul expands or shrinks with the presence or absence of an audience.

Reader, where disparagement has been the poison, omnipotence will be the antidote, and my mistress quaffed the latter lustily, until the female flesh which had so discountenanced her mother and repulsed her husband became magnificent in her own regard, with breasts pointed and uplifting, wrists strong and graceful as sequoia trunks, full flanks, escarpments for eyebrows, and a belly suave and swelling as the Sussex Downs. Daily Mary surrendered the territories of her person to the multiple ministrations of her handmaidens, sighing contentedly, and preening a little, and on occasion even fancying that she saw in the Temple dome her own reflection, great and golden, suspended like an enchanted island in an azure sea, and compassed all around by a host of tiny cherubim.

Such, then, are the compensations fantasy provides in times of adversity, and I trust that you will no more grudge them to poor Mary than you would snatch the last cheroot from the mouth of a dying soldier. Let the trump sound, then, and the host sing out as gaily as birds at the gateway of April, for there is as yet no harm in it, and self-aggrandizement will equip her better for what is to come than self-depreciation.

*   *   *

Friends, countrywomen, I take my hat off to you, for you have followed me this far, and who is to say what quirks of coincidence will beset the reader who, like the traveller, leaves his native land ten thousand miles behind? Viz., if the ill-starred *Aphrodite* never reached Valdivia, where rivers of white gold flow like milk from the high peaks of the Cordilleras, a certain naturalist had gained those very shores, in the pursuit of other riches.

Valverde, in the province of Valdivia in Chili.

My dearest Marguerite,
Señor de Rozas has given me his assurance that he will bring this letter to a Biscayan ship presently at anchor off the town, whose captain may be trusted to carry it to our cousins in Asturias. Do not miss me too sorely, or concern yourself about my safety, for I may pass for a Basque among the encomenderos, *and the* inquilinos *do not seem inclined to distinguish between one European and another. To them we are all* chiapi, *or 'vile soldiers', for it is not so very long ago that the Indians were everywhere enslaved by the Spaniards, and many of them still bear their master's brand upon their brows.*

Seeing that I am covetous neither of land nor gold, but only of a fruit which proliferates almost like a weed (it is of such little value that at the market one may buy a great bundle wrapped in a tobacco-leaf for next to nothing), the haughty Hispanics give me leave to rove, and grub in their fields for likely specimens. I need not tell you that I encourage the view that I am a bird-witted botanist who is unworthy of their curiosity. A view which may well be the truth, dear sister, for I live in a mud hut and sleep on a straw bed like a peon, and in the full glare of the sun may be discovered flat on my belly in the field, with my nose pressed up against a bush, muttering like a madman to my gauges.

As to the provenance of the frutillar, I can find no consensus. It is generally regarded by the Spaniards as indigenous, yet the Indians – who I daresay have sharper memories for such matters – swear that it came in the wake of the conquerors, with other foreign seeds like the plum, peach and cherry, which also grow in profusion in these fertile valleys. I can no longer be certain, therefore, that the capiton and frutillier are two true species, or whether the latter is a strain of the former, altered and enhanced by the richer soil and milder climate of its new environs. You will appreciate that there is a great deal of work to be done if we are to discover the origins of both these strains, but I am less dismayed by this prospect than by certain practical obstacles which a more sagacious man would surely have foreseen! Valverde is an orchard in bloom, Marguerite, with blossoms which stretch as far as the eye can see, even to the foothills of the Cordilleras, and bees – of Spanish pedigree, I do not doubt – swarm everywhere, and drone about the flowers from morn till night. To be sure, I have female frutilliers enough to match my foreign males, but how is the experiment to be effected, if I cannot keep them in isolation from their countrymen? I have attempted to purchase stuffs to make a canopy, but they are in very short supply – indeed, the ladies hoard their grandmothers' silk gowns like precious treasures, and not a one will be persuaded to part with her poorest petticoat!

Yet all is not lost, if I may place my specimens at some remove, and throw myself upon the mercy of the sisters of Sant'Ana, some of whom are skilful spinsters, and so well-disposed towards the peaceful art of horticulture that they have kindly offered me a corner of their cloistered garden. In addition they are very adept at making artificial flowers and fruits of sugar, with which they decorate the church, and after Mass distribute to the congregation – which I daresay attends the more eagerly on that account. For Feast-Days they carve charming angels from preserved citrón, in mezzo-relievo, one of which I salvaged for Céleste, though it was sentimental of me, for I fear that heat and hungry ants will have the best of it before I set my foot on France! It pains me to think of the months that must pass before I give my little niece the kisses she deserves, so kiss her quickly for me, Marguerite, a dozen times or more, and hope that Fortune favours my experiments, and restores me before too long to Solutré.

Farewell, then, from the fields of the Lord, where the good nuns pray that they may harvest souls, while I pray as fervently for hybrids . . .

I embrace you
Your devoted brother
Antoine

Chapter VIII

An A–Z of Depravity . . . A Maiden Saved by a Nettle . . . The Eye of the Matriarch . . . A Murder Averted . . . Several Troubling Epiphanies . . . On Shame and Curiosity . . .

It did not go unnoticed by certain citizens that Mary was lit by an inner light, and lay in her Palace like a queen bee fattened on the nectar of devotion. We speak here of a Gentlemen's Supper Club, whose members were rich enough to pay weekly for the privilege of exclusive access to the exhibit, and whose sole aim in life was to advance the theory and practice of debauchery. Neither boy nor girl was sacred to those libertines, nor arse nor quim, sow nor sheep, nor even the meanest rodent that grubbed in the ground; indeed, so refined were their appetites that they had bored themselves with every protruberance in the province, and exhausted themselves in every orifice. Not even the Royal swan was safe from despoilment, not the bower-bird's arching nest, and on how many mornings had Dawn's first candid rays discerned on tulip-bole and topiary hedge alike their alien dew?

Such was the impudence of these fellows that the latter exploits had fired them with a lust to mimic the fertilization of flowers by flying insects. To this unnatural end they mounted their spies on the shrubbery and kitchen-garden of a certain town-house, so that they might study the ladies at their embroidery-frames, and the maidservants culling the fruit from the raspberry-canes. By and by each female must creep away to heed the call of nature, and each had been observed to return again and again to a favoured nook, this one to hide in the hollyhocks, that one to squat above a clump of celandines, and yet another to steal a piss among the tickling bluebells.

The intelligence thus gathered was collated with much excitement, and tongues ran away with themselves as the gentlemen waxed poetic in their cups.

'Would you not agree, comrades,' cried the Chairman, a rake by the name of Edesad, who sported a vest and slippers of daffodil-coloured silk, 'that the *calyx* is comprised of the sepalled skirt, while the petticoats may be compared to the concealing petals of the *corolla*? It is this pretty *perianth* that flutters in the breeze, seducing our senses with bright hues and sweet perfumes, so that we must plunge our feelers under its folds and discover the divine *gynaecium*, whose projecting *stigma* eagerly awaits the gifts we carry on our iridescent wings!'

Applause greeted the Chairman's analogy, which was, however, quite inappropriate. As she who has the slightest acquaintance with botany will know, the flower contains both masculine stamens and feminine ovules, whereas in the human the reproductive functions are strictly differentiated, no doubt for good reason. But such considerations did not deter the plausible Edesad, who had attended the university for a full semester, unlike his aristocratic companions, and knew how to tailor his scant knowledge to flatter their measureless vanity. Rising on the tips of his daffodil slippers he exhorted them: 'And now, gentlemen, attend to your *anthers*, for tonight we must become *palynologists*, and apply ourselves to the production of pollen!'

How lewdly they laughed at this, for if the science befogged them the obscenity of his gesture was plain, and they romped out roguishly, and stumbled through the midnight streets till they came to the gates of the appointed garden. Since they did not wish to leave anything to chance, a map had been made of the micturitions, and once inside the wall the young bloods spread out stealthily to cover all the sites. Then they must go to it with gusto, hands on their hot members in the chilly moonlight, and woe betide the one whose mettle fail him at the mid-point of the matter. The odds being against success, they had made a pact that their pollination, at least, should be ubiquitous, and so not a worker among them dared fail at his task, for honour would not tolerate the droop; thus when Dawn came every clover-clump and dandelion patch had been anointed, and the hollyhocks streamed like fountains, and the bluebells hung their slippery heads in surprise.

Morning brought the ladies out to the garden with their

teacups, and the kitchenmaid with her clippers, and though straw hats shield their faces from the sun, and veils keep off marauding insects, and gloves protect their fingers from the prick of the rose-tree thorn, no such precaution was taken for the tender parts.

Imagine the wild surmise of the spectators when they saw the sepalled skirts spread out, and heard the peaceful sighing stream descend between the thighs. What could be more clandestine, they agreed, than to imagine the quim caught up in its private musings, minding, as it were, its own sweet business, without a thought to spare for alarms? In all ignorance it grazes the couch-grass, carelessly allows ingress to the sticky nose of the larkspur, even smiles at the quivering caress of coltsfoot and campion, never for a moment suspecting the snare which lies in wait!

'O joyous prank!' breathed the onlookers, excited beyond measure. 'O importunate pollen! Even as she knows it not, her filaments gather in our glistening harvest.'

Reader, you may think it a cowardly trick, and quite supreme in its silliness, but the truth is that Nature is not so scrupulous, and, like a fading doxy, will snatch at any chance. So it came about in the fullness of time that every female of the household was assailed by the same unmistakable symptoms – with the lucky exception of one young maid, who had inadvertently sat on a thistle and jumped up crying for vinegar!

In telling this tale, I assure you, my intention is not at all to titillate, but rather to give you the measure of these gentlemen – to provide a Natural History, if you like, of what was presently to become the Queen Bee Club. For it will not surprise you to hear that these jaded roués saw in Mary's arrival the answer to their prayers. To these thoroughbreds guilt was the sole spur sharp enough to goad them on to galloping ecstasy, and it had long been dulled by excessive use, for even the piercing eye of Conscience, when it sees too much, will turn away in torpor. Might not the athletics which had long since bored them in the bedchamber take on a new spice when enacted under the matriarchal eye of the Colossus? Might not each *frisson* be greatly enhanced by the severity of her regard, each exploit thrillingly magnified? If it is true that dull senses delight in novelty, Fate could have offered no finer deliverance than this Great Dame who had landed so fortuitously on their doorstep!

Egged on by the loquacious Edesad, the blades resolved that henceforth their supper-parties would be held in Mary's shadow. Moreover, they agreed to return to first principles, and accordingly began with servant-girls, chasing them into corners and tossing their homespun skirts over their heads, delighted that the sauce and savour had come back to the meat, and declaring themselves quite content, after all, with simple shagging.

I must take issue, however, with such fundamentalism, for it seems to me that shagging is the very opposite of simple, being a human business, and thereby bearing imagination's taint. Nay, Mary's was the galvanizing glance which lent a new lustre to antique improprieties, so that if she was a debutante at the outset, as the weeks went by she witnessed willy-nilly not only the ABC of sensuality but the XYZ of depravity. Picture, if you will, as if through the wrong end of a spyglass, rites which amazed her and rites which alarmed. Consider the crab-race for instance, run on a circuit around her shackled form, where couples in their birthday suits must scuttle to the finishing-post, the females with their limbs locked tight around their partners' necks, and the males on all fours, puffing and panting at their double duty. Or the spectacle of the wheelbarrow-race, where youths must hurry on their hands with air-borne arses pinioned on their drivers' pricks . . .

Those were the scandalous sights my mistress was obliged to witness, and you may imagine the initial shock, which presently gave way to outright scorn. How else, indeed, could she defend herself against the saturnalia played out before her eyes, how else deny her secret interest, and her surreptitious quickening? The truth is, reader, that her body relished what her mind abhorred: such are the troubling epiphanies which seem to lie in wait for those who undertake, by chance or by design, a sentimental education.

A paradox indeed – and one too human for a doll to comprehend, if I may say so. *Shame* is a gentleman whose acquaintance I have yet to make, so far he stands above my lowly station, but by all accounts he is a substantial fellow in the hearts of men, and takes the rod to those who entertain his poorer cousin, *Curiosity* by name. Him I know well, and do consider it a privilege to keep his calling card . . .

As for my mistress, plain disgust perplexed her less than subtle excitation, and for this the Chairman offered every opportunity. One day he set a ladder up against her ear, and Mary feared the worst, yet what transpired was even more outlandish than she had expected. He had hoped that an earring graced her earlobe, but finding none therein, he climbed up to her hatpin, and attached a rope. The jewelled pin lassoed, a little noose was quickly made, through which the Chairman thrust his little head.

My mistress strained to see what was afoot, at first supposing that the roué had repented of his sins and meant to make a scaffold from which he might dispatch himself. To be sure, she had no wish to be the site of a suicide, but since the slightest movement might have hastened his demise she dared not intercede, and held her breath instead, lest she dislodge him from the gallows. Then from the corner of her eye she saw he had secured himself, in fact had fixed a belay to the ladder rungs, and did not hurl himself to an abyssal doom, but rather fumbled with the buttons of his breeches.

Why, he tightens the noose only to augment his pleasure! thought Mary, watching him incredulously, for his little eyes bulged, and his face was as blotched as a bad apple, but he showed no signs of desisting. How galling to be so ill-used, and at the same time hardly to be noticed! Suddenly all she had suffered was as nothing compared with this pique to her female pride, and she reflected bitterly that the entire race of men was incorrigible, for they would rather flirt with death than with a living breathing woman. Why, they are nothing but pirates, she thought, every last one of them, who fly the skull and crossbones while they hold our hearts to ransom. Excepting Mr. Gulliver, she reminded herself hurriedly, thanking her lucky stars that she had married the one dear man in a race of wretches.

Yet the image of the husband she had conjured up to console her did the very opposite, and mysteriously incited her further, so that the more she excused him, the more savagely did spleen assail her. Years of wrath rose up in her breast, and for a moment she was quite primed to play the executioner, and show the tiny Chairman what it meant to dice with danger. If I were to make an example of him, she fumed, it would be no more than he deserved, and might serve to teach the other rogues a lesson. The slightest shrug of her shoulder would have sent the fellow on his way, but at the last moment Conscience, I am glad to say, commanded her otherwise, and brought her back from the very brink of murder. Instead, ladies, she did what her mother had taught her, which was to close her eyes and concentrate on England, while the mannikin jerked on his rope like a jack-in-the-box, half-strangled himself, and had his gratification.

Chapter IX

Observations on Intimate Matters . . . How the Queen Bee Club was Formed . . . A Little Odyssey . . . On the Phenomenon of the Sneeze . . .

It is said that the male of the species feels sadness after the act, yet I have never heard a female complain of it. On the contrary, should the outcome be successful, it seems that she is more likely to gloat over the pleasure she has gained than lament the losing of it, and think her lover churlish to talk of *tristesse* and *petit mort* while she basks languidly in the afterglow. It is said also that of the two sexes the weaker feels the more encompassing delight, while the stronger merely undergoes a spasm; if there is a lesson, therefore, to be learnt by the latter, perhaps it is that enjoyment may be all the keener the less it is taken for granted!

You will be forgiven a certain impatience, then, with those gentlemen who have run the gamut, and who now sit sullen at their supper, for once unpartnered and somewhat at a loss. Their *ennui* discountenanced Edesad, who snatched up his snuff-box and strolled a pensive circuit round the sanctum, sneezing from time to time, and clicking his little satin heels. As he toured the recumbent giantess – who had dropped off and was dozing fitfully – his reponsibilities bore down on him, and he fell into a brown study. Undoubtedly his cohorts would soon fall to bickering, and tear themselves asunder with sectarianism, like a political party which lacks a unifying cause. If, as he feared, the future of the Supper Club was in jeopardy, then so was his chairmanship, with all the perquisites that flowed from it: the gifts of game, the bolts of satin, and, most importantly, the jewels which fetched a pretty price at the pawnbrokers.

Meanwhile Mary, who had abandoned herself to a dream of Mr. Gulliver, emitted a sigh which stirred the silence of the Pleasure Drome like the eerie rustle of a hundred bats. Since sleep speaks frankly of what consciousness will always seek to hide, her body transmitted a trembling message, and she reared up her hips like a rocking-horse, and spread her splendid thighs.

Chairman Edesad, at that moment circumambulating the twin promontories of her feet, dropped his snuff-box in surprise, and stared at the panorama which had opened out before him. There were the synclines of the calves, and the two fine buttresses of the knees, and between them an ever-narrowing canyon which culminated in a shadowy but imposing *couloir*. The captive slumbered sweetly on, all unaware of her examiner who, careless of the risks attached to the enterprise, advanced into the gulley until he stood transfixed before the buttons of her giant gusset.

'How stupid I have been!' he marvelled. 'Young hearts demand a challenge, and here is one worthy of the great explorers, an expedition perilous as any undertaken by . . . (He searched his mind for illustrious explorers, but since learning in Lilliput was sadly stunted he was forced to stop short at the ancients) . . . Why, by Menander, Patrocles, or Crassus!' Greatly pleased with himself, he clapped his hands to command attention, and proposed a toast.

'Gentlemen, I give you . . . the Giantess! Is she not truly a continent fit for heroes? See how she pulses in slumber like a queen bee in her hive, pining for a multitude of mates. Yet we drones have been remiss in our duty, and have not paid our hostess the homage she deserves. How will she fulfil her destiny if her courtiers hang back like cowards and will not serve her? It is a shame on all our heads, that we have shown such little regard for royalty.' After he had chaffed them, Edesad proposed the inception of a superior Society, which would go by the name of the Queen Bee Club, and would apply strict rules of selection.

Summoning them to the mouth of the canyon, he indicated the trials the incumbents must face, and if the bloods fell back from the beetling precipices, then so might a Herakles have been daunted, or Odysseus on the deadly brink of Charybdis. 'Here at last is a labour worthy of our manhood,' cried the Chairman. 'For only he who is brave enough to breach the barricade and feed the bee with Royal Jelly will be admitted to membership.'

Honour dictated that the audacious Edesad be the first to undergo the test, and presently he advanced between the unpredictable precipices, well aware that he could be crushed between them like a thumb in a slammed door. But faint heart, as they say, never won fair lady, and he could take comfort from the thought that if his goose was to be cooked he had none but himself to blame for it. No general had ordered him into the breach, and no bugler would sound the Post should he fall on the battlefield. Self-consequence was the sole Standard that spurred him on to valour, and such were its snares that, unmindful of his peril, he pressed on impatiently, all but persuaded that it was as grave and glorious to die for cunt as it was for country.

At last he came to the head of the *cul-de-sac* and stood before the buttons, but since each was fashioned from a giant turtle shell and very weighty he could not summon the strength to undo them. So great was his chagrin that he stamped his foot like a child in a tantrum, but still he would not call for help. By now his companions had lost sight of him and, forgetting that silence was the *sine qua non*, they cried out clamorously 'Go to it!' and 'Have at her!'

Edesad stood frozen as the giant stirred above him, and her thighs drew closer in on either side. He could go neither forward nor back, and panic gripped his heart as Time, that accursed creditor, told him that his debt was due.

It is said that the wisest generals leave the routed enemy a line of retreat, knowing that a trapped army will fight more savagely than beasts; so it was with Edesad, who recklessly seized his sword and slashed and sawed at the buttons until he had severed their threads. Turtle shells fell with the hollow clang of dinner-gongs, yet as the silken gusset parted he saw a thicket dense as any that ever defended the Sleeping Beauty: a veritable barricade of hairs, all tangled and obdurate as mangrove roots. There was nothing for it but to hack a path forward and advance without compass or map, in the blind hope of gaining the interior. In the meantime the cries of his companions grew fainter, and were soon cut off entirely by the undergrowth.

The cave-mouth which now confronted him was tall and narrow, surmounted by a bulbous pillar, flanked by winged buttresses, and with a floor irregularly rutted and slippery from subterranean streams. How his heart quailed before this straitest of gates for, like many of his fellow-men, nothing filled him with such fear as the prospect of enclosure. Nevertheless, summoning what courage remained to him, he slithered into the cleft.

Presently his eyes adjusted to the dimness, and when he saw the infernal colours of the place, its pinks and purples, crimsons and carmines, he thought he had been swallowed up by the mouth of Hell itself. Here, surely, was the source of those dreadful visions depicted by the great artists: the fiery hues and licking oriflammes, the strange and shifting lights and the terrible obscurities. How far was far enough? he asked himself, but, shamed by the cowardly answer, he resolved to set his fear aside and penetrate the very heart of darkness.

Superstition is a cunning foe, however, and far superior to simple fright, for while the latter makes a man tremble for his earthly body, the former stirs the profounder terrors of the soul. Weak-limbed and divided against himself, the champion sank down against the slippery sides, certain that he had glimpsed in the abyss the horrible head of a Gorgon, and he with no shining shield to counter its accusing gaze. An Oracle, of course, could have told him it was his own soul in its feminine aspect that stared back at him from the depths, for what is left for long enough in darkness will turn crippled and ugly, and appear in the fearsome guise of a hag in a halo of snakes. But there was none such on hand to advise the Chairman, and so he must shake and shiver in his ignorance, and clutch at the cavern walls, and find no purchase thereupon.

Though but a tickle to the slumbering Mary, the travails of the trapped mite were irritant enough to provoke a sudden fit of sneezing. Before you consider the effect of her spasm on the beleaguered Edesad, however, will you not stand for a moment in the slippers of a doll who has known neither common cold nor the excitation of snuff or dust-mote on the mucous membrane, and savour as if for the first time the strangeness of this phenomenon.

So democratic is the sneeze, it seems, that the prince, like the pauper, must suffer it, and so peremptory that he may pinch his nose and hold his breath but the process will neither be hurried nor halted. From the moment that he knows he cannot stop it, his lips contort into a gargoyle's snarl, his nostrils flare fiercely, his lungs gulp in a gasping breath. Stone-deaf and blinded he launches himself, with muscles tensed tremendously, like a horse at a high hurdle. In that split-second Time stops and consciousness surrenders to a blissful obliteration: here indeed is his *petit mort* (though there are few enough who sing its praises), for this passionate paralysis brings him very close to death. Here, within a whisker of oblivion, both Papist and Puritan are but fragile pivots of a sky black and blessed and pinpointed implacably with stars; here also, one might imagine, is the end of all doctrine and schism, for whoever has heard the laughter of the Apocalypse would surely be a fool if he resume his dogmas!

Freed, finally, from the convulsion, his eyes wide and his spirit startled, he returns rejuvenated to the everyday, for his body has drawn much benefit from the exercise. After the deluge the lungs are cleansed and content, the spleen is refreshed, and the blood flows more briskly, lending a healthy glow to the skin and aiding the purgative work of the liver. As to the effects on the quim, there is little study and less speculation, but I suspect they may be equally advantageous.

What was tonic for the Sleeping Beauty, however, was poison to the encircled Edesad, since the narrow funnel was squeezed quite flat by the spasm, crushing the breath from his lungs and all but cracking his ribs. Once again his eyes bulged and he thought his head would burst like an ear of corn in a grindstone. Mercifully there was a swift end to the pulverising pressure, and the walls of the cavern relaxed once more and resumed their regular pulsing.

Now you might expect a man who has narrowly escaped the fate of the common flea to be suitably chastened, and henceforth go in awe of that potent passage through which new life is thrust upon the world. But Edesad was an incorrigible fellow, and now that the immediate danger had passed, was very loath to abort his mission. Pride raised its head and prinked up his member (I believe I have already noted that his appetites were enlivened, rather than dulled, by the onset of asphyxia). Hastily he threw open his breeches and, bringing out his booty, belaboured it like a cook beating cream, for although *festina lente* is the wisest motto in such intimate matters, the Chairman's mind was on the end and not the means. Other adventurers might build their cairns and fly their flags from conquered mountain tops, but Edesad's sole ambition was to enter his spoor in the annals. And so the thing was done speedily, and the little Chairman slithered towards the chink of light that marked the exit, whence he emerged bald and bedraggled as a new-born. His wig was lost, his waistcoat waterlogged, and his yellow slippers woefully stained, but in his heart he was huge in stature, and his triumph was august as Alexander's at the battle of Arbela.

That night Edesad surpassed himself at banqueting, and finished his feast with every liquor to be found in Lilliput, imbibing small-beer and stout, hippocras and posset, claret-cup, eau-de-vie, and astonishing quantities of eggnog.

The Supper Club were all agog for an epic, and here the hero was faced with a dilemma, for he must disaffirm his fear while at the same time doing justice to the danger. In truth he did not want them to try for entry lest he lose every man jack of them, and thereby be a leader without followers. Nothing he could say, however, would dissuade the candidates, and like a fretting female he must content himself with cautions.

'You will do well to equip yourself with a lantern', he told the first in line, 'and carry pit-props with which to brace the unstable sides.' Then one by one he must bid them God-speed, like a mother who waves her sons away to the war, convinced that they are going to their graves.

CHAPTER X

*A Sheep called Dolly . . . Mr. Burton makes his Fortune . . . On the
Mysterious Laws of Attachment . . . The Flight of the Oracle . . .*

Meanwhile, in a holier precinct, I continued to be concerned for my mistress, of whom I had heard nothing since we two had been parted by the pounding waves. If my pious priestesses knew of her fate they breathed not a word of it, so I could not but assume that Mary was dead and drowned, or else, God willing, alive and adrift on her dressing-chest.

In the long nights my temple, though lonely, was far from silent, for bats flitted squealing through the open well of the roof, and the doors were invariably left ajar for sleepless supplicants, allowing easy ingress to stray dogs and nocturnal snakes. One hot night I was disturbed in the small hours by a bleating faint at first but unmistakably mournful, for being solidly Scotch in my pedigree, I not only know the cry of the curlew from that of the capercailzie, but also when a hill sheep laments a loss.

It is seldom that my thoughts turn to my homeland, since, not being of a morbid humour, I prefer to avoid melancholy recollections rather than dwell on them. How many farmers' daughters, after all, have hugged me by night in their truckle beds, yet in the morning, turning contrary, cursed me for a witch and ducked me in the rain-barrel, or even threatened to throw me in the turnip-cutter? Indeed, I can hardly count on my fingers the generations of girls I have belonged to, who did with me as they pleased, and thought it their prerogative to put me in my place. Mary was the latest of this lineage, and in no wise better than the rest of them, but since a doll by her nature must belong to someone, it made me sad to think that she might be the last.

The sheep's cry grew closer, and a pale shape moved through the doorway. This spectre, upon examination, turned out to be a ewe advanced in years, with an appearance of wild dejection. Her fleece, which was ensnarled with briars, moulted in swatches like a mangy wig, while strings of vetch and bindweed entwined her tail and trailed in a dismal bower behind her. The animal proceeded up the aisle, and to my surprise I heard her muttering a morose litany:

'Is her fleece not white like daisies or the moon? Is not her milk as sweet as the grass is green and good? What has driven her black-footed daughters away?' The ewe walked forward a few steps, then distractedly backwards. Then she took several sidesteps, and raising her muzzle to search the air, continued gloomily, 'They are not on the cliffs nor in the pasture, has the tide taken them? They are not ensnared in the blackthorn thicket, and the fence-posts bear no trace of their wool; they have not hidden themselves mischievously among the meadowsweet of the hedgerows, nor yet are they astray in the marram grass of the marshes. Did the crows steal their eyes, that they cannot find their way back to me?'

To eavesdrop on misery is poor amusement, and I felt impelled to make my presence known. Had the poor beast lost her lambs? I wondered, but before I could put the question the ewe wheeled round to face me and, spreading her legs, pissed long and loudly on the floor, as sheep will when other species surprise them. The animal had undoubtedly heard herself addressed, and, far from being afraid of me, seemed glad to have an audience for her appeal. Blinking a rheumy eye, the sheep petitioned me anxiously.

'If they have fled across the mountains, madam, who will keep them warm in the high ice-falls? Tell me, are your eyes keen, can you see the snow-patches above the scree, are they not the white fleeces of my flock, lost and cold and lit by the moon?'

'You poor dear,' I said, seeing nothing in the distance but the starkest tip of the mountain. 'How long have they been gone?'

'Long as a league, long as an albatross wing, long as the shepherd's stick which beats us when we stray from the field! How should I know, madam?'

'I meant only to establish whether you had been searching for a brief or an extended time,' I said hastily.

'Pray do not trifle with me, madam. I know the difference between a day and a night, and that my feet are weary from following my heart, but if you would have me count the moons you must teach me the abacus!'

Just then there was a small sound among the colonnades and, turning sharply towards it, the sheep gave a little skip. 'Oh!' she cried roguishly, shedding her years with her despondency. 'What naughty scamps you are, to play such tricks on me! Come here, now. Come to your Dolly!' Eager as any bride she trotted toward the shadows, hope hoisting her old knees high, and her flower-tangled fleece trailing behind her like a train.

'You have found them?' I cried, glad to discover that she was my namesake, and hopeful of a happy outcome. The sheep had vanished behind the pillars and did not answer. When she returned she was alone, and it was clear that her hectic heart had played the trickster, and persuaded her feet to follow a phantom. This setback was hardly supportable and, beckoning her to approach, I urged her to rest on the rug at the foot of my throne. So wretched was the ewe that she readily accepted, and even nuzzled disconsolately at my china hand, and climbed at length into my lap, where she lay hot and burly as a new-made barrel, her fleece flea-ridden and full of pricking thorns.

Reader, understand that I am quite accustomed to being petted, but not at all to petting, since beasts in general have been too big for me: the tabby-cat as threatening as a tiger, the canary the size of an eagle, and the Scottish sheep like woolly mammoths. Thus was I denied the apprenticeship in cradling and caring which is incumbent on everyone, and of which the doll is often the earliest instrument. Inept and untutored as I was, I did my level best, plucking the burrs from the coat of the pathetic creature, and rocking her awkwardly, and crooning *there, Dolly* and *poor Dolly*, and the like. Yet – since inexperience will always tend toward zealotry – it was not enough for me to bear her weight and buoy her up, but I must also set my shoulder to the earnest wheel of encouragement.

'But, my dear Dolly, have you asked others of your kind if they can tell you their whereabouts?' I enquired of the sheep, which, evidently fearing that I might kill her with kindness, struggled a little, and looked at me askance.

'Indeed! But they are so stupid that they will believe in any nonsense. They are also scaremongers, who insist on spreading the most sensational kind of rumour!' She shook her head, and snorted with derision. 'Giants, I ask you!'

Needless to say I was immediately alert, and pressed my charge further. But here you need not wait to hear it, as it were, from the horse's mouth. Being already familiar, no doubt, with Mr. Gulliver's escape from the island, and the practicalities he faced in provisioning himself for his home-ward journey, you will quickly solve the riddle of the flock's disappearance, which, far from being the fault of dilatory mothering, was in fact a cruel kidnap.

Without dwelling too long on the tragic circumstances, it must be admitted that some of the flock had been devoured *en route*, while the survivors travelled to England in a medical bag, and arrived at length in Redriff. Those hardy specimens, originally earmarked for presentation to the Royal Society, had been forgotten in the subsequent upheavals, and left in darkness to their own devices. Having gnawed a way out of their leather cage, the beasts grazed profitably at first on the giant grasses in the suburbs of the stable, and grew quickly fat on their new-found Plenty.

Life in the sheepfolds of Lilliput, however, had ill-prepared them for the perils of an English country garden, where the natives were xenophobes to a man, and presently made it plain they would have no truck at all with foreigners. Thus Death stalked them daily without rhyme or reason – or so it seemed to the innocent interlopers. One yearling died from the poisonous nip of a dung-beetle, while her twin was felled by a snail-shell dropped from the beak of a chaffinch. Several were stung by horseflies or snatched by starlings, and other unfortunates perished in the jaws of marauding cats. One reckless ram, standing his ground, butted the shrew which had savaged his fellows, but his temerity was his undoing, for tough horn proved no match for piercing teeth; an elderly ewe, meanwhile, surprised at midnight by the striped stare of a badger, promptly dropped dead of heart failure . . . But enough is enough. I have made my point, and see no need to supply a complete catalogue of the carnage. Suffice it to say that the flock – initially large in number – was well nigh decimated, and had it not been for a singular stroke of fortune, would soon have gone the way of Herr Scheuchzer's *homo diluvii testis*, or the fossil-dragons of Ohningen.

To cut a long story short, the survivors were discovered by the sharp-eyed William, transported by chaise to Newgate Street, and bred up on a billiard table by the industrious Mr. Burton, on whose like the prosperity of the British Isles is founded, and who, seeing that the sheep bore fleeces finer than the thread of any silkworm, sheared them with his nail-scissors, sent to Scotland for the best spinsters, and presently was the proud purveyor of *cobweb-hose*, by appointment to His Majesty.

*　　*　　*

For the moment, however, I knew no more of this than did the unfortunate Dolly, who continued to reject the notion that they had been carried off by a giant, huffing and puffing, and swearing that it was all stuff and nonsense. Yet one man's rumour, as they say, is another man's intelligence, and I was much intrigued by what the sheep dismissed. Civilization, after all, is but a thin veneer, and I thought it by no means impossible that my mistress – if still alive, Praise Be! – had been obliged to turn huntress like Diana, and prowl the shores in search of morsels for her larder.

'It is true, I'm afraid, that there are giants about,' I said gently, not wishing to distress poor Dolly further. 'Why, my own mistress is rather large, to say the least!'

'Well, it shouldn't be allowed!' cried the ewe. And she launched into one of these bitter tirades to which the elderly, bless their hearts, are terribly prone, for all change is a scandal to them – as it will be to you, dear reader, as time goes by. Rather than admit you are outflanked by the march of modernity, I hazard that you will be every bit as tiresome as the sheep, and defend yourselves by flying into a fury, and loudly demand to know what the world is coming to.

Sensing that Dolly would rather berate herself than suffer a slight to her vanity, I regretted my candour, and wished I could undo every word I had said, as one may erase a written indiscretion with sea-salt or china-white, and start again with a clean slate. What price truth, after all, if it be a torment over and above a sheep's self-appointed suffering? And what price the proleptic powers of an Oracle, if they did not also embrace analepsis? If I could channel time and tide and see the future, why could I not turn the same talents about-face, as it were, and render smooth and blank the sands of memory?

Yet the miracle I could not make was to be accomplished soon enough by ordinary infirmity, for by and by the ewe forgot both outburst and inciting factor, and losing the thread of things, resumed her mournful muttering.

'Let us go, you and I,' said I on a reckless impulse. 'If you will only let me sit astride you, we may kill two birds with one stone, for we may yet find your flock where we seek my Mary.'

Reader, you may be forgiven for asking why a doll who had been so exalted should wish to step down from her throne and cast her lot once more with a far from perfect mistress. It is true, of course, that one who dines too long on ostrich fillets will presently pine for oatmeal brose, but I cannot pretend this is the whole answer. Yet on one matter I do not deceive myself: to be rich in wisdom is not in itself entitlement to the mantle of Divinity. To be an Oracle it is not enough to have visions; one must also believe in them. And in any case nothing is holier to most folk than old habits, for will we not stubbornly seek out our other halves even when they do not suit us? In Lilliput, as you have seen, I had the ear of hundreds, and priestesses to puzzle over my every pronouncement, but the powers invested in me as Oracle were as nothing next to a doll's need to be deciphered by her mistress.

What assigns us to this destiny I cannot say, for regrettably I am not privy to the laws which rule our shadowy quest for recognition, and even if Mr. Bates were to dissect each one of us like his baby elephant, and examine every ounce of our brain matter, he should bring us no closer to a conclusion. If it comes to that, why did my mistress risk life and limb to pursue a dilatory husband, when she might easily have sought a divorce and washed her hands of him? Reader, I have no explanation, except there be an unseen hand which, guiding the soul to greater growth, matches it up with mysterious teachers, and keeps us at our desks till we have learnt our lesson.

CHAPTER XI

*The Itch that cannot be Scratched . . . On Virility . . . Divers
Attempts are made on Mary's Virtue . . . Some Observations upon the
English Abroad . . . In Praise of Taxidermy . . .*

So what did Mary learn in the meantime, while the busy
drones infested her hive? For the most part, mercifully,
she was oblivious, since the tiny things had vanished from
her line of sight; none the less she was affected by their
presence, if only in the subtle disturbance of her dreams. One
morning she woke in dread, for she had seen a tiny Gulliver
tossed like a china cup in the air to shatter in smithereens
upon the marble floor. He is surely dead, she thought, and
tears of remorse rolled hugely down her cheeks, for like the
poor distracted sheep she must carry the blame on her own

shoulders. It was as if her very largeness was his obscure executioner, and had propelled him to his doom. I have killed him, said her heart in its confusion, and never, he has left me, and I hate him for it.

Reader, you must understand that she could not bear the brunt of her own fury, for mind and will were set on preserving the fellow. Thus she subjected herself to an unbearable tension, for the more passionately did she mount the attack, the more strenuously must she spring to the defence. She would have run a million miles, if she could, to escape the rage which made its object so frail and friable, yet she was shackled to it like an ox to a treadmill. It was the itch that could not be scratched, the bridge that could not be crossed, the delicious morsel that could not be eaten. She boiled, but no steam came from her. She begged the heavens to send her a vision of a Lemuel so hale and huge and hearty she could do no harm to him. She bit her lip to ribbons but did not bleed.

Reader, you and I know that a hateful thought is not at all the same thing as a murder, but my meek mistress knew of no such separation. Accordingly she forbade the first as firmly as she did the second, and thus stored up an abominable surfeit of temper. If she annihilate the man she wished to save her, she could have no hope for herself or pity for her own predicament, for one cannot sail in a ship whose planks are staved and splintered by one's own cannon, and one cannot live in a house one's own breath has blown down. To continue the conundrum, if a small thing is lonely it may make friends with its longing, and conjure up some large and luxurious rescue, for then it may feel itself safely enveloped. Whereas a large thing will envisage no lap great enough to lie in, except it belong to the very gods, and, flying into a frenzy of frustration, will fear its every angry thought a thousand-fold!

In what confused condition, then, should I find my mistress, if indeed I found her at all, bearing in mind that Temple and Pleasure Palace were placed on opposite sides of the capital, and in between them were crescents and crossroads, tinkers' camps and traders' awnings, and many a raucous band to bar my way with a coin thrown down and a cry of Tell my fortune? Nevertheless I rode my Dolly through the thronging streets, enquiring after my mistress in Akkadian – that being the prayer tongue of the Temple – and meeting with no more comprehension than you would, reader, if at the butcher's shop you asked for your oxtails in Ancient Latin.

After long days of fruitless searching I came one evening to the western outskirts of the city, and there in the distance, if my eyes did not deceive me, was the hooped cage – praise be – of my mistress's petticoat, propped on a pole and rotating majestically in the last red rays of the setting sun.

Tiny chariots depended from the structure, and as I drew nearer, I saw that a strange merry-go-round had been made of it, on which rode Lilliputians in happy hundreds, whooping and squeaking with terror. Since a lady will not generally stray too far from her underwear, I reasoned that my mistress must be close at hand, and turned my attention to the adjacent building, which was surrounded by souvenir stalls and shooting galleries . . . But you are already acquainted with the uncommon attractions housed therein, and so I shall abridge a little, and consider what the members of the Queen Bee Club have been up to in the interim.

Despite Edesad's apprehensions, all but one had passed the perilous test, and were duly inducted as drones. Yet if each had had his triumph, so had he felt the terror of envelopment and, venturing no farther than honour required, had seen his seed fall lamentably short of its goal. By no means did they share their failures in fellowship, however, but rather doubted themselves in silence, each one smarting at the memory of his puny arc, and quite convinced that his comrades had come off better. Beset by such anxieties, the roués suffered a marked inhibition of appetite, and fretted themselves to a fever, lest their potency fall even deeper into decline. Evenings found them in a disconsolate circle, each with his eye on his neighbour and his hand on his member, and together they clouted and cuffed them, beat and bullied them, rapped and slapped them, belaboured them and boxed their ears, until finally, dwarfed by the shadowy bulk of the giant, they spouted feebly and gave up the ghost.

Vessel their Queen Bee was, but sadly too vast a one for the little fellows! Nor would she afford them that other proof of their virility, for even if they made common cause to mount a siege, a brotherhood of battering-rams would not suffice to stir her senses. The Chairman saw the crisis clearly, yet to solve it he must move mountains, for only the complete surrender of the matriarch would salve the wounds of his comrades and restore their self-esteem.

'Do not wallow in despair,' he urged them. 'If you ask me, not a man on earth could move her. But all is not lost, my friends, for our monster may yet be wooed by mechanical wiles.'

Somewhat mollified by his remarks, his comrades listened

eagerly enough to the proposition he put to them. Since they were all of private fortune, why should they not endow a prize handsome enough to attract the best inventors, whose skills, sharpened by competition, would surely supply the solution?

Unanimously approved, the plan was swiftly set in motion, and soon the blueprints started to arrive, of which a shortlist of six was selected, those to be constructed within the week and tested out for efficacy, for the final arbiter must be the giant's pleasure.

(Forgive me, reader, if in the following passages I offend against Propriety, but I have pledged myself to a stricter master, and am compelled to tell the Truth.)

The first proposal to be tested involved a great gang of grouse-beaters with ostrich-feather flails, who mounted a simultaneous assault upon the giant's nether parts. Mary sensed that something was afoot, and might have allowed she felt the faintest tickle, had her grim mood not negated anything that smacked of pleasure, and closed the door on all external stimulation.

The second attempt on her virtue was more ingenious still, for it harnessed the power of the wind to woo her. Trim sails mounted atop the temple roof by the Worshipful Guild of Carpenters propelled a wooden carousel which spun within an inch of her, making a pleasant breeze. Yet to its poles were strapped no painted swans or plunging nags, but a hundred baying hounds whose tongues licked at her lustily, and never missed their turn.

Still the Colossus did not melt or moan, but watched the contraption curiously, wondering what gratification the members of the Queen Bee club could glean from it. 'How asinine,' she sighed. 'Is there no end to their absurdity?' And yet . . . and yet again. It could not be . . . or could it? Were hers the senses they intended to inflame, in preference to their own? For Pity's sake, thought she, who had been butt, and sport, and guy, and game. I do believe they mean to make a jade of me!

The notion was as odious as it was novel – nay, ladies, entirely unprecedented, for nothing heretofore had prepared her for it, and she could not but conclude that the unnatural rascals were determined to degrade her. Have they not taken enough liberties already, she thought wrathfully, that they must drag me down to their level? And she let out a cry of outrage which raised the hackles of the hounds and sent the spectators scurrying for cover.

With shock, however, came sensation, for energy too long enchained had found an outlet, and now enlivened her indiscriminately, heightening her colour, opening her pores, and causing a subtle change of climate in her southern latitudes – a certain warming, as it were, as if a parasol had been tilted sideways to allow the rays of the sun to smile on English skin; a distinct tropicality, in fact, as alien as the land she lay on. But still she shied away and struggled, until a vehement thrust of her pelvis fractured the ratchets of the carousel, thus crushing the hopes of the Carpenters, who were obliged to retire from the contest. The way was now left clear for the Armourers who, having affixed a kind of canopy to the ceiling, filled it with a million balls of lead shot which at the tug of a cord would shower down a chute and pitter-patter on the giant's private parts. Alas, it was all over as swiftly as a summer thunderstorm, for the Armourers, to be honest, had underestimated, and must regretfully admit that fifty million balls would scarce have been enough!

Next a treadmill was tried out, this to be turned by several brace of oxen, and the water pumped upwards on a millwheel to spout from a spigot in a powerful stream which, being conserved beneath the giant in a trough, and thenceforth channelled through a wooden aqueduct, assured the engine of a constant flow. If the method lacked refinement, the principle of continuity was sound, for now that there was no lull or let-up her sensation went unhindered, and her opposition weakened, and she sighed voluptuously. She was not in England, after all, where the sun-starved flesh of the apple is for ever cool and resistant, but among foreign fruits that could not help but swell with juice in the insistent heat: the papaya opening eagerly to show its gleaming pips, the cantaloup oozing, and the vulgar guava brimming like a rain-barrel. And sweet, yes, reader, all of them steeped in a honeyed sweetness half-known to her and seldom sampled . . .

Thus, with scandalous and infinite slowness, the whole land with its alien tongues inveigled itself into her being: the odd inverted moon, the feathered shade of the palm-fronds on the shore, the turquoise tranquillity of the shoal-waters, and the indigo depths beyond the reef. You will say she was too easily seduced, and that a true Englishwoman is made of sterner stuff than this: in reply I must insist that of all races the English are the most impressionable, for when foreign sunlight thins their skin and melts their marrow-bone they turn quite dizzy with delight, and are avid for any amount of entrancement!

My mistress did not lose her bearings all at once, however,

but held to her meridian a while longer, and stoutly fought for the fading memory of London's spires, and her own green garden with its whitewashed gate. Yet what should restrain her now that no cloud crawled across the sun and no slap came like an Atlantic squall to quell her pleasure? If she did not succumb entirely to the waterfall, she was at least aroused by it, and this fact did not escape the observant Edesad, who promptly ordered in the waiting Fishermen.

Imagine, reader, if only for the sake of science, how their crustacean cargo might exacerbate her craving – for they had filled a net with countless tiny crabs, as well as crayfish, shrimps and prawns, and now applied this lively poultice to the part. How pleasantly the pincers tickled, and what a seductive sea-smell emanated from their bluish shells, and how excitably they scurried to and fro upon the shores of Mary's island! Her breath is in abeyance . . . heart apounding . . . skin all moistening and aglow. (In this way, dear reader, in becoming acquainted with another country, a woman may abjure her own if it not nurture her, and see it as a far land she can no longer fathom, or even as a harsh outcrop on a Northern seaboard where dolls and children are accustomed to be beaten.)

Of the professions, Taxidermy is supposed to be the stuffiest, yet as we approach the crux, I beg you to consider an example of the talents daily wasted on the late lamented lapdog and the vanquished stag. The bold inventiveness of the apprentice-boys was evidenced as follows: some days before, on receiving notice of the contest, they had salvaged from the strand a Manatee, that amiable cow which grazes on the sea-wrack of the southern oceans. Making an incision at the muzzle of the beast, they slit its belly to the tail, and gutted it, and having scoured it out with salt and stuffed the cavity with straw, they sewed it up neatly, and treated the tough hide with oil and beeswax, till it was soft and sleek. This simulacrum was suspended from a sturdy frame, so that it might be pushed like a swingboat at the hinder end, and move as sweetly to and fro.

Twenty men it took, to push the thing, and several teams of twenty in reserve. Delighted with the contrivance, the Chairman urged them to maintain a constant swing, clapping his hands and crying, 'Haul away, my hearties, for I'll lay odds that Manatee succeed where Man has failed!'

(Ridiculous, aye – but I hazard that it is no more absurd, ladies, than your everyday mechanics, since I do not think you would pretend that it is love alone which sets you swooning, and it would be shabby to deny the journeyman tongue some credit, or belittle the part played by the busy labouring fingers. Oh, I do not doubt it is sweet indeed when the soul lends its blessing to the enterprise, but although not every building will be consecrated by a Lord Archbishop, each one requires the same honest toil of its masons!)

Up bobbed Mary's head to inspect the source of the sensation, but the ropes tugged so irksomely at her scalp that it was far less incommodious to lie back and let the strange beast have its way with her. If the incursions of the Queen Bee Club had made a negligible impact, here she encountered a first-rate fit, slick and sizeable, and no sooner had the device advanced than it retreated, and then, relinquished, was restored again, and famously received, till Manatee and matron rocked not recklessly but with the rhyme and reason of a piston driven by an engine, back and forth, with such a clack and clatter that she might have thought herself a child again, encompassed by the hectic rhythm of machines.

Here, indeed, was an endeavour great as any industry, though it produce no actual wealth! Such an expenditure of energy could certainly have founded far-off Colonies and generated fortunes, yet it filled no coffers but her own; she and she alone drew profit from it! This, thought Mary, was the very reason it was frowned upon – insofar as she had the wits to think at all, for her limbs trembled with exertion, and perspiration streamed from her indecorous belly. Eagerly she heaved and strained, and her bosoms, growing mightily engorged, sundered their silken bonds and thrust their twin planets upwards as if to suckle the heavens with their bounteous milk. Yet even as her body burgeoned to immensity, her thoughts grew distant, and diminished, till they were as small as any Lilliputian.

A formless lump I am, she thought, *unfashion'd and un-fram'd*, yet it was of little consequence, and in no wise devalued the newly minted currency of her pleasure. 'Aye sir' and 'Please' and 'I entreat you' were the sole notions left to one who saw what marvels might be made from her own raw material, and so it was that Mary, urged and amazed by a dark decisive tremor, raced headlong towards her ruin. And did she regret it for a moment, did she attempt to recollect herself? One might as well require the stag to stint his rutting, or the birds to contort their hearts with guilt and stay their cheerful congress! Nay, reader, she was unravelled, could not record it, sighed, swooned, shuddered, swam on silken seas, was sucked like a whirlpool into the interior, faded from view like her rapturous island, fell, in fact, utterly out of sight.

The temple trembled; the mill-wheel tottered; the crew leapt for safety as the Manatee broke from its moorings. Yet even as chaos quaked around her Mary was restored to herself, knit newly, as it were, by Cupid's skilful hand, all formed and framed and fully fashioned. Careless of Propriety she rested where she lay, undone, indecent, yet content, for though the effort had been great, great also was her pride in the achievement. O well-kept secret! she reflected, as with a superlative shrug her shoulder snapped a dozen shackles. O blissful ambition, that leads to wonders such as this! Her brow was smooth, her eyes a-sparkle, her bosom flushed with felicity. What am I seeking that I have not found? she asked herself, weeping tears of copious happiness.

Chapter XII

A Doll's Discontents . . . Mary's Liberation . . . A Prince Resurrected
. . . The Rout of the Queen Bee Club . . . A Family Portrait . . .

Reader, in speaking so frankly of what happened in the Pleasure Drome, I have tried to do justice to my mistress's experience. Yet the neutrality which befits a narrator has not always been easy to preserve. You will recall that I had arrived at the temple in the meantime, and insofar as I myself was a witness – perched on the sheep's back, with my nose to the window – I confess I was greatly shocked by the spectacle. With my own eyes I had observed the hounds' tongues and the crabs' claws, and the miraculous motion of the Manatee. I had overheard the fevered cries, too, and the ecstatic farts of the quim, and had been quite confounded by the phenomena, for though in my role as confidante I was privy to many female secrets, I had been relegated, in the main, when my mistresses bade farewell to their childhood. On manners and morals I believe I was always able to offer a trenchant opinion, but on the earthier issues I was lamentably ignorant, this being a conversation cut off, as it were, in mid-stream.

Needless to say my colleagues were no better informed than I, and no less resentful of the loss of status which was the dismal adjunct of our mistresses' maturity. Such rites of passage always brought rebellion to the ranks, for dolls, I assure you, do not take kindly to redundancy.

'How women do deceive themselves,' Belinda would grumble, 'if they imagine they may banish us so easily!'

'Indeed!' Arethusa would agree. 'One wonders what they will do with their fits and fevers, and what heads beside their own they will beat against the walls!'

'And with whom will they share their thoughts? And who else but us will give a fig for their complaints?'

'Ladies, ladies!' Charlotte would cry, in a vain attempt to play the prefect. 'We should be gullible indeed if we believed that marriage recompenses them in the slightest for what they forfeit when they abandon us. From what we have been able to observe, there is little companionship in it, less happiness, and a good deal of frustration which is allowed no outlet!'

'Indeed, they are the ones who gull themselves!' said Lady Anne, swelling the chorus of disgruntlement.

'Are they contented?'

'Do their eyes flash?'

'Do we hear the trill of their laughter?'

'Do they sing with the birds in the morning, do they dance with delight for their mirror?'

'Nay, 'tis pity that they do but fret and mourn in front of it!'

No man, we were agreed, could satisfy their burgeoning dreams, nor match their girlish pleasures. Thus bolstered, we continued to circle the conundrum, the blind leading the blind, never asking the central question, yet aching always for the answer: What did women want that we ourselves could not provide?

By peeping over the brink, then, I had said farewell to innocence for ever. In this, to be sure, I had the advantage of my colleagues, yet it did not seem so, since unlike them, I must plainly face the pain of being supplanted.

'Why, it is no more than dogs do, or the bull with the cow,' I scoffed at first, for envy will always make little of what it cannot have. 'What the poets sing of, and what flowers and furbelows invite, is at base a loud and liquid business, more suited to the farmyard than to the human female!'

Even the wisest of us will fight shy of unwanted intelligence, so be patient with your poor Oracle, who is made of wood and pride and sawdust, and pity her dilemma, which unlike yours, is quite without solution. What is carnal must remain as foreign to her as a far land she may spend her whole life studying in the accounts of others, until she know its every aspect, but she may never set her foot on it, or smell its air, or taste the startling savour of its fruit.

Stoics are not born but made, dear reader, and the best that might be hoped for in this instance was that by acknowledging the existence of a world beyond my ken, I might enlarge my understanding of the forces which operated in my own small universe. One law I had already learned, for instance, is that if the mistress be tormented by repressed desires, it is sad but certain that the doll will somehow bear the brunt of them . . . But I did not intend to stray so far from my proper subject, and beg your pardon for my digression.

Now that the bonds of her breast were sundered, my mistress was able to raise herself to a sitting position. Chains sheared away from their cleats, and the ropes which had bound her hips unravelled like knitting-stitches. She flexed a leg and rose on to her knees, so that the onlookers fled in frenzy for the exits. With only her ankles restrained, she asked her magnificent thighs to obey her, and stood at last unsteady as a colt, testing the margins of her freedom. She stamped her feet, for pins and needles stabbed her limbs as the blood coursed fitfully through them, and took a step . . . aye . . . she could walk . . . and took another, clanking in her ankle-chains. Straightening her back until her headdress grazed the dome, she practised her deportment like a green girl setting out for Sunday School, though somewhat less strict in her dignity, and with no black-browed Bible to weigh her down.

And now, reader, summoned like a shy bridegroom from the distance, Bluebottle moves towards my mistress through the darkness. Not dead at all, as I had thought – no ghost or dream, but large and lively, and with a tale or two to tell, as you will shortly hear!

If Edesad's profligates had been diminished by the giantess, each measuring his puny prowess against a superior shadow, here was proof positive of their inadequacies. To be sure, the young rakes had heard tell of a great Gulliver, but long ago in nursery days, when the world was full of giants which they plotted in their jealous cribs to conquer. Night after night they waited to grow great enough to kill the one parent and claim the other as their rightful prize, for were they not assured that age and stature alone would remove all impediment to their desires? 'When you are bigger . . .' goes the tired refrain of the nursemaid, who never stops to consider that the expectations thus implanted may taint her charges' lives, unless they are fortunate enough to forget them! Such, then, were the poisonous promises which dragged the members back to futile infancy. As if it were not a cruel enough fate to be dwarfed by the female, they must now acknowledge that she had a mighty mate! For what now loomed over them was a rival of the utmost vim and vigour, in fact, the outsize epitome of manliness! In this way Bluebottle dealt the death-blow to the Queen Bee Club, not by crushing their persons, but rather by crushing their hopes, for though they wait a hundred years to grow they never could surpass him.

Gathering his tattered cloak of leopard-skins around him, Bluebottle stooped to enter the door of the temple, and gazed in astonishment at the scanty clothing of the shackled deity, at the torn net and the scuttling crabs, at the fallen fish and the foaming fountain and the drifting debris of machines. Believing himself to be in the presence of a sea-goddess, and much perplexed by the strangeness of her rites, he was loath, at first, to approach her. Such was his history, however, that he could not abide the sight of manacles on any living soul, and stepping determinedly forward he wrenched the remaining chains from the walls.

'Bluebottle!' cried Mary, believing she had seen a ghost, albeit an uncommonly princely one.

'Madam Gull?' cried he, recognizing with some difficulty the strait-laced lady of the *Aphrodite*, for while Mary had met but the one black in her life, to a man who had moved for years among Europeans one white face was as like to another as the spumy waves of the sea.

Observing that she was not dressed with the customary modesty of an Englishwoman, he wrapped his cloak around her with the gallantry of a Raleigh, and hurried her from the chamber, hardly allowing her the time to collect her dressing-chest from the vestibule.

'We must go quickly, Madam Gull,' he urged, and I daresay my mistress would have gone ahead and left me stranded there on Lilliput, had I not at that very moment spurred my poor mount towards her.

So bald was my head and so arcane my garb that her eyes would not at first believe what her heart, at least, should have remembered. 'My poor girl!' she cried at last. 'We have been through the mill, you and I.' And clasping both doll and sheep to the sanctuary of her bosom, she followed the Nubian northwards towards the thin gold line the dying sun had drawn along the crests of the mountains, never daring to consider what her toes stubbed against, or what small things were crushed under her soles like caterpillars.

By sun-up we had reached the wooded foothills, and rested for a while in the seclusion of a steep-sided gully, under a spreading cedar the size of a hawthorn bush.

Reader, if you had seen us there, still and settled in the brilliant shade, I fancy that you would have remarked, as I did, how we made a fair imitation of the kind of family one of our modern painters might group together for a portrait. A black man cloaked in leopardskin is the patriarch, ramrod-straight, a man of evident substance; Mary is the matron, dishevelled delightfully, like a French shepherdess; in her lap, with pride of place, sits the precious infant; and lo and behold a pet sheep lolls on the sward before them, her fleece winsomely woven with garlands, and her neck be-ribboned by an embroidered garter! As for the background, here is no park cunningly landscaped to within an inch of wilderness, but the wild itself with its hauteur and hazes, its troubled torrents, its snarling mists and saw-toothed crags. (From this whimsy you will understand that, despite the disquieting events she had been unfortunate enough to witness, the doll was overjoyed to be reunited with the mistress!)

Bluebottle fetched water from a stream, with which the two refreshed themselves, and said presently, 'Mrs. Gull, we may speak in English?' Having received my mistress's assent, he began to tell of his adventures in the interim. He spoke at first stumblingly, but then with relish, savouring every syllable with the pleasure of a man long denied his favourite food, for though he could acquit himself fairly in Spanish, fluently in the several languages of the African coast, and elegantly in the French dialect of the interior, English was the tongue he had grown accustomed to, and Lilliput had left him hungry for a taste of any talk at all.

CHAPTER XIII

A Mountain eyrie ... On Manners and Measurements ... Cupid's Dart ... Bluebottle Builds a House which Breaks his Heart ...

He had landed, he told us, on the northern tip of the island, beyond the snowy mountains. He was at first quite certain that he was dead, yet found that he encountered a very curious Heaven, for its tallest trees would hardly shelter him, nor its tiny fruits provide him with nourishment. As for the birds which buzzed inquisitively around him, why, he took them for biting bugs which had no business in Paradise, and swatted out at them until the sight of tiny feathers bright among the blood smears filled him with remorse for his great arrogance, that could not tell one thing from another.

The shock sharpened his eyes, and now there was no mistaking the dwarf coco-nut palms, and the swamp oaks which would have reached a height of eighty feet in Guinea, but which were shrunk here to the size of parasols. This Heaven, if such it was, was modelled entirely in miniature! The realization was accompanied by a feeling acutely familiar to one so long misplaced, and he stared around him with bitter resentment in his heart. Not even in death, then, would he see his own image reflected in the faces of his kith and kin; not even in the afterlife would he be reunited with his homeland. He glared at his great black feet and spat angrily upon them, cursing the gods of his race, who had played such an ugly joke on him, and doomed him to be a black blot even on the face of Eternity. For if a black man stand out like a sore thumb among whites of similar size, how much worse his position in a nether world inhabited by midgets? Now Bluebottle feared nothing on earth that did not speak the Spanish tongue, but here was a prospect to fill the staunchest heart with dread.

And yet, did he not bleed? Was not that his own red blood seeping from the lacerations made by the coral reef, and puddling in the sand around his feet? The sweat of relief broke out upon his body, and he let out a stifled cry. Far from being a spirit, was he not, after all, entirely embodied? Like a rabbit set free from a snare his instincts returned to him, and he bolted into the underbrush, there to conceal himself from midget and Spaniard alike. Only when his frantic heart quieted was his cunning restored to him, and he clasped his knees, and rocked himself in his burrow of palm branches, and began to appraise his prospects. Once again he was a stranger in a strange land, and whatever the size of the natives, there was no reason to suppose them friendly. Therefore they must no more stumble upon him than he on them, and to that end he must seek out regions which were thinly populated, and whose terrain would afford sufficient concealment.

Half a day's march to the south lay a range of inhospitable mountains, with slopes deeply wooded and cleft by inaccessible gorges; from the peaks he could spy out the land, and find game, if he were fortunate, in the forests. These snowy cornices were his compass-point as he strode through marshy everglades, forded several slow-running rivers, and came at last to higher ground where the trees were tall enough to hide him. Not until he had reached the very summit of the ridge did he pause to take stock, throwing himself down on his belly in the snow and peering cautiously over the lip of the precipice.

Spread out below him was the southern half of the island, with patchwork fields and small towns dotted here and there on the central plain, and a distant haze of city smoke at the farthest tip. In the wooded foothills of the mountains, he saw clearings where clustered huts were flanked by plots of vegetables and little fields of maize, yet no road led towards his rocky crest, from which he deduced that the population had neither appetite nor ambition to conquer the northern peaks or negotiate the mountain passes.

Satisfied that he was safe enough in his eyrie, he made it his business to seek out bed and board before night fell in the icy slopes. A cave served him tolerably for a lodging, and as for his supper, well, the whole forest would be his larder. A dozen bounds took him down to the tree line, and then the stalker went stealthily, his hand poised on the knife at his belt, anticipating a full-sized stag or raging tusk, and quite forgetting to examine the very ground at his feet, where the real game moved in miniature. At last, stooping to attend to an annoying itch, he was startled to see a wild boar rooting at his toe like a pig nosing out truffles. Without more ado he scooped the creature up and thrust it wriggling into his pocket; he had learnt his lesson, and henceforth he would keep his head down and his eyes peeled.

Still as an oak by a stream he waited for his prey to come unsuspectingly to drink. First came a herd of deer, from which he culled three dappled does; then a wolverine, and by and by he added to his store a brace of wildcat, and a barrel-shaped bird which resembled an ostrich. This quarrelsome menagerie he despatched rapidly, roasted whole, and ate skins and bones and all, like a gourmet gobbling up a dainty plate of quails.

In the days that followed Bluebottle became aware of the scattered homesteads of the mountain folk, and despite his caution they in turn noticed his presence, fleetingly, like a tall thundercloud glimpsed in the corner of an eye.

Had the southerners encountered the giant they would have fallen upon him without mercy but, fortunately for Bluebottle, the northern shepherds, insulated by the mountain barrier from boom and slump alike, lacked the prejudices currently rife among their volatile neighbours. Those whose lives are constantly hard are not so quick to blame, and if they had heard, some years before, rumours of a great white giant, the news had become so garbled in its tortuous passage across the mountains that it took on the hazy status of myth, for in airy regions where earth rises dizzily to meet the embrace of sky, folk do not make the same distinction between the possible and the impossible, nor force as strict a standard on reality.

Presently, sensing their tolerance, Bluebottle took to leaving a portion of his bag at the door of one or other cottage, so that a hard-pressed crofter or goatherd might wake next morning to a haunch of venison or a whole roast pig, and be assured the immigrant had no desire to harm him.

Meanwhile he dwelt much upon the shipwreck and his lost comrades. Melancholy among the *seracs* which guarded the glacier like stoic sentinels, his eyes reddened by snow-glare, his shoulders clad noisomely in uncured hides, he who had been prince in his own country peered south to the flatlands, pining now not only for his own kin but for a glimpse of a human person of any colour under the sun. Day after day he spied from the ridge, but saw no fellow giant rising from the plains, no Lionel Sims or Leopold Scurrup, no cooper or carpenter or coxswain, and finally he was forced to the gloomy conclusion that all hands had been lost, and that he was the sole and wretched survivor.

Since it is not in man's nature to be solitary for long, but rather to seek out any available relation, his loneliness led him more and more often to the huts and homesteads of the natives where he would spy on them at their harvest, or milling their maize, or sawing logs hauled down from the forest.

To his credit, Bluebottle was not a measuring man, and by and by his study of the inhabitants altered his vision of them, so that the more he observed them, the less stunted they appeared to be, and soon he would have sworn that any difference between his hosts and himself was negligible. (If this seem to you incredible, reader, consider the fire which was kindled in my own small breast, on hearing how radically longing swells the stature of its object!) Moreover, since there is no gap on earth, it seems, that reckless lust will not leap over, he readily convinced himself that once they had become accustomed to the blackness of his skin, the sturdy locals might accept him not only as a fellow citizen, but even as a suitor. His life heretofore had been no less improbable, and if circumstance compelled him to remain for ever on the island, why then should he not marry and settle? Man, he told himself, was not born to crouch like a bear in a cave, but to be conjugal, and multiply.

Is it surprising that one who has prepared the ground of love so well, who has tilled and harrowed it, and watered it by day, and paced its boundaries by night, should quickly find a flower to grow on it? So it happened that one morning in bright drizzle Bluebottle saw a girl carrying a jug of milk to the sawmill, and suddenly set his heart on her. Her cheeks were mottled pink with the cold, and her hair was as ruddy as the sawdust which formed a thick carpet on the forest floor, but to him she was matchless, and his limbs trembled, and his soul turned a silent somersault in the rain.

Impulsively he reached out his hand, and would certainly have revealed himself, had not a squadron of sparrows surged from the underbrush and startled his quarry. Milk spilled on the sawdust, and the girl cried out in dismay, for now the workers would go thirsty, and her father would certainly scold her.

In the clearing, all was industry. Here an axeman trimmed branches while another stripped bark; here men unchained the redwood logs which had been dragged by mules from the upper reaches of the forest, and there a great cedar log lay on cross-pieces over a pit, with one man below and one atop, each toiling at his handle-end of a double saw, with the aim of turning raw lumber into rough planks. From the lower slopes of the mountain came the hardwoods: mahogany, sweet gum, and tupelo, and these must be fed through a mechanical saw turned by the force of the mill-stream.

At a bench shaded by a lean-to a ginger-bearded fellow bent in concentration over the blade, calling out commands to his companions. He it was that rebuked the girl for her clumsiness, so that she hung her head and bit her lip in remorse – whereupon he swiftly tousled her hair, kissed her brow, and was exceeding fond with her. Bluebottle could be in no doubt that this was the one to whom he must recommend himself, if he were to gain permission to court her.

The tools were less crude on the sawing-bench, yet the labour was no less arduous. Meanwhile the power of twenty woodsmen slept unused in the ball of his own thumb, and a log he could have lifted as easily as a tallow candle took a dozen men to guide it through the saw. If he could find a secret way to ease the workers' burden, would he not thus make a formidable impression on their overseer?

On the moonless nights that followed Bluebottle crept down from his eyrie to expedite his plan, felling a few firs with his pocket-knife on the way and carrying them to the sawmill like a bundle of kindling sticks. With the same blade he trimmed every log in the clearing and guided each one through the whirring saw, until the stacked planks were as high as his waist. Then he turned his hand to the intransigent swamp-oak and mahogany, and their hard hearts yielded so readily that he was certain no obstacle would now be placed in the way of his suit.

Cosy at his camp-fire he busied his mind with plans for his wedding. In this instance, he decided, he would be willing to abjure the rites of his tribe – for in Guinea a royal betrothal required the sacrifice of more livestock than lived in the whole of Lilliput, not to mention a brace of giraffe, six ocelot cubs and a rhinoceros in rut. That he was marrying beneath him was a fact which deserved consideration, for his bride's family were not of comparable estate, yet here Pride must simply step aside and Rank submit to Love's imperative.

Having settled the nuptials, he set his mind to the approach to be made to the patriarch. He had no wealth, to be sure, in this hemisphere, and he knew very well that the peasant sets more store by pork on the plate than absent emeralds. Yet his prodigious power would be his pledge, and the royal ruby on the hilt of his pocket-knife would prove his pedigree. In the meantime he would turn his hand to the joiners' trade, and build a fine house for his fiancée. (An ordinary Jack Tar, as we have seen, is in a position to amass more skills than any prince, and if he could take his sail-makers' needle to a dozen tiny leopardskins and sew his wedding-cloak, so could he square a pretty joist, and fit a ridgeboard sweetly to a rafter.)

Now the objection will be raised that such a match were very incredible, if for the sole reason that certain other parts would not fit so snugly. But has it not often been argued that crude anatomy should prove no deterrent to the higher emotions, since love's blessed blindness admits of no blemish? To be fair, I must admit that the partisans of this position belong in the main to the female sex, and to those among them least favoured by Nature. Whereas here was a man in his prime, fair of face, upright of limb, and an aristocrat to boot. Yet to Bluebottle it seemed that the match was not only congruous, but as good as made, and if any impediment rose to mind he simply abridged it (as you are quite at liberty to do, reader, with the passages herein that do not please you!).

Far from being incompatible with his requirements, the girl had become the apotheosis of all he longed for, and before long the roof-joists rose solid above him, and the window-frames on either side. While his fingers took pains with plane and saw, so his imagination worked as cunningly at its own craft, until the known and the unknown slipped together and locked like the tongue-board with the groove, one life into another, and each comprising all that was mysterious and hidden, and all that was manifest and magnificent. As a joiner joins the well-honed timbers together so that no storm can put the ship asunder, in the same way Bluebottle trued his love's edges, and in the alignment made his fiancée fit and familiar and settled her into place, so that she could count his camels like a desert princess and never find a reason for leaving him. So absorbed was he in this dual task that he did not notice the small figures who, spying from the fringes of the forest, talked in awe-struck whispers of the great temple the giant was constructing.

In the meeting-house of the village some of the elders argued that the generous gifts of game and the miraculous productivity enjoyed by the sawmill were proof enough of the giant's benevolence, and urged that he be formally welcomed among them. Others complained that the visitor had built a basilica upon their doorstep without so much as a by your leave. One sharp-eyed elder, advising the others that the giant had been mooning over the forester's girl, warned that even gods could be foolish, and overreach themselves. Meanwhile the forester twirled his hat in his hand and smiled absently, as if it were quite beneath his dignity to heed such gossip, but in fact his mind was busy as a hawk at harvest time, for he had profited handsomely from the giant's labours, and could not help but consider the wealth that would accrue to him from such a brilliant match.

Presently the debate floundered on to the subject of immigration, intermarriage, and the like, and drowned itself in a sea of abstraction, so that no decision was taken about the giant or his temple, and the elders fell back on the maxim which had served them well enough in the past and had kept them, one might suppose, from much foolishness: *If in doubt, wait it out*.

That night the forester went home pensive, and for some time gazed moodily at his daughter, who was husking corn at the kitchen table. How stunted she appeared to him all of a sudden! Not but that she was a woman fully formed, and she was in no way deficient of figure. How curious, then, that he should find himself irritated by a presence usually so pleasing to him, and exceeding exasperated by the tender little ears, the soft little chin, and the small bare feet, much scuffed by stubble and freckled by fierce weathers. There was simply no substance to her, he reflected angrily, and he would have stuffed her, if he could, with corn meal like a goose, and fattened her up for her future. Failing that, he barked at the wife who had conspired to starve her, and slammed out to the porch to puff his angry pipe-smoke at the stars.

At last the house was finished and Bluebottle made his

way to the sawmill, where on the earth floor of the lean-to he laid his ruby-hilted knife. Beside it he scratched an image of the forester's daughter, and marked the eyes with two blue pebbles, and the hair with a handful of ruddy sawdust, having no other language with which to speak his suit.

When the forester saw the image graven on the floor he could no longer doubt the giant's intentions. A shudder of confusion racked his limbs, and he sank down by the mill-stream to consider what must be done. Assuredly the elders must be told that the stranger had shown his hand, but the harder task, and one for which he must brace himself, was breaking the news to his daughter. Again a vague and vast frustration overtook him, and since a simple man will always resist a complicated emotion, he stamped a foot on his daughter's facsimile, and with a swift kick scattered her sawdust hair. Then, employing all his strength, he hoisted the haft of the knife to his shoulder and hauled it back to the village.

So what will happen now in the depths of the forest where Bluebottle, against the odds, has staked his all on happiness? On the edge of the clearing small birds dart among the blackberry bushes as the sun rises above the treetops, its pristine light as naked as his waiting heart. Will she come to him alone or accompanied, a shy bride or a glad one? Will she hang back behind her father or run up the steps impulsively and take her place beside him? Ah, reader, no matter what the outcome, in such lovely aching moments are our souls sincerely shown to us, for in their weightless play they weave the truths we will carry with us to our coffins!

Before long the tiny deputation stands at the mouth of the

clearing: a half-dozen elders, two workmen balancing the knife across their shoulders, the frowning forester, and the daughter dragging her feet and squinting up at the man who, just as she has been told, is tall and dark and passing handsome.

It has to be said that flattery will move a flirtatious heart far more than any call to duty and, being young, the girl cared little for wealth, but a great deal for pride, gossip, and the particular approval of her peers. 'Your strange prince is a fine catch,' her girlfriends whispered, 'We will none of us find a better,' and this envy was a precious nugget which proved more persuasive than her father's pleas.

Do not judge her too harshly on this account, however, or take her for a nincompoop, for although a novice in matters of the heart, she was strong of will, deft at milking, skilful at trapping thrushes, a not inconsiderable wood-carver, and a solid performer on the finger-organ. In short, she was the type of girl who would not go far, simply because she did not choose to, being quite content, nay, quite determined to secure a neat and cosy nook for her life rather than waste it in wandering the untrammelled lands of the imagination.

If we enquire further we will discover the ominous fact that she has a positive passion for small spaces, and finds no greater pleasure than in poring over her collection of thrushes' nests, or filling her dolls' house with tiny dressing-chests, each one of which she has fashioned with her own hand, and stocked with sheets stitched lovingly from scraps of linen. Let us not dwell too long on these propensities, however, lest we lose all hope of the giant's cause, but for the moment allow the elders to proceed with their protocol, and offer the obligatory gifts of salt and tobacco, which their guest received graciously, bending on one knee and striking the soft ground with his forehead, his cloak of leopardskins spread out around him.

In the amplitude of his heart the man who knew himself as Prince Yussuf Bel'Ablil held a girl huge enough to blot out the sun, and in passionate dumb-show began to plead his suit.

All eyes turned to the girl who must make the decision, and even those elders who objected to the match were still and silent. The forester, meanwhile, crossed his fingers behind his back and spat twice, viciously, for fortune. But his damnably good daughter, she who loved nothing better than a snug parlour and a linen-drawer in perfect order, shrugged, simply, at the fabulous knife, and scowled at the lofty eaves of the house, sensing its terrible draughts. In this barn of a place she was expected to make a home? Was she to shiver under a beetling chimney-breast, lose her way on an acre of carpet, spend her life on a ladder with her duster for company? Such a marriage-bed it would be, moreover, with pillows bigger than clouds and devilish to launder . . .

'I would rattle in there,' she declared with a shudder, 'like a pea in a drum!' And much aggrieved by this gross affront to her aspirations, she turned on her heel and flounced from the clearing – thus proving, reader, that however glorious the courtship, it cannot but fail if it speaks not to the fundamental nature, and offers a palace to one who pines for a doll's house!

But what of the hard-pressed forester, whose expectations tumbled about her recalcitrant heels? How darkly the wicked ruby winked at him, and how his cheeks flushed with outrage, that the matter should be so rudely settled. No daughter should gainsay her father and escape a whipping: aye, yet at the same time he could not but look on his stubborn offspring with a revival of affection, seeing all of a sudden what a good and suitable size she was, in fact faultless, and concluding, somewhat to his surprise, that the fault must therefore lie in the scale of her suitor. Could it be that avarice, blinding him with its delusions, had promised opportunities where there were none? Thus released from the snare of complexity, his simple heart fled free like an animal, yelping in wild relief. Assuredly he would chastise his darling, as was proper, but how light would be his stroke, and how sweet his shining tears of happiness!

The same cannot be said of the black prince, however, for if the meaning of her words escaped him he could not mistake the import of her scornful frown. An immense sorrow contorted his features, and despair was writ large in every limb. Boneless he sank down, as if he would liquefy and vanish into the earth like summer rain. Who could now doubt the sincerity of his attachment, or breathe the word absurd, or fail to see, in the fallen Colossus, their own sorrows, magnified to a degree well-nigh unbearable? Massive in its speechlessness, the great chest heaved and strained with sobs, and the great hands tore the wedding cloak asunder, until the elders took it upon themselves to throw the magnificent knife in a bramble-thicket, lest the poor soul seek to harm himself.

'Forgive us,' they muttered in dismay, stroking his hair and seeking to assure him it was the palace that the girl had spurned, and not the prince. But he did not understand them, nor, needing the embrace of solid arms, could he take consolation from their tiny kisses. All he knew was that his beloved had foresworn the place assigned to her, and he wished for nothing more than to sink into the yawning emptiness to which she had condemned his heart.

At last the chief elder, who had searched her heart for something that might assuage the giant's grief, called the others to a consultation. She had heard tell, by way of a tinker recently come from the city, that a great goddess had risen from the sea, and had been placed by the people in a temple. Being of an unusually rational cast of mind, she had initially discarded this as one of the many rumours which rose from the boiling mists of the mountains. Yet if it were truly so, then to be in the company of one of his own kind, and a female at that, might prove a comfort to him. The other elders readily clutched at the straw she offered, for they had wrung their hands to ribbons and were quite worn out with worrying.

When Bluebottle opened his eyes he found himself enormously alone. Behind him the sun sank through the rags of the trees, leaving scarcely enough light to read the pictograms the elders had drawn in the dust beside him. He saw a lady and a temple, both of goodly size. Prostrate before her throne were tiny worshippers, and tiny streets and spires, to indicate a city. All this was compassed by an exact geography of coasts and mountains, and flanked by a series of emphatic arrows. Go south, the message clearly said, for we have troubles of our own and cannot salve your sorrows here. Wail he might, and grind his teeth, but there was nothing for it but to obey the stark banishment, and lock and bar the house, and leave the place to the sighing wind. Let the dew fall on it and the moss and ivy cover it over; thus it would stand as a monument to his unrequited love. He, meanwhile, had no choice but to erase it from his mind and journey in search of his fellow castaway. This thought brought on another bout of weeping, for his heart knew that the red-haired girl was irreplaceable. And since nothing confounds an angry man like gratitude, as he marched across the mountain screes he brooded bitterly upon the tact with which the villagers had sought to ease his disappointment even as they sent him into exile.

(Imagine, if you will, the impact of this tale on one who heretofore had thought herself excluded from the lists of love! Gratitude, indeed, was not the word for the emotion that suffused me when I heard of that incongruous affair. How can a poor pen convey my joy, or the desires which, formerly constrained by sober practicality, were now set free like thrushes from a net? At that moment, reader, you would have sworn I knew what it was to possess a human soul, with all its fervent expectations. Thus illumined, I did not spare a thought for my inferior size, nor even for my bald dilapidated brokenness. Here was the evidence that a love existed which could leap the hurdle of dimension, and bedeck my head with victors' laurels. Rights accrued to me as well as prizes, and believable visions burned in me, and though there might be no happy ending – as there had not been for Bluebottle – was it not enough to weep, to laugh, to tremble, to be lit by an inner light? Such are the abundant treasures the soul holds in store for humans, though the scornful mind consider them as valueless as dross.

Reader, I marvelled at it all, my heart shuddered in my straw-filled breast, my eyes rolled entranced in their sockets;

185

I would even say a tear ran warmly down my china cheek, if I did not think you would take me for a Papist!)

That a man should confess his feelings without the slightest dissimulation moved my mistress exceedingly, and if to her the negro's tale was tragic in its foolishness, she found that there was honour in it all the same. Had he not stooped from the heights to grant his generous heart to the girl, stinting his passion not at all, and asking nothing in return? She could not but compare his recklessness with the notable lack of ardour shown by Mr. Gulliver, and though she judge herself disloyal for making it, the comparison would not be banished summarily but, like an importunate hawker, lodged its foot determinedly in the door.

'I accept *maintenant* that it can never be,' Bluebottle concluded sadly. 'The size of it is, the lady does not love me.'

'Perhaps, dear sir, this was not the sole obstruction,' suggested Mary, but Bluebottle looked at her so wanly that she was not cruel enough to be candid. He has relinquished his hopes of the girl, she thought. I cannot insist that he also relinquish his folly.

Reader, we climbed and climbed, and finally gained the mountain crest where Bluebottle's cave would be a safe if painful haven, for no red-head gazed out from a high spur like Dido on the rock at Carthage, mourning her missed opportunities.

The fire was quickly built, the tiny roe-deer roasted and devoured. So great was her relief to have escaped the hated temple that my mistress was light-hearted as a child who sets out on a Sunday treat. To her the savage place was like a fairytale, with bluish beards of lichen on the rocks and jewelled icicles. So cosy was she in this eyrie that she ventured from her bed of birch-twigs, 'Might we not be safe here for a time, Mr. Yussuf, since by your account the natives are not hostile?'

'Mrs. Gull, I have decided,' said Bluebottle. 'They are solid folk who will not harm us, but I think this island is a place we cannot stay. There is timber enough in my house to furnish us with a *piragua*, in which we may escape across the sea.'

Mary was too drowsy to question his resolve, indeed, having none herself to speak of, she was very glad of it. All her affections, I rejoice to say, she now turned upon her doll. Embracing me warmly, she covered my face with sentimental kisses, whispering, 'Don't fret, my dear. I'll sew you a wig from my very own hair. You must have a new gown too . . . there's that paduasoy wrapper, and the green petticoat could be cut up, if I knew where my scissors were . . . But yes, something must be managed. You'll see, we'll fix you up properly for the journey.'

Reader, I luxuriated in her arms. Warmth tingled in my limbs; my heart expanded. What bliss it was to feel myself in the bosom of a family, and to be loved not only by a mistress, but also – dare I say so? – by a master! I was in possession of so many riches – indeed, an embarrassment – that I could not regret the few pleasures that were barred to me. Now that we were one again, I stared into the red heart of the fire and forgave my mistress everything. Aye, reader, it was an idyll, which I hoped would never end. Aeons passed, it seemed, in drowsy happiness, and sleep sailed me strangely to a scarlet field: strawberries, as far as the eye could see; no timid woodland clump but a great bed of them, a bed for giants to sleep on, with banked walls crisped and creamy white, like snow-capped mountains, or meringues.

Wolves howl below the timber-line; old Dolly, meanwhile, stands distrustful in the doorway. You will say that a sheep cannot go mad as humans do, you will say that the river of instinct flows too strongly in her to admit diversion. Thus far I agree with you – that the beasts of the wild may be free of contamination, but look only at those which daily rub shoulders with *homo sapiens* and you will see lap-dogs fattened on vanity, cowering carriage-horses, lisping parrots, and every evidence of eccentricity. Millennia have passed, remember, since the sheep's ancestors roamed free on the Mesopotamian marshes, and in the intervening aeons, bred up solely to save us from the hazards of the hunt, she has lived with the certainty of sudden slaughter, has suffered her fleece to be shorn each spring and her lambs to be marched off each year to the market, for whole peoples have fed on her, and her flesh has founded dynasties. It should not surprise us, then, if now she loses her way in delusion, and sees in the foam-banks at the bend of the torrent the fleeces of her naughty flock, and scolds them from on high, and takes a last leap into space to gather her loved ones in.

Such, reader, was the sight that met my eyes in the morning: the snowy crest of the mountain, the shadowed gorge and, wedged in the abysmal waters, the poor bedraggled morkin, her fleece all flattened and her flower-trails floating on the barbarous current.

Alas poor Dolly, who had rescued me, yet failed to find her happy end! How selfish is felicity, that makes the

fortunate forgetful of all else. I had been dazzled and entranced, a butterfly about to fly free from its mute and
landlocked chrysalis, but now I saw that her unhappy corpse
bespoke a parlous bargain. The light of life gone out! Yet
my companions, seeing nothing, assumed that she had
wandered off in search of better pastures, and, in comfortable
ignorance, concerned themselves no further. A sheep is a
small thing, to be sure, and easily overlooked; it pained
me greatly, though, to think that henceforth it must be my
habit to ape their carelessness, and leave a fellow creature
unlamented. Should I aspire to be human, yet indict
humanity? Thus was a doll divided, reader, as we all may be,
by a desire for advancement, and a dislike of the advance.

But enough of Conscience, for I am duty bound to move
the story on, and bring you to the clearing where the house
Bluebottle had not thought to see again stood locked and
empty as his aching heart. Yet if the sight of it pained him,
he relished the prospect of the work that must be done.
What love's affliction had constructed, anger would dis-
mantle, plank by plank, and from the timbers he would build
an ocean-going raft, for the gods who had disqualified his
settled nest might yet approve a craft more fitting for a
wanderer.

When the shutters were thrown back, a dewy glitter veiled
the interior, as if an evanescent fog had spread itself across
the floor and walls and rafters. The four chairs wore a ghostly
sparkle, and the table legs dissolved in floating frost. To
Bluebottle it was as if his love had left imprinted on the place
that first morning of bright mist which had kindled it,
so that he must be constantly mocked by the memory, and
feel his strength sapped by a halo of unhappiness. Speechless,

he strode into the bedchamber, and set to work immediately on the demolition, as if the task would rip the haunting from his heart. The miasma, meanwhile, was found to be but a common infestation of arachnids, albeit tiny ones, with tiny webs, which were shown no mercy by a lady who had too recently been overrun, and who now took vengeance with a rancorous broom.

As the days passed the place resounded with the noise of hammering, and soon enough the walls came down, leaving half a parlour and a porch for a frontispiece, with hardly a house at the back of it. News of our arrival had spread in the meantime, and though my companions did not know it, their every move was now a public marvel. Among the spies who clustered on the fringes of the glade was the red-haired girl, who came without remorse for any heartache she had caused her ex-fiancé. Cool curiosity alone had brought her to the clearing, since a female giant was a spectacle the village girls could not forego. Such massive breasts and megalithic feet, and such voluminous stockings, not to mention the barbaric hanks of hair! And such unwomanly incompetence with cooking-pot and darning-needle! Now it is true that sewing is a soothing task which settles the mind, but not, I believe, if one has lost the habit of it. My mistress had promised to outfit me properly, and so she did to the best of her ability, lamenting the crudeness of her cutting and the gracelessness of her stitches. When it came to the matter of a new wig, however, the work was so finicky that only a spider's skill could have fashioned the skullcap, let alone affixed the hairs.

By and by the forester's daughter became so exasperated with her clumsiness that she hurried off to fetch a crochet-hook, and clambered up to instruct the gormless creature.

Banging on a thimble to announce herself, she seized a single hair and looped it round the hook. Two swift passes through the weave, a slip-knot, and the hair was fixed fast to the cap. My mistress gazed in admiration at the skilful imp, who shrugged, as if to say that any fool could do as much and, settling down in Mary's lap, toiled unceasingly till sunset. By nightfall the wig was trimmed and touched up with the curling-tongs, and ready to be fitted. The little sempstress stared at me, and I stared back at her, for though I was very glad to be hirsute again, I will confess my mind was full of other matters. Small she was, indeed, and not at all distinguished in her person – her skin was freckled, her eyebrows imperceptible, and her arms weatherbeaten to the elbows – but none could doubt the magnitude of her effect on Bluebottle, who went tight-lipped about his tasks, evincing every wary sign of bruised affection. In short, dear reader, I blessed the girl, I blessed her every mouse-like bone and sinew, for in her tiny form was dream made flesh, and thrilling power, and opportunity. If she had been loved despite her size, then so might I be!

There being little left of the house, that night my mistress made the beds up on the stoop where, in the small hours, the following exchange took place.

'Do you find her *jolie*, Mrs. Mary?'

'In her way, Mr. Yussuf.'

'But do you find her strange, in any way?' Bluebottle persisted.

'Strange, Mr. Yussuf?'

'Do you find her . . . somewhat small?'

Mary sent a brief sigh up at the Lilliputian stars. 'I believe

I do, Mr. Yussuf,' she replied, at which the prince sprang up from his pallet, cleared the steps with one bound, and ran off into the forest. There he remained at his own business, prone under the branches in the chatter of insects, drawing on the strength of his self until the sun had wheeled through a whole cycle and lit up the darkest corners of his addiction; and in the dusk of the day after, though far from cured, he came back quietly and started to stitch up the mainsail.

Chapter XIV

A Sojourn with our Dutch Allies . . . A Scientific Castaway . . . On the Monopoly in Cloves and Nutmegs . . . Captain Sparrow's Prejudice . . . Bluebottle's Honour . . . On Bribery and Corruption . . .

Reader, they launched the raft before the tar was dry on it, and in an improbable fog, for Bluebottle was adamant, and would not wait for clement weather. They had not asked the villagers for provisions, nor had they refused those deposited on the doorstep, which led now to no interior, for a house will become a ship if it must, and leave only thin air and a blank threshold to mark its passing. Before you extrapolate, however, bewailing the transitoriness of modern times, and the unstable flux of populations, remember that history will do the same to every house in the long run, and in any case no man can stay in a country where he is not wanted.

They sailed, then, with the aid of a few instruments, north towards the Equator, hoping to gain the Straits of Molucca, and thence to reach Batavia, where passage might be found on a Dutch East Indiaman. Here the two were at odds, for while Bluebottle's thoughts were on Bristol, Mary could not yet bring herself to return to England, having come too far for that, and risked everything. She had in her dressing-chest Mr. Moll's invaluable chart, as well as a quantity of sovereigns sufficient to secure her onward passage to the Pacific. Bluebottle, on the other hand, had half a handful of florins and a ruby-hafted knife, but he was very hopeful of employment, for the seafaring world is a small one, and not a bos'n he had sailed with could but recommend his skills.

In the several weeks of the voyage hardly a sandbar or palm-tree broke the stark horizon, though we saw miracles of coral below us, and swimming shapes, and birds' wings in the balmy air above. My mistress had put the chart at Bluebottle's disposal, and if at first he seemed content to pore over it, nodding to himself and quietly humming, he came to her one evening clicking his tongue in disapproval.

'This Mr. Molly – I think he has not sailed in Oceania!'

Mary bridled at this, and sprang to the German's defence. 'Mr. Moll's maps are reputed throughout Europe. He relies only on the most up-to-date information, I assure you.'

'Then Europe,' said the black man baldly, 'is very wrong.' He stabbed at the chart, indicating the island Mr. Moll had drawn from the coordinates. 'Here there is no land at all. Yet where' – indicating an empty space to the east – 'is Pra'ana?

Where too' – moving his finger some degrees to the west – 'is the archipelago of Spechy?'

As Mary scanned the blank expanse she was seized by the same excitement she had felt that day in Devereux Street. He had put his indignant finger on the very spot, she was sure of it. Here the tantalizing island had raised its mist-wreathed peak above the painted sea, only to sink back into oblivion! Dry-lipped and with a pounding heart, she pressed him to speak further of Spechy.

'It belongs to no crown,' said Bluebottle. 'Yet the *habitants* speak, on the whole, English. There are several islands, of which I saw only Sumina, and its sister Amina across the strait. The port of Allegria is *très agréable*, though they are constantly rebuilding it.' He regarded her keenly. 'I am to believe that Mr. Gull has business there?'

'I confess I am persuaded of it.' Blushing furiously at the mention of her husband's name, Mary retired into the private shade of her parasol, and picked up her Plato, whereupon Bluebottle left her to the solitude she craved. A flock of sea-birds circled overhead; she plucked a fallen feather from my wig, and granted me a brimming smile. 'Well, my Lady Mary, I think we will pass muster,' she said at last, conjuring up an island where English was spoken, a Governor's residence with colonnades and calling-cards, and even a ball, aye, with a passable orchestra. And there in the midst of the dancers – O illustrious mirage – a husband who was snipped and shaven and adept, a husband with his wig in place and all his wits about him.

She held the feather to her cheek, and then consigned it to the waves as swiftly as a skimming thought, and it struck me in that moment, though I had not the slightest evidence for it, that she would find her Lemuel only to discover that she did not want him. The truth is, of course, that I was not without prejudice, and between you and me I thought Mr. Gulliver a poor specimen compared with Bluebottle, in whose debt I was, and henceforth would remain.

Meanwhile, on that self-same day (if a good deal earlier, owing to the difference in time at the Meridian) Mr. Moll received a letter from that self-same archipelago.

My dear Herman,
I write in haste, for the ship sails this very night which will bring this packet to England, leaving your old friend to take his chances on the South Sea island of Sumina. Note the name well, Herman, lest I disappear entirely from the world's remark, for there are few ships that call here, and I may wait a year or more for a homeward passage. Fear not, however: I am no mutineer but a willing castaway, and have marooned myself solely for the sake of science — nay, for the love of it, Herman, since my lovely frutilliers *languished on the long and arduous voyage, as did their faithful swains, the* capitons. *Having been unable to establish the controlled conditions required by my experiment, I was obliged to fetch them out of Chili, only to find that plants will no more mate in motion than clocks will keep their proper time, and indeed I cannot blame them, since I myself prefer the stalwart earth to all these shifting seas. Instead they yellowed and they drooped, and despite all care and encouragement could not be induced to fruit. Yet I am undeterred, being certain that both species will flourish in the stable plot I have procured for them, that they may become acquainted at their leisure, and*

thus discover a partiality which will lead to a successful exchange! Do not take me for a sentimentalist on this account, however, for I may not sound like a scientist but should I die unrecognized I shall at least have the satisfaction of knowing I have lived like one!

  Ever your affectionate
  Antoine

Reader, I have tarried too long in the back of beyond, and have tested your patience enough. Lest you forget that civilization exists, I will hurry you on to the Indies, where our Dutch allies are the guarantors of its graces. The fugitives had hoped for Batavia, but all Bluebottle's skills could not steer against the stinging tail of the southerly monsoon, which drove us through a narrow channel far from the Strait of Sunda, and whipped us ever east across the Flores Sea, until we came in sight of the isle of Amboyna, which commands the trade in cloves and nutmegs from the Moluccoes.

A word, however, before we gain the harbour, for I would be derelict in my duty if I did not impart what I have learned of the business of spice-trading. For instance, consider the clove-tree – for I wager you have never seen one. It is not very great of body, but slender, and at most will reach a height of thirty feet. The leaves are five inches long and tapering, and the cloves grow only at the tips of the branches, in clusters of ten or twelve, which are at first white in colour, then green, and finally dark copper in their ripest stage. Each tree will produce 70 or 80 lb. of the fruit, which is gathered in by spreading sheets around the bottom of the bole, and briskly shaking the tree until the ripe cloves fall to the ground. An exact register of the trees on the island is entered once a year in the Company's book, and beyond that certain number all others must be destroyed. The free Mallatians of Amboyna, moreover, must keep within their strict allowance, and sell to the Dutch at 6d. a pound, and if they contravene this order their goods are forfeited, and they are made slaves for the rest of their lives.

Now most of the neighbouring islands of the Moluccoes produce nutmegs and cloves, but the Dutch Company will not suffer them to do so, for they have enough at Amboyna to supply all Europe and fill a hundred China-junks to boot. For this reason they lodge a small garrison on each island, to make sure no new trees are planted, and to cut down those which spring up plentifully of their own accord. In addition October sees the Governor set forth with seventy-five *orambies* of eighty paddles apiece to survey the outlying islands, taking with him the native king and his princes to serve as hostages in the event of a rebellion. This great fleet spends six weeks felling and burning all clove and nutmeg trees except those reserved for the Company's use, thus ensuring that the monopoly rests secure in the hands of the Hollanders. It goes without saying that a high price is thereby guaranteed for the commodities; that an even higher price has been paid in blood is something we shall come to by and by.

But the clove has a pretty scent whatever the cost of it, and presently this aroma wafted towards us on the off-shore breeze, as if the whole island were a giant-sized pomander floating on the azure sea.

We entered a narrow bay flanked by watchtowers and came at length to a well-made harbour below a town of some hundred houses, all built of brick and timber in the Dutch manner, yet none above one storey high, for in those regions earthquakes are a regular occurrence, and the ground, swelling up like the waves of the sea, may do a great deal of mischief. On a high rock overlooking the town stood a stone citadel, well ditched and bastioned, its turretted walls surmounted by numerous brass cannon. The harbour was very busy with native *sampans*, and yawls plying to the Dutch ships at anchor in the bay, and China-junks whose crews loaded their cargoes in a frantic hurry, hoping to snatch a speedy passage homeward on the monsoon winds.

Think of it, reader: a rough-hewn raft, a black man bared to the waist, in the company of a European lady, yet such was the imperative of trade that the sight hardly raised a single eyebrow. Their presence had not passed unremarked, however, for on disembarking they were immediately apprehended by a custom-master, and taken in charge of two corporals to a lodgement near the citadel. Here my companions were informed that they would be detained at the Governor's pleasure, until they had satisfied His Excellency by supplying an abstract of their voyage, together with the exact whereabouts of their ship.

My mistress was not pleased with such high-handedness, for she had thought herself among allies and after the indignities she had suffered on Lilliput, had expected to be treated like a gentlewoman. Yet no maid was sent to attend her, and no bedclothes were spread upon her pallet, and though she was sorely in need of refreshment not a morsel was offered save the putrid meat that must be purchased from the keeper. If she would have better victuals, the rascal said, he would be pleased to purchase them from the market;

then he proceeded to relieve her of several sovereigns, and on his return presented her with a piece of belly-pork and a brace of inferior yams. Mary protested vehemently, but the fellow replied that he had been obliged to change her currency for Dutch *skillings*, and could not be blamed if the rate was disadvantageous to her. Bluebottle did no better, I have to say, and was parted quickly from his florins for a poor return, so that the two had no more provisions for their outlay than they might have had for half a crown had they been at liberty to venture out to the market. Resolved to leave their uncongenial lodging as soon as possible, they prepared a deposition to be conveyed to the Governor.

Your Excellency,

We hereby swear that we embarked on the Aphrodite *at Bristol on the 6th January of this year, bound for the Indies. Having been driven off our course near the coast of Chili, the ship foundered in a great storm off New Zeeland, and to the best of our knowledge Captain Fitzallan and all hands perished in the wreck. After being held captive by the hostile natives of Lilliput, we contrived to escape by means of a makeshift raft, hoping to reach the safe haven of Batavia. Illustrious Sir, depend upon it that we are arrived at Amboyna through no fault or false intent, but rather by the accident of squalls; we beg your indulgence, therefore, and respectfully ask to be granted an audience, that our departure from these shores may be expedited.*

(signed)

Mrs. Mary Gulliver of Redriff

Prince Yussuf Bel'Ablil

Days of damp heat passed, yet no word came back from the Governor. By the end of the week my mistress had succumbed to a slight fever, which owing to the unhealthy conditions rapidly worsened. In vain did Bluebottle plead for a physician to be fetched, for though he sponge her brow and douse her limbs with water in the worst of it, he feared the onset of convulsions. That Sunday, as the bells of the Protestant churches tolled out gloomily for service, he summoned the keeper from the guardhouse and poured his remaining silver into his hands.

'*Mon ami*,' he begged, 'if you do not send for assistance the lady's death may well be on your conscience.'

I was much impressed by his chivalry, but wished that I could direct him to the sovereigns my mistress had secreted in the hem of my petticoat, for I did not see why honour need be stretched so far as to render him penniless. Now I own you may find the African's goodness hard to credit, and since I am the only one to vouch for him, you may accuse me of a loss of objectivity. Yet I have tried, believe me, to be vigilant; I have done my level best to winkle out a blemish. He is proud, certainly, and I shall not pretend he is entirely wise. But reader, I can go no further. If my eye does not perceive a fault my pen will not invent it, and the truth is that I have shown you more than one fellow with the moral stature of a lampshade, so it ill befits you to take me to task if now I offer an exemplar!

'Lady, is it?' said the guard (who was no worse or better than he should be), casting a scornful glance at Mary's *déshabillée*. 'Surgeons cost more than your sort can afford, I warrant.'

At his wits' end, Bluebottle pulled the ruby knife from his

pocket. '*Prenez ça*,' he cried, as the frightened keeper levelled his musket. 'I have no more to offer you! It is worth much, and will surely pay a surgeon's fee!'

Greed conquered caution in a trice, and the guard reached out and snatched up the item. 'It's a pretty enough weapon, to be sure. We'll see, though, what it will fetch at the market.' And he hid the knife in his jerkin and hurried from the room, locking the door behind him.

Hours passed, and congregations, the black-hatted Dutch and the bare-limbed Mallatians filing quietly past the barred window. Again and again Bluebottle gazed anxiously out, but saw no surgeon coming. 'What keeps him, what keeps him?' he muttered and, returning to the invalid, sat by her bed in an attitude of great dejection. He looked at Mary's senseless face, and looked at me, and cried despairingly, 'So many comrades dead, dear friend, and I can do no more for you than your little wooden maid! We are both helpless!' Then a frenzy of frustration took him and he seized me, reader, by the throat and shook me violently, so that my wig flew off, and if I had owned a set of human teeth they would have rattled in my china head. My arms and legs were windmills, and my skirts awry – ah, but for far too brief a moment, when in truth I would have settled for eternity. His eyes flashed; he cursed wildly in an unknown dialect. O sweet memory! Would that he had torn me limb from limb like a leopard, if it pleased him. (Better to be mishandled, reader, than never touched at all – thus speaks starvation, forthrightly, so call it flagrant if you will!) I trembled, aye, in his magnificent rage, yet I was not one bit affrighted, for was I not at last the object of a passion close enough to love?

Too soon it was over, and with a look of shame he set me

down again upon my mistress's pillow, replaced my little wig, and turned his back on me. Morose and impatient, he sat cross-legged on the floor, and did not know that though he forgot me, reader, still he was forgiven.

Presently a commotion sounded at the door, and the guard was marched in by two soldiers, ashen-faced and heartily protesting.

'This man gave it to me, on my honour,' he cried, pointing at Bluebottle, who could not but agree that it was so.

'And where would a blackfellow get such a costly thing, if he did not steal it from a gentleman, and as likely as not cut his throat in the process?' the corporal demanded, throwing the African down upon the bed, where his wrists and ankles were soon made fast with ropes.

'I am a Prince of the Malinke,' Bluebottle protested. 'The knife is the birthright of my mother's line.'

'And your doxy, no doubt, is the Queen of Sheba!' jeered the corporal.

'My companion,' said Bluebottle icily, 'is an English gentlewoman, the gravity of whose *maladie* must be evident even to a fool like you. On my life it will be the worse for you when the Governor hears of this affair!'

'Enough of your insolence!' cried the corporal, threatening him with his musket. 'May you have time enough before your trial to regret it.' And he ordered the soldier to take him out forthwith, and confine him in the common prison with his own kind.

Now it has been said that the discipline of the Dutch, both in civil and military affairs, is admirable, and it cannot be denied that they keep the natives very much in awe of their governance, since they cut the ears and noses off the petty criminals, and chain their legs in irons, and sign them into slavery. Those wretches thereafter must saw timber, and hew stone from sunrise till sundown, eating a pint of coarse rice at noon, and lying down at night on bare boards with a piece of wood which serves five or six for a pillow. If the chronicles of the excellent Mr. Funnell are to be believed, those who escape are so severely handled when recaptured that some will cut their own throats rather than face their appointed punishment. Among the Dutch population, on the other hand, since 'a small matter of money will buy off a great fault', even the severest crimes receive but lenient treatment.

I was not wrong, reader, to fear for the African more than I feared for my mistress, since the forthrightness of the one in fact convinced the corporal that it would be prudent to fetch the surgeon for the other. With the advent of this gentleman the condition of the invalid was quickly ameliorated, for though he smelled of *schnapps* and had an odd habit of muttering Ovid's *Epistulae ex Ponto* during his examinations, he had lost none of his skills in his lengthy exile in the Colonies. Thus Mary was bled and purged and poulticed, and clean linen was brought, and plain gruels, semolinas, and all the wholesome victuals necessary for her recovery.

When her days and nights had settled once more into place, and the parliament in the rafters was revealed as a plain and simple spider's web alive with buzzing flies, her first concern was for the whereabouts of Bluebottle. On discovering from the new guard that he was accused of theft and would soon stand trial before the Fiscal, she sent off a heartfelt petition to the State-House, vouching on her honour as an Englishwoman for his innocence, and begging the Governor to release him from captivity.

In the meantime our lodging saw a new influx of hostages, those being the Captain and several officers of the *Loyal Bliss*, which had lately arrived from Bengal. Captain Sparrow, a stout and sonsy gentleman from the northern counties, had no more reason to boast of his birth than the famous Captain Dampier, but as keen a nose for fortune, and as great a genius for navigation. Indeed it was later said of him that he could sail his way out of a beagle's quim, but I am not equipped to be the judge of that, and like Mary must take him as I found him: bluff, broad, and remarkably hairy of nostril, but kind enough, and very punctilious in his dealings with the ladies.

'William Sparrow at your service, madam,' said he with a creaky bow. 'I wish that the circumstances of our acquaintance might have been happier; however, it seems that we must be cellmates for the moment, so we must heave to and make the best of it, must we not?'

Mary rose weakly to introduce herself, and when she had done so the Captain exclaimed, 'By God! Begging your pardon, ma'am, but may I ask if Mr. Lemuel Gulliver is some relation?'

'You are acquainted with my husband?' cried Mary, fanning herself feverishly. 'Tell me, have you even seen him?'

'I am doubly glad to know his good lady,' said the Captain, wringing her hand in his, 'but I regret I have not set eyes on the good fellow for a number of years, in fact, I had quite lost track of him. He keeps good health, I hope?'

At this my mistress could not hold back her tears, and before too long had poured out the tale of her trials. At last, throwing herself on the Captain's mercy, she begged, 'Only find me a passage to the South Seas, sir, and I will be greatly in your debt, for I am certain that my husband is in the vicinity of Spechy.'

The Captain moved quickly to the door to check the corridor, and seeing that the guard was still within earshot, said in a booming voice, 'Madam, we are bound for Batavia for caulking, but thereafter it will be my pleasure to conduct you back to England.' Seeing Mary's dismay, he put a finger to his lips. 'Say nothing. We must kow-tow to the Dutch for the moment, but be assured I will take you onward to your archipelago.' And with that he bade her a hearty goodnight, having promised to speak more of the matter anon.

Next day smoke-clouds dulled the sun and a fine white ash blew across from the plantations, whirling through the harbour like a snowstorm, dusting the sober hats of the Dutch merchants, and settling in sweet-smelling screes against doorsteps and sills. In the lodging-house the spider's web on the ceiling hung thick with it, and the air was hot and dusky and caught at the throat.

When Captain Sparrow announced himself he wore a wetted kerchief tied across his nose, and carried a paper bearing the seal of the State-House. Advising my mistress to adopt the same piratical fashion rather than risk adding to her ills a gross inflammation of the lungs, he told her that they were summoned by the *Sabander* to appear before the Governor on the following afternoon. 'Depend upon it, we shall be on the high seas before the week is out,' he said warmly. 'In addition, you will have an opportunity to petition the Fiscal on behalf of your Mr. Yussuf.' Lowering his voice, he continued, 'I have buttered our keeper up with brandy and enough silver to purchase a lass, so he will be too far gone to eavesdrop. As that poet fellow said, though I recall not his name, these Hollanders require *Brandee* to exalt them above their natural phlegm, and the same spirit that makes them fight and destroy men makes them beget 'em!'

It was evident that he had had a tot himself, and needed no more encouragement to confide that the *Loyal Bliss* was bound not west towards Batavia, but eastward, outwith the dominion of the Dutch, where he aimed to make a survey of all the islands that might augment the English share of the spice trade. 'So you see, madam, why we must be hugger-mugger, for the Dutch are bitter guardians of their prerogative. Let me say only that they have broken the Treaty time and again without a stroke of punishment, and there are those among us who do not see the reason for such complaisance to a cruel encroaching people, unless the aim be to bring England under the total subjection of that State! As for our South Sea Company, those rogues would debar their own countrymen from enterprise in distant regions, while making no use at all of the privileges granted to them!'

To Mary's ignorant ear here was riddle upon riddle, and her enquiries prompted the Captain to launch into the following tale, which I set down without apology for any prejudice contained therein, knowing you will recognize a Tory when you see one, if not an outright Jacobin. Yet you may get the gist of it, and spit the pamphleteering gristle out, and still digest the facts – which are that in the last hundred years the Dutch have massacred more Protestants for their own private interest than ever did the King of France under zealous pretence of religion. As Mr. Dryden wrote,

Well Monarchies may own Religion's name
But States are Atheists in their very frame.

To our tale of terror, then – which is told through a kerchief and takes several pages, if the tender-hearted reader has a mind to abridge them.

'Madam,' began Captain Sparrow, 'I swear it would be no exaggeration to say that the canals and summerhouses and fine lemon-tree gardens of Batavia are all built on blood! I will not talk of the rout of the Portuguese from these islands, nor of the paltry Treaty which allowed us but a few outposts in the Indies – no, nor even of the horrible massacre of the Mallatians at Polorone, but only of the bald facts of Amboyna, and the manner by which the English were ejected from it.

'This island, dear lady, is a thorn in my heart, for it was here, many years ago, that my own mother's uncle perished. In those days the English had factories in Amboyna town, at Hitto, and at Larica, as well as others on Ceram, but the Dutch were not satisfied with their presence and, having tortured a Japanese to a false confession, accused the English of plotting to take the citadel. One by one the plain merchants of Hitto and Larica were taken and tortured, and Captain Towerson, being His Majesty's representative, was kept under house arrest, until false accusations were wrung from the men that he was the ringleader. Abel Price was the first to come under the water-torture, and Timothy Johnson, Ephraim Ramsay, and many others, each of whom was forced to accuse another, and thus they went down like ninepins. John Clark from Hitto refused all blandishments, and suffered the water-torture till he swelled up thrice his size, his cheeks as big as bladders and his eyes starting out beyond his forehead, but still would not confess. They took him to the rack, then, and burned him about the feet and armpits till he answered yes to every question, upon which they threw him in the dungeon where, after six days in darkness, great maggots were seen to crawl from his wounds. Then they took Captain Towerson out, and brought them all before the Fiscal Court, and finding every man jack of them guilty of conspiracy, sentenced them to death.

'But that, dear lady, is not the worst of it. As merciless as any cat with a captive mouse, the Dutch lighted on three Factors: Mr. Tomson and Mr. Collins, and my own dear uncle Colson. In a cruel humour they declared they would pardon two of the three, if they would draw lots to see who would be spared. They prayed and drew, those men, and kissed each other. The loser was my uncle. I knew him not, but he was a braver Englishman than ever I shall be!'

Breathing harshly, the Captain held a hand to his heart. For a moment he could not speak. 'Ah, pardon me, madam!'

(Reader, if I had had hackles to rise they would have stood up straight at this juncture, for a rage that finds no words is always the most affecting, and attacks the sensibility like a molten shower of meteors. The air around the Captain spat and crackled, and the very floorboards heaved beneath his feet, as if the dead were trying to rise and make their plaints. Apoplectic, he held his sorrow captive, while we white-knuckled females bore the brunt of it . . .)

'And the next morning they were all taken out to the yard

and done away with in the Dutch manner – forgive me, madam – not beheaded, merely, but sliced clean in two with the sword.'

My mistress begged the Captain not to distress himself, but still he would continue, as if he could not bear to leave the boil unlanced. 'Madam, though the prisoners were allowed no writing materials, two men among them contrived to leave their testament. On the night before the executions a clerk was allowed to visit Captain Towerson's cell, only insofar as he must guarantee a debt contracted by the English Company. On this bill, which was later smuggled out to Banda, the Captain wrote that he died guiltless of all charges laid against him, and prayed that God forgive his accusers their sins, and receive them into His mercy.

'Yet it was the deposition of my own uncle that brought the infamous business into the open – though it took a half-century – for he detailed every trick and torture that had led the Dutch to their villainous verdict. Bear with me, madam, if you please, for the words I never will forget are those plain and final ones, written in the loose-leaf of his Prayer Book:

Understand that I Samuel Colson, late Factor of Hitto, was apprehended for suspicion of conspiracy, and for anything I know must die for it. Wherefore having no better means to make my innocency known, I have writ my confession in this book, hoping some good English men will see it. I do here upon my Salvation, as I hope by His death and Passion to have redemption for my sins, vow that I am clear of all such conspiracy and know no more than an unborn child of this

business, neither do I know any Englishman guilty thereof,
nor other person in the world. Written with my own hand
this fifth of March. I was born in Newcastle Upon Tyne,
where I hope this Book will come, that all there may know
of my innocency.

Captain Sparrow had recited this sad testament with his
eyes tight shut, but now he gazed out at the smoke-ruddied
sun, and coughed prodigiously, so that the phlegm growled
like an angry dog in his throat. 'So now the Dutch slash and
burn with impunity, secure in the possession of their stolen
goods, and will not suffer any other nation's ships to stray
along their shores, and make false draughts, which wreck us
on their shoals. Such are the allies you and I must wait upon
tomorrow, madam, and bow and scrape to them, and make a
good account of ourselves – nay, a solid sterling one – if we
would not moulder in captivity for ever!'

That night there was little sleep for my mistress, since she
must go on wrestling in darkness with the Captain's demons,
as well as bear her own alarms for the fate of Bluebottle. Her
poor bed lay in tussocks; elves spied on her with scarlet eyes.
Only cold fury could rout them and temper her will for
tomorrow, for she had seen now clearly what the world was,
and it was not passion, she thought, that was the worst fault
in it, nor even the sins of the flesh, but rather crime in the
cause of commerce, cool and judicial, bolstered up by business, and smiled upon by States.

In the morning she rose resolved like a Christian Englishwoman and sponged her face and brushed the white ash from
her hair. 'Slippery are the foundations of wealth which are
not laid upon the principles of justice,' she told me gravely,

but reader, I have spent lifetimes in consideration of such matters, and while I applauded her idealism, I had a mind to ask her why those foundations did not fall. But since the theme of justice will occupy us in no small measure, let us return to it hereafter, and press on in the meantime to the Citadel, wherein lies the Council Chamber, a grim hall hung with gleaming armour, and flags and ensigns taken by the Dutch from divers nations.

There was a teak table the length of a pinnace behind which tall chairbacks stood starkly to attention, dwarfing the ordinary men upon them, whose wide white collars wore a trim of Flanders lace, and whose skin was quite unsullied by the Tropick sun. So black and so white were the colours of gravity that I was glad my mistress had dressed with all due soberness, though I have to say that I wore my regular frills and fancies, and my skirt, weighed down by secret sovereigns, made me jingle like a gypsy bride.

'Will the woman speak on her own behalf?' asked the Governor, yet his vague blue eyes did not regard her.

'I will, sir,' said Mary meekly, taking a lead from the Captain – who had made his pleas with such a surfeit of flattery for Governor and Fiscal, that none would have supposed he had a rebel bone in the whole of him – and she swore on the lines of her statement, which the Koop-man stamped with the Company seal. 'I beg leave to plead also for my fellow signatory, Mr. Yussuf,' she said, before they could dismiss her. 'On my life I will vouch for his honesty, for it is his own property he is wrongly accused of stealing!'

Silencing her with a rap of the gavel, the Fiscal spoke in the ear of the Governor.

'The Blackamoor?' said he with thin distaste.

'With respect, sir, the fellow is the lady's servant,' Captain Sparrow interjected. 'Should he have incurred a fine I'm sure his mistress will make prompt settlement.'

Mary's eyes sparked, and her mouth flew open – indignant truth, I fear, was on the point of gainsaying him, though anyone could see that Captain Sparrow's lie was far superior in cunning. 'By your leave, Your Excellency,' the Captain pressed, 'a trial would greatly delay our departure for Batavia, and thenceforth we are at the mercy of the Trades . . .'

Heads bent and bobbed together; brows furrowed; there was a solemn discourse of wigs. The Koop-man's thoughts were all for the coffers, and the Fiscal was not inclined to fault him; the Governor, meanwhile, had endured a long and tedious morning, and was impatient to be rid of any blessed soul who kept him from his luncheon.

'We are agreed, then?' he said with unaccustomed energy. 'Madam, have you the means to purchase the wretched fellow?'

'I believe so, Your Excellency,' said Mary, bowing her head to hide a blush of purest rancour, 'if you would advise me as to the figure.'

'A sum, Meinheer Van Speult! Stir yourself!' the Governor snapped at the Fiscal, but it was the Koop-man's eyes which were keen as a cardsharp's and more than able to assess the lady's value. A rapid whisper in the Fiscal's ear, and a sum was named that would have beggared her. 'In coin, if you please. Come forward, madam.'

Mary approached the bench as bidden, and tossing up my skirt to show my very pantaloons, shook out a shower of sovereigns.

Brighter than armour, the coins rang loud on the table.

'This sum is correct?' the Governor demanded, frowning at the pile. 'Well, is it, Meinheer Meulenbelt?'

'I know only the rate of exchange given by my Keeper, sirs,' my wily mistress murmured in reply, 'for goods he fetched me from the market.'

'It is somewhat in excess,' the Koop-man said reluctantly. 'Evidently the fellow was mistaken.'

'Evidently the fellow was a scoundrel and a fleece! Be so good as to make the proper adjustment, Meinheer Van Speult, and reimburse the lady.' The Governor smote at an importunate fly, and watched it expire on his handsome blotter. His pen was poised; he nudged the corpse towards the inkwell with his nib. At last his glance fell fair and square on Mary, and for a brief moment a memory of justice glimmered wearily therein. 'We are not robbers here, madam. Your servant will be returned to you in the morning. You will then proceed to Batavia with Captain Sparrow.'

If Mary felt she had been favoured, and even let a foolish tear well up, the Captain knew that a small pinch of scruple is the best spice for the dish of tyranny, for as well as enhancing the flavour it greatly disguises the smell of it. When they had gained the lodging he cried heartily, 'Well, Mistress Mary, we have certainly outwitted the rascals!' but thereafter fell into a mood of moroseness, for petty triumph could not slake his anger any more than the brandy-flask. The grudge he bore was historical – fuelled, as he saw it, not by solitary spleen but by the massed rancour of his dead fellows – and could not be discharged, as it could not be borne, by one individual alone, but must have allies, nay, armies of avengers to march behind its Standard and spur its horses to the final rout. Reader, in his dreams the Captain was a soldier among soldiers, but if daybreak misplaced him as a mere merchantman, then he would be as fervent in the cause of English trade as Hector in the glorious fight for Troy. In short, there was no risk he would not take if it embarrass the hated Hollanders, injure their interests, or undermine the state of their economy. (Indeed, in the morning you shall have the measure of his rashness, for what else would have persuaded him, *a*) to give the slip to the Dutch ships that were to escort the *Loyal Bliss* to Batavia, *b*) to stand about in a storm and steer a course towards a *cul-de-sac*, *c*) to launch a cannonade against the pursuing galleys?)

CHAPTER XV

The Escape from Amboyna . . . Why a Black Man May Turn his Back on Africa . . . Mary Gains a Servant and Loses a Friend . . . A Doll's Despair . . . A Fortuitous Tempest . . . Señor Torres Vindicated . . .

Dawn had seen the release of Bluebottle, red-eyed from a surfeit of darkness, bitten by scorpions and livid with bruises, yet outfitted according to Dutch decorum, in a straw hat, second-hand breeches, and a calico weskit. He would say nothing of his days in the dungeon, but ate ravenously all that was offered, and afterwards sat sullen in a corner, stirring himself only to shake his head at Captain Sparrow's offer, and swear that, far from having any inclination for the South Seas, he wanted nothing more than a prompt return to England.

Why a plain lodging in Bristol and a sailor's living should satisfy one who was born a *nyancho* is surely a perplexing question, yet a hard look at Africa may answer it. Only observe the coastlands from the Gambia river to the Bight of Benin and you will see how they have been named for commodities, be they gold or grain, or slaves or ivory. Observe also how that great littoral is blazoned by a thousand forts whose ramparts bear the flags of all the European nations, which vie there for the mastery of trade. So if a black man should seek to slip ashore there in the night, would he not be speedily apprehended, and shipped once more to the mines of Potosí? And if by some stroke of fortune the man evaded capture by the *caboceers*, and the Kru of the coastal marshes did not take him, how would he then pass safely through the hinterland to gain his own domains? Do not imagine for a moment that the Dyula merchants of Kaur would not sell a renegade Malinke to the slavers, or that the local chieftains stand aloof from that shameful trade, and enrich themselves solely by trafficking in ostrich plumes. Nay, depend upon it, when the bidding is bullish there will be no lack of vendors, and who then may count upon the colour of brotherhood?

Reader, our prince had said a long goodbye to Africa, and in this life had no expectation of Paradise, but a stubborn desire to remain at liberty. And if he have common cause with a few fellows lodged in Shift Street on the Bristol Quay, so much the better, for the plain truth is that he missed the company of Mrs. Lily Withers, so-called wishfully by her dying mother, as if a name could bleach away the definite touch of the tar-brush and turn the babe as pale as the Kerry man who sired her. Laundress or no, had she been a Muslim he might even have married the lady, for she was his Moor and his mistress, strong-armed, constant, and slow to rebuke. All the more reason for remorse, then, if in the meantime he had given his heart to another!

But it is Mary's shame that takes the centre stage now, since her confession may be delayed no longer. She had procured the African's release only on the basis that he was her servant; she had paid cash, and though she had not bought him she had bought him out, but Bluebottle's mood would not allow the nice distinction. If she had expected gratitude she was to have none; instead the bitter look he bestowed on her brought tears to her eyes, and she stood before him undefended, drowning in the tide of his reproaches. Not only was he dressed up like a Dutchman, and his tribal knife taken from him – without which a Malinke is like a *maribout* without his *greegree* – but now he, Yussuf Bel'Ablil, must play the lackey to an Englishwoman?

'No doubt you will purchase a dog-collar from Duck Lane,' he sneered, 'and call me your Pompey like the other ladies?'

Though Mary's cheeks were whipped to wretched scarlet, Bluebottle was so beside himself that no apology on earth could stay him, and at last she could bear no more, and rushed in distress from the room.

'Desist, man, desist!' cried the Captain, who had witnessed the scene with growing consternation. 'Have you taken leave of your senses? The good lady has saved your skin, yet you malign her for it!' Bluebottle stood silent, his eyes alight with mutiny. 'You have no choice, my fine friend,' said the Captain testily. 'Only pass the harbour-bar with us, and play the fool for the sake of the exit papers, then you may go where you please. Upon my word, I have no intention of hindering you from Batavia!'

'*C'est vrai?*' scowled Bluebottle, who was very far from being persuaded. Dutch cudgels, after all, had revived the memory of older scars got by Spanish Rhetorick – which, reader, is but a sweeter way of saying by fire and the sword. He saw the Captain's countenance, round and raw and ruddy as the sun, and fought a war within himself, for he whom the whites have wounded must always be wary of forbearance, lest he love that race so well, and himself so little, that he lose the soul he was born with. Face facts he must, however, and when the Captain promised there were China-sloops aplenty which for a bribe would convey him to Batavia, face facts he did. But it does not follow that he could as readily forgive, even when the Captain swore that Mary had no wish to wrong him, but had seen no other way to save him from the rope.

Time pressed on the party, and hurried them down to the harbour where, their papers having passed muster, they boarded the pinnace and were soon alongside the *Loyal Bliss*, which stood at anchor in the deeper waters of the bay. The sky was the colour of the phlegm which the Captain spat on the waters as he cursed Amboyna past and present, and the gulls which swooped down to the gob and fought for it, so greedy had they become for easy pickings.

Nearby stood a Manila-ship which several *sampans* were competing to provision, and on the pretext of haggling for a hundredweight of coco-nuts, the Captain struck a different bargain. Under the very noses of the Dutch, Bluebottle passed darkly from one ship to another, to merge there with the colours of the crew, and if he hardly had the time to shake my saddened mistress by the hand, is that not the way of things, that the light of affection may be so obscured, and a friendship which might have been mended end, rather, with a shrug and a shamefaced mumble?

Yet on this occasion I do believe that my own loss was the greater, for instinct told me that every increment in the distance between me and the African would decrease the total sum of what might be hoped for. Latitude, longitude – each has its established principle, but the law is not yet written that can account for those interior noons or angles of declination, nor instrument made that is accurate enough to measure them. Gone was the peerless dream of Lilliput, gone irretrievably with the dreamer, slid away senselessly on a square-rigged Manila-ship, and all because I had not discovered how to fix its coordinates. I could not hold my happiness without it, and thus was left reduced – in fact, as meagre as ever I had been – or, if you prefer, cut down to my proper size.

Pain it was, indeed, and all the worse because I could not languish, nor tear my hair, nor give vent to public and excessive mourning. Nor might I go the way of the ewe and cast myself despairingly upon the waters, since as few folks will weep for a doll's demise as will lament the passing of a sheep, or a slave who lies interred in the *poço dos negros* of Lisbon. A broken china skull, a leathered hand, a rag or two of petticoat or pantaloons, even the glimpse of a half-buried necklace – have you not glimpsed such decay in ditches and diggings, and passed on by without a thought, seeing only the unremarkable remnants of the less than human? Nay, she who cannot comfort herself with the prospect of tears and orations must eschew grand gestures and become adaptable – though this is not a virtue held in very high esteem, stemming as it does from dire necessity. Before you abandon me to its slender satisfactions, however, allow that even a doll has every right to rage, and rage I did at all who had what was denied me, seeing the whole world as a swill-pit and a swine's-alley, and a dung-heap, and a sewer full of scrabbling rats, and wishing upon it the pox, the flux, and the plague-fire on which it might burn at last to blazes. Here I was not entirely in accord with Mr. Gulliver, however, my wrath being reserved for the female *Yahoo*, who, though she found no colonies, suppress no populations, prattle in no Parliament, and declare no foreign wars, should not be judged a total innocent, insofar as she holds dominion over the smaller classes!

But that is by the by. With hindsight, reader, I will not swear that I was not deranged by simple Envy, which, as a function of emptiness, seeks to destroy the very thing it would be filled by. Thus my dear mistress was dear no longer, any more than women were the gentler sex, to be loved and honoured, served and emulated, but rather belonged to a cruel confederacy of bloated doxies; primps and simperers; fat harridans; waddling witches; bitches; back-stabbers; slappers and grabbers; cock-grinders; shit-picklers; man-trappers; gin-swillers; church-sniffers, ass-pizzles; child-beaters; cesspools and sophists; eunuchs; bawds; ball-bags; pleaders and piners; lice and leeches; tyrants and termagants; thumb-screwers; cream-curdlers, bleeders, and sob-squeezers! (Needless to say such a great rage, being kept within small confines, made a dreadful noise in the skull of the subject, while its human object heard not a single whimper, and ate and slept and walked the decks in ignorance, her thoughts awash with her suffering self.)

If the events of our first hours aboard are already sketched in, I have not yet described the tempest sent by the stars to aid the Captain's getaway. This storm started as a dark mushroom which burgeoned from the morbid smoke above the island and, swelling to an immensity, turned the sky as brown as peat, and struck us with its full force in the centre of the channel, pouring a putrid deluge down upon our heads. The ship laboured so much on the swell that none thought she could hold out; the sea took her ahead, and astern, and on both her sides, so that we were well-nigh inundated, and were spared the unfortunate fate of our escort only by the superior seamanship of Captain Sparrow.

League after league he made his feint southwards, where few would think to sail in search of him, it being generally considered that the sea was landlocked in that airt, and would not admit of passage. He had heard, however, of a Spanish seaman who had passed through a strait there a hundred years before, or so it was said by the grizzled *cognoscenti* on the quays of Manila. That the fellow had had no profit from his discovery and made no impression on the world's cartographers might yet be to the Captain's advantage, and he had too keen a nose for fortune's winds to rule out a possibility which, although remote, might even save his bacon. There existed, he was sure, such a channel; instinct assured him of it, and with every nerve and sinew he strained to slide the ship towards the place where the land would part decisively: this weather-vane of a man, whose feet, flat-planted on the deck-boards, read the subtleties of the swell in the same way as the thighs of a rider gauge the mettle of a frisky horse; his knees loquacious, his belly swivelling its eyes from port to starboard, his heart trained to a hunter's quiet, his brain afire with the effort of fathoming each encrypted sign.

We passed a pumice island, and one which growled with packs of yellow dogs; we stood off another for watering, to be repelled by hosts of ravening flies. On the port side lay New Guinea, safe in its stockade of reefs and shoals, its wild copses of clove-trees teasing the avaricious eye of the spyglass. At 10d. south of latitude sandhills were sighted to the starboard, and the flood of the tide bore the ship eastwards with such a velocity that the Captain did not doubt the Spaniard's strait was near, for such a tide as this must have a far greater indraught than a paltry river or lagoon, must be pulled, indeed, by the mighty magnet of the Southern Sea.

Making his punctilious observations, he measured 218d. to the west of the Meridian, and lit a pipe, and marked it in his log. Señor Torres had not erred in supposing New Holland to be the Austral continent itself! He, Captain William Sparrow, who had this very moment seen its northern spur, would bear witness to the man's integrity, though his be the sole voice of faith in a dissenting world. His heart fled forward, and came once more in sight of Sunderland. Trembling, he heard the crowd's cry and felt the thrill of greatness, for he was a man who had seen too many triumphs slip away from him while others claimed the credit, (though he had too grand a scorn for whiners to complain of it!). He clutched his pipe, and crossed himself, and stared at the running sea, and the wraith of his uncle rose before him as if it had been summoned, dimming his eyes with such a mist that he could decipher neither deeps nor shallows. 'By God's Grace,' he vowed, 'I will take the news to Europe!'

CHAPTER XVI

Divers Observations En Route to Spechy . . . The Peculiar Music of the Celts . . . A Wailing Ship . . . Mary Envisions an English Hedgerow . . . A Comparison of the Rosehip and the Strawberry . . .

And what of Mary's straits on this auspicious Day of Discovery? Her friend was lost and gone from her, and I, her little oracle, would grant her not a word of consolation. Downcast she was, but braced herself, I have to say, against the blows, and did not break. Somewhere beyond the south horizon lay that heartfelt island which had beckoned from the depths, and though it lie for the moment in the dark and quiet, like a child with the measles, she would not forget it, but patiently endure the miles and weeks between. Indeed her faith in it was all the stronger, now that Mr. Moll was proved at fault – for his chart showed a seamless land mass where Captain Sparrow found an aperture affording supple entry to the Southern Seas. Yet one man's fallibility may be another's opportunity: thus my mistress no longer felt it would be impertinent to add in her own small way to the German's geographies, or even to amend them. With this aim in mind she devoted the ensuing days to a detailed observation of undiscovered territories – an abstract of which I append below, so none may fairly say that I depreciate her contribution to the cause of science.

New Holland

Topography:
The land to the south of the northern promontory continues boggy and watery, with an abundance of mangrove trees, and few hills to be seen which are above the height of the ship's top-mast. Ten leagues eastward from the shore the surf breaks mountainously on a wall of coral rock which rises almost perpendicular from the unfathomable ocean. This great reef is overflown at high water by six or seven feet, and is dry in places at low water, and though breaks may be detected here and there I fear it would be a drastic task to take the ship through the treacherous passages which lead out to the Main. We steer S.W., therefore, and stay within the reef, where the channel affords us thirty fathoms and calmer water, though the Captain is constant at the watch lest the ebb tide take us seaward to the shoals, or the flood tide run us aground in the mangrove shallows.

Habitants:
The natives that were observed have skins the colour of

wood-soot, though they anoint themselves with a white pigment, black hair either lank or curly, and black beards which they sometimes singe off with coals. Even the women do not so much as wear a clout across the privates, though the men guard them so jealously that they kept them on the far side of the estuary to hide them from the ship, having, of course, no concept of the spyglass. They seemed amiable enough fellows, despite their redoubtable weapons — which are long throwing-sticks barbed with the stings of rays or sharks' teeth — and appeared to get a great amusement from our company, notably when the Captain, who has named the river here for his poor dead uncle Colson, took the East Coast in the name of His Majesty, and hoisted the English colours on the shore. Three volleys of small arms were fired to conclude the ceremony, which unfortunately caused great alarm among the natives, who fled immediately to the bushes.

Fauna:

We saw few mammals but the stately kanguru, which makes good eating, though alligators abounded in the swamps, and there were many varieties of land- and sea-fowls, such as bustards, eagles, quails, pelicans, cockatoes, and a very beautiful parrot called the lorryquet. The shoals were rich in many kinds of fish, and also clams, cockles, crawfish, and mussels, which make up the native diet for the most part.

At 14d. 32´ S the Captain sighted a group of three islands to the East which marked a decided passage to the ocean. The yawl and pinnace were sent ahead to guide us through, and by his own cunning blend of Timorousness and Temerity *the Captain brought us once more to the blue vastness of the untrammelled Main.*

The Trades in these low latitudes being so variable as to seem entirely capricious, the *Loyal Bliss* sailed sometimes southwards, and sometimes east on the advantage of an unknown current, and for many days sighted no other land than ringed atolls, distant and emerald, like many watching eyes. Sapped by the ceaseless seduction of the sea, the crew went sluggishly about their tasks, standing up only to sit down again, and walking the one way only to turn about; irascible at one moment, and at the next one drugged and forgetful, like autumn wasps.

There was a man aboard from Monaghan who played the Irish pipes like the devil himself, and when he took them on his knee on the mizzen-deck at dusk it was as if the sea itself clung close to the ship to listen, and the sun too was caught on the hook of the song and could not bear to sink away from them, when every Gaelic note already wrung the heart with thoughts of separation, of lands lost, and loved ones left behind. Not a man among them, be he ever so quarrelsome, would interrupt the play, but instead would drop his voice to a whisper, so great a thrall the fellow held over them with his bald pate bowed to his tune and what was left of his hair tumbling in grey strings over eyes that were now fixed on his instrument, now raised to regard the miles between the ship and the blank horizon. The cat purred and suckled at his bare feet, and the Captain wept in secret on the quarterdeck, for the drone with its mewls and skirls, its ascents and descents, spun a web as strong as any rigging, and not only the Celts aboard were caught in it, but Dane and Dutchman,

Moor and Mahometan, and every migrant race that ever mixed and briefly mated from the Bay of Biscay to Bengal. Indeed it was a sound fit for wanderers, harsh yet unholy sweet; without sentiment or excuse; dour and dolorous, yet possessed of a passionate vivacity; of the earth and the green furrow, yet speaking of the wide and borderless spaces; holding out no hope, at least none that was false, yet mourning the loss of it; praising no gods, or none that was particular; flattering neither vice nor vanity; elevating no estate above another, nor even favouring the living over the multitudinous dead.

As for the volume of tears which was wrung from the listeners, to speak of fifty casks would be conservative. Nor would it be an overstatement to say that the wood of the planks was waterlogged, and the belowdecks drenched by a constant downpour, and geysers spurted seaward from the gunwales. You may think it unseemly, that a shipload of brawny sailors should forego all self-control and bawl their heads off, but I aver there is no harm in it, for they do say that if enough salt water swab the decks of the soul it will come up spick and sparkling in the morning.

I give you, then, a wailing ship, a generosity of grief – indeed, a democracy of mourning from which no flotsam or jetsam is excluded. And yet I could not weep, though I lay awash in soggy petticoats, and suffered an abominable drip upon my forehead, for I was not my own woman, nor even a woman at all, but a mere mite, a neuter, if the truth be told, with a sewn seam where my sex should be, and eyes of glass, and lips immovable.

(Reader, I do not often dwell upon my motherland, which was no mother to me, I assure you, but permit me a word to

229

my countryfolk, who may detect herein a common strand. Being from the Lowlands, I do not speak the Gaelic, but there is no sound more affecting to the ear than that sorrowful sister of the Irish. Sibilant as a dove in the eaves, shyer than a corncrake in the field, it is the lullaby we would hear, I swear, were we rocked in the arms of Paradise. Yet Mr. Knox's shadow bars us at the gate, and his voice girns at us, stopping our ears with its litany of forbidding. *No* to desire and *no* to promise, *no* to the gentle wash of tears and the dreams of women, *no* to the fulsome flesh and the luxurious fires of laughter. And a triple *no*, aye, a multiplicity of *nos* to softness of any shape or form on earth or in heaven.

No no

230

no no no no no no no no no no no no no no no no no no no no no
no no no no no no no no no no no no no no no no no no no no no
no no no no no no no no no no no no no no no no no no no no no
no no no no no no

Reader, what a dark cargo it is that some must carry; indeed, I can hardly bear to think on it; indeed, I will no longer. If Scotland silence me, or ire or envy keep me in the pit, my mistress, God be thanked, is made of softer stuff, and may weep on my behalf, if she pleases. For I have foisted upon you more than enough of my own troubles, and I would not have you think that I aspire to rival her in your attention. Henceforth I will be amanuensis only. I shall turn over a new leaf. Silence, I swear to you, will be my middle name. There, I have promised it, and should I fail in my resolve you have my permit to strike me from the page.

In her curtained chamber, Mary mopped her eyes to the music of melancholy. 'Oh Mr. Moll,' she murmured, laying her pen down on a ploughed page where inky tears had puddled in the furrows, 'I know I am privileged to set eyes upon the wonders of the Southern Seas, but tonight my heart is a simple homebody, and yearns far less for science than for the sight of a hedgerow in Somerset!'

She saw it clearly now, and sighed, and sobbed, and gave way utterly to sentiment. Nothing, surely, in the whole wide world could compare with the decorous dog-rose, whose temperate spires were leaved in lightest green, and upon them, the perched pink flowers, all frail and differentiate, their stems so slight and imperceptible that they might just have lighted there like butterflies, to flutter unprotected, for there was not one of them which took shelter, or hid its head in the shade of another. Indeed, so airy were the florets, and so transparent the petals, one would be hard put to see a single shadow within them, nor even in the bush itself, which had no solid trunk but rather many spurs which rose in separate fountains from the ground, so that a gale might rush straight through and nowhere meet a dense opposing mass. Thus they flew their flags tenaciously on hedgetop and headland, pale scraps of silk that yielding, were not torn, and bending, did not break, nor seemed to shed their petals in a vanquished litter like other blossoms, nay, not even when the bees had done their work and the hips swelled scarlet in the sunshine, for their faithful choreography inscribed the air-currents, and gave an exact account of the wind. And she thought that this was how she should like to dance, with a light heart and the wind in her hair and a partner to suit her step. To be shaken, yet rooted . . . was not that the long and the short of marriage?

That night her sleep was sweet as tears, yet she could not be idle for long, and next morning found her stationed early on the deck, the light aslant her eyes, and her hand clasped firmly on the ubiquitous spyglass.

Balade
This island is about 250 miles long, with a breadth of 35 miles, and situated between 20d. and 22d. South, and between 166d. and 167d. East, lying diagonally N.W. to S.E.

At the two extremities parallel ridges of mountains enclose deep valleys; for the rest the island consists essentially of mountain peaks, rising to 6,000 feet in Captain Sparrow's estimate, and clothed in fine timber trees which greatly excite his interest.

Some 30 miles to the south lies the island of Kunie, where we remained some time to take on fresh water and carry out repairs — the ship's hull being by now in a very ordinary condition — and were afforded every hospitality by the natives. These folk are well-proportioned and tall, with reddish-golden skin and long straight hair of which they are very vain. Their villages are orderly, consisting of beehive-shaped huts clustered around a central compound where stands the great meeting-house, which is generally rectangular and built up high on stilts. They are excellent agriculturalists and fishermen, and make a tremendous art of tattooing — although only the women are thus decorated — and have a great love of flowers, in which the village plots abound, and of which necklaces are fashioned to honour feast-days or visitors.

Small as Kunie is, I have observed that several languages or dialects are spoken by the various tribes, of which there is a unifying strand, this being that all are similarly deficient in abstracting the general concept from the particular act or object. Thus they have a confusing number of words for eating, each one applicable to a different article of food. Their reckoning, I noted, showed a similar peculiarity. Their numbers were counted to five, and for <u>living</u> objects the word <u>bird</u> was added, for inanimate objects <u>yam</u> and for large objects <u>ship</u>.

To count to 10, they must say two 5s; to 15, three 5s. 20 was <u>a man</u>, however, and 100, <u>five men</u>.

233

Despite its obvious deficiencies when judged by the standards of Europe, I must say I was pleased with a system rooted so stubbornly in the stuff of daily life. There is a niceness to it I would not see sacrificed — for is it not true that 10 <u>gold bars</u> as an entity has nothing of quality in common with 10 <u>kisses</u> (or bridesmaids, love-letters, or the like), and could quite properly be seen as a different concept which requires a different term?

I amused myself for some hours with concocting a numerical order to fit the obsessions of various acquaintances. To 'inanimate' numbers Mr. Moll must append the suffix <u>map</u>, while Captain Sparrow must surely count <u>cloves</u>, and for 'animate', <u>Dutch dogs</u>, no doubt. For large objects he would have <u>citadels</u>, but for his proud 20 he would certainly take <u>Englishmen</u>. As for myself, doubtless I would count small things in <u>dolls</u> or even <u>Lilliputs</u>, while all that was great and animate I would calculate in <u>Gullivers!</u>

Jesting aside, I fear that this leisurely tongue will not survive the curt transactions of commerce that must follow upon Captain Sparrow's survey — for although he has found no clove-trees, he is convinced that the soil and climate are very suitable for their cultivation. Should his assessment turn out to be faulty, he assures me he will settle for a stake in ginger, vanilla, or the superior sandalwood of the region.

Elsewhere, reader, in the meantime, another servant of science turned from his scrutiny of his strawberry-plants and scratched his pen once more across his page.

. . . The genus fragaria *consists of some eight known species to date, native to the north temperate regions of both*

hemispheres as well as to mountain districts in warmer climes; one such species has recently come to light in Chili. The leaves have usually three leaflets palmately arranged, but the number of leaflets may be increased to five or reduced to one. While the flower has the typical Rosaceous structure, the so-called fruit is very peculiar, but it may be understood by the contrast it presents with the 'hip' of the rose. In the last-named plant the top of the flower-stalk expands as it grows into a vase-shaped cavity – the 'hip' – in which are concealed the true fruits or seed vessels. In the rose the extremity of the floral axis is concave and bears its carpels in the interior. In the strawberry, by contrast, the floral axis, instead of becoming concave, swells into a fleshy, dome-shaped mass in which the carpels or true fruits, commonly called pips or seeds, are more or less embedded, but never wholly concealed. Thus a ripe strawberry may aptly be compared to the 'fruit' of a rose turned inside out, for the rose-hip bears its seeds in the <u>interior</u>, whereas the strawberry blazons them on its <u>exterior</u> . . .

The natives of Kunie being very adept at navigation, they conveyed to Captain Sparrow that he must ply south-eastwards for sixteen days to reach the archipelago, and so he did, and on the seventeenth day we came in sight of Spechy. Mary's excitement knew no bounds as she stared at the islands through her spyglass. Sumina itself, of which she had the clearest view, was a rocky terrain of pinkish granite, well-elevated and lightly wooded, while to the west of it, across a narrow strait, lay an island for the most part obscured by clouds, through which a great volcano thrust its smoking summit. She looked wildly from the one to the other, and her hand trembled, and her heart raced, and glad tears played havoc with her vision. Here lay her journey's end, she could not doubt it; here lay recompense for her trials and reward for her sufferings – for none could say that she had deviated from her aim, despite the many hurdles laid before her. Faithful as any albatross, she had flown across the seas to find her mate; she had judged the winds and the waymarks, and now at last, unerring, neared the nest. 'I am the happiest woman in the world!' she told herself, and her poor heart was seized by a spasm of fright (because, dear reader, she was thereby the most enviable!).

She slapped her wrist for silliness and chased away the superstitious shadows. She must be all action now, and pack her dear doll with her belongings, and thank the Captain from the bottom of her heart. The canoes were already scudding out to meet the *Loyal Bliss*, cutting white-toothed across the bottomless blue of the sea. The boat was lowered; she bade an affectionate farewell to Captain Sparrow. Then, giving her last few florins to the boys, she stepped into the pinnace which, led by the canoes, would take her through the reef and set her safely down on Sumina.

CHAPTER XVII

---

*The Archipelago of Spechy . . . A Concert Tree . . . How the Town of
Allegria was Misnamed . . . Some Observations on Crime and
Punishment . . .*

As my mistress approached the port she saw wooden
houses painted in agreeable pastel shades of which
all varieties of blue predominated. Those on the waterfront
were built on sturdy piles, while others clung steeply to the
hill that rose behind, yet all were well-proportioned and
surrounded by verandahs which, from a distance, appeared to
be ablaze with brilliant flowers. On entering the harbour,
however, she saw to her surprise that the vivid hues were not
petals but plumage, for each verandah boasted a bird-table,
on which the birds were perched like gay bouquets.

Yet if this was the one eccentricity her eye detected, elsewhere was ordinariness in abundance, and she gazed upon it like a starving man. No dungeons here, she thought, or dark perversities, no midgets and no giants: rather, all was normality, in scale at least, if not in system. Moreover, there was about the houses such a civil air, and in the neat streets such a bustling industry that but for the acute angle of the October sun she might have disembarked at one of southern England's smaller ports – at Exmouth, for example, or at Rye.

Her spirits soared, for there could have been no place more suitable for a reunion: an island for a honeymoon, where one might find a simple lodging and survive a six-month on a sovereign – in short, a Tropick Paradise! She scanned the quay excitedly, and for a moment thought she glimpsed her husband in the throng – his hat, his sober coat, his gold-topped surgeon's cane – but no, it was not he, but a mirage the scintillating air had summoned up to tease her. Or else he might have sent a chaise, she thought, if he had heard of her arrival. (She did not see one, reader, even through her spyglass, but since when did reason silence raging hope?) She touched her hair, her face, and tied a ribbon, and imagined that he trained a steadier glass on her, and saw . . . a willing wife, well-travelled, and much ripened by experience. She was no doubting maiden now – so why did doubt's draught creep beneath the door to cool anticipation? How hesitate when she had almost reached her journey's end? What was done could not be undone; each sea-change and each fructifying insight was her very own, that she might hide, at first, but not repudiate. The harbour wall flew by; the pinnace docked decisively, and once again she was impatient to deliver all her bounties to a spouse who would delight in them. I will forgive his foibles, if he will forgive my own! she thought, and with this resolve she gathered up her skirts and gladly leapt ashore.

Reader, no anxious husband reached out a hand to steady her, and since our oarsmen quickly fled into a tavern, my mistress stood confounded on the quay like any common immigrant, weighed down by luggage, and with none to offer her assistance.

On the harbourfront, market-stalls were heavy with the produce of the region: sacks of black beans and vanilla-pods, trays of dates and tamarinds, and pyramids of coco-nuts. Yet as the minor key serves to offset the solidity of the major, so did the few peculiarities lend savour to the scene, for there was an inordinate number of stalls which sold watering-cans, and intriguing stacks of bamboo cages, some of which held shrews and mice, and others black bats pendulous and sleeping.

If here and there a head of russet hair bespoke the heritage of Norse invaders, in the main the islanders were olive-skinned and dark, and of a pleasing evenness of feature, although they had about them a decided air of aloofness which discouraged any casual approach. Accordingly it was some time before my mistress plucked up the courage to accost a barrow-boy who, indicating an octagonal building surmounted by an imposing clock-tower, gave her to understand that she should present herself to the Harbourmaster.

Reader, you will agree that it was an inauspicious arrival, for where she had dreamed of bearers and bouquets, she was met instead by bureaucracy. Having dragged her dressing-chest to the lobby, she addressed herself to the clerk at the counter, only to be rudely repulsed. *Queue here*, said a peremptory sign, from which she deduced that the local patois was a hybrid – *queue* being, as far as she remembered, the French for an animal's tail. She must wait in line, it seemed, like a pauper at the poorhouse, and shuffle along with her uncomplaining fellows, until she passed from the cow's tail to its *tête*!

After a tiresome half-hour she regained her place before the counter, and endured the terse inquiries of the immigration clerk. This young man had a pale, mulish face and an English rendered formidable not on account of its foreign terms but by being spoken strictly through the teeth, so that the vowels were greatly shortened, and at first one could not tell *hat* from *hot*, or *hut* from *height*, for all were uniformly turned to *hit*. The fellow interrogated her at length, inscribing her replies on a printed form, and repeating them aloud as he did so. '*Ship-ricked*,' he intoned. '*Silled on a rift . . . ribbed by the Ditch*.' Finally he stamped the document with a self-important flourish and, pointing to the dressing-chest, barked '*Tin Hill*' at a porter, from which she understood that the interview was over, and that she and her luggage were to proceed to the *Town Hall* forthwith. The clerk, it seemed, intended to escort her there himself, for he took from the stand a veiled hat like a bee-keeper's, brushed a speck or two of down from the brim, and ushered her into the street. His uniform, if it could be so described, was of a plain white stuff, loose-cut and unfrogged, with breeches which flapped like sails around the ankles, and his bare feet were clad in the goatskin sandals favoured by the majority of the islanders.

As we penetrated the narrow alleys behind the port, it became evident that although no beggars stretched their hands out from the shadowed doorways, some of the natives must resign themselves to penury. Here an old woman with a frangipani bloom behind her withered ear sold a lone salt-cellar and a pair of wooden spoons; there a madman in the cockaded hat of His Majesty's Forces grinned proudly over his wares, which consisted of a rusty musket, a leaky powder-horn, and a book of which little remained but the salt-stained binding. Thinking to ask which wreck the sorry item had been salvaged from, my mistress picked it up – pray God 'twere no Captain's log from some drowned East Indiaman! – at which the salesman, emitting an unholy shriek, snatched back the book, and clutched it to his breast as if it were as precious as an emerald necklace, or a baby son. Her escort was displeased and threatened to chastise him for his impudence, but as she begged him to release the wretch, two white-clad officers stepped smartly from the throng and seized the man, and gave a curt salute.

'Your pardon, citizens,' said one. 'Old Isaac is as slippery as a Palolo worm, and cannot resist the crowds on market day.'

'Where are they taking the poor soul?' asked Mary in concern, as they marched the madman off towards the harbour.

'To Ogé,' said the clerk indifferently, leading the way towards the main street of the town, 'to the Hospital, where he belongs.'

The bustle of the harbour was behind us now, and presently we came upon a strangely silent square with café tables set out in the open air, where waiters mutely served, and white-clad men and women ate their lunch without a word. The reason for the hush was soon revealed, for at the epicentre of the quiet stood a broad-leaved oak, from which burst, suddenly, a peal of purest birdsong. Trio followed upon solo, and octet swelled to oratorio; *carillon* melted into *barcarolle*, and *rondo* burst gladly from the gravest plainsong. This polyphony was enlivened, moreover, by rhythms which shifted so subtly between *largo* and *pizzicato, sostenuto* and *tremolo* as to pose a far greater threat to Mr. Handel's pre-eminence than any Signor Bononcini!

Our guide, who was in a famous hurry to deliver my mistress to his superiors, responded reluctantly to her enquiries, giving her to understand that although the 'Concert Tree', as it was called, was seen by many as a national shrine, in his opinion it was but another sorry symptom of a national nuisance.

Indeed, as we approached the apex of the town, it was apparent that the dry blue air above was busier than any marketplace, for a constant flicker filled the sky as multitudes of momentary wings disturbed the flow of sunlight. Below in the lagoon were the lugubrious pelicans, and pink flotillas of flamingo, but here on the heights were the swifts and the swallows, the larks in their steep flight, the flaring garrulous parrots, and the sparrowhawks clenched like fists in the firmament. Tournaments of smaller birds jousted in the shrubberies and in the eaves, and everywhere down-feathers spiralled in gentle flurries to the streets beneath – all of which were named in honour of the aviary, being called Rosella Street, or Sparrow Walk, or Pelican Lane – to lie in steep soft banks against the gutters.

'But I have never seen so many birds!' cried Mary in delight. 'Is there no species that preys on them, that they should multiply to such a degree?'

'Unfortunately there is none,' replied the clerk. 'Of course if the citizens would not stuff them with mice and millet seeds I daresay we should see fewer! But these folk will starve their families before their bird tables go empty.' Perceiving that she had lit upon his hobby-horse, my mistress observed that she knew of no other country which lavished such devotion on its fauna. Adjusting his veil to keep his nose protected from the floating down, the fellow shook his head, and sighed a martyr's sigh. 'What can one do, madam, in the face of ignorance? In their superstition they believe that the birds are the souls of the dead, and that by feeding them they do honour to their ancestors!'

(Here, reader, I cannot but invoke that famous follower of Vulcan, Mr. Knox. How thunderously the old firebrand would have denounced a heresy so convivial that it consigned not a single soul to Hell but rather hoisted all aloft in such a feathery Assumption!)

'But might not such beliefs provide some comfort,' ventured Mary, 'while causing no great harm to anyone?'

'No harm? I beg you, listen to the incidence of sneezing, and ask yourself, is it not an irony that the very thing the people worship is the same that makes them sickest? To be sure, Allegria is a pretty name for a town, but *Allergia* would be closer to the mark! . . .'

By now we stood before a white wooden building on the roof of which was mounted a pair of golden scales. 'Here you see the emblem of Sumina,' announced the clerk, throwing back his veil and gazing upwards with a countenance softened, suddenly, by simple pride. 'Of all the islands of the archipelago, we have been charged with devising the machinery with which to administer the practical affairs of society in the most enlightened manner possible.' Then, shaking her hand like a democrat, he drew down his veil and was gone.

In the lobby Mary was relieved to see no evidence of the dreaded *queue*, and instead was greeted pleasantly by a rotund clerk, and ushered to an anteroom, wherein were many small partitioned booths, each of which was furnished with an *escritoire* complete with quills and inkwell. On the far wall a high window, screened by a curtain woven from multicoloured feathers, looked out upon a courtyard in which stood a very dry and dusty fountain.

At length the door opened, admitting not only a draught which stirred the drifts of down that had accumulated in the corners of the room, but also a dignitary with a bald head round as the moon and a belly to match, who bore down upon Mary with an egregious smile.

'Great pleasure, dear lady!' he cried, seizing her hand and kissing it, to her consternation, in the soft and private centre of her palm. 'Honorary Consul Absalom, at your service. I trust you are enjoying your visit to Sumina? There is so much of interest, you will find, on our little island. The coral caves in Windward Bay are a most impressive feature, and of course our obsidian reliefs are quite renowned . . .' Mr. Absalom chatted in this hospitable manner for some time and, after inviting her to take advantage of the Official Rooming-House the State reserved for visitors from overseas, concluded, on a vaguer note, 'There is an enquiry, I believe, about a Mr. Gullible?'

'Mr. Gulliver,' said Mary shortly, 'is my husband. I am certainly anxious to have news of his whereabouts, and hope that in your capacity as British Consul you will be able to assist me.'

'Not British, Madam,' the man demurred. 'All lands. All.' Glancing warily around, as if suspecting eavesdroppers in the shadowy booths, he whispered, 'Am I to understand that you wish to enter a formal claim for this husband?'

'This husband, my dear sir, is the only one I have!' retorted Mary. 'As such, I consider my claim a natural one!'

'In that case you must forgive me, madam,' said the Consul, studying his gold-ringed fingers with a shifty air, 'for I do not believe we have records of such a person.'

The lie was perfectly apparent, and for a moment her heart hung suspended like a hawk in the heavens; her mind, meanwhile, marvelled that the guileless Absalom should occupy a position which, at least in England, requires a proven talent for deceit. Yet she was not to be fobbed off so easily, and determined to use her native cunning to gain a foothold. Reader, her head drooped forward like a dying daffodil, her lips quivered; her eyes were bedewed with mournful tears which, overflowing, rained upon her cheeks and fell unchecked upon her bosom. 'Dear lady!' cried the Consul in alarm as, sagging in her chair, she succumbed to a credible fit of the vapours.

Mr. Absalom hurried to fetch water, and fanned her wildly with his handkerchief, and in fact seemed so confounded by her outburst that one must suppose the ways of the Suminian ladies differ quite considerably from our own! At last her sobs subsided a little, and, lifting a tear-stained face to him, she appealed, 'Dear Sir, is there no avenue that remains unexplored?'

By now the Consul was in torment, and wrung his hands

despairingly, and bit his nails, and coughed and sneezed, and finally allowed, 'It may be possible . . . perhaps some other department can assist us . . . I will make inquiries at the Census Bureau . . .'

'You are my last hope, Mr. Absalom!' cried Mary, overwhelming him with thanks that were in part sincere, for she could not sustain a grudge against a man so patently ill-suited to dissembling.

Having secured an appointment for the following day, my mistress allowed herself to be conducted to the Rooming-House, which was but a few streets distant. This was a white-washed wooden building which, surrounded by a verandah and flanked by sloping lawns, commanded a fine panorama not only of the steep streets and crazy rooftops of the town below, but also of the harbour, and the sunlit Sound beyond. The lawns were sprucely kept, and fringed by imposing mulberry-trees and araucarias, and, if there was not a single flower-bed to be seen, under the dappled shade of a cedar a kitchen-garden was in the process of construction. Gauze canopies protected invisible plants from the sun's heat, and a section of the site had been newly dug and levelled, and the soil banked up at the side. There was no gardener in evidence, however; nor hide nor hair of any servant, although certainly one existed, for on the balcony a table had been laid with a cold repast of roast kid and cucumbers.

In no time at all we were installed in our new lodging – which consisted of a chamber simple as the cell of any novice, furnished with a cot, a plain chair, and a dresser which served as a washstand – whereupon my mistress betook herself to the balcony and sat down to a solitary supper.

Presently she was suffused by a curious calm, occasioned, perhaps, by her high vantage point, for the sky was glorious with whirring wings, and the blue distances she gazed out upon infected her with an optimism so airy that you will forgive me if I reflect for a moment on the Laws of Perspective, and ponder whether they might not equally be applied to the trajectory of a Quest, whose end is always at the vanishing-point, while the objects that more closely abut the senses take on an ever greater substance. Despite the Consul's clumsy attempts to frustrate her, she was convinced that the pursuit of Mr. Gulliver was all but over; she was within sight of her Grail, and herein lay the source of a sudden *sang-froid* which made her toss her head, and shrug, and say – *Tant pis*.

Reader, you will accuse her of capriciousness, you will cry out for a constant heroine. But such a one I cannot supply, for it would be a poor storyteller who banished from his tale all human inconsistency. Allow me to insist, then, on that insouciant moment in which she said No matter, and thrust aside her parasol, and let the bright sun strike her open face. And if in that aberrant instant she was indifferent to her Lemuel, then so might have Aeneas, as he gazed down on Latium, paused doubting on the brink of sure success. (The truth is, however, that as soon as our triumph is threatened, we will dispense with dithering, and hesitate not half as long as hungry dogs!)

At length the sun sank into the sea, and the birds flew away to roost, and the skies above became immeasurably quiet. Being quite wrung out by the day's exigencies, she joined me in the narrow cot, and soon was fast asleep. If there was scarce a flower or blossom on the island, nor was there a buzzing fly or biting gnat to bother her, or interrupt her vivid dreams – and odd enough they were, for she could have sworn her very body left the room, and in its lace-trimmed nightgown lightly took the steps and flowed across the lawn towards the kitchen-garden.

The gauzy canopies were laid aside, the furrowed soil revealed. The low moon was behind her as she climbed the bank and stood barefoot above the pit, and gazed on . . . Pluto! A man like a menhir stood waist-deep, well-planted in the earth – a veritable seed! She strained and stared, and though her mud-man did not move she thought she saw the elvish angle of his smile. She knew him but did not; she swore his Rhadamanthine presence was familiar, yet even as she turned this way and that, and ducked and dived, and craned to see what manner of a man or god was down below, her long moon-shadow darkly followed her and, like a trickster, screened his chthonic face.

Next morning my mistress was awakened by a tap-tapping above her head, and hurried out to the verandah to discover a gaggle of parrots spitting the seeds of mulberries promiscuously on the metal roof, and making a great deal of noise in the doing of it. She could not but be amused by the sight of the birds at their slatternly breakfast, and dressed light-heartedly, and sped through the streets to the Town Hall.

Here she found the entrance obstructed by ladders and carpenters, and on presenting herself at the desk she was met by the same portly clerk who had assisted her the previous day, but who now answered her request to see the Consul with an unhappy shrug. 'Mr. Absalom is on leave, regrettably,' said he, 'on account of his allergies.'

Insisting that the matter was most urgent, Mary demanded to see a higher authority, indeed, she swore she would not budge from the lobby until she had satisfaction. The clerk blenched at this, and vanished into the nether regions, returning at length with the important air of someone who is party to an intrigue. The matter, he announced, had been referred to the Ministry of Justice, and if Madam would make herself comfortable in the anteroom, Chief Justice Abernethy would join her presently.

Had Mr. Gulliver committed a heinous crime? Did he languish in some rat-infested prison, while maggots feasted on his open wounds? Reader, you will understand the chill that fell upon my mistress, and how laughable was the notion that she might wait at all comfortably; indeed, she had her handkerchief in tatters long before the door opened to admit the Chief Justice.

Though not advanced in years, Mr. Abernethy had a face whose severity was little softened by a left eye which looked not fair and square upon the world but obliquely, as if by turning inward it might better train itself on esoteric themes. A sharp-bladed nose, surmounted by two pedagogic furrows twixt the brows, added to the impression of *gravitas*. 'Begging your indulgence, dear lady,' said he, raising a finger to stem her impassioned flow, 'I have been made aware of your claim regarding Mr. Gulliver, and I will come to it all in good time. Before addressing that vexing question, however, I feel obliged to impart certain information regarding the Juridical system of our archipelago.'

(Reader, I beg you, be as meek as Mary, and fold your

hands in your lap like an obedient schoolgirl, lest you discompose the lofty gentleman, and thereby prejudice her Lemuel's case. Have patience, as she must, with long-windedness, for what will be revealed lends such a twist to my tale that it were better said in Mr. Abernethy's very words.)

'Let me explain immediately,' the Chief Justice began, 'that here on Sumina we have come to see that incarceration is not only inhumane, but very far from being a deterrent to prospective criminals. Of course, as soon as one dispenses with custodial sentencing, however, one is faced with the problem of what kind of punishment will take its place. What you see here, madam,' – he indicated the booths around the room – 'in part supplies the answer. Here it is that every citizen who has reached the age of majority is duty-bound to cast his vote in the Sentencing Lottery. In the space available to him on the ballot-paper he must specify a punishment, without a prior knowledge of the nature of the crime. Thus, according as his temperament be cruel or magnanimous, he may decree anything from a few hours' labour at street-sweeping to the most elaborate death-sentence. Here in the Polling Station the votes are collated, and form the basis of all sentences meted out by the Judiciary for a period of seven years.

'As soon as the Court has reached a guilty verdict, a notary plucks a vote at random from the ballot-box, in accordance with which the felon will be sentenced. For example, dear madam, the crime may be child-beating, but the sentence will not deviate from what the ballot-paper stipulates. And herein lies the beauty of the system, for of course the fraudster will be no less fearful of his sentence than the murderer, since it is quite possible that the luck of the draw condemn the former to be hung over Amina's volcano, where he will roast to death. Conversely, the murderer may receive a sentence which is so lenient as to be derisory. For instance, records show that fifty years ago a Mr. Arcturus, who had murdered a deaf-mute, was ordered to sleep for the nights of the full moon on the grave of his victim's mother. A light enough sentence, it would seem, yet I am assured that never was there such a regenerate, who retired to a monastery and devoted himself for the rest of his days to the care of the sick and needy!'

So shocked was Mary by this barbaric jurisprudence that she could hold her tongue no longer, and demanded to know by what means the guilt or innocence of the plaintiff was decided: whether he have Counsel, and be tried before a Jury or a Magistrate, et cetera, et cetera. But reader, before you join my mistress in condemning the Suminian system, and comparing it unfavourably with English justice, let me prevail upon you to take a doll's-eye view for a moment, and focus on the notion of legitimate chastisement.

Consider the train of events that follows when Parliament impeaches a Royal Minister, and strips him of his privileges. The disgraced lord spends the evening brawling in the taverns, then comes home in his cups to set about his wife, who consoles herself thereafter by belabouring the nurse-maid, who does not hesitate to take a mean revenge by tugging at the daughter's hair, and slapping her across the thighs, and putting her to bed without a light. Do not think for a moment, however, that the victim of these incremental abuses is without redress. For always there will be a scapegoat lowlier than she, a miniature citizen with fewer rights than has a piglet in a sty, or a partridge in a poacher's sights, to whom the girl will play both judge and jury, and subject without scruple to every kind of purge and scourge, as well as trouncing, drubbing, cuffing, striping, paddling, flaying, drowning, garrotting, beheading, *auto-da-fé*, et cetera, et cetera. Reader, forgive my jaundiced viewpoint, which cannot but reiterate that she who is clutched close for comfort at the one moment never knows what the next will bring, whether she may be hung up by the thumbs, or forced to sleep face-down in the chamberpot, or strapped on the operating table to suffer the excision of her parts. Such is the martyrdom endured by one who has enjoyed an hour before her mistress's caresses, and has repaid her dear a thousandfold in that sweet currency which is companionship.

While we are on the subject, there is another matter which I would disclose – though gentlefolk will always do their level best to gloss it over – whose symptoms I had suffered, yet had been ignorant of their cause, until my rude awakening in the Pleasure Drome. If I offend, forgive me, but a case that bears upon the common good should not be held *in camera*, and so will have both prosecution and defence in one brief summing up, which is as follows. Should the girl be punished for exploring her most secret parts, and prudishly denied the pleasant charge that may be gained from them, depend upon it that the oppressed will turn oppressor! In duplication of denial, she will be as strict a warder to her doll, and have her in a chastity-belt as quick as winking, thence deriving a gratification all the keener for being gained at such a cruel remove! The lesson that may be drawn from this by students of morality is that perversion loves nothing better than the strait gate of constraint . . .

But we are come off our track a little, for my intention was not to polemise, rather to speak up for the disenfranchised – who are already quite accustomed to the arbitrary cudgels of their masters – and to suggest that dolls, like other humble folk, might fare no worse in Sumina than at the very hub of the Enlightenment.

The Chief Justice, meanwhile, had little patience with my mistress's objections. 'We have found it quite adequate to have one spokesman for the accused,' he said, 'and one for the accuser. The Judge, of course, presides over the proceedings, and his is the final decision.' Before she could interrogate him further, tea was brought in and poured by the desk-clerk, whom the Chief Justice addressed as Mr. Aurore. Offering her a dish of plain cake over which he had grated a nutmeg, he continued, 'There are some citizens who, abhorring punishment in any shape or form, cast their votes exclusively for leniency. Yet they do this without benefit of the knowledge accumulated by the Judiciary over many decades. If they would take the trouble to examine the records they would see that the worst punishment, paradoxically, is often the mildest one, for it exposes the tender feelings to the stern assaults of conscience. To the brute, believe me, indulgence is more threatening than severity. Why, I myself have seen hardened criminals beg for mercy when ordered to bathe the Mayoress's tiger-cubs, or tend the nestlings in the Public Aviary! A harmless chicken-thief, on the other hand, may find that the Lottery has delivered a sentence of Death Probable – being cast into the river, perhaps, to take his chances with the crocodiles – or Death

Inevitable – which might condemn him to be lashed between two mule-trains which will be driven in opposite directions – and this appears, at least initially, to be a thornier problem. Nevertheless, the mere possibility of such an outcome has stamped out most of the petty offences of pilfering, bullying, and house-breaking, thus freeing the energies of the Judiciary not only to deal with serious crime, but also to engage in scholarly research.

'Sadly it is true that there will always be enough voters of a bloodthirsty disposition to ensure that the ballot-box contains many ingenious variations on the death sentence. On one famous occasion, for example, a woman accused of stealing a kid from a neighbour's pen was publicly flayed and boiled in a bath of brine, and on another a Clerk of Works who had accepted bribes from contractors was sentenced to be taken to the silver mines of Ogé, where he was cast, while still alive, as a municipal statue.

'Yet such an uncanny correlation was noted between punishment and crime in those and other similar instances that a far-reaching study was embarked upon. In the ensuing examination of the laws of Chance it was one of our foremost statisticians, Mr. Anamaxander, who elucidated what we now call the First Law of Synjury. Though I hesitate to summarize a lifetime's work in a few sentences, the Law states that in 72 per cent of cases the structures of Synchronicity will supply a fitting punishment for any given crime, due to the operation of a factor C, or Charm – a supra-rational nexus which for the moment can only be denoted by an algebraic formula. Because of this, unfortunately, the powers-that-be have decreed that the First Law may not be broadcast among the general population, who continue to believe in the vagaries of luck, and thus go on casting their votes with the morbid lust of gamblers! I do think it is lamentable that a theory of such elegance should be the secret of a tiny clique, when its publication could inspire the many!'

The Chief Justice concluded with a catastrophic sigh, and sniffed, and blinked erratically, as if he might break down at any moment. Indeed, the unhappy enthusiast could hardly stutter a few more words in praise of Truth and Beauty before he must reach for his handkerchief, to stop the tears from coursing down his carven cheeks. Stricken by embarrassment, my mistress sat in silence, for she could not offer counsel on a quandary so far beyond her ken — nor, I confess, did she feel much sympathy for one who wept for the general principle, yet appeared to be unmoved by any individual plight. Moreover, he had avoided any mention of her husband, which filled her with the fear that his excursus was a lengthy prelude to a tragedy both brief and brutal.

'I implore you, Mr. Abernethy, tell me the truth about my husband, for I am no weak woman who craves the comforting falsehood! Even if he has committed some bad deed, have pity and obfuscate no longer. I swear to you he is an upright man and, despite some eccentric traits, neither a lunatic nor a felon.'

If the Chief Justice was not best pleased to be recalled from abstract realms, he made an effort to collect himself, and mopped his eyes, and fixed her once again with his equivocal gaze. 'Please do not mistake me, madam. Your husband was involved in a misunderstanding, rather than a crime. Nevertheless he insists on doing work in the community, as recompense, pending an application for asylum.'

Relief arrived at a trot, but on its heels there galloped sheer dismay. 'It is not still that silly business with the horses!' she exclaimed.

Mr. Abernethy availed himself of the nutmeg grater, and blushingly addressed the plate of cake. 'I am assured that he has put that sorry incident behind him. Fortunately the owner of the nag did not wish to press charges.'

'Charges?' breathed Mary, hand on racing heart.

'Forgive me for raising a matter which pains me equally, and accept my assurance that Mr. Gulliver is perfectly safe, although he continues to suffer an oppression of spirits which stems from the inequities of his native country, where the marital system is abhorrent to him. For this reason he has secured our pledge to protect him against the claims of all litigious wives.'

'Wives?' cried Mary, utterly nonplussed. 'Pray tell me what he has said to you, Mr. Abernethy.'

'With respect, madam, Mr. Gulliver informed me that, like all gentlemen in England, he was burdened with the support of many wives, whose accumulated pressures had become intolerable. For is it not true that an English wife may chastise her husband with impunity, secure in the knowledge that she is quite within her legal rights to do so? Whereas a husband may never refuse a wife's – forgive me – conjugal demands, on pain of litigation? Accordingly he finds himself, in middle years, debilitated by his efforts, and, moreover, dogged by a vast brood of children he is legally obliged to support.' Mr. Abernethy shook his head severely. 'An unfortunate state of affairs, if you will forgive my saying so.'

Mary listened open-mouthed, for she could not believe

that she had heard aright. Surely this fantastical fiction had come not from the lips of her Lemuel, but from the vulgar pen of some Neapolitan librettist! 'I assume you have never visited my country, sir, and must therefore take an Englishman's word on it?'

'I regret that I have not. By all accounts it is a country marvellously advanced in the sciences, if somewhat retarded in social relations . . .'

She could contain her ire no longer, and cut the man off in mid-sentence, declaring that she had never heard such nonsense in her life. 'On this, dear sir, you must take the word of an Englishwoman,' she added with asperity. 'Mr. Gulliver has no wife but me under the sun, and I have never made a single claim against him, nor one demand he could not easily refuse. Furthermore, he has been absent from England for most of our married life. So you will hardly quarrel with me if I say that I have every right to see him, wherever he may be, and in whatever state of mind.'

The Chief Justice eyed her with dismay. 'Madam, you have me at a loss. Whomever am I to believe?'

'Let Mr. Gulliver himself decide,' she urged. 'If you cannot reveal his whereabouts, at least let a letter be conveyed to him.'

'But his whereabouts are no secret,' he said with surprise. 'You were not informed that he is currently on the island of Ogé?'

Her hand flew to her breast and hovered there. 'Ogé? But that is the hospital island!'

'You will find him in good health, none the less,' he said irascibly. 'Allow me to apologize for the oversight, and assure you that those responsible will be reprimanded.' And with that he swept out in a dudgeon, leaving Mary to ponder on the great good fortune of finding that her husband lived, and was at liberty. Revelation had followed revelation, like blows that rain upon a boxer's head, and she had scarce been able to absorb them. Now that she had a moment to consider their import, however – not least the hint of impropriety regarding horses – she was exceedingly disturbed. Yet if she had learned anything in the course of her travels, it was that cool reason may be relied upon to come when it is needed; hence she set aside wild speculation in favour of reviewing the substantive facts, which were as follows:

1) Mr. Gulliver was employed in an unknown capacity on the neighbouring island.

2) He had placed himself under the protection of the State.

3) For reasons yet unclear, he had become a frightful liar.

So satisfied was she to have driven off the predators of the imagination and fenced her plain conclusions safely in, that for a moment she knew the same security as a squire might, who has surveyed his ordered acres, and sits at his hearth with no more pressing concern than the dinner gong, and which oloroso to fetch up from his cellar. Like the squire, then, she took out her fob watch, and like the squire consulted it, finding to her surprise that her audience with the Chief Justice had lasted above four hours.

From the lobby came the muffled din of hammering, while outside the window of the anteroom a stifled sneeze announced the arrival of a carpenter. Mounting a ladder, the man applied a measure to the window frame, at the same time instructing his apprentice. In the dusty yard beyond, the desk-clerk filled the basin on the fountain from a watering-can, while birds swooped down from the cypress tree to douse themselves. The sight evoked a longing for her own luxuriant garden, for peony and gillyflower and morning glory, all washed to a wholesome sparkle by the English rain, and it occurred to her that she was very parched, not only by anxiety, but by the desiccated air itself, with its admixture of dust and spores and feathers. Indeed, she began to cough and sneeze a little, so that the apprentice-boy caught sight of her in the interior and, discomfited, struck up a tuneless whistling.

Two things followed immediately on this event, although she could not swear that they were caused by it. Firstly, the carpenter silenced the apprentice with a muttered oath; secondly, the birds swerved up affrighted from the fountain and fled in a body into the cypress tree, as if sucked in there by a whirlwind. How curious it was, she thought, that those same creatures which were unperturbed by workmen's dust and din should flee in panic from an inoffensive whistle! It was as if a mysterious reflex had alerted them to some species-memory of danger – to a fellow imitating their call to lure them, perhaps, or a sly hunter signalling his retriever dogs. And even stranger was the evident remorse of the apprentice, and the censure of his master – one might have thought the lad had spat on a cathedral floor, or otherwise blasphemed against the Host!

Her speculations were cut short by the return of Mr. Abernethy, who informed her that a letter had been sanctioned. Thanking him effusively, she hurried to a booth where, banishing all thought of the macabre Sentences composed therein, she inked a quill and wrote:

My dear Lemuel,
Chief Justice Abernethy has been kind enough to inform me
that you are alive and well, and this alone has amply
recompensed me for the privations of my journey. Mr.
Abernethy has told me many things which require clarifi-
cation, not the least of those being your request for protection
from claimants and visitors. I believe I have not asked a
great deal of you heretofore, nor do I now ask more than the
solace of a brief interview to reward me for the travails and
shipwrecks which have cast upon these shores
Your sincere and loving wife
Mary Gulliver.

She read it back, and thought the tone was too obsequious
by far. Why fawn so, and ask so little, when he owed her so
much more? Concern and rancour skirmished in her breast,
yet lacked the time for a protracted war, for Mr. Abernethy
overlooked her, and she must show the same decisiveness and speed as Admiral Byng before the fortress of
Gibraltar.

Having vetted the contents, the Chief Justice folded the
missive and stamped it with his seal. 'If you would be so good
as to address it to Mr. Arbuthnot,' he instructed stiffly.

'Mr. Arbuthnot is with my husband?' cried Mary, amazed
to hear the name of Mr. Gulliver's intimate.

'No, no, madam. It is the name he has assumed, in
deference to our custom, since Gulliver would be unseemly
for a man, and would attract attention from the vulgar.'

Reader, though it occurred to her that so far she had
encountered on the island not a single soul whose surname
did not start with A., she had no wish to catechize her

mentor and invite another florid disquisition. She therefore set aside her curiosity, and wrote the name of John Bull's infamous inventor – who, having assigned that universal alias to the Englishman, could hardly blame an Englishwoman who purloined his own.

Chapter XVIII

*A Most Attractive Thief . . . Empiricism's Limits . . . An Ally from
Amina . . . A Curious Card-game . . .*

Her business concluded, my mistress took her leave without regret and made her way towards her lodging. The
sky was glazed blue and white like a Chinese vase, and
flocked with tiny clouds which drew wistful glances from the
few citizens who were still abroad. The shops and emporia
were closed, and the streets almost empty; all activity, meanwhile, centred on the shady balconies, where bird baths were
being filled to the brim, and bird tables replenished, and
foodstuffs laid out for the family. Envying the loose house-
robes in which these folk enjoyed their leisure hours, she
hurried through the sultry streets, and on reaching the Guest

House approached her quarters by way of the verandah, in the hope of encountering her lunch. In this, however, she was disappointed, for while the birds fed gluttonously, her own small table was entirely bare. Just then a slight noise issued from within, and as she gazed from dazzle into darkness she made out a ghostly shape, and gave a cry of consternation.

'I beg your pardon!' said a voice as shocked as hers, and the intruder spun round from the mirror, wherein she had been peering at herself, as well she might, for reader, let me assure you, she was as lovely a creature as ever graced a Greenwich drawing-room, if a little strong-boned for the English taste, and with a skin unfashionably darkened by the sun. The footpad's hair was raven black, her startled eyes a luminous lavender-grey, and her figure – which was laced tightly into Mary's satin stomacher – would have tempted the customers away from Mrs. Sally Salisbury!

(In addition, reader, let me remark that there was a certain queenly solitude about her, a striking stillness such as one discovers in the interval between the deep bass inrush of a wave and the lighter trill and trickle as its outflow tugs the pebbles down the sloping strand. An air of mystery, indeed – a whiff of sulphur, even, and a glint of mercury! But more than that I will not say, nor answer anybody's whys and wherefores. Some things one cannot speak of, nor approach too closely, for they serve to remind us that the purest wisdom loves the question better than the answer. But how tell this to Englishmen, empiricists, or poor embattled Mary?)

'I meant no offence, madam,' said the intruder hastily, 'but in my whole life I never saw such finery!'

She did not curtsey, and her apology was far from servile, yet Mary found she could not take offence, but rather was inclined by loneliness and curiosity to further their acquaintance. 'As for the stays,' she said, 'you are very welcome to them, for they are devilish uncomfortable, and I would gladly exchange them for a garment more suited to the climate here on Sumina!'

'I may keep it on?' asked the girl in disbelief, caressing the scarlet satin with a desire both innocent and avid.

'You may indeed,' said Mary recklessly, 'if you will lunch with me!' If a servant could dispense with the proprieties, she thought, then why not she? She was delighted with her newfound daring, which for friendship's sake would flout the rules of privilege, yet when the girl accepted graciously, as would an equal, she found herself abashed, for where no taboo exists transgression loses all its lustre.

'Mrs. Tinker,' said the girl, shaking her hand as brusquely as a stable groom. 'I am the Keeper of the Guest-House. And you, of course, are Mrs. Gulliver. I am very sorry I was not here to welcome you before, but I was called away to nurse a relative on Amina.' She hurried off to fetch the victuals, and presently returned to lay the table with a meal of leafy radishes and tunnyfish. Then, spendid in her cherry-coloured corset, with a sapphire parrot's feather wound into her coiffure, she sat down to luncheon with a somewhat startled Mary.

Viewed in the brilliant sunlight of the balcony, the House-keeper was not as young as she had first supposed, being around thirty years old, but very ravishing; in fact, her only fault lay in her figure which, although voluptuous, was lent a masculine cast by a pair of wide and well-developed shoulders. Entirely female, however, was her indignation when she heard of Mary's interview with Mr. Abernethy. 'He has forgot he ever suckled at a woman's breast,' she said. 'He thinks that great abstractions best befit his elevated station but, as we say on Amina, show me the babe that ever cried in Latin! The man is smaller than life, and that's the truth of it . . . but I am concerned about your husband – he is not ill, I hope?'

'I am assured that he is not,' said Mary, but even as she spoke her limbs were shaken by a tremor, for she could not but recall the downright Lie, and the humiliation heaped upon her by a spouse who had impugned her rightful status. Indeed, the chair and table trembled too, and fruit fell from the mulberry tree, and across the shivering waters of the Sound smoke belched from the mighty peak of Amina. A drip of lava eked like blood from the volcano's lip and leaked a runnel down its wooded slope . . . *enantiodromia*, reader, is the term which signifies that Nature's trope is suddenly reversed, whereby the Mother who has nurtured shows us her devouring face. Now Mary shrank in terror from the sight, yet her companion's face was blithe and bonny.

'Our Mistress Pele, bless her, is a demon at her monthly time,' said Mrs. Tinker wryly. 'We may not take kindly to it, but we must take it all the same.'

'How can you tolerate such terrors?' Mary cried and, to her great dismay, gave way to tears of wounded pride, and fright, and misery. No tactic this, or pantomime to win a point, but pure abjection, and before a living breathing female! Defenceless as a babe before its mother, and as mute, she did not know if tenderness was more imperilling than reprimand, or love's envelopment more treacherous than any vengeful slap! Here, reader, was the true volcano that she feared – capricious rage, and cloying swamps of sentiment, and lust, mansuetude, and rapture – the untapped powers which lived within her and in every other member of her sex, not least in Mrs. Tinker. Here was no frank-eyed friend, but the abyssal mirror in which her infant terrors were reflected, and in her confusion she cried out, 'The same! The same! The venom is within me!' and hid her eyes, and vomited across the balcony.

No scolding came, however, for her helplessness, but hugs instead, cool cloths across the brow, and quiet mops and buckets; meanwhile the earthquake eased, and all the rattling crockery fell silent. 'Forgive me,' she muttered, but was quickly hushed, and held in two strong arms till she was solid once again, and fear gave way to gratitude, and soft exhausted tears.

'To bed,' said Mrs. Tinker presently, 'for sleep's a great restorer. We shall talk again at supper time, and see how we may clarify the situation.' She led my mistress to the cot, wherein she fell through thickets of distress and slept at last, and later, when she woke, was greeted by her cheerful ally with the news that Mr. Aurore would shortly join them.

'Mr. Aurore is my fiancé,' she explained, to Mary's great discomfiture, for to her mind the portly little clerk could never partner such a paragon. 'You must accompany us this evening when we take a turn around the town, for I believe he has the ear of Mr. Abernethy, and may be able to unearth the truth about your husband.'

*   *   *

When the gentleman arrived, however, it was evident that he viewed the prospect of a threesome with little enthusiasm, having no doubt anticipated a tête-à-tête with his fiancée. Mary, if the truth be told, was hardly more complaisant, and as the trio set off for the town she judged his figure bovine, and his manner awkward, and his teeth protruberant – indeed, she thought him a decidedly unworthy Consort!

Foolish is the friend, however, who would cast aspersions on a woman's choice, even with a sincere intent to save her, for she will succeed only in wounding the self-pride the lady has transferred to her beloved, to augment his worth, and boost his meagre stature. Thus the desired result will never be achieved, but rather its antithesis – a rashly steeled resolve, a headlong marriage, and a friendship ruined!

No less oblivious, it seemed, to Mary's jealousy than to the shortcomings of her lover, Mrs. Tinker slipped an arm through hers, and one through his, and thus linked they paraded down the boulevard towards the port, as incongruous a trio, I daresay, as ever was seen in the South Seas, with the Housekeeper in her scarlet stays, and the clerk in his workaday white, and my mistress in a green silk mantua somewhat the worse for being so well travelled.

Before long Mrs. Tinker's attentions sweetened her fiancé's temper, and he stirred himself to politeness, pointing out for Mary's benefit the thunder-clouds that hovered over Amina. 'How strange it is but true, that we will always covet what we have not,' he said with an ingratiating smile. 'The citizens of Sumina look longingly towards the rain-clouds of Amina, while the Aminians complain about their swamps and sulphurous airs, and yearn for the parched blue skies of Sumina!'

'The Suminians, however, will go to any length to avoid admitting their envy of us,' retorted his fiancée. 'Really, it is laughable, Aurore.'

The clerk was much discountenanced, and hurried to defend himself. 'Yet in private, my dear, we do the island honour,' he appealed. 'Perhaps it is a law of nature that one will deny most fiercely what one most desires, and build all kinds of barriers to conceal one's true turn of mind from others, lest they gain the advantage of us. There is a danger, however, that we may eventually contrive to hide our longings even from ourselves – not to mention our loved ones – for does not habit, like coral, secrete a calcareous substance which, as the years go by, enamours the tender organisms of feeling?'

'Bravo, Aurore!' cried his fiancée, as this lavish discourse was cut short by a lamentable bout of sneezing. 'Such talents are quite wasted on a clerk. We must spirit you away from all those feathers, and find you a quiet cave where you can contemplate in comfort!'

'Are all Suminians besotted with philosophy?' asked Mary, piqued to think that Mrs. Tinker had forgotten her or, even worse, had merely brought her to play gooseberry.

'I daresay my fiancée would say so!' exclaimed the clerk. 'No doubt she would also point out that poets and artists are as rare on Sumina as flying insects – but she herself is from Amina, of course.' Being rewarded by an affectionate tap of his fiancée's fan, he continued with reckless gaiety, 'I grant it is a stupid habit, to be forever belittling the place, but at least we are not so misguided as those idiots on Ogé!' He indicated a rocky outcrop on the north horizon, which glowed with the pale translucency of alabaster. 'Some swear their logic proves that Amina does not exist at all!'

This jocular remark was altogether lost on Mary, so chilled was she by the prospect of the island. Dumbstruck, she shivered and she stared, for here was no clement atoll, of golden beach and feathered palm, but beetling cliffs and barren crags whose ghostly pallor was not warmed even by the livid rags of the setting sun. How hollow were her hopes! Hollow too the heart that had deceived her by conjuring from the map a spot most happy and hospitable, where she might consummate a blissful union. Her voyage, truly, was in vain, if that frigid and forbidding place must be her final destination! 'Twere bad enough to be imprisoned there, she thought, but what manner of a man would choose of his own free will to live in such a cheerless sanctuary?

Since nothing is more perturbing than to be repelled by what one rightly should desire, Mary strove mightily to reinstate love's captaincy, and thereby steered her ship from shoal to whirlpool. Mistaking her stricken silence for advertence, Mr. Aurore embarked on a description of the silver-mines from which Ogé derived its income, and of the well-appointed hospital, in which the most advanced techniques were practised. The wily Mrs. Tinker, meanwhile, read the signals of distress and, declaring that they must take a cordial at a café on the harbourside, sent her lover on ahead to find the perfect table.

'You must not mind my fiancé,' she said kindly. 'He is so eager to please that he forgets himself. But be patient, for he has a good heart, and will quickly be won over to your side.'

Being of the opinion, rightly or wrongly, that sentimen-
talists are not to be depended on, for they are blown this way
and that by the winds of approval, Mary could but answer
with a dumb beseeching look, and thought that she had far
rather be in the capable hands of her Amazon than entrust
her cause to the irresolute Aurore.

(Reader, I own that she is very quick to condemn in others
faults which are her own; but bear with her, for I have never
promised you heroics, nor do I pretend to show a lady free of
failings, believing that the truth, though plain enough fare,
nourishes better than the banquet of flattery.)

'No, no, do not frown so,' said Mrs. Tinker, 'for it only
compounds your troubles. Trust me, and in the meantime let
us bide our time as pleasantly as possible.'

They were soon seated outside one of the establishments
which fronted on the harbour, the better to savour the cool
evening breezes, and enjoy the view across the basin, in
which were berthed not only fishing smacks, but canoes
and outriggers of the most elaborate workmanship. At the
surrounding tables the citizens of Sumina amused themselves
with a vivacity untainted by excess. Ancients coddled infants,
and young bloods played backgammon, and sweethearts
talked but did not touch, although no chaperone constrained
them: nowhere in the measured gaiety, in fact, was any hint
of the propensities described by Mr. Abernethy. Mary sipped
the cordial obediently, and even said that it reminded her of
elderberry wine, to please her friend (which it did not,
although she wished it had), and dully saw the sights and
heard the sounds, and tried to hide the fact that she was
altogether sick and tired of strangeness.

If the islanders were circumspect with folk from foreign

parts, and hardly glanced at Mary's hoops and petticoats, they showed no such scruple about one of their own, particularly when the one in question was laced tightly into a cherry-coloured stomacher, from which her generous breasts upheaved like Venus rising from her conch. Far from being discomfited, however, Mrs. Tinker seemed to accept the attention as her due, and even to relish it, for her eyes brightened, and her voice deepened, and her fiancé wore the look of a man who did not know whether to be proud of his peacock, or jealous of the glances she attracted.

Meanwhile, the tethered boats swayed listless on the evening tide, and on the harbour wall the fishermen disbursed their catch of eels and crayfish, and repaired their nets by lantern light. No place could have been more pleasant, and no sight more soothing, yet not even the haunting advent of moonrise lifted the pall of gloom that hung about my mistress: indeed, its very fullness made her dwell on lack, for was it not to this same moon that the sinner Cain was banished, there to live cold and alone, and walk stooped over, and carry a bundle of thorns for ever on his bleeding back?

Reader, should you detect herein a note of satisfaction, I will not deceive you by denying it. Though I aspire to objectivity, I am no paragon, and I cannot swear that I was quite recovered, at the time, from my own injuries. Of course, it can be said that my disappointments were my own doing: I had got above myself, no doubt; I had soared too near the sun, and like Icarus had fallen down to earth. Many sermons may be squeezed, I'm sure, from such material, with which the *haves* will seek to resign the *have nots* to their condition. But reader, I was very far from being resigned, nor had I forgot a single grievance, as will presently be seen. For the moment, however, I stood on the sidelines, and while my mistress was swept along by the increasing momentum of events, my own days were dull and humdrum, and such excitements as could be had must be enjoyed, as it were, by proxy.

CHAPTER XIX

*An Encounter with a Naturalist . . . The Bat-harvest . . . On the
Function of the Scapecoat . . . The Perils of Gardening . . .*

At this very moment, in the carved prow of an outrigger
canoe, Fate spurred his oars towards the harbour – or
such was the figure cut by Monsieur Antoine Duchesne, who
came bare-chested, with a wild cravat at his neck, and a
riband of feathers about his weather-beaten brow, and his
hair flying behind him, and his arms gesticulating with that
graceful alacrity only to be found in the French.

'Ola!' he cried to the watching fishermen, and again 'Ola',
cleaving the waters till he reached the quay where, throwing
a faded velvet jerkin around his shoulders, he leapt ashore
and roped the craft to its mooring. In a trice he had

273

commanded a mule-cart and a clutch of wooden pails, with which he and his crew began to unload a noxious cargo. This, reader, consisted of a large heap of volcanic soil from the alluvial plains of Amina, and several hundredweight of dung, the purpose of which will presently become clear. The sudden commotion in the quiet harbour attracted the attention of the customers on the café terrace, and appeared to cause them some amusement.

'Why, it is Monsieur Antoine,' cried Mrs. Tinker, rising eagerly to hail him. 'He is our other guest,' she explained to the startled Mary. 'A famous botanist from France!' Mr. Aurore, on the other hand, seemed less than gratified by the appearance of the gentleman, who strode across the terrace, bestowing a smile here and a *bonsoir* there, and wiping his dirty hands upon his breeches.

'Mrs. Tinker!' cried the vagabond, planting a resounding kiss on each of her ruddy cheeks and eyeing her *toilette* with interest. '*Charmante*,' he murmured gallantly, and gave a bow to the clerk, who returned the compliment as punctiliously as any Prussian.

'And here is dear Mrs. Gulliver, who has come all the way from England!'

'Madame,' said the Frenchman respectfully, yet stopped mid-bow and stared. 'But it is *la belle dame en robe de soir*!' he exclaimed, with a merry laugh. 'We have met, I believe, by moonlight. It seems that you arrived on Sumina by stealth, and your ship left likewise, or it might have done me the favour of carrying my mail to Europe!'

Mary was all confusion, and could but stutter and blush, for she who had thought herself dreamer was now unveiled as sleepwalker, and by the very mud-man she had gazed upon so fervently. 'Sir, you have the advantage of me,' she said, when she had summoned up sufficient sternness. 'It would have been kinder, I think, to make your presence known.'

'Forgive me, Madame, but your appearance was so sudden that I was startled. And you stared at me with such fixity that I was afraid to speak, lest it cause a shock to your senses – for they say, do they not, that it is dangerous to wake a *somnambule*? And then you turned away and were gone, like an apparition – though, with respect, Madame Gulliver, a very charming one . . .' All this was delivered with many glowing glances from a pair of tawny eyes, and wild shrugs of the shoulders, and black locks which danced with heady energy about a sunburned neck. Mere severity, as you can see, would not suppress this scalliwag, who smelled like no bouquet, yet flirted as gracefully as if he had been a courtier at the Palace of Versailles, for he had youth on his side, with all its rash vitality, and the very good fortune of being born a Frenchman, and an only son besides, so that *no* was not a word he was accustomed to, except it be a mild rebuke from a pretty mother, or a *non*? with a tender question mark appended, or a *mais* applied before, as salve to take the sting away. Other ladies would have countered the onslaught of flattery, returned the volleys with interest, and made amusing sport of it, but Mary lacked the coquetry, and nodded silently, prim-lipped, and thus was left susceptible.

Declaring that he must avail himself of the water-pump before he would sit down with them, Monsieur Antoine sluiced himself in public on the quay, and returned to the table with his jerkin soaked and his breeches splashed, and his hair sleeked down like a retriever-dog's. More cordials were brought, and the Frenchman declined a game of cards. '*Mais jouez donc,*' he urged, 'for I must eat some bread and cheese, and set to work at once.'

Tossing her head flirtatiously, Mrs. Tinker demanded, 'So you have found your precious soil, Monsieur, but will we ever see your precious crop?'

'*S'il plaît à Dieu!*' cried the botanist, with a radiant glance towards the heavens, which allowed Mary a surreptitious study of the beauty-mark which sat astride his chin. 'They say that all plants flourish in the earth of Amina, and so I am as confident as any scientist may ever be. The tulips there, Madame,' he said, turning suddenly to fix his gaze on Mary, so that she was obliged to collect herself, 'must be seen to be believed. Six feet high if they are an inch, *je vous assure.*'

'And the crop you speak of, sir – may I know what it is?'

'My *fraisiers*, Madame Gulliver. They have languished on their long voyage and, like fretful invalids, require a great amount of cosseting. Yet when their convalescence is complete, I trust they will do what is required of them.'

'And that is, Monsieur?' said Mary, who was entirely ignorant of the horticulturalist's art.

'Why, to mate, Madame – which is no more than Nature requires of all of us. To cross the ballroom floor and choose a partner, which is a nervous enough voyage for a gentleman, believe me, yet my swains must be braver still, and take a blind leap across the barrier of race!' A loaf and a platter of cheeses were set before the Frenchman, and he set to his meal with gusto, filling up his mouth and talking all the while. 'Hybrids, Madame! I aim to create hybrids, or half-breeds if you prefer, from the conjunction of two different species of the same genus. I am determined to prove to science that our French *capiton* is not always, as is the general belief, hermaphrodite, but may fertilize my Chilian females – which are, by the by, so much greater in size and more luscious to the taste that any new stock which stems from them must not only benefit horticulture, but the economy itself! Where once we saw dwarves on our dinner-tables, Madame, now we shall feast on giants!' With this the young scientist, gobbling down the last morsel of his cheese, took his leave of the trio – to the regret of the two of them and the considerable relief of the third – and led his stinking mule-cart off towards the boulevard.

'Monsieur Antoine works always in the cool of the evening, when he may remove the nets without fear of the birds,' said Mrs. Tinker in a distinctly proprietorial manner. 'In the day he sleeps, and must not be disturbed.' To this her fiancé replied with a positive pout, and said archly that he would think himself a lucky man, were he the subject of such keen surveillance.

A lovers' tiff would doubtless have ensued, had a group of boys and girls not approached at that moment, drawing all eyes to them with their clamorous high spirits. Positioning themselves along the harbour wall, these young folk launched into the air rude kites made from dried palm-leaves, which were swiftly borne aloft by the sea breeze. Yet Mary was soon aware that this was not the harmless pastime it appeared to be, for Mrs. Tinker gave her to understand that the lines, being made from the webs of poisonous spiders, were most hazardous to manufacture, and were fixed with sharp hooks on which morsels of rotten fruit made tempting lures for bats.

Reader, my mistress watched in horror as the creatures

which had darted above her, fleet and invisible as thoughts, were one by one outsmarted and attached, until they fluttered steeply in the night sky like rags on some infernal washing line. As the dark harvest was reeled in, she saw that here was the very source of the enigma she had glimpsed in the market-place, where the bats, still living, suffered in their cages. She was not slow to express her distaste for such cruelty, thus rousing the clerk to a peevish defence of the benefits the sport provided in the way of remedies distilled from the organs of the creatures, which were used by the physicians of Ogé to treat all ills from melancholia to kidney stones, not to mention the asthma endemic on Sumina.

'If you will not spare my feelings, sir,' cried Mary, who had been kept dangling like the poor tormented bats, and could not bear another careless mention of the island, 'at least do me the kindness of telling me why my husband is on Ogé, and what work he is engaged upon!'

The clerk was flustered, and looked beseechingly at his fiancée, whose face was all reproach. So it is that the weak, being forgetful of all frailties but their own, will continue to be the cruellest, and if taken to task for it will be all injured innocence, and swear they are too tender-hearted to hurt a living soul. 'I beg pardon if I am at fault, madam,' he said stiffly, 'but I do not have the information you seek. I know only that all those who live on Ogé must be surgeons or patients, except they toil in the silver mines, which seems unlikely, since I assume your husband is no common labourer.'

'He is a physician of repute,' retorted Mary, 'who wishes only to alleviate suffering, and improve the condition of humanity!'

'Then be assured that he is well placed on Ogé,' said the clerk glumly, and shook his head, and sighed, as if it pained him to dwell on such a locus of affliction. 'Those wretched souls are certainly in need of some improvement.'

The most meagre endorsement was enough to touch poor Mary, who said unsteadily, 'Believe me, sir, he is a good and dedicated man.' The thought of Mr. Gulliver's goodness was the straw that almost broke her back and brought her perilously close to tears.

'Oh, madam, do not cry, or you will have us both awash!' the clerk appealed with an unhappy laugh, and looked, indeed, as if he might brim over. He cleared his throat, continuing, 'Your loyalty does you credit – for I must confess that I consider it the highest of the virtues. I know nothing of your husband's situation, but I will move heaven and earth, I promise you, to discover it. After all,' he added, with a misty glance at his fiancée, 'what kind of a man is he who will not do his utmost, who will not risk everything, if need be, to reunite true lovers?'

'Dear Aurore,' murmured Mrs. Tinker. 'Everything, I trust, will not be necessary. Just a little earnest effort will suffice.'

Next morning the door opened to admit the Housekeeper with a breakfast tray and a jug half-full of washing-water. 'The cistern is almost dry,' she announced. 'I think you must do a rain dance for us, Mrs. English!'

'Is there no well, then, in the garden?' Mary asked.

'No, nor even a pump in the street. I am forever saying that we must bore for one, but they are still shilly-shallying over the expense. They argue – quite mistakenly, of course –

that there is no real need for such an outlay, since foreigners do not care to wash, but prefer to douse themselves with perfume.' Whisking a duster across the dressing-table, Mrs. Tinker retired to the balcony to sweep away the fallen feathers.

Mary, meanwhile, saw on her plate the paw-paw and the passion-fruit from fertile Amina, which never knew a drought, and brooded for a moment on the botanist. Last night, from the verandah, she had glimpsed the tidy rows of plants and the spade stuck upright in the ground, and the nets thrown down beside it, but of the gardener himself there was no evidence. She allowed herself to linger, though reflecting that it was a strange ambition which would lead a gentleman to devote his life to the humble strawberry, yet somehow it was a sweet one . . . and lost herself for once in pleasant thoughts, and did not know her lips were smiling. At length, however, alerted by the sound of snapping twigs, she saw a stealthy shape creep from the hedge at the perimeter of the lawn, carrying in each hand a wooden pail which brimmed with water.

Unwilling to be discovered, she drew back under the shadowed eaves the better to observe him. How carefully he filled his watering-can, so that not a drop would be spilled, and how steadily moved up and down the trenches, so that not a plant would go thirsty, or drink a surplus, but would receive exactly what accorded with its needs! She smelled the rankness rise afresh from the damp manure around the roots, and dwelt awhile on agriculture and the open air, on hoe and plough and loving husbandry.

(Thus, reader, is the Future comically constructed: for each and any object may be unwittingly selected as a prop for the dreaming of it, and when the little roots of the heart steal out in search of nutriment, even a heap of dung may furnish them with a felicitous narrative!)

She washed sparingly, and dressed rapidly, and took her tray out to the verandah, where she found Mrs. Tinker seated in a rocking chair, with a basket of sewing beside her. 'But why does not Monsieur Antoine make his garden on Amina,' she enquired, 'since by all accounts one may grow anything there?'

'Because Monsieur Antoine is a man, my friend – as I believe you have already noticed – and men may stay no more than two consecutive nights there.'

'Surely you do not mean that Amina is an island of women?' asked Mary in astonishment.

'I agree that the system is a little old-fashioned,' said Mrs. Tinker hastily, drawing a piece of mending from her basket. 'My mother would have had it no other way, but, as for myself, I confess I made a great to-do whenever my father was obliged to leave. I daresay the tears I wept on that wretched shore would have irrigated the whole of Sumina! Custom is a strange thing, to be sure . . . and yet, one may come to see that it performs a useful function.'

'But you prefer to live on Sumina,' said Mary, eyeing the curious garment she had spread across her lap, which a travelling player might have worn in the *Commedia dell'Arte*.

'For the moment, yes,' said Mrs. Tinker, shrugging her sturdy shoulders. 'When I have my children, however – and certainly when I am old, and need companions to rely on – I expect I shall return.'

'But you intend to marry Mr. Aurore, do you not?'

'Of course, but I am not so green as to suppose that one

man will be my lifelong helpmeet. One needs a certain continuity in life, yet the male, as we say on Amina, has the attention-span of a *Palolo* worm, and it does not do to depend on him for the basic necessaries. He will come and he will go, and others will replace him – is this not the inevitable way of things?'

Mary was dismayed by this reply, and decided that there was no end to the perversity of these islands, whose inhabitants practised neither conjugal fidelity, nor the proven procedures of law, nor any faith that she could see, except it be in the birds whose feathers were the cause of so much sickness. To speak of continuity, yet live on boiling lava, and disdain the solid structures of the male – surely the fleeting play of light and shadow was more permanent than such a sorority! And yet, one glance at Mrs. Tinker was enough to make a woman thirst for suckling rain and seeping milk, to miss a sister and lament a mother, to thrill with admiration and to fume with rivalry, and finally to gaze at the uncharted realms within, and wonder at the mists that circled there . . . She drew back from the brink and shook a prudish head, as common sense commanded. 'Well, I could not talk so lightly of replacing Mr. Gulliver!' she declared, in such an acrimonious tone that Mrs. Tinker stopped mid-stitch to stare at her.

'Nothing is taken lightly on Amina, I assure you! Look. Let me show you my *Scapecoat*, in which I shall be married, and in which they will bury me when the time comes.' She spread the queer cloak out for Mary, revealing its ragamuffin splendour. Although of plain unbleached cotton, it was much decorated with silver-thread embroidery, and appliquéd with brilliant scraps of silk, and hung about with sticks and stones and gewgaws. 'It begins when I was twelve years old,' explained the sempstress, pointing to a sleeve on which an abalone shell was sewn. 'Here is the shell I gashed my arm upon while playing in the surf. And here' – indicating an embroidered moon on which a wild boar rode – 'is my first female flow. This braid is a lock of my father's hair, and, beside it, dried flowers from his funeral. The sickle embroidered at the hem marks the first time I betrayed a friend. The canoe is for the leaving of my homeland, and the feathered crown, soon after, is the loss of my virginity . . .'

'But you expose to public view what is best kept private,' protested Mary, who like any lady had been brought up to believe in the virtues of concealment. Why, it were better to go stark naked, she thought, than wear one's history upon one's back!

'Spoken like a true Suminian!' the Housekeeper retorted. 'On Amina we do not think so much of secrecy, believing that wounds heal faster in the open air. All that has marked us with pain or with pleasure we work upon the coat, so that we will forget nothing, and therefore wear remembrance without undue regret. She who owns her wounds, as the saying goes, will not make others pay for them.' Slipping her arms into the billowing sleeves, she stood up and spun around, and tinkled like a Christmas tree. 'Do you not think there is beauty in biography, when it is worn with pride?'

'Beauty – aye, but that depends on the biography,' said Mary, with a shiver, staring with fascination at the empty fields upon the Scapecoat, where the future waited to be written. Were she to put her needle to her past, how might its major characters appear? There was a silk stocking, for her beloved father, a Bible for her mother, and as for her own travels . . . no, she certainly could not reveal the sleek leviathan that stood for Lilliput! Snapping up her parasol to hide the fever in her cheeks, she rose in agitation from the table. If only she could calm herself, and concentrate on Mr. Gulliver, and visualize . . . a globe, perhaps . . . or surgeon's staff . . . or astrolabe? But now she blushed a fierier red, for truth would not embroider any silken symbol of her love, and sewed instead a meagre hank of straw from the stables!

Reader, as a wise man once wrote, the articulation of the self is the transformation of the same; to speak is to become different. Not that Mary's lips had said the words aloud, but her mind had sung them like a Town Crier who so deafens the winter morning that only the worst slug-a-bed may sink back into sleep. Could she ignore its rousing call and tell a lie, and sew a hero once again upon her inner cloak? Reader, she could not, and fell to silent brooding on her quest, which had done, as far as she could see, no good to anyone, and might even be likened – dare I suggest it? – to flogging a dead horse. Yet having come so far she could not now turn tail and flee to England, for wife she was – for worse, in this case, as for better – and still subscribed to the belief that wherever disappointment is, lies solemn duty!

Thus preoccupied, and finding that her gaze had fixed upon the kitchen garden, she asked on a morbid impulse, 'But it would be no crime to borrow water from a neighbour's well? To borrow, that is, without asking?'

'Dear friend, do not think of it!' the Housekeeper exclaimed. 'You shall have my ration with pleasure, if only you will promise me never to trifle with the laws of Sumina!'

Chapter XX

An afternoon in the Museum . . . a History of Aviation . . . Some Secrets of Onomatology . . . Cupid's Dart hits home . . . An Embarrassing Encounter with a Mermaid . . .

One more worry, then, had been added to the list of my mistress's concerns, and she resolved to have words with Monsieur Antoine, and alert him to the danger. There was as yet no news from the Chief Justice, nor message from the clerk, and so she filled the anxious hours with application, bending over her journals in the shady coolness of her chamber, annotating her charts, and collating for Mr. Moll what she had so far learned of Spechy.

Morning slipped into sultry afternoon, and presently her studies were disturbed by the advent of the Frenchman himself, who sailed into her room and informed her that he had every intention of diverting her from her cares – of which he had been apprised by Mrs. Tinker – for it would do no good to sit about fretting, since a watched pot never boils, and so on and so forth, dancing about the place, picking me up, reader, and peering at me with a lively interest, patting my head and putting me down again, sniffing at a crystal scent-bottle, and stroking a satin mantua or silver hair-brush with delicate and discerning fingers, which were made for measuring anthers, passing pollen with a sable brush from stamen to stigma, and nipping out superfluous leaves to swell the fruit.

'Let us use the afternoon to enjoy ourselves,' he declared, 'since I may do no work till sunset. You must come with me to the Museum, for I think we will be very well amused there.' And with that he snatched up Mary's parasol and presented it to her with a bow, confounding any thought of refusal.

'My dear Monsieur Antoine,' Mary retorted, 'I will come with you gladly, but first I must caution you about your midnight forays.'

The Frenchman raised a merry eyebrow. '*Mon Dieu!* I am undone! You have observed me!'

'You would be advised to take the matter seriously! Have you not heard of the cruel Lottery which passes for a legal system here, and renders perilous the pettiest of crimes?'

'Indeed, I have heard of it,' said the Frenchman airily. 'But water cannot be had at any price, and I must irrigate my garden by fair means or foul.'

'If you were to be caught in the act,' said Mary with

a shudder, 'I dare not think what might become of you!'

Monsieur Antoine sobered at the sight of her distress and, forswearing his bravado, took possession of her hand. 'Forgive me, madame, for I forgot myself and spoke like a selfish oaf. Please do not upset yourself on my behalf. Though I have proved myself unworthy of your concern, I promise that I will take every care in the future. But should the worst come to the worst, I am confident that the Courts must deal more leniently with foreigners.'

Although in the course of her travels Mary had seen precious little evidence of clemency, she sincerely hoped it might be so, and indeed before long had been persuaded by the plausible young man that were he to plead ignorance, and throw himself upon the mercy of his hosts, his little misdemeanour might be easily forgiven. Such is the arrogance of Europe, of which I shall say no more for the moment, but rather heed the insistent *Allons-y* of the Frenchman who, tossing his winsome curls, whisked my mistress off to the Museum.

This, reader, was a building in the Colonial style, greenwashed and formerly grand, with a verandah of wrought-iron, and a dry lawn paced with all due pomp by a solitary peacock. At first sight the interior was very unremarkable, for the same artefacts might equally be seen in London or in Leipzig – the broken pikes, and verdigris-encrusted coins, and gloomy portraits of dignitaries who stared, cross-eyed as Mr. Abernethy, from their gilded frames.

The light was dim; their timid footsteps echoed on the polished floorboards of the empty halls, while the coughs of the custodian yielded only to the salvoes of his sneezes. 'Is there nothing here of Amina?' whispered Mary, who had noticed not a cookbook or a curling-tongs, nor any other vestige of the feminine.

'*Je crois que non*,' the Frenchman whispered back. 'Our Suminians are very proud, and give such a lofty account of themselves that we might suppose they reproduce by perfect parthenogenesis.'

He had spoken Mary's thoughts exactly; indeed, so rare and apposite were his words that for a moment the two shared the most concordant of glances. Breaths were briefly held, and pupils infinitesimally widened, and noses scented hungrily as hounds at bay, so that startled Reason cowered and ran for cover, and forgot its Greek and Latin, and its very name besides. Their skin prickled, and their ears rang with silence, for in the speaking air between them their separate solos for a second were conjoined, and sang a thundering duet. They stood, they stared, and could not come together, nor bear to stand apart. Comets passed, and epochs, and *nydroi* fell to earth, and though neither one had laid a finger on the other, thought, in that dazzling interval, had tangled them a thousand times, and thrown them on a thousand avid beds.

If ardent curiosity had launched its dart, propriety as quickly raised its cowardly shield. 'Why, look at this!' cried Mary, advancing businesslike upon the next exhibit. 'It is some kind of lexicon, is it not?' She pored over a glass case in which was displayed a number of pages from a dictionary, much yellowed by age and stained by wine and weather.

'Little boys are given names from it, as soon as they arrive from Amina,' the Frenchman explained, for which Mary was obliged to him, since she had been studying the book so diligently that she had not understood a single word. 'Do you see how it goes no further than the letter A? Thus even I, who am *Duchesne*, must be *Antoine* for the duration.'

The mystery of *Arbuthnot* was thereby solved – and yet, she found the Frenchman's tone too intimate by half, his glance too tender. Determinedly she focused on the alphabet, which started with *Aaron* and ended suddenly at *Auchinloss*, and found the string of memory was strangely tugged. Those pages were from a book which in her girl-hood had graced her father's shelf! 'But it is *Mr. Outram's Onomatology!*' she exclaimed, 'although they have not come by the half of it!' And before she knew it she was whooping with laughter – to the evident gratification of her com-panion, who tapped triumphant fingers on the case.

'Did I not guarantee that we should find diversion? But there is better yet to come, Madame. If you permit, I will show you *une petite histoire d'oiseaux!*' The mirthful Mary gave her assent gladly, and allowed herself to be steered through a doorway which was surmounted by the giant jawbone of a whale. Indeed she found it all too easy to forget her cares; in fact, she found it altogether lamentable, so that she would walk with him, yet had a mind to walk without him, would think to lead, but then would rather follow. And he would turn, bemused, or she, and each would halt or blunder, thus occasioning several collisions, a bruised instep, and a positive chorus of apologies.

The Frenchman's cheeks were reddening; his lips set into a puzzled pout. He had thought to impress an eager pupil with his grasp of *Histoire Naturelle*, but instead was thwarted by a darting dervish whose skirts whisked here, then there – and who cursed herself, had he but known it, since sadly she must spoil his pleasure if she would forbid her own.

Reader, there were birds to the right of them, and birds to the left of them, not high and glorious on the wing, but solid, stuffed, and uniformly woeful: the emerald-tailed *Kunai*, the *Boa-boa*, and the *Burra-bird*; the *Rusty caria*, the *Mulah* and the *White-beaked Millet-thrush*, extinct to the very last man. '*S'il vous plaît*, madame,' begged the brave botanist – who thought his world might fall like theirs about his ears – drawing her towards a case which contained a rough and ancient sketch . . .

. . . 'Here is the story of the first settlers, of whom the birds were so unafraid that they flew down to perch upon their hats, little knowing the human hunger for poultry-meat, or the thriving market in tail-feathers. Within a generation, madame, there was not a single species to be found on Sumina, for each and every one had succumbed to the madness of the musket!' Seeing that he had the lady's attention, the naturalist pressed gamely on. 'Our present day Suminians, however, do not care to trace their lineage from these ruffians, but insist that the Gods sent a tidal wave to engulf the island, in which all the guilty perished. As for the righteous few that were spared, it is said that to atone for the sins of the others their souls at death took the form of birds, thus repopulating the ravished island . . .' (Thus, reader, may a cheerful man turn leaden and lecturing, if another inhibit his instincts and bedevil his hopes of happiness.) '. . . It is a fine fable, is it not,' the Frenchman concluded earnestly, 'that can contrive to reject the darker heritage, and claim the light.'

'Perhaps one simply cannot face all that is in oneself,' murmured the lady who had reined him in, and who now was the very picture of composure. 'To plumb the depths must require great strength of character.'

No remark could have been more judicious, yet it only depressed the young man's spirits further. '*Certainement*,' said he in a strangled voice, and offered her a formal arm, and so they proceeded up the hall, sober as a pair of Puritans and as sedate, pausing to look at this, and nod at that, though time hung heavy on their heads, and listless interest failed them.

At length Mary consulted her fob watch and found the hour surprisingly advanced, thus opening for both a legitimate escape from their embarrassment. Had Monsieur Antoine been a more prudent man, he might even have accepted it, but he had never mastered the miserly art of saving face, and instead made one last attempt to engage her. 'But we cannot leave, madame,' he protested, 'without seeing the *pièce de résistance*!'

Politeness said she must concur, and so was guided to a threshold all alight with sun, and entered a conservatory-annexe, which appeared to feature all varieties of fish. As dazzled as she was dejected, Mary squinted at a beast as yet obscured by glare. *'Voila la vraie Sirène!'* announced the Frenchman, presenting the item with a desperate bow.

She stood, she peered obediently, she forced a smile . . . and saw . . . but no, it was no Mermaid . . . but instead, by cruel Fate's impertinence – a sad stuffed *Manatee!*

O site of her delirium! O author of her Fall! O vile persuader! – What she had thrust away swung back towards her, what she had put behind her was once again athwart. Reader, she smouldered and she sighed; her flesh was fired by aberrant blushes; her eyes grew round, as miniature crustaceans swarmed across her breast; her thighs thundered, beset by traitorous memories; her knees shook like saplings in a storm, and hardly deigned to hold her. The chaste constrictions of her corset might have stiffened her resolve – and also nipped sensation in the bud – but she had given the garment to the Housekeeper, thus ridding herself of every last let and hindrance, and every rudiment of decency!

Monsieur Antoine, who had only hoped to penetrate her reserve, not to make such a profound impression on her senses, observed her with dismay. 'Madame, you are unwell?' he said, taking an uncertain step towards her. 'Shall I fetch salts?'

A beauty-mole, two very graceful hands . . . a rosy earlobe, and a curl that smelt of sweet pomade . . . shoulders she had first glimpsed powering the paddle of an outrigger, shrouded now in silk but not forgotten . . . the smile she had sought to discern in the cedary shadows . . . Here, to be sure, was the fusillade that would fell her, if she did not immediately put a stop to it!

'Do not approach me, sir!' she commanded, holding him at bay with the point of her parasol, lest she be undone by increments of breathless pleasure. Outside the window the peacock cried out for his missing mate, and as he hoisted up his tail a hundred emerald eyes stared in at her and saw her shame . . . She gasped, and sank, half-fainting, cried for mercy, and succumbed, falling senseless as a rag-doll at the foot of the *Sirène*.

She lay there in a disarray of dewy sweat and, it must be said, smelling distinctly of the sea, while the Frenchman was very flummoxed, and feared he was somehow to blame – for in their short acquaintance she had been as often insensate as awake – and fanned her wildly with his hat and flew for vinegar, and when her eyes, albeit languorously, had opened, he implored her forgiveness for tiring her.

Now there is not a woman in the world, I wager, who will not turn Thespian when it suits her, and so it was with Mary, who lay immobile for a while to save her bacon – though she kept perfectly well, and could have sprung up and toured the gardens at a trot – sighing tragically, and calling for water, and swearing she was overcome by heat. So remorseful was Monsieur Antoine that he was happy to pay the custodian handsomely for half a cup, which he administered on bended knee, holding her head with a solicitous hand, till she had sipped it all down like a strawberry plant . . .

Chapter XXI

On the Curious Habits of the Palolo Worm . . . A Doll's Revenge . . .
Monsieur Antoine makes a Great Contribution to Science . . . An
Invitation to Ogé . . .

Reader, it was October in the Southern Hemisphere, and while Scotland shivered in its Hallowe'en, and turnip lanterns grinned like devils in the gloomy darkness, here we were enlivened by uproarious Spring. If few flowers bloomed on the island – there being no insects left alive which could pollinate them – none the less the season was self-evident, for all the birds in the sky, it seemed, were simultaneously struck by Cupid's dart, and sang their courtship songs, and bustled and nestled, and prinked and pecked, till down fell everywhere, and no clouds formed but were of rainbow feathers: saffron and lavender, and scarlet, tobacco-brown, and indigo.

In the seas, as in the air, all was fecund industry, for in the shallow waters inland of the reef the *Palolo* worms were stirring. This creature, reader, resembles our British lugworm, yet it is of the genus *Nereida*, and propagates most particularly. As the last quarter of the October moon dawns in the Pacific – to the very day, mind you – the *Palolo*, heeding a peremptory instruction, breaks off the posterior half of its body, which protrudes already from its burrow in the coral reef, and looses this vestige to the waves. Those fragments flurry to the surface in such great quantities that all the waters writhe with the worms, and later, when they discharge their eggs and sperms, the lagoon churns cloudy-white, and Sumina stands like a baked meringue in a whipped-cream sea. Birds leave the land then, for their courtship feast, and gulls dive deadly from the heights, and maidens frolic in the strand and bathe in milk like Cleopatra.

To sum up, there was something in the air – or so it may be said by those who have a mind to make excuses for my mistress – though I admit that on that afternoon I was not one of them. I saw the lady ushered palely in, I saw her bid the primmest of goodbyes to her companion, and I will tell you now that it is an ill thing to be life's dupe and pauper, to partake of nothing, yet peep from the lattice at the whole wide world and its weddings!

How she flounced at me, reader, when the botanist was gone, how she kissed and caressed me, and set me up and spread my skirts, and called me Sister Oracle. 'Dear heart,' she mooned, 'tell me what I must do, for I am all at sixes and sevens over this Frenchman! . . .'

(Reader, it galled me that the question should be put so gaily, for my mood was so far from generous that I even envied the little birds at their mating.)

. . . 'In his presence I tremble and flush, yet for all that I find I am not silenced; rather it is as if we had been acquainted for many centuries. No sooner did I shake him by the hand than a shock assailed my senses, and a strange rapture stole over me, a bliss that I have never felt before . . .'

Reader, her fecund tides gushed over me and would not cease, so that I wished only to absent myself, lest I be drowned by the torrent. But a doll must sit still, however she shrink, and cannot plug her ears, and that is the damnable way of it.

. . . 'I became huge in my happiness,' sighed she with shining eyes, 'yet I was as small and skittish as a little girl. And ever since the moment of our parting I can think only of his dear face, his laughter, and the music of his voice, that tender voice which is both foreign and familiar . . .'

'Pray remember that he is but a stripling,' said I sternly, 'and you, madam, are no longer a young woman!'

So the axe-blade fell, but the corpse would not lie down and die, but sat up straight and set the severed head upon its neck, protesting: 'Why, he is nine and twenty if he is a day, and I am but five and thirty! Moreover, he is my very twin, I swear, for all that I would keep hidden, out of shame, the sweet gentleman expresses openly and artlessly.'

'Aye, and does he not blazon it to all and sundry?' I countered. 'His light, forgive me, does not shine for you alone. In short, he is a ladies' man. Surely you have noticed his effect on Mrs. Tinker, how she preens herself at his approach, how her eyes flash, and her bosom quivers like an eager spaniel?'

'But she is soon to be married!' the matron cried, affronted.

'Just because one swears by swede,' said I, 'does not mean one will never try a taste of artichoke. The minx cannot be said to lack forwardness, and since the Frenchman has resided here for several months, would you not say they have had ample opportunity for dalliance?'

'No, no,' cried Mary, horrified. 'She is too loyal, and too honourable!'

'But are you not also loyal, madam?' I pursued, relentless. 'What of the good Mr. Gulliver, on whom you have lavished your devotion? What of the recompense he owes you for your lonely years? Are you so light-minded that you will forfeit your rights at the eleventh hour, and so faithless that you will abandon him?'

At last I had her; her hands flew to her betraying cheeks. She blenched, she wept, she ran to the balcony and begged forgiveness of the very birds. In truth it was pitiful, and if my heart did not exactly brim, it was at least a quarter full . . .

Aye, reader, I am a hypocrite, but not so much of a one that I would cozen you as I had cozened Mary, or swear to you that my advice was in her better interest. Disappointment, depend upon it, makes a delinquent counsellor. As a servant I had served her ill, for I who was barred from bliss had turned like the worm to savour the alternative delights of wickedness. And very inspiriting it was – indeed, I would recommend it to any female who is in the dumps, for it will brace her far better than Cinchona Bark or Carmelite Water, and to every other soul of whom Fate has made a minion. No basis, I believe, could be more equal: as I loved her, so did I hate her; as I hated, so did I contrive to wound. In short, I had found my mettle, and was quite myself again! My little eye was bright once more, my cheeks as hectic as the churning seas. How blue the sky! How fresh the salty air! How wild and strange and fair the winds of freedom!

Let her stew — I told myself — let her have a taste of torment, for assuredly she is my debtor, and by mourning only pays her dues!

Alas, poor Mary. And again alas, for is it not one of Fortune's laws that news long hoped for will arrive at the very instant it becomes redundant? Presently the House-keeper burst breathless into the chamber, crying: 'Be glad, my dear, be glad! I have spoken with Aurore. A letter has come from Ogé, and you are to attend on Mr. Abernethy in the morning!'

What Mary would have welcomed yesterday with tears of joy she could look on now with no enthusiasm, and turned her swollen face from her friend, and from her constricted heart squeezed out a stony thanks. Duty was all, she was determined on it: let others flirt and wanton, if inconstant be their nature! Suffer she might, but find her reward therein, for guiltless she would go to Mr. Gulliver, and play her persevering part, and pursue her rightful grievances.

The Housekeeper dismissed, the door was barred, the diary opened soberly. Each one of Monsieur Antoine's en-quiries was rebuffed, and though the lady's lamp burned all through the night, neither angels nor devils could have gained admittance to her chamber.

*   *   *

Distressed as he was, the Frenchman was none the less a scientist, and no woman on earth, I daresay, would have kept him from his assignation with his *fraisiers*. Dully he drew aside the muslin nets, thus baring his darlings to the anemophilic breezes of the evening, for the bees were too scarce to depend upon, and though he play the marriage-broker with his little sable brush, he doubted his own delicacy, and feared that too much tampering might cause irreparable damage to the perianths.

His shy and tardy greenhorns were drawn up in segregated lines, each one directly opposite its dancing-partner: *capitons* to the right, *frutilliers* to the left, and not a male *frutillier* among the foreign females, nor a female *capiton* among the males, so that any fertilization that occurred must have crossed by necessity between the species, whether on the bridge of the wind, the point of his brush, or the anxious breath of his own *animus*.

Bent like a rheumatick on the Pilgrim's Path he moved along the trench, setting his lamp down on the earth to study every pair, and note the pedicels, and count the fallen petals. Who but a poor fool, he arraigned himself, would practise horticulture in a bird-infested land? – forgetting, in his furious self-reproach, that his plants would surely have died barren before the ship had reached a better landfall. Who but a worse fool, moreover, would seek a sterile match – and not, it must be said, for the first time – with a female who already had a mate?

The moon shone down relentlessly on his mistakes, while the lamp illuminated pale florets numerous as the suitable girls he had shunned. Failure is my very name, he decided – mulching a root, and making a gloomy measurement, and plodding on, as will every scientist who, knowing he may never reach the promised land, lets habit take the place of hope, and finds his only consolation in routine. Here was a stem which shivered in the breeze – a wild rose of a female, her petals scarcely fallen. The lamplight flickered; overhead the bats were out. He paused to peer again, afraid that passion had informed his glance, and crouched down carefully to examine the corolla. Did he detect a change, or could he be mistaken? A little mound, an evening Venus rising? He glimpsed a creamy dome: it was distinct, no trick or apparition. Yet a single swallow, as they say, does not make a summer, and though one plant was fecund, he must find others to uphold his proof. On hands and knees he crawled along the row, and said a prayer for fusion. Here was a palpable swelling, and here – *O jolie bouton!* – the faint beginnings of a blush.

He counted twelve, and then a score, weeping freely, and thanking God that so many fruitful matches had been made, for he was no Francis Bacon, who sought to harness Nature in the service of his overweening pride, but humble enough to bow before her might and call her Mistress.

'Une race nouvelle!' he sobbed. *'Une race métisse!'* Thus blessed, the botanist dwelt no longer on his failures, and danced a stumbling jig instead, tripped on an empty water-pail, and fell down laughing in the friendly dung.

(Picture it, if you will, as a scene in an opera. The moon, lovely over Allegria, the sweep of the cedar branches. The naturalist, carolling his triumph to the stars, while behind the lattice the voice of the lady flickers in a *tremolo* of doubt. The duet becomes a trio, to which the villain doll contributes, from the depths of the interior, a dark ignoble chord

– muted at first, but swelling presently to drown the other voices out. Now it becomes an aria in the minor, which is a key that connotes conflict in a character – for if I aimed to thwart the mistress, I swear I meant the man no harm, and I am not so hard-hearted that I cannot sound a single remorseful note!)

Nothing, reader, could be more glorious than the open doors of Spring, and nothing more painful to those who close their hearts to it. Such a one was Mary, who rose next morning without relish, and dressed as soberly as a churchwarden, so that no rakish patch or promiscuous ribbon should perturb Mr. Gulliver at their reunion. She made it her business to be gone from the Guest-House long before breakfast – thus avoiding an encounter with Mrs. Tinker – and on presenting herself at the Town Hall was hailed by an excited Mr. Aurore. Mr. Abernethy was indisposed, he told her, but had given him the authority not only to pass on her husband's letter, but also to escort her immediately to Ogé.

She broke the seal; he watched her open it with ardent eyes. Yet what she now read must have disappointed the most rabid sentimentalist, for by no stretch of the imagination could it have been called a *billet-doux*.

My dear wife,
I trust it will not inconvenience you to arrive at noon, but no earlier, for there is much to do here and too few hands. Time is of the essence, yet am I surrounded as ever by idiots and incompetents. I would be very much obliged if you would procure a cage of bats from the market – a half-dozen at least – 14 oz. of squill, the same of black bryony, and 8 oz.

*dried marsh-mallow, which may be got from the Apothecary
on Grebe Street.*

  Yr. affcte. husband
  L. Gulliver

Sunlight shone sorely bright upon the words, and though
duty's iron bonnet squeezed her poor head to a baker's
dough, it could not armour her against the blow, but rather
multiplied familiar echoes. Resounding disappointment is a
force that may inflame, but more often saps the spirit, and
shrivels up the little blushing fruits of self-esteem: in short, it
makes a female frantic for approval. At its behest the most
intrepid voyager will lose her daring, and become a maiden
so ill-favoured that she will even call starvation love, and sell
herself for a shopping-list!

I need err no more, thought Mary, gazing at the uninspir-
ing missive, since by God's grace I have a living husband to
correct me. 'Let us wait no longer,' she implored the clerk,
'but leave at once, for Mr. Gulliver has need of me.' Though
very curious to hear the contents of the letter, Mr. Aurore
was circumspect, and did not incommode her with a single
query, but toured her through the town with all the pomp at
his disposal, clearing a path ahead wherever possible, since so
much down descended from the honeymooning skies that
they might have disappeared for ever in the drifts, and by the
time they reached the port both wide-brimmed hat and
parasol were inches deep in feathers.

They chartered a twin-prowed outrigger at the quay, and
sped over the milky churn of the lagoon until they reached
the reef, whose needling eye the oarsmen threaded more
skilfully than any Captain Sparrow, and brought them

through unscathed to start across the open waters of the Sound. The pallid cliffs of Ogé lay but a league or two off, rising and falling as the light craft rode the rolling sea. The sand was scarce around the island, and the shore-line tide-scoured, since there was no reef to act as arbitrator with the raging waves, and salt-encrusted pinnacles rose directly from the deep, and formed into tortured arches, with here and here a Cornish zawn or secret cove.

They came at length to a narrow bay sheltered to east and west by blinding buttresses, where craft of all kinds lay alongside an infernal quay. Here the raw ores were off-loaded, and ingots too, and lead for the smelter ferried up the track by fly-blown mules with cataracted eyes. White dust, and glaring ash, and lime-infested waters, and mule-keepers blindfolded against the sun, and bearers bent double, with backs blackened and ridged as ancient oyster shells, who walked wordless, without saliva left to spit, or strength to curse the indignity of their labour . . . All this the stricken Mary observed from the scant shade of her parasol, while the clerk secured a brace of mules to carry them up the cliff. This journey was so vertiginous that it does not bear telling; suffice it to say that yard by yard they rose above the hellish scene below, and presently arrived at the parapet where, gazing inland, they thought that they had come to Purgatory.

If Sumina was airy and azure, and its sister island damp and occluded, their cousin was fiercer by far, for what spread before them was a landscape of blistering barrenness. Alabaster outcrops rose up from the plateau in place of trees, and in the scrub-filled gulleys dried-up streams were guarded by the eerie ghosts of juniper, each branch and thorn salt-frosted. A rough road led inland to the hospital, or so said the muleteer who set them down and would not be induced to take them farther. His mules were indentured to the mine alone, he said, so they must go on foot, or wait the day out for the train which took provisions of an evening. Since it is no easy task to argue with a man whose eyes are shrouded in a mole-black scarf, they set out along the unforgiving road, though the sun stood at noon, without a drop of water between them, nor even any notion of the distance.

Chapter XXII

Intimate Confessions . . . The Wooden Wooed . . . Lady Mary Makes a Decision to Emigrate . . . A Refutation of Plato . . .

All this, reader, I was to learn later, but in the meantime I remained in the literal dark, for I had been left behind in the shuttered chamber, where I had ample opportunity to brood upon my sins. Presently there were sounds without: a soft persistent knocking, and a muttered conversation, which concluded with a sharp remonstrance from the Housekeeper: 'You may batter the door down if you wish, but she has gone already to Mr. Gulliver!'

Silence reigned thereafter, though I cannot say it brought me peace of mind, and I was not displeased when it was broken by a creaking hinge. The door eased open, and

Monsieur Antoine entered surreptitiously. He stood bemused for a moment, as if unable to recall the business that
had brought him, and picked up a petticoat and pressed it to
his cheek, and set it down again, and lined his foot up with a
ladies' buckled shoe, and smiled at the comparison. Such is
sentiment, that it will make a miracle of daintiness from a
medium size, and all the more so in a man with a message he
cannot deliver! His eyes, believe me, brimmed with Mary's
absence; he shook his head; his lips, meanwhile, were all
mobility, and made as if to mutter.

His agitation took him first to the dresser, and next, to the
discovery of Mary's diary. A page, a pen, a slanting script:
these plain things were enough to stir a tempest in his lover's
heart, for he trembled, reader, as he read, seeing the name of
his old friend Mr. Moll before his very eyes and howled out
an astounded 'Herman!', and leapt up buffeted by storms of
jealousy.

I watched this spectacle with interest from the bed, until
at length I found myself observed, indeed approached, indeed borne down upon, until finally I was snatched up in an
embrace which was both brutal and agreeable. Reader, so
close was I clutched that I heard the beating of his Frenchman's heart, and felt the tickle of his Frenchman's hair, and
cared not at all that I was but a straw-filled stand-in for my
mistress.

'*Poupette*,' he murmured as we lay together on the cot
(such a pretty word, *poupette*, for one cannot underestimate
the importance of onomatopoeia, and *doll*, by contrast, has a
drab and grudging sound to it). '*Poupette*, I envy you, for
night after night you may lie by her side and listen to her
secrets' . . . (this said in the singing French of the South, and

rendered here in rough translation) . . . 'You have been her companion since childhood, and each one of those darling years I envy you – nay, each day and hour you two have spent together' . . . (this with a kiss and a thrilling sigh, so that Heaven's angels danced before my eyes as he envisioned the untarnished bliss that could have been, and should have been, perhaps, but frankly was not – sweet laughter and loyalty, a pair of heads upon a scented pillow, soft lips incarnadine, and kisses shared, and picnics on a summer lawn – everything, in fact, that a man may wistfully attribute to the feminine). At this whimsy he even shed a tear, whereupon it was but a short step to rhapsodizing his own childhood, and fabricating another in which Mary also figured. Herein they gathered lilies-of-the-valley in the forests of the Solutré, and measured lizards captured on the summer wall, and stole on to the forbidden balcony to watch the dawn light move through the lavender-fields. 'Ah, I envy you for every precious moment you have shared with her, *Poupette* – but love you for them, too, as I am sure your mistress must' . . .

Here I was too dizzy to demur, for if he could make a paradise of my imperfect past, what might he not do with my future? He stroked my hair, and kissed me on my china nose, and I cared not that I was only wooed by proxy. Reader, I purred and was persuaded, for I had glimpsed the promised land, and from that moment on my heart was an ardent emigrant which, shunning Scotland's snows and even all of England's graces, plotted a course for France.

All that remained, then, was to instill the same ambition in my mistress – a not inconsiderable task, you will agree, since I had already done my best to steer her in the opposite direction! I must blow hot now, where I had once blown cold, and if it was not too late to turn the ship about, I might yet bring us two in sight of more harmonious shores, where each might take possession of her happiness.

'As for myself,' sighed the Frenchman, 'I am very far from that felicitous condition, since your mistress does not give me a single thought. Last night, *Poupette*, I made a great discovery for science, yet today I find no pleasure in it. Although my reputation is secured at last, such success is hollow if Mary does not hear of it, and will not share my triumph. I have no right to require her indulgence, yet I cannot bear to relinquish all hope that she may concern herself with me. Indeed, I am convinced that were she to learn of my achievement she could not be entirely indifferent . . .' Monsieur Antoine regarded me with a sombre face for some moments and then, seized by a fit of anger, demanded: 'Tell me, is my vocation so feeble that love may unman it and bring it to its knees? How low have I sunk, when my work must win a lady's favour before it have the slightest substance?'

Reader, I was touched by his torment, for I saw that even such a fine fellow as he could succumb to the canker of loneliness, which wreaks such havoc on the self-esteem. Had it been within my powers to soothe him, I would gladly have placed myself at his disposal; as it was, I resolved to aid and abet him with clandestine schemes. Henceforth I would be his champion, and sing his praises in a stubborn ear. To be sure, his little dove had flown, and meant to make her nest with Mr. Gulliver, yet I did not think that she would be altogether deaf to my persuasions. Right choice requires the heart, you see, where I hold sway, and here the tug of war was over. If mate she was to have, then let her choose the one who would not clip her wings or turn a cold shoulder on her companion. To this end alone would I direct my efforts, and connive most earnestly at the outcome, now that our interests, once opposed, were finally allied.

Soft light, warm scents of thyme, a life begun anew . . . my mistress would be swayed and wooed, as I had been, and since she was not wooden, hers would be the greater share of happiness, if she were won. Yet I should have my own, for if history had heretofore excluded me, the heartfelt embrace of the Frenchman had restored me to love's graces. *Animus* had smiled on *anima*, had warmed her with his generous breath, and salved her wounds with his sublime affection. Reader, though one's heritage be meagre, it need not altogether define one's destiny, and I am not Platonist enough to believe that fulfilment can only be had by sacrificing all desire for its possession – a grand notion indeed, dispensed from an even grander altitude! But the choices of privilege are not for the multitude, who know they have no claim to the aggregate, yet still cherish hopes of a decent portion. In short, dear friend, it was sufficiency of bliss: no doll could ask for more . . .

CHAPTER XXIII

*On Aerophilia . . . Mary Encounters her Husband at last . . . The
Great Benefits of Distilled Water . . . Mr. Gulliver's Charts . . . A
Catalogue of Modern Madmen . . . On Geese and Swans . . .*

My mistress, meanwhile, wandered in the wilderness.
White dust, and scanty shrubs whose ragged shadows
scarcely breached the road, parched lips, and blinded eyes,
and feet that blistered with each savage mile . . .

'I wish that I had never set eyes on the place,' complained
the clerk, who, being unaccustomed to exercise, had rapidly
tired of the adventure. 'I swear I shall lie down and die before
I walk another yard.' And much to Mary's chagrin he sat
down once again at the roadside, and made a great show of
removing a pebble from his sandal.

'Do bear up, Mr. Aurore,' said Mary, who, being encumbered by a cage of bats, had little sympathy to spare. 'Is that not a wall on the breast of the bluff, with a gate-house to the left of it?'

Wall it was indeed, and the sight of it spurred the sweating clerk across the final distance. Having presented their papers at the lodge, and received the assurance that it was but a quarter-mile to the Hospital, they refreshed themselves at a water-pump, and set out along a path which was straight as a die, and perfectly white, being surfaced entirely with salt-crystals. It soon became apparent that the path was one of many which converged like the spokes of a wheel on the hub of the Hospital. At regular intervals upon the rocky beds between, sundials were set instead of flowers, each with its *gnomon* pointing north, and stony face of graduated hours. A disconcerting sight, indeed, to greet the travellers, yet at least there could be no mistake as to the time, which was a quarter past two o'clock, stated here, and proven there, and everywhere endorsed by an authoritative chorus.

Mary braced herself – for such a decisive landscape made a crime of doubt – and hurried her companion on through sunlight pure and pitiless as intellect, until at last they stood before the Hospital. This was a building of unpillared elegance, a regular Villa Malcontenta, styled after Signor Palladio, three-storeyed, bricked in alabaster, and stuccoed in a pure patrician white. A monkish silence reigned about the place, and shuttered windows obscured a view of the interior; indeed, she would have thought it uninhabited, had a fellow not approached across the courtyard, walking at speed, and waving his arms back and forth with great expenditure of energy. His breath came fast and furious, in lusty gulps and beatific sighs, and his lips smiled indiscriminately, as did his glassy eyes.

Once hailed, he would not halt the motion of his feet or still his windmill arms, but, beaming, spoke the one word '*Aerophile*', and briefly pointed them towards a small brass bell within the portico, before proceeding draughtily and at the double.

'Now there is a comical name for a man,' said the perspiring clerk. 'Mr. Aerophile, I ask you! I'm sure I never heard the like.'

'Surely it is a general term,' said Mary, 'from the Greek roots *aer* and *philos* – literally, a lover of air. Apparently he means to cure his ills by inhalation!' Reassured by this rationale, she rang the bell, reflecting that where Mr. Gulliver ruled, all things must have their rhyme and reason. 'No doubt the unpolluted atmosphere of Ogé is an antidote to allergies,' she extrapolated, feeling that she stood on a little patch of order and of England, no longer liminal or lost, or led astray, or tossed on tropick seas of sensuality.

A grille was opened; on the announcement of their names they were admitted by a warder unremarkable in aspect, but for the jaunty stalk of celery he wore behind his ear. The cage of bats was gladly seized and borne before them down a corridor which echoed with the sound of sweeping, and Mary thought that she had never seen a floor so clean or walls so bare, with not a picture or a tapestry to break their blankness. Yet if the establishment was far from homely, she did not doubt it was humane, for there were no bars of Bedlam here, nor cells that she could see, nor any evidence of desperation. This theme evoked an image she had endeavoured to suppress – that last material sighting of her husband, straw-streaked and foul, and ravaged by incomprehensible distress. For a moment fear befogged her head, of what she might encounter, but such forebodings are more easily dismissed by those who follow duty rather than desire, and choose the Right, and not the Reckless path. (Believing, reader, that they have paid their self-denying dues, the fools anticipate no further punishment.) So Mary drew the credit she was owed by dignity, and, head held high, sailed forth with her unlikely Charon to an unknown fate.

The latter, meanwhile, crooned to the wretched creatures in the cage, and poked a finger fondly through the bamboo bars. 'Well, am I glad to see these little beauties,' he crowed, skirting a pair of polishers who buffed the floor ferociously on hands and knees. 'There's not a moment's peace, you see, if Mr. Arbuthnot runs out of livers!'

'You are taking us to the laboratory?' asked Mary, afraid that some tender squeamishness might overtake her there.

'No, no, madam. He'll be in the distillery, since it's already afternoon. The gentleman's as regular as clockwork, bless his soul, and expects the same of everyone. But here we are, the very door.' The warder knocked and entered, warning his charges that they must keep their voices low and stay well clear of any apparatus.

At first she could not see him, for a glass contraption filled the room, with tubes and filter-pipes, and tanks above, and empty vessels everywhere below. Clear liquid flowed in a steady stream from the spigot, while labourers filled demijohns and rolled them to the storage racks. What kind of alcohol was under manufacture here she could not tell, for it was too pale for brandy or *uisge beatha*, and in quantity was so prodigious that it might have kept the whole of sober Sumina inebriated for a twelvemonth.

Her eye fell on a white-robed man who sipped the brew, pronounced it good, and quaffed a beaker down in one. Yet this unlikely tippler was no red-cheeked Dionysos, but starkly pale, with narrowed lips and closely shaven pate . . . an alchemist, perhaps, or wigless anchorite . . . She blenched, and looked again. Could it be he? Her love? Her long-lost Lemuel? Turning, the foreman fixed the new arrivals with a vigilant stare, and curtly asked if he could be of some assistance.

She curtseyed crazily, as if she were once again that green girl who, clinging to her mother's arm, had met him on the lawn at Lady Chesingham's. Did he admire her now, as he had then? Did his hundred watchful eyes adduce her qualities, or merely see and censure her dilapidation? With head still bowed – she dared not look – she waited fearfully for his approach, and in the interim forgot her case. Judgement was his once more; he was her husband, after all, and she the wife he could forswear, if her aspect did not please him. So thought Mary with a mind as tousled as her hair, and shrank in stature till she was a nonentity, a sorry scrap before an august giant.

She risked a glance, and saw with consternation that his Argus eyes were avid for the bats, and not a single one regarded her. Those blind mice with their devil's wings were objects of desire, it seemed, far preferable to her! As for her rounded limbs, her breast, her brow – they were invisible. Hurt heaped upon hurt, reader, for surely there are few among our sex who will not prefer a disapproving look above indifference, for the first at least takes notice, while the second is a sentence of oblivion!

'You have the herbs?' he asked her absently, like a man requesting that the marrow-bone be passed to him at luncheon.

She thrust the packet at him, on the prickling point of tears. She would not cry. What fault there is cannot be mine alone, she told herself, and gained an inch or two in stature. Would he not greet his helpmeet, or do her honour, or say a single word of thanks? Would he not even call her by her name?

Vexation gave poor Mary voice at last, or simply slighted vanity. 'Will you not kiss me, Lemuel?' she asked him fair and square.

A hand flew to his pate and, finding it buck-naked, hovered in mid-air; he frowned in angry memory. England. O England, so long ago and far away! He took a halting step towards his wife, his lips a foreign shore, his smile a castaway marooned so long it cringes from its rescue. 'Forgive me,' he barked, 'I have quite forgot my manners!' and pecked her scantily, and backed away. At a loss for words, he stood and pondered, till his eye fell on the still. 'But you must take a taste of our nectar, friends!' he cried, with an exaggerated hospitality, filling a beaker from the spigot and urging them to drink. 'I guarantee you will not find a better vintage anywhere.'

'Thank you, no!' retorted Mary.

'I'll taste it gladly, sir,' said the clerk in the same instant, and drank the liquid greedily, but then, ungracious, cried, 'Why, it is not alcohol at all, but only water!'

'*Only?*' echoed Mr. Gulliver, advancing on him with a

beetling brow. 'Did I hear *only*? It is the very purest of waters, I assure you: every drop has been distilled for fifty days. It is the *nonpareil*, unsullied as a Vestal, and purer than any piety . . .'

'Then I will drink,' said Mary hastily, thinking to humour him, and thus forestall the fit she feared, or even fisticuffs, for you will recall that she had seen him run amuck before, 'if you will kindly pour me some.'

His temper checked, he filled another glass and held it out to her.

'Clear as a bell,' said Mary to oblige him.

'You will not find a better purge,' he told her earnestly, 'nor one more palatable. As to its tonic properties, I can guarantee that it surpasses squill in stimulation of the lungs and heart, and thereby cleans the blood, and heightens the complexion. Dull and melancholic humours are invariably dispersed by half a quart a day, and even hysterics may be helped by sipping a spoonful on the stroke of every hour . . .'

His hobby-horse once mounted, it was apparent that he meant to ride it to the death, and the devil take his listener. Mary could but nod and drink, and though she found the water anodyne, for it tasted neither of this nor of that, she thought it better to declare herself refreshed. To stem his diagnostic flow, she introduced the topic of the drought, suggesting that any surplus he could spare would certainly alleviate the sorry plight of Sumina – a proposal far from controversial, one would have thought, to a humanitarian like Mr. Gulliver.

'What we produce here is too precious to be wasted on that feckless crew on Sumina,' he retorted. 'If I thought for a moment that it would be put to prudent use, they should have all the casks they asked for! But there is no profit in helping those who will not help themselves, and I shall sit on my stockpile like a miser — nay, I will bathe in lakes of it — before I see it squandered on their feathered friends!'

A dismal pang assailed her as her husband spoke, for she had wished to think well of him, and found she could not. Despite herself she saw the Frenchman's empty pails and desiccated beds, and in her frustration prayed for thunderstorms, and gutters torrenting, and gardens fruitful as the charitable swamps of Amina.

In short, the lady seethed, but stayed her tongue judiciously. As well perform a Rain-dance to invoke the flood, she thought, as try to argue with a man who worships Reason; indeed, I daresay I might wring more mercy from the savage gods than I would ever get from Mr. Gulliver! 'Lemuel,' she interjected, making no small effort to control her tone. 'I believe you promised me an hour alone. I would be very grateful if we might withdraw, to talk of private matters.'

A flush darkened his face at her forthrightness, and he answered shortly, 'If that is so, then let us waste no time, then, since I am not a man to break a promise. I shall be in my chamber, Anstruther, if anyone requires my attentions, but pray do not inconvenience me with trifling queries.'

'Depend upon it, Mr. Arbuthnot,' replied the warder. 'I'll see that all is kept in order here, and feed the bats while I'm about it, if I may.'

'No you may not!' came the peremptory reply. 'Have I not told you before that I will not have pets made of my specimens?'

'Aye aye, sir,' said the warder, so crestfallen that one might have supposed he had been denied his keenest pleasure and his perquisite.

'*Chiropteromania*,' said Mr. Gulliver, whisking Mary from the room and starting down the corridor. 'The fellow has a passion for the creatures. His is a chronic case I fear may prove incurable, although the symptoms have been moderated by a strictly regulated diet.'

'Thus he must chew his stick of celery?' said Mary, striding long and hard in an attempt to match her husband's break-neck pace.

'Indeed, though it is a pity he will not be weaned of his old habits, and insists on wearing the item. Small gains have been made, though, for not so long ago he would not stir abroad without an offering of putrid fruit upon his shoulder!'

Breathless, she trotted at his heel, her mind uneasy with the subject of disorders, and said no more as they ascended several flights of stairs, and reached the threshold of his chamber. This was an attic room, lit by a round window like a ship's porthole, and furnished with a meagre bunk and monumental desk. Yet it was the four walls that commanded her attention, for they were entirely papered with writings, sheet after restless sheet which the draught had set a-fluttering, each one inscribed with divers charts and complex diagrams.

'You have been keeping very busy,' she remarked acerbically, and turned away, before emotion choked her. (Reader, you will recall that Mr. Gulliver had not penned a single line to William or Caroline in years, nor yet to his forbearing wife, though no doubt he had scribbled, as he scribbled still, unceasingly. Let none be surprised, then, if she had little inclination to applaud his labours!)

'For the most part,' he said, 'the charts you see pertain to my most challenging cases, for I have many patients in my care whose diets must be monitored from day to day. I am also become my own guinea-pig,' he added modestly, 'as should every physician who is worth his salt.' With unaccustomed warmth he pressed my mistress to peruse the calendars he had compiled, which kept a most meticulous account of his condition since the day of his arrival on Ogé. She stood perplexed, reluctant to inspect the wretched charts, yet loth to deal him a rebuff. At the top of each page were marked the days of every month, and phases of the moon, while, listed in a column on the left-hand side, were all the elements of human disposition. For example:

April 1 2 3 4 5 6 7 8 9 10 11 12 13 14 15 16 17 18 19 20 etc.

repose

pulse

breath

appetite

digestion

sputum

tongue

vision

olfactory

spleen

vitality

mental vigour

sharpness of memory

Each element was graded daily on a scale of 1 to 10, according if it were good, bad, or middling; appended at the bottom was the weight and nature of the foodstuffs which had been consumed at any meal, and volume of water – distilled, no doubt – and the exact dimensions of every stool . . . Thus were his fluctuations charted to the very last degree – *ad nauseam*, in fact – yet if she had ever yearned to know her husband intimately, here was his mystery exposed, through scientific evidence . . .

O primacy of intellect! she thought, and could not conquer her distaste. O chilly computation! What of the galling absence of the heart, the emptiness that should be filled by kith and kin? On not a single graph was *wife* inscribed, or *love* or *loneliness*, so singleminded was this sovereign of the void!

'And do you think, ever, of your children?' she demanded, believing that his sense of duty must indict him.

'My children?' he echoed absently. 'Do they keep well? It does occur to me that I have been remiss in supervision of their diet. Do they drink water in sufficient quantity? Enzymes are the cornerstone, you see, and cannot operate in equilibrium when undermined by sultry foods and toxic humours. These charts are ample evidence of the disturbances that may occur when Nature's laws are flouted constantly – not only bodily disease but aberrations of the mind, and every malady that can afflict the human spirit.

Coarse meats and raucous spices will condemn us to a crueller death than hemlock, and a slower one! We shall have our just deserts if we continue to indulge in them, when with a little self-discipline we might take the straiter gate, abjure the grosser pleasures, and achieve proportion, health, and sanity . . . Why, I believe we may extend our lifespan by a hundred years eventually, if irrigation be our daily watchword!'

(Damn it, dear reader, is there no limit to humankind's ambition? Yours, I grant, the comforts and the sorrows of the flesh, but mine alone the privilege of longevity!)

'Lemuel,' cried Mary, maddened by this homily, 'I can hold my tongue no longer! Will you not do me the simple courtesy of hearing what I have to say?'

He gazed on her with bafflement, as if he beheld the fabled cockatrice, with forelegs like a crocodile, and hindlegs held aloft by wings. Ego was all, and though it tried to comprehend her indignation, where was its tiller and its chart? Troubles turned down the corners of his mouth, and dark confusion came and went across his brow. Was it a woman's place to challenge one who only did his best to serve, and, if it was not, should he admonish her for impudence? He stood accused, it seemed, but where was her right, and where the justice of her case, and for what crime did she arraign him? He pawed his hoof – he could not let a female *Yahoo* pen him in – and offered her the single chair, that she might know she had been granted every courtesy, and given leave to speak. His 'Very well' was said with all authority; he stood above her as she sat, and put a finger to his chin: thoughtful, fair-minded, and aloof – this was the proper attitude to take, for dignity must triumph over disputation, like Reason over impulse, and husband over wife.

Folding her hands before her like a girl who has forgot the Catechism that she must recite, Mary began bravely, 'Contrary to the account you gave – no doubt for your own good reasons – to Mr. Abernethy, I demand nothing of you, except that you tell me honestly whether I must go or stay. I have crossed the Globe to find you, but I have yet to hear you say my name. Am I your wife, and are you my husband still, or no? Say what you want of me, and if I please you not . . . if you are tired of me . . . then let me go.'

Rash words, reader, from a woman twice deserted! Indeed too bold an initiative by far, which once more raised the horrid spectre of abandonment. Unhappy ultimatum! Such a weapon never should be wielded by a wife, thought Mary, shivering in her shoes. To forsake a husband would subvert an inner rule – as for the reverse, it was a husband's right, though it be wrong. She had been wronged, then? – or had she been merely wrong, and therefore culpable, a poor and paltry thing that got her just deserts?

Confusion and chaos reigned within, and her voice withered in her throat like a thirsty seedling, till she must water it with pails of tears, and sob and sniff and blow her nose, to the evident discomfiture of Mr. Gulliver. So low was her condition that she might have clung to him for comfort if he had come within a yard, but still her husband stood apart, and though he did not deny she was his only lawful wife, his haughty manner said that he begrudged the truth that had been wrung from him. 'Forgive me,' she muttered through her handkerchief, making a mighty effort to control herself, lest she fall even further into disfavour.

An intemperate silence reigned between the two, in which unspoken questions rattled at their chains, indictments were made, claims filed, appeals refused, and rioting emotions barred and bonded. At length Mr. Gulliver strode to the window, and stood in speechless contemplation of the sundials. The hour, at least, was universal, the sky irreproachably blue, the shadows of the slanting vanes both stark and irrefutable. Consoled, if not restored, he turned back to his wife and addressed her with a certain magnanimity.

'Come now, Mary, it is hardly a crime if a man tell a tall tale to assure himself of a little peace and quiet! After the shipwreck I was not myself, I fear, for several months . . .' A reckless memory came back to him, and strained to canter off apace, till conscience reined it roughly in. He gave a startled little snort, if not a downright neigh, before continuing, 'My work, as always, was my saviour, and for that I must have solitude, though I admit that my responsibilities have become so onerous of late I would be grateful for a measure of assistance . . . I am no longer a stripling, as you can see, although I flatter myself that I am not quite a dotard, and have many useful years ahead of me . . . In short, a sober person, very neat and competent at paperwork, would be a boon . . . a helpmeet who could relieve me of the routine tasks and free my faculties for study . . . For practice requires its theory, and without it dies a pauper's death and moulders in an unmarked grave, where it cannot benefit humanity! To come to the point, I do believe my burden would be greatly eased should a cultivated person . . . that is to say, a person such as yourself . . . should you . . . if you saw fit, that is, for I am told I am the devil of a taskmaster!'

He held the straw, and Mary clutched it desperately. 'Can

it be true that you require my help? Oh, nothing could make me happier, I swear!'

'Let bygones be bygones, then!' said he with a rigorous smile. 'We shall be colleagues, and shake hands on it. But first you must inspect the wards, where you will see soon enough whether you have the stomach for it. These are unhappy souls whose ships have lost their masters, and a firm hand at the helm will guide them to their wits, but a bleeding heart will surely scupper them. One must avoid the swells and storms of sentiment, and keep a cool brain, and impose a strict regime . . .'

'I will do my very best!' cried Mary, resolved to keep her sympathies in check lest she reveal herself as weak and womanish. Such was her husband's impetus that she hardly felt herself descend the hundred steps that took them to the Still, but flew instead on wings of inspiration. Had she not yearned for years to be his cohort, privy to his sacrosanct concerns? What joy to be invited, and to know at last which Aphrodite was her fate: without a doubt she was the elder one, man's soulmate, born of no woman but stemming from Uranus alone! As for the earth-bound body, well, that common daughter could not attain the Universal love that touched the spirit, nor sacrifice her carnal lusts to an Olympian ideal of partnership, and thereby must for ever be dismissed . . .

They reached the Still, where Mr. Anstruther obliged them with the keys. 'And I'll accompany you,' he said, 'in case I'm needed.'

'Please don't trouble yourself,' Mr. Gulliver replied, and then, when the determined fellow would not be dislodged, he gave a haughty sigh, and said, 'Oh, if you must.'

At the first door Mary braced herself to pass the test. She had expected horrors, but within the room was cool and clean, with walls as white as Aphrodite's teeth, and a chequered floor laid out in varicoloured marble. Seated on a stool was a fellow in his middle years, white-robed and shaven-headed, and of a morose yet not unpleasing appearance. When addressed by Mr. Gulliver, however, he shut his eyes in anguish and set up a muttered litany, of which every single sentence was constructed as follows, in the negative. '*I never thought of a knapsack, nor a summer-house, nor a flying squirrel in America, nor of the hinges of Mr. Southwick's cellar door, nor a hen's foot, nor the river Potowmack. I never thought of a bustard or a mainmast, nor a swan's nest, nor the Mint, nor a periwig nor featherbed, nor a Dunstable lark, nor a crystal glass of Frontinac . . .*'

'You may take notes, if you wish,' said her husband. 'This is Mr. Abelard, who believes that by a mere thought he can destroy America, or Hastings, or Mr. So and So's pigsty in Sussex, so he must think everything he has ever thought of all over again, that he may *un*think it, and thereby remedy the mischief. Unfortunately, having been a seaman, he has travelled much, and absorbed many experiences, and thus has a great deal to *un*see and *un*do. One might say he is afflicted by an uncontrollable nostalgia.'

'How sad that he may never savour its pleasures, but only feel its pains,' murmured Mary, and was reprimanded by a most forbidding frown.

'Our task is simply to cure delusions,' said Mr. Gulliver. 'Pleasures – take my word on it – are neither here nor there! But let us pass on, for we will get no sense from the fellow.'

Chastened, she followed her husband to the second room,

wherein stood a giant by the name of Mr. Alexander. 'But is he not another Englishman?' she whispered in surprise.

'Certainly,' said her husband. 'You will find your countrymen in the majority, although we have also French and Dutch, and even several Russians here. All the flotsam of Europe washes up eventually upon these shores – and in increasing numbers recently, as if some curious current brings them here. It has become a major problem, I assure you, for the archipelago. If I did not know better, I would suppose that England exports her surplus lunatics in prison ships, in the hope that the four winds will scatter them abroad . . . This Alexander, for instance, is no seaman, but a well-digger by trade, and would have us believe he came to the Southern Hemisphere by means of a tunnel.'

'He has twice jumped into a ninety-foot well to kill himself,' the warder added eagerly. 'And if water be brought to him he will fill a bucket with it and immerse his head.'

'His is a baptism delusion,' Mr. Gulliver explained. 'Of the religious manias it is currently the most common. Since dissenting from the Church of England he has become conscious of the enormity of his sins, which he fears cannot be pardoned, and constantly quotes texts from the Scriptures that corroborate his despondent notions. He is a danger to no one but himself, but I do not advise you to approach him, for he will seize your elbow and engage you with his never-ending sermons.'

The door slammed shut, although the giant had not moved an inch or said a word for the duration of the visit, but stared at nothing, with a look of guilty misery. The next door was not opened, and instead they must observe the patient through a hatch, this being Mr. Abbot, a.k.a. the Slaughterer of Brentford, a butcher by trade, who sparred with unseen adversaries, slicing and stabbing at the empty air.

'Meat is forbidden in the Hospital,' confided Mr. Anstruther. 'I do believe he takes it as a slight to his professional vanity.'

'Pray keep your opinions to yourself,' snapped Mr. Gulliver, while Mary nodded solemnly. 'They are no substitute for proper diagnosis!'

'Begging your pardon, sir, I'm sure!' replied the warder with a furtive wink, as if he meant to make of Mary a conspirator, though she had not the faintest inkling of the plot.

'This Abbot fellow boasts incessantly of his capacities for killing,' said Mr. Gulliver. 'It seems he mistook the keeper of his Parish work-house for a hog, and ever since then has been sticking imaginary pigs, felling fictitious bullocks, carving visionary veal, and dressing conjectural joints. Of the vocational delusions his is the most rabid, and resists all treatment. But there are others less harmful in this category. We have a hatter, for instance, whose skill is so great that he can make hats from old bellows, blankets, mops, no matter what, yet he despises his trade, and instead aspires to build churches all over Derbyshire which are higher and more commodious than any that exist in Europe. And a watch-smith too, who says he has made a chronometer that will go for a whole year without losing the thirtieth part of a second, and begs me to apply to the Astronomer Royal, who he swears is in possession of the certificates that vouch for its perfection . . .'

They left the butcher to his gruesome jig, and as they proceeded Mary thought to ask her husband whether there were female patients in the hospital.

'Oh, very few,' he said, 'and those are queens and princesses for the most part. Their cases are far less interesting, I fear. But we shall see our monotonous Annes and Elizabeths anon.'

'The wish to elevate one's status might be taken as a common factor, then, among the inmates?' she ventured, hoping that her humble observation might pass muster. Her husband, however, would have none of it.

'We do not talk of *wishes* here,' he scolded, 'but of lost wits, and how they may be regained by the application of enlightened methods.'

Ah well, she was a fool, as she had feared – she bit her lip to stop the tears, and hung her head.

'Come now,' said her mentor kindly. 'We may all make mistakes at the outset. Ignorance cannot be regarded as an outright sin, for it may easily be cured with a little earnest effort . . . Shall we continue, if you are up for it?'

'Indeed I am,' she said with fervent gratitude, and forced her lips to form a cheerful smile. They entered yet another room, where sat a man so thin that had there been a breeze his bones might have rattled together like the bare winter branches of the alder bush. As soon as he set eyes on the visitors he begged them piteously for food, and even tried to snatch the warder's stalk of celery, so that Mary could not but conclude the poor wretch was in the final stages of starvation.

'Good afternoon to you, Mr. Addison,' said Mr. Gulliver genially. 'I see you have refused your food again today. You will not get better, you know, if you do not take proper nourishment!' At this the fellow backed away and, covering his mouth with his hands, looked most affrighted. 'This patient is very contrary,' Mr. Gulliver explained, 'for though he cries out to be fed, he will strive with all his might to avoid it. When the warders attempt to place a morsel in his mouth he resists them strenuously, saying that it is too vile a place to put one's meat, for he supposes his true mouth to be quite the opposite orifice. Indeed, in the course of his extraordinary misconceptions he begs them to feed him through – forgive me, but I will not mince words on this occasion – the anus.'

Of all the predicaments in which one might find oneself, surely this must be the saddest, thought Mary, for he is so topsy-turvy that he cannot tell *up* from *down*, or *in* from *out*! Had she been bolder she might have suggested that the fellow take his meals while standing on his head, but did not, lest she invite another reprimand from Mr. Gulliver.

At that moment another warder hailed her husband, requesting that he attend immediately upon a patient with convulsions, and Mary was entrusted to the temporary care of Mr. Anstruther. The *chiropteromaniac* seemed unperturbed by the responsibility, and toured her down the corridor with evident delight, opening a hatch from time to time, and discoursing happily upon the inmates.

'Here we have Mr. Allcott, who commands the sun,' he said, peeping in on a man who stood on tiptoe at the window and appeared entranced by some celestial spectacle. 'Believing that he has the entire management and regulation of the great luminary, he watches it from its rising to its setting since, were it not for his constant care, much mischief might befall it.'

Opening the next hatch, he cried jovially, 'Now this young fellow, a surgeon formerly, is also much concerned with *globes*, and herein lies an entertaining tale. You see how he holds himself as rigid as a ramrod, and clutches anxiously at certain parts, like a hen who guards her precious eggs? Well, between you and me, madam, the fellow fears he is no *cock*, and, believing that he has mislaid his bollocks, constantly laments his fate!'

'Certainly he seems quite inconsolable,' said Mary, affronted by the warder's laxity, and disinclined to be amused by such a tragic spectacle.

'That he is,' said Mr. Anstruther, 'although there are some who have attempted to console him. Such a one was Mrs. X – forgive me, but I must not give her name, for she is a most illustrious patron . . .' With a gleeful chuckle, he continued, 'Hearing the fellow's plaints, and failing to get the gist of them, this lady applied for explanation to the keeper who, not wishing to embarrass her, told a downright lie. The patient, he said, collected flints and pebbles which he imagined to be jewels, and having recently had some taken from him, thought he had been robbed of all his wealth. At this the tender-hearted lady promised to bring him some very pretty gems, much handsomer than those which he had lost, but the poor lad, quite nonplussed, cried out: 'I will have none but my very own!' And so they parted in confusion, each entirely unsuspicious of the other's meaning!' The warder laughed immoderately until, perceiving that he laughed alone, he humbly begged her pardon. This Mary granted graciously, for after all the man was but a patient, to be pitied like the other detainees, although his malady was somewhat less apparent.

'I am sure you did not mean to offend,' she murmured. 'Let us speak of it no more. No doubt my husband will rejoin us very soon, but in the meantime I should like to rest for a moment, for I am rather fatigued.'

'Forgive me!' he cried remorsefully, guiding her to a nearby bench. 'Such a gallery of gloom is guaranteed to lower the spirits, if one is not immured to it.' Fussing like a mother hen, the warder made an effort to divert her with animated conversation, remarking, by way of encouragement, 'But Mr. Arbuthnot keeps very well, do you not think? With respect, I'd say he was a changed man . . . aye, and quite the reformer, as you can see . . . indeed, we are all very proud of him.'

'And why should he not keep well?' said Mary sharply, having a mind to put the warder in his place. 'You are impertinent, sir, to speak of him as if he were a patient!'

Mr. Anstruther stared at her with evident surprise. 'Meaning no mischief, ma'am, but may we not all be physicians the one day and patients the next?'

The fellow was ridiculous, she thought: he raved; indeed, he was deranged. 'I never heard the like!' she cried, yet suffered, if the truth be told, a sudden cruel resurgence of her doubts. 'Next you will tell me you are a diagnostician, and offer an expert opinion on his case!'

'Well, since you ask me, ma'am, I will give you an answer, for I would not cozen you on Mr. Arbuthnot's account. He is a dear fellow, and a very clever one, I'm sure. However, not to put too fine a point on it, one day he forgot himself, and mounted a mare . . . an unfortunate lapse which, I'm glad to say, brought him very swiftly to his senses . . .'

Her heart's reaction was delayed – first came anger, at the man's effrontery, and then a tremor of suspicion, and at last the seismic shock which ravaged her foundations. The truth, if such it was, was madness – or was madness truth? She could no longer tell, only that her roof-beams shook and dusty rubble fell around her, and hearth and chimney-breast were naught but ash and soot. How could it be, that in a moment all should crumble to absurdity: not least the high ideal of duty which had replaced her youthful hopes? Where was her hero, where the husband she had held in such esteem, and whom should she serve, if he not be the master?

'Do not take on so, madam,' implored the warder. 'We all have our little problems here, but your husband has a kind heart, I warrant, if one can find it, and a sterling intellect . . .'

She let out a wail of fury, like an infant wrested from the darling breast. 'He led me to believe he was in charge,' she cried, 'and a proper fool he has made of me!'

'No, no, not a fool, madam, though I daresay you should not have indulged him, no more than I should. But it is hard to be strict with such a persuasive fellow, and who can say for certain that he will not one day purge the world of allergies and ills, and bring its inmates closer to perfection? Indeed, I do believe my innards never were so pure as recently!'

As if reminded of his regimen, the man retrieved his stalk of celery and took a hasty bite, and set up such a lusty crunching sound that Mary clenched her fists and had a mind to turn assassin. Hell hath no fury, as I have said, like a woman disappointed; as for a woman duped, let alone one who is invited to be apprentice to a lunatic, and in the most lordly manner possible – reader, I need elaborate no further, and leave it to you to imagine her condition!

And what now should she do, if Mr. Gulliver returned? She could not still the ferment in her mind, and, jumping up, declared she was in desperate need of air and meant to take a turn around the garden. Indeed, she might have been an *aerophile*, so violent was her stride, and loud her step upon the crystal path, and adamant her breath.

Each sundial she passed advanced the time by seconds, yet the seconds dragged like hours – nay, like her very lifetime, whose disparities were now paraded for review: the dreams that had become delusions, and the credulity that had led to self-deceit. And each and every *gnomon* pointed to the self-same truth: she had been well gulled, for sure, but not only by Mr. Gulliver! Madman or no, that she was married to an egoist she could no longer doubt, nor could she deny she had misjudged unerringly, and thus made sure that, famished as she was, she received as little nourishment as poor tormented Mr. Addison. Could she forgive him? Aye, at least more quickly than she could forgive herself! For she it was who had contrived to settle on the very one most likely to repulse her: a frugal fellow, pale and pernickety – in fact, dear reader, a man devoid of heart, yet full of zeal.

As the poet once said, *More geese than swans now live, more fools than wise*, and I will leave it to you to decide which spouse, on this occasion, was the bigger goose! Yet Mr. Gulliver must have his swansong, else Mary will sleep in a cold bed forthwith, forgo all fevers and felicities, and never eat her fill of what she fancies – which I'm sure you will agree is no fate at all for a female. *Love is not love*, another wrote, *that alters when it alteration finds* – but that, I think, depends on the degree of alteration!

She saw her husband issue from the door and fly towards her, his vestments whiter than the salty path, and haloed silver by the sun. How she had wished for this, yet now, as he approached, she felt no sweet sensation in her, no fluttering wingbeat or accelerated breath.

'Are you unwell?' he asked, although the frown conferred upon her was more reproachful than concerned. 'You must be made of sterner stuff, if you would help me in my work! And you must not stand bare-headed in the sun, for I assure you it will cause mortiferous growths upon your skin. Put up your parasol, and let it shade us to the door.'

They stood, they stared; she did not stamp her foot, although she might have done, but simply shook her head. 'I fear I am not as you would have me be, for I am not fit to fetch and carry, or serve you faithfully. In fact, dear Lemuel, I would say I am *"a formless lump, unfashion'd and unfram'd"*, and you may name me Chaos if you will, but I would rather be a foolish fleshly woman than a perfect paragon, for such a one you seem to seek.'

She laid ironic accent on the *seem*, but was not cruel enough to speak her thoughts aloud, and say outright that woman was redundant, for none who walked on two hind legs alone would fit his bill!

He blenched, he flushed; waiting, she heard his stomach rumble hungrily, and saw him fumble for his wig with amnemonic hands which, finding nothing, rearranged a shaven pate. Speechless, he stood and stared, and pityingly she: Man and his mate, she thought, without the least affinity!

'Farewell, then, Lemuel,' she said, and shook his hand, and turned away.

Chapter XXIV

*On Chaos, and its Consistency . . . The Law of Synjury Proven . . .
The Judgement . . . Why Love is the Best Linguist . . . Mary Commits
a Felony . . .*

Reader, if I have said little, so far, of Amina, whose soil
is damp and sweet and whose womenfolk sew the
Scapecoat, it is because the island hides in cloud and
bashfully resists discovery. Nor shall we decipher her by
archaeology, for such is her volcanic flux that homes and
hearths are regularly swept away by lava tides, so that not
a potsherd or a pig-pen stands as witness to their passing. Again and again the inhabitants must take to their
canoes and flee, and from a distance watch their villages
destroyed, and then, when Mother Pele's wrath subsides,

return and start from scratch. Little wonder that they erect no temples, or any other noble artefacts, for each night they fall asleep to her abyssal lullaby and, ear to the pillow, hear her grumbling bowels. Yet to those souls their island is as safe a lap as any on the earth, for they believe that in Chaos lies her consistency, in Formlessness her form: such is the grace, epitomized in poetry and decorative arts, that limns these Atlanteans. Oh, that we should all be so commendably light-footed and bright-browed, so careless of History, yet so attuned to Flux! Reader, though egos quake and fall like sundered cliffs, when fire embraces sea it makes a black flower with a scarlet heart which seethes with steam and burns and boils beneath the waves and, cooling, spreads its roots of pumice-stone, on which rise coral reefs, and sundry soils and trees – and so the island, gaining what it loses, grows . . .

Enough, however, of philosophy, for in the psittacotic streets of Sumina a singular catastrophe is brewing. You will recall, no doubt, that on the previous evening Monsieur Antoine had achieved the summit of success, yet had accomplished this, at least in part, by subterfuge and petty larceny. In the process he had all but drained the neighbouring well, so that its abstemious owner, seeing the level fall by several feet a day, could not but become suspicious. The man had kept a watch throughout that culminating night, and soon his labours bore the bitter fruit of satisfaction. Here was his thief and here his proof: the muddy footprints and the spilling pails, and, irrefutably, the fertile bed and juicy crop of strawberries. Had he had youth and strength he might have thrashed the Frenchman then and there, but being emphysemic, and advanced in years, he spent the early hours composing a complaint, which in the morning he delivered to the Ministry.

On Sumina the wheels of Justice were not slow to turn, and by afternoon the culprit had been summoned to appear before the Court, and a half-hour later apprehended by the Guard and taken to the Gaol, where, shortly after, he was ordered to appoint his spokesman, since his trial was scheduled for the following day.

Meanwhile an unsuspecting Mary sailed across the Sound, savouring the sunset and the distant lights that came on one by one as if to welcome her return. Full to the brim with the insouciance that often follows an ordeal, yet she was solemn, for the test she had survived had not been set by any husband, but by her alone. Henceforth she must be judge, and take responsibility for all her deeds, and live without recourse to a supreme authority.

In freedom try, and lose or win, in freedom love or hate! Oh thrilling thought which, alchemistic, might transform her! Such a delicious anguish racked her as she flew towards her Frenchman that she was ill-prepared to find that he had fallen foul of Fate – forgetting, in her excitement, that the man was not a part of her, but separate.

At last she reached the garden gate, and hurled a wish up at the crescent moon before she dared to climb the stairs. The quiet beds were shrouded, and a single lantern lit the balcony on which her erstwhile rival stood, her hair in ruins and her lovely face awash with tears.

'Where is Aurore?' Mrs. Tinker cried. 'Is he not with you?'

'Why, I have shooed him off to his lodgings, for the poor man was asleep on his feet! My dear, whatever is the matter?'

She hurried to the Housekeeper, who stammered out the dreadful news, and clung to Mary, who, though she tried to comfort her, was hampered by a heart transmuted into stone. What she had feared had happened. Yet in her chill bewilderment she could not countenance the cruel facts.

How can it be? she thought, and dully shook her head, and even blamed herself, for had she been sterner with the Frenchman, might the disaster not have been avoided?

'He has appointed me to speak for him,' continued Mrs. Tinker wretchedly, 'but since he refuses to believe he is in danger, he will not suffer me to lie on his behalf, and plead his innocence. Yet if they find him guilty there is no machinery to mitigate the sentence, or make an exception to the rule. See what a burden he has laid on me, that I must bear alone!'

'You shall not!' said Mary, marshalling her forces. 'I will stand up with you, if only to testify to his good character, and dedication to the cause of science . . .'

The Housekeeper shook her head despairingly. 'The Protocol does not allow a second advocate, nor even another person in the Court, whatever their relation to the accused.'

'Then let us prepare a speech, and passionately plead his case! Although we cannot predict the outcome, we shall not forgive ourselves if we give in to despair, and do not do our very best for him. I should not like to sew such squeamishness on *my* Scapecoat,' she added, hoping to rally the Housekeeper with her vehemence, 'for I could not bear the world to think me a defeatist! Come now, I shall fetch pens and paper, and we shall make a start.'

Thus incited, Mrs. Tinker dried her tears and, though still resigned to failure, reluctantly allowed that no act was futile, if it occupied their agitated minds. They spent a sober hour or two in composition, and having appended a final plea for mercy, tremulously kissed, and drank a glass, and did not speak of matters of the heart but reached an understanding all the same.

When Mary came to bed she held me, reader, with an awful tenderness, confessing that, despite my counsel to the contrary, she had decided she was done with Mr. Gulliver, and pressing on me all her divers reasons. I did not point out that, as *I* had changed my tune, then so had *she*, but delicately heard her out, and interposed judicious comments, until she did not doubt she was the one who had persuaded me!

'The trouble is, though Mr. Gulliver purports to serve humanity, he has no pity!' she said at last, as if to clinch the argument.

(Aye, and had she? I might have asked, had not self-interest stayed my tongue. Truth was less dear to me, I have to say, than my designs, therefore I would be prudent, bury the hatchet, if need be, and pray for Monsieur Antoine, on whose fate depended not only the mistress's happiness, but the doll's delivery!)

Reader, I may not penetrate the Court, and therefore cannot satisfy your curiosity as to the tenor of the Judge, or his response to Mrs. Tinker's eloquence. Outside a crowd had gathered, in which Mary took her trembling place, but spoke to no one, for she could not tell if friendship or acquaintance brought them there, or merely prurience. These punters peered and craned, ate candied fruits, and turned their hat-brims down against the climbing sun, and made adjustments to their veils to shield them from the birds which, having breakfasted, enjoyed their morning exercise above, wheeling and diving in displays of aerobatic courtship. How blue the air, as Mary waited for the verdict; how still the trees and pinpoint buds which perched, expectant, on the branches; how obdurate the golden scales atop the roof. She stared ahead, and closed her ears, but could not fail to overhear the rumours that, begun as ripples, gathered strength like tidal waves, imperilling her on every side.

At length a white-robed clerk appeared and nailed a notice to the door.

'*Guilty,*' the cry came back to her, and instantly a grave and gloating silence fell, and cheerful birdsong echoed like an outrage in her ears. Uncharitable Justice, that would not exonerate her sweetheart, or add her dearest hopes to its accounting!

The hushed crowd waited for the outcome of the draw, and now, incensed, she saw that their Suminian democracy assured, if nothing else, the right of every gambler to his stake. On this account alone they were agog, she realized, since each and every one of them might be the author of her lover's fate!

The dignitaries issued from the door; behind them Mary glimpsed the crimson corset of her friend, and Monsieur Antoine, ashen-faced and flanked by guards. She thrust herself forward till she was athwart the steps, and saw her darling strain towards her, and heard him desperately call her name.

The ballot-paper, first held aloft, was now unfolded, and perused by Mr. Abernethy's eldritch eye. He passed it to the duty-clerk, who donned a pair of spectacles and stumblingly pronounced:

'Sentence. Ahem. To be carried out forthwith, that is, this very day at twelve noon . . .

' "*Whatever be the trade of the accused, he must witness the destruction of his product. If he be a wheelwright, let his axles be broken; if a cooper, let his barrels be staved; if a farmer, let his crops and livestock be laid waste.*" '

A sigh swept through the crowd, yet who but the prisoner understood the awful aptness of the sentence, which cruelly proved the principle of Synjury? To see his strawberries, in the very moment of their secret swelling, trampled to the dust – none could conceive of a retribution which was less haphazard, or more commensurate! The Frenchman doubled up with shock and let a banshee wail escape his lips.

'My *bears*!' the flabbergasted Mary thought she heard him cry. 'Oh, but my *bears*!' – and stood there uncomprehending, as her lover, felled by algebraic odds, was dragged away.

What message was encoded in his desperate words, his pleading gaze? She racked her brains, but found his meaning untranslatable. *My bears*? she thought: *mes ours*? *mes ourses*? and took a phonetic side-step to *mes sources*, which might suggest – oh joy! – that he was no thief at all, but rather had stumbled on a secret spring . . .

With Mr. Aurore beside her, Mrs. Tinker hurried down the steps. 'My dear, my dear, he is a very lucky man! He will not like to lose his garden, but when one considers that he might have lost his life . . .' She stopped, and feebly shook her head, and leaned on her fiancé's arm.

Subdued, the three proceeded to the Guest-House, where the sentence must be carried out: thereafter, with his seedling plants laid waste, their friend would be in need of all the comfort they could offer. They reached the house a half-hour in advance of the executives, and Mrs. Tinker, her fiancé at her heel, flew to her kitchen to prepare the cordials that must be served to all the company.

Mary was left to contemplate the garden and the shrouded beds which must be sacrificed, their soil dug up or scorched . . . and yet her mind would not abandon its attempt to fathom the conundrum of the *bears*, and fumbled wildly with the French *barreur* – a helmsman – and *beaux-rêves*, and even *barrière*. She sounded their cadences, tested their timbre, scanned them for diphthongs and spirants, and, making no sense of anything, turned back to English. *My beards?* she thought, *my barns? my bees?* – for love's obsession makes the most fanatical interpreter.

She shed a tear, recalling the night when she had first encountered him, and thought him dream or archetype, earth-bedded in the dark recesses of her sleeping mind. A half-forgotten snatch of German echoed in her inner ear: the guttural *Erde*, rich as an autumn furrow, and then *Erdbeer*, its literal earth-berry – or strawberry to you and me. But then, *Eureka*, as they say! The lode was struck at last! She saw the lustre of the vein, and leapt up crying, 'Why, he meant to say my *berries*, and mistakenly said *bears!*'

Did the Frenchman have fruit, then, where she had seen only florets – had he achieved his miracle? She took the steps at speed and, rushing to the beds, drew back a corner of the net. Crouching, she saw a glint of red among the green, and bent back the leaves with trembling fingers, to reveal not one, but half a dozen plump and peerless hybrids. What should she do? She could not simply leave them there to be

342

despoiled, yet if she plucked the fruit without permission she would contravene the order of the Court.

There was no time to lose, and though in her befuddlement she could not see how the berries, once harvested, could be of any use to Botany, blind instinct won the day, and seized a stem, and snatched a fragrant handful.

Reader, my mistress gained the safety of the chamber just as the official party reached the gate, and, throwing herself upon me, hid the strawberries beneath my petticoats, wherein the precious hoard must damply incubate! And then she fled out to the balcony, and stood, benumbed, to watch the dreadful ceremony.

Down by the seed-beds stood the Judge, the guards, the sullen Frenchman, and his accuser, sheepish now, who at a signal from Mr. Abernethy stripped away the netting to expose the verdant rows. A silence followed, full of gall and wormwood, in which the prisoner raised his head and saw his ruin. No pick or spade had yet been hoist, nor need be, for the scarlet berries were a blazon to the busy skies, their lustrous flesh a naked offering to the birds!

The parrots and the razorbills struck first, and soon the other species came in fatal clouds; even the Concert Tree fell silent as its songsters, drawn by the distant clamour, suspended their arpeggios and flew to join the fury of the feast. The Frenchman closed his eyes and let the tears course freely down, but Mary witnessed every moment of the gluttony. The bower-birds, those aesthetes of the aviary, took their plunder off to beautify their nests, but all the rest, dishevelled, fought for primacy. The larger species, slovenly and savage, lunged at the fattest fruits, and crimson pulpy flesh flew everywhere. Each morsel tossed into the air incited an affray among the smaller birds, and raiding-parties of the very smallest scavenged the residues which smeared the breasts and claws of their superiors, and sipped the squalid juices from their beaks.

Before a quarter-hour had passed the spoilage was complete, and where the nursery had been was but a midden-heap of fallen feathers, broken stems, and dung-splashed leaves. The pile was quickly torched, and acrid smoke rose skywards as – not for the first time, reader – Science perished on the pyre.

Now you will think, as Mary did, that having paid the price, the Frenchman must be instantly released. Unfortunately she had not bargained for the Judge's thoroughness. 'The premises,' said Mr. Abernethy, 'will be searched, and any produce that is discovered there will be destroyed forthwith.'

Reader, my mistress dashed within, and having retrieved the berries from my petticoats, swallowed six in one celestial mouthful, conserved the last, and looked around her wildly for a hiding place. A pitcher, or a powder-jar, or shoe or reticule? – containers all, but none of them inviolable. Her thoughts were frenzied, but in the meantime sensation went its topsy-turvy way, transferred the sweetness of its taste, and by association took up lodging in another secret niche which, thus enlivened, sent libidinous signals to her brain.

(On this account, I have to say, no serpent was more diligent than I in his persuasiveness; indeed, it was my shining hour, for mere cogitation is no match for genius, whose consummate insight is none other than the child of heart and mind conjoined in the corporeal marriage-bed.)

In short, my mistress was inspired, and, seizing her

scissors, snipped at my most intimate seam, and slipped the single fruit inside. Her fingers trembled so immoderately I was afraid she would not thread her needle, but this was accomplished in the nick of time, and when the guards came to the door they found a lady busy with repairs, and mended stockings flung about the room, and feminine trappings everywhere. With bluff apologies, they bowed and left, and never saw the contraband that was concealed inside me, nestling in its bed of straw!

CHAPTER XXV

A Vulva Sweeter than Date Wine . . . On the Very Necessary
Combination of Animus and Anima . . . Captain Sparrow Returns
. . . A Smuggling Operation . . . A Doll's Destiny . . .

Reader, do you not think the hunter's heritage lives on, and flays with scorn the man who goes back empty-handed to his cave? No other hypothesis could explain the mood of Monsieur Antoine who, confronted with a shy and eager Mary, glowered at her as if she were his enemy. What had he to offer her, indeed, but ignominious failure, and a love that laughed aloud at his presumption? His hair was thick with ash, his cheeks were grey; he turned away from her, but gallantly she drew him back. Emboldened by pity, she took him firmly in her arms and whispered, 'All is not lost, Antoine. Look to the doll, if you would find forbidden fruit,' whereupon she unpicked a single stitch, and held an inch of seam apart to reveal the damp and gleaming red within . . .

No response, reader, could have been more reverent than his, and none more gratifying. His eyes grew round and filled with tears of joy; he struck his brow repeatedly and cried, 'Miraculous Mary! In this one berry you have preserved the very seeds in which the separate strains commingle. If dried, and subsequently sown, these jewels will generate the first true race of hybrids!'

Words warmer than a dozen suns, and fertilizing tears – this happy confluence intoxicated Mary, and all but released her from the thrall of Mr. Gulliver, whose frigid shade diminished with each kiss that rained upon her hand, her foot, her nose, her flaring throat, and finally upon her parted lips.

How shall one measure boundless bliss – in multiples of *ships* or *yams*, or *men* in legions, or else in *fruits*, or *humming-birds*, or *frangipani blooms*? Reader, I am too bashful to anatomize the congress that took place before my startled eyes, and lack a surgeon's nicety in naming parts or pinning down the physiology of love's endeavours. Only believe that they clove to each other with such alacrity that if Hephaestus with his instruments had come upon the pair he would have thought himself required to melt and fuse them into a single entity, and let them live as one . . .

I hope I may be forgiven, therefore, if I shy off at a tangent and elaborate a variation on this cogent theme. When *animus* and *anima* combine a *race métisse* is born, a strain as rare and sweet as the *fragaria* which ever since has worn the suffix of

Duchesne . . . The metaphor may be excused, I think, if it identify a process which occurs so seldom in the individual that very few may stand alone, and therefore very few conjoin wholeheartedly, and say an outright yes, and yes again.

My point is this: true union, like charity, begins at home, though some may travel countless leagues in search of it, and anchor, all expectant, at the most exotic islands. Reader, if concordance is what you seek, look inward first and last, and see who speaks with whom, and who stands speechless in the shadows, and which sex plays the slave and which the cruel master, and which is dispossessed, tabooed, enchained, or banished to a foreign shore!

There, I have said my piece, and between you and me I feel the lighter for it! As young Mr. Sterne said the other evening at supper, an hypothesis, once conceived, assimilates everything to itself as proper nourishment, and from the first moment of begetting it, grows stronger by everything one sees, and hears, and reads. (Yet he did not say how it burns to be aired, and, if unheard, lies as heavily on the heart as undigested partridge on the stomach . . .)

But enough of philosophy, for our Odyssey is not yet over, and you will wish to know how we escaped that palindromic archipelago. In the meantime, you will recall, I bore the veritable sire and dam within me, cradled in a bed of straw, and though it is not given me to procreate as women do, I leave it to you, good ladies, to decide the meaning of fecundity, define its length and breadth, extend its provinces and colonies, and draw its boundaries beyond our present ken. Although my belly cannot grow a greening shoot, History, I hope, will one day recognize the part I played in propagation, since by my agency, as you will shortly see, the seed was spread abroad, from nation unto nation.

Yet I would not claim more credit than is my due, for our exodus could not have been effected without the fortuitous arrival of an old friend, in the form of Captain Sparrow. This benevolent bird, having been turned back by storms northwest of the Horn, had retraced his course and, in the hope of provisioning his vessel for the homeward journey, had anchored in the bay that very afternoon. Needless to say, he was very eager to encounter my mistress, and, after an affectionate reunion, generously placed his ship at our disposal.

Before we embarked, however, we first must run the gauntlet of the Custom-Master, whose orders were that every member of the Frenchman's party should be scrupulously searched, their persons scrutinized from top to toe, and their effects punctiliously itemized. The sting, it seemed, was in the *queue*, and now a chilling interlude ensued on which I shall not dwell for long, for Mary and her lover, hand in hand and deathly pale, could hardly bear to watch while I was turned about, and ogled, tilted, tapped, and splayed . . . Suffice it to say, dear reader, that the *dill pissed mister* in the *inspiction*; the strawberry was safely smuggled through, the pinnace swiftly boarded, and then, on the good ship *Loyal Bliss*, we bade adieu to Sumina.

Reader, if the Queen of Scots began her life as a *Marie* and ended it more drearily as *Mary*, my fate was to be the converse, for having disembarked at Le Havre, and subsequently journeyed south to the Duchesne estates at Solutré, I was surrendered to the care of Monsieur Antoine's little ward Céleste, the daughter of his widowed sister Marguerite. Her eyes were blue and limpid as her name, and her heart unclouded by the bitter legacy of black-browed Mr. Knox, whose trumpetings unthroned an earthly queen and sought to tear the very name of woman from the heavens!

In France, moreover, children are not banished to the nursery, but sit at table and converse like little adults, and are tenderly indulged – indeed, it seems the French prefer them far above their dogs, and do not care to punish them as Anglo-Saxons do. Accordingly my new-found mistress doted on her dolls, and never raised a hand to them: in other words, no pall lay over her patrimony, and as she had been cherished, so she cherished me.

As for my erstwhile mistress, I may report with all confidence that she ripens daily on a diet of inflammatory discourse, dances, masques, and glees, and *vins de marque*, and piccolos and clavichords, and hammock days and thrilling nights, and the companionship – you will be very glad to hear – of Sparrows, Bluebottles, and other refugees from England's doleful fogs, not least her father and her long-lost son and daughter.

In the meantime Monsieur Antoine's *bears* have brought him a deserved renown in Scientific circles, but I do believe he is a peasant at heart, for he has turned his rich valley-acres to excellent account, and in the early morning rises with the birds and adds his sprightly discords to their harmonies, and rides his filly down the hill to rake and hoe and dibble with his gardeners.

To conclude, then – for every Odyssey must end, and each adventurer must find his domicile – I will confess I am contented, insofar as any doll can be, for I am well coddled and cosseted, and may bask in blessed sun all summer, and at the winter window gaze the whole day long on glittering snows.

Nobody, of course, may know the future, but for the present I have little to complain of, for when *entente cordiale* replaces strife one is inclined to pardon age-old injuries. I would not have you believe, however, that my life is a rose garden. Nay, reader – it is a bed of strawberries!